Planet X

EVANGELINE
ANDERSON

ELLORA'S CAVE
ROMANTICA PUBLISHING

What the critics are saying...

ഇ

5 Stars "When Krisa first sees Teague, he is bound and covered with a blindfold, but neither helpless nor defeated. [...] Ms. Anderson allows some real heat to build between the two that will have the reader doing some twisting as well. [...] I loved the pacing throughout this story. Nothing seemed forced. There was plenty of action and sexual tension, but the intense attraction built into a believable relationship. [...] This is a terrific hot story with several twists along the way that kept me staying up late and turning pages. I'm happy to recommend it." ~ *Just Erotic Romance Reviews*

5 cups "Ms. Anderson has penned a wonderful adventure, full of exciting landscapes and other worldly characters. Krisa is the perfect model of modesty until her survival depends on her acknowledging her passionate nature. Teague is a convict with a code of conduct that rivals many a gentle man. The sexual awakening of Krisa and Teague's restraint combine to make this book impossible to put down. The sexual encounters left me totally captivated and engaged till the last page." ~ *Coffee Time Romance*

"The writing blew this reader's mind. Planet X is fully engaging, believable, and you will not want to put it down. The crafting of this tale is so well done, you can visualize all of the wild and creative surrounding, clothing, characters and the planet they inhabit! Ms. Anderson has a mind like a steel trap and an erotic pen that will leave the reader hungering for more. Her pastel paradise is not for the faint of heart, but the erotic readers looking for hot and how!" ~ *Love Romances*

An Ellora's Cave Romantica Publication

www.ellorascave.com

Planet X

ISBN 9781419953859
ALL RIGHTS RESERVED.
Planet X Copyright © 2006 Evangeline Anderson
Edited by Shannon Combs.
Cover art by Syneca.

This book printed in the U.S.A. by Jasmine–Jade Enterprises, LLC.

Electronic book Publication March 2006
Trade paperback Publication September 2007

Also by Evangeline Anderson

ഇ

About the Author

৪৩

Evangeline Anderson is a registered MRI tech who would rather be writing. She is thirty-something and lives in Florida with a husband, three cats and a college-age sister but no kids because enough is enough already. She had been writing erotic stories for her own gratification for a number of years before it occurred to her to try to get paid for it. To her delight, she found it was actually possible to get money for having a dirty mind and she has been writing steadily ever since.

Evangeline welcomes comments from readers. You can find her website and email address on her author bio page at www.ellorascave.com.

Tell Us What You Think

We appreciate hearing reader opinions about our books. You can email us at Comments@EllorasCave.com.

PLANET X

ဘ

Dedication

∽

This book is dedicated with love and gratitude to Treasure. Thanks for always being there to cheer me on and for being my constant reader.

Chapter One

ဧၚ

"No, no, Krisa! Come away *at once*."

"But who is he? *What* is he?"

Krisa Elyison stared with fascination at the huge, blindfolded man who was chained in the metal-lined hold of the *Star Princess*. He was the biggest man she had ever seen, and it wasn't just that he was tall, which was obvious even though he was sitting on a narrow metal bench. He was massive as well.

The prisoner had a broad chest and thick arms roped with muscle that led down to a narrow waist and powerful thighs spread wide in a lazy slouch. Spiky, bluish-black hair was buzzed close to his scalp and his skin was a dusky, exotic tan that Krisa had never seen before. Everyone on her home planet was quite pale, owing to the configuration of their sun. There was a coiled tension in his muscular form that reminded her of a wild animal in repose.

"Krisa, come away."

"But what's he doing here, Percy?" Krisa turned to the small, nervous man behind her, one delicate eyebrow arched in question. The *Star Princess* was a light tonnage merchant-class cruise ship that carried an equal amount of cargo and passengers, but Krisa couldn't remember anything in the glossy holo-brochure about it doubling as a prison transport.

"That's none of your concern, my dear. Now if you've got your luggage settled, then we need to go back to the blast couches and prepare for liftoff." Percy gave her the small, tight grimace that passed for his frown.

Percy DeCampeaux was her chaperone, sent to accompany her from her home planet of Capellia to Lynix

11

Prime. Krisa had never met a more nervous and prissy person, despite the fact that a genetic variation in the Capellian population ensured that two-thirds of its inhabitants were female.

Ignoring her chaperone's orders, Krisa took a step closer to the bound and blindfolded man. She was supposed to be stowing her pale pink carryall cube in the hold and preparing for liftoff, but she couldn't take her eyes off the massive figure chained to the dull silver wall of the hold. There was something fascinating about him, a masculinity so intense it was nearly primal. She patted the thick roll of hair at the back of her neck nervously, making sure all her chocolate-brown curls were securely in place, though the prisoner couldn't possibly see her through the thick black blindfold he wore.

"Krisa," Percy said, in that high, nasal voice she found so annoying. Krisa glanced over her shoulder and saw that he was standing well back from the bound man, fiddling with his monogrammed luggage nervously.

"Just a moment." She took another step, moving around a mountain of luggage that had been strapped down securely for liftoff. Her long, sateen skirts rustled across the metal floor plates with a sound like the uneasy whispering of ghosts. Krisa had been hoping for a little adventure on her first and only interstellar trip, but she'd never imagined it would start the minute she set foot aboard the ship.

It was her first trip off-planet and very likely her last. She was going to meet Lord Radisson, her future husband, who was the planetary envoy to Lynix Prime. Soon her only function would be to serve as a dutiful wife and hostess to one of the wealthiest men in the galaxy, and there would be no call for any further adventures in space. Which was why Krisa was determined to make the most of this one, no matter what Percy said.

She took another step and the prisoner raised his head, his nostrils flaring in her direction. *Almost as though he was scenting me.* The thought made Krisa shiver even as she studied the man's face. He had a full, red, cruel-looking mouth and his jaw was covered with dark stubble. Plain black trousers molded to his powerfully built legs and the black tank shirt he wore left his muscular arms and shoulders bare. She wondered if he wouldn't get cold in the metal-lined hold.

"Hello?" she said hesitantly. She was close enough now that she could smell a warm, musky scent coming from the chained man. It had a wild tang that, like his appearance, was utterly masculine. Somehow, that scent seemed to invade all her senses at once, making her feel restless in a way she couldn't understand.

His nostrils flared and he turned his head, as though tracking her somehow. Krisa felt suddenly breathless. She tugged at the high, confining collar of her dress, wondering why it suddenly seemed so warm in the previously chilly hold.

"I wouldn't do that if I were you. He'd as soon bite you as pass a civil word."

Krisa gave a little scream and jumped back, putting a hand between her breasts to still her rapidly pounding heart. The tight cincher she wore beneath her clothes to give her a perfect hourglass shape pinched her sharply at the sudden motion, and she stumbled, falling into the chained prisoner's lap. Reaching out blindly, she caught herself on one rock-hard thigh, feeling the blindfolded man's muscles tense immediately beneath her palm. Krisa got a brief, blurred impression of immense strength, barely held in check by his bonds, and heard Percy shout a belated warning somewhere behind her. A low growl was building in the prisoner's corded throat, but before he could say anything to her, she was yanked backwards and away from him.

"Here, that won't do at all." The man who had spoken to her was giving her a look that was half concerned and half reproving. "You're lucky he didn't take off your face." He wore a short maroon jacket trimmed with gold braid and narrow black pants that ended in shiny black boots.

Krisa recognized the uniform of the Royal Space Corps at once. The man who was speaking certainly wore it well, but despite the broad shoulders which filled out the braided jacket admirably and his thick head of blond hair that gleamed in the dim overhead glows of the hold, Krisa's eyes kept returning to the chained man. She wondered what he might have said to her if the officer hadn't pulled her away. Indeed, she barely registered the fact that the man who had spoken was still holding her arm, but the inappropriate contact was certainly not lost on her chaperone.

"I'm sorry, and you are?" Percy, who had been cowering in the corner of the hold, now stepped forward, bristling at the stranger's audacity. "Be so kind as to unhand the future Lady Radisson," he added, drawing himself up to his full height of five foot four, and looking the newcomer squarely in his delightfully cleft chin.

"Terribly sorry, so rude of me, but I was concerned for the lady's safety." He released his hold on her forearm and stepped back a pace. "Allow me to introduce myself. Captain Owen Ketchum at your service."

He sketched a charming little salute and actually bowed over her hand when Krisa held it out to him. She caught a whiff of expensive Tazzenberry cologne and wondered where his accent was from. New Britton, maybe?

"I'm Krisa Elyison of Capellia, and this is Percy DeCampeaux, my chaperone. We're going to Lynix Prime," Krisa answered before Percy could stop her. "Where are you headed, Captain Ketchum?"

"Making my way back to Lynix Omega to deliver that brute." He jerked his chin at the chained man who sat silently on the narrow metal bench. "Kurt Teague. He's a Feral from Al'hora. He's already escaped once, which is no mean feat when you consider the Lynix Omega Correctional Facility's a triple-X maximum-security prison." He shook his head grimly. "This time, as you can see, we're taking no chances. Those magno-locks are rated for over ten thousand psi each." He gave her a condescending little smile. "That's quite a lot, in case you're wondering, Miss Elyison."

No chances indeed, Krisa thought, as she returned her attention to the silent, blindfolded prisoner. Both of his muscular forearms were indeed encased in the unbreakable magno-locks, which were attached to chains affixed firmly to the walls on either side, forcing his upper body into a very uncomfortable-looking spread-eagle position. The thick titanium-steel manacles certainly *looked* strong enough to hold anyone in place but, remembering her earlier impression of his immense strength, Krisa wondered if looks might not be deceiving in this case.

As she watched, the prisoner tilted his head back and bared white teeth in a frightening grin, just as though he knew she was staring at him. But that wasn't possible, was it? Krisa shuddered and looked away quickly, squeezing the hand that had touched Teague's muscled thigh tightly into a fist at her side. To think she had come so close to such a dangerous man! It gave her a curious little thrill along the length of her spine, even though she knew her interest in the huge prisoner was decidedly unladylike.

"What...did he do?" she asked the captain in a low voice, ignoring Percy's obvious wish to be away from the hold of the ship and the blindfolded man chained to the wall.

"Oh, he's a murderer many times over, favors the knife for his dirty work. A regular sociopathic killing machine, aren't you, Teague?" Captain Ketchum turned his head to direct his last words to the prisoner himself, but Teague's only answer was that wild, white grin again.

Krisa thought his teeth looked much sharper than normal, almost animalistic. She wouldn't have been surprised to see a smile like that staring back at her from behind the bars at the large predator exhibit at Capellia's Imperial Menagerie.

"He seems to enjoy killing," Ketchum went on with grim good humor. "But then, what can you expect from a brute like that? More animal than man, these Ferals."

"I'm surprised he's on a merchant-class ship with normal people if he's as dangerous as you say," Percy said nervously. He had evidently decided to resign himself to being acquainted with Captain Ketchum.

"Oh he's dangerous all right, deadly as they come. But you needn't worry, Mister DeCampeaux, Miss Elyison." He nodded, and a grim look passed briefly over his handsome, regular features. "I had a job to catch him, I can tell you. But now he's going back where he belongs, the Deep Freeze. That's what the chaps who live there call the Lynix Omega Correctional Facility," he explained. "Because the temperature never gets much above zero, you know."

"But why the blindfold?" Krisa couldn't help asking. Her eyes were drawn again to the silently snarling Teague.

"The blindfold is actually a kindness," Ketchum replied. "Ferals are indigenous to the Night side of Al'hora. They never see the sun, so the brutes have adapted to do without it, light is painful to their underdeveloped eyes. If I wished to be cruel I should transport him without it, but I've never seen the need for unnecessary brutality, even to an animal like Teague." He grinned charmingly at Krisa who returned the smile hesitantly.

"But what about—" She was cut off by an announcement from the ship's overhead system.

"Would all passengers please report to the blast couches? Liftoff is scheduled in ten minutes."

"Well," Percy twittered with obvious relief. "I expect we ought to be going."

"Quite right," Captain Ketchum agreed. "I shouldn't like to try a liftoff if I wasn't safely tucked in. Fairly painful, I should think." He offered Krisa his arm. She noticed a modest row of medals on his maroon jacket which gleamed with muted brilliance in the dim light of the overhead glows. "May I escort you to the blast compartment?" he gravely enquired.

"All right." She took his arm, ignoring Percy's grumbling. "But..." She looked back at the chained man. "But what about *him*?"

Ketchum laughed, a delightfully mellow tenor sound that fell pleasantly on her ears. "Don't worry about Teague, my dear. Ferals are extraordinarily tough, he'll be just fine without a blast couch. Unless you want me to unchain him and let him have the couch next to yours?" The pleasant tone was lightly mocking.

Krisa looked at the enormous man and felt that cool tingle of interest run along the length of her spine again. For some reason, her cheeks grew hot, and she forced herself to look away from Teague quickly. "No," she said in a voice that was little more than a whisper.

"I didn't think so. Let's go, shall we?" He turned them toward the metal frame of the doorway and they left the hold with a fuming Percy in tow. Still, Krisa couldn't resist one last look over her shoulder at the hulking figure chained to the wall of the hold.

As she looked, Teague raised his head and turned his face toward her, just as though he was looking back.

The last thing she saw as they exited the hold was that white, predatory grin.

Chapter Two

ဆ

Even though she had taken off the waist-pinching cincher that gave her curvy figure a perfect hourglass shape and taken a nice, warm sonic shower to relax herself, Krisa still couldn't sleep. She punched the flat, gelafoam pillow and rolled over again in her narrow cot for what had to be the fiftieth time. According to Percy, the cot would double as a cryo-sleep chamber in another week when the ship had built enough momentum to use the hyperdrive.

Krisa knew, also thanks to Percy, that the *Star Princess* was too large to use its hyperdrive immediately as a smaller, more cramped craft would have been able to. Her chaperone had impressed on her that Lord Radisson had chosen a more luxurious mode of travel over a faster one for Krisa's own pleasure and convenience.

While Percy had explained the cot, he had been blushing furiously. Twin spots of red burning high on his skinny cheeks, as though the very thought of Krisa lying in bed, even for the purpose of cryo-sleep, was positively indecent. Krisa had only known him a week but she was beginning to believe that Percy thought almost everything was indecent. She was more than tired of him twittering around her, like a tiny moon circling a planet with an erratic orbit, and only hoped that he wouldn't play a very big part in her new life on Lynix Prime.

She sighed and sat up in the darkness of her sleep cubicle, aptly named since it was a claustrophobically small six-by-six-foot compartment, which barely had room for the cot she slept on. Still, Krisa felt lucky because at least the tiny cube had a fresher in one corner. It was one of the few aboard the *Star Princess* that did. She knew, because Percy had told her several times that this little luxury had cost Lord Radisson thousands of credits more. She supposed she ought to feel grateful that her future husband cared enough to spend so much to see she was comfortably accommodated, but it was difficult to feel grateful to a man she had never met.

Standing in the darkness beside her cot, Krisa murmured, "Lights, dim." At once a thin strip of radiance cells along the bottom of the faux-wood wall illuminated, so that she could step inside the tiny fresher without stumbling.

The fresher door slid shut behind her with a nearly silent whooshing hiss of compressed air, and Krisa stood undecided for a minute in the middle of the postage stamp-sized room. She didn't really need to relieve herself and though another sonic shower might have been nice, she was well aware that every one she took cost Lord Radisson additional credits. She didn't want to seem to appear wasteful, although by all accounts her future husband had plenty of credit to waste. Reluctantly, she decided to save another shower for the morning. She contented herself with flicking on the holo-viewer over the tiny sink instead.

A low, humming buzz announced that the viewer was warming up. Soon Krisa was greeted by a 3D version of her own head, hovering just above the sink, looking as tired and scared as she felt.

A pale, oval face dominated by almond-shaped, chocolate-brown eyes, and framed by a profusion of ringlets almost the exact same color, stared back at her. She looked anxiously at the unsightly dark circles that were forming under her eyes, hoping that she could get enough rest to erase them before she had to meet Lord Radisson for the first time. It wouldn't do to look less than her best at the Lynix Prime spaceport, considering the staggering Bride Price he had paid for her.

Krisa pushed the directional buttons on the viewer, causing the 3D image to rotate so she could study the back of her head and then flipped it so she was staring at her face upside down. The viewer was a novelty since plain mirrors were considered more than adequate on straightlaced Capellia.

Really, she didn't know why she was so nervous. It wasn't like the match had been sprung on her at the last minute like some unlucky girls at the Briar Rose Finishing Academy. Lord Radisson had held her contract for eight years, since she was thirteen years old.

Krisa had known for years that as soon as she reached the age of consent her future husband would be coming to collect her. She had been a little disappointed to see that he had sent Percy DeCampeaux instead of coming himself, but she knew he was a busy man. He probably couldn't be bothered with small details like coming to get his future wife in person.

Nothing to be afraid of, she told herself. Just because she was going to strange planet to be married to a man she had never met, a man whom she had only seen holo-vids and pictures of, was no reason to act like a nervous little twit. Krisa made a face at herself in the viewer and then pressed the distort button and watched her creamy skin twist like rubber into a grinning clown mask that winked and nodded at her knowingly.

Abruptly she slapped the holo-viewer's off button. There was no point in trying to sleep with so much on her mind. It was late but maybe someone who wanted to talk would still be up in the main lounge. Maybe even Captain Ketchum, if she was lucky.

Of course, it wasn't strictly proper to be in the captain's company without a chaperone, and without the all-important cincher that gave a true lady her perfect shape. *But we'll be in a public place,* Krisa reasoned to herself. Still, Percy wouldn't like it if he found out.

Krisa knew that her chaperone disapproved of her acquaintance with the captain, but she couldn't see any harm in it. After all, it wasn't like she would *do* anything. Her Certificate of Virginity had been verified and stamped before leaving Capellia and the fact that said virginity was a sacred trust was strongly impressed on all Briar Rose girls.

Captain Ketchum seemed to be a perfect gentleman and he was full of entertaining stories and anecdotes. He was much more amusing than Percy, with his continual harping about how much Lord Radisson had paid for every little luxury that was bestowed upon her.

She took a few hairpins and secured her curls in a loose but proper chignon, wincing as one of the pins scraped the tiny, fingernail-sized bump at the back of her neck where her ID chip was implanted. It wouldn't do to let the captain see her hair down around her shoulders—there *were* limits to the improprieties she was willing to commit. Then, grabbing a white dressing gown, and making sure she was modestly covered from neck to heels as was proper for a future Briar Rose bride, Krisa made her way out into the main corridor and went looking for company.

The main lounge was deserted and a quick tour of the long, narrow halls of the ship revealed that, aside from the pilot and a few of the crew, everyone was asleep. Morning and night didn't mean much in the middle of space, but everyone aboard the *Star Princess* kept more or less to the twenty-five-hour cycle they were used to, sleeping and rising at basically the same time.

The *Star Princess*—Krisa had loved the name of the ship she would be traveling on from the moment she heard it. *A name straight out of a fairy tale*, she'd thought. One where the beautiful princess ends up with the handsome prince in the end.

Now, as she wandered the empty corridors, listening to the slow, even breathing coming from the twenty-odd other sleep cubes, the thought seemed juvenile and silly. Her own fairy tale was nothing more than a simple case of supply and demand. Capellia, sometimes known as Bride Planet, produced double the number of females needed to keep its population going. Conversely, women were scarce in the

Lynix System. Krisa was a commodity like any of the other imports stowed in the ship's hold. A rare and valuable one, but a commodity just the same.

Stop being such a ninny, she scolded herself. *You're lucky a man like Lord Radisson was interested enough to buy your contract.* Some of the girls at Briar Rose had nothing more to look forward to than Ring miners who had struck it rich, or colonists that had a Federal dispensation to buy a wife for reproductive purposes. Krisa was grateful she wasn't one of those unlucky girls. Instead of uncertainty and poverty, she had a life of luxury to look forward to.

Lord Radisson had first seen her picture on the Rose Garden, Briar Rose's interstellar web site, and he had been waiting for her to come of age for eight years. He insisted that she was the only girl who would fit his station and lifestyle. Though she knew it was supposed to be a compliment, his words made Krisa feel more like a beautiful acquisition meant to complete an expensive collection than a cherished wife-to-be.

Sighing, she turned to go back down along the corridors to her sleep cubicle and try to rest when another thought occurred to her. Bypassing the cube she slipped silently back to the cargo section of the ship. She held her breath as she passed Percy's cubicle, where she could hear a high, whistling snore issuing from inside the metal walls.

Back near the hold the *Star Princess* gave up any pretense of luxury and became ugly in a practical way. The faux-wood floor gave way to metal plate flooring that was cold on her bare feet and the almost silent hush of compressed air circulating through the ship was the only sound. Krisa knew she shouldn't be doing what she was doing, but there was a part of her that craved adventure, a part that just couldn't resist a forbidden situation.

Back at Briar Rose she had been legendary for her escapades and escapes from the locked dormitory to wander the grounds at night. The Briar Rose grounds were too vast to actually get anywhere and back by foot in a single night, but that hadn't been the point for Krisa. The point was the escape itself, the surge of adrenaline though her veins when she picked the lock or went out the window and roamed the dewy grass, soaking up the light from Capellia's double moons, and breathing the fresh night air. It was the only time she felt really free — really *alive*.

Now Krisa felt that same electric thrill running down the length of her spine as she crept soundlessly into the darkened hold and tiptoed toward the sleeping prisoner who was still chained to the wall. Biting her lip, she admitted to herself that this was the real reason she had come out of her sleep cube tonight. She moved carefully because the overhead glows were dark and the radiance strips at the base of the metal walls threw a faint, sinister green glow that made only minimal visibility possible.

Krisa breathed quietly through her mouth and came to a stop four feet from the chained man. *A sociopath,* she heard Captain Ketchum's pleasant tenor echoing ominously in her head. *Kills with no remorse. Butchered any number of innocents. Caught up with him on Sirius Six — followed the trail of victims — some with hearts carved right out of their chests. Superb knife work — rather like a homicidal surgeon.*

Ketchum was more than willing to talk about Teague's horrible deeds though he was less definite on the details of his recapture. He had assured Krisa that it was too bloody for a lady to hear about. *Believe me, my dear, you don't really want to know.*

Krisa stared in fascination at the man in chains. She'd never seen a sociopath before, let alone a homicidal murdering one. The only people who visited Briar Rose Academy, besides prospective husbands, were guest lecturers. The lecturers tended to be plump, middle-aged ladies who spoke on topics like "Running a Household on a Budget" and "Pleasing Your Husband-to-be". None of them were half as fascinating as Teague.

He sat motionless on the narrow metal bench, wrapped in shadows. His square chin was slumped against his broad chest and his arms were still held in the uncomfortable-looking spread-eagle position by the magno-locks. Despite the locks, he was sprawled in an attitude of catlike grace and his massive thighs were spread, revealing a large bulge in the crotch of his black trousers, highlighted by the greenish light from below.

That part of a man's anatomy was one Krisa had yet to see and she had only spoken of in giggling whispers to other girls at the academy. *His cock*, she thought, feeling her cheeks glow red at the forbidden word. *Goddess, it must be huge.* Of course she had no real idea of how big that part of a man was supposed to be, but she knew what she was seeing in Teague's trousers looked bigger than anything she could ever imagine being able to handle herself. She hoped nervously that Lord Radisson's was a bit smaller.

Teague stirred a little, his muscular chest moving up and down as he took a particularly deep breath. Krisa held perfectly still, watching the blindfolded face carefully, to judge for signs of waking. He settled again however, and she felt brave enough to creep forward another foot. She was close enough to see each tiny bristle on his square-cut jaw and trace the massive biceps and broad shoulders with her eyes. An animal, Ketchum had called him, and Krisa could see why.

Once when she was twelve, before she'd entered Briar Rose and was still living at home with her family, a traveling menagerie of wild animals had come to their part of Capellia. Krisa still remembered the excitement of watching them unload the animals at the port. The enormous cages had been floated on hydro-cushions to the arena they'd erected only that morning. There had been a huge, sleek cat in one of the cages. *Felidae Panthera*, the metal plaque on the cage had said and, *Native to Old Earth.*

The panther had been all muscular grace, its black pelt gleaming and its eyes like two green stones, blazing with barely controlled violence. Krisa still remembered how badly she had wanted to reach through the stasis bars and stroke the panther, though she knew it would be a stupid, dangerous thing to do.

Now she reached out a hand, knowing she shouldn't, but somehow drawn to touch the sleeping prisoner. *Krisa, this isn't smart,* warned a little voice inside her head, but she felt powerless to stop. Her senses filled with Teague's spicy, somehow unsettling scent, strong but not unpleasant, and she was reminded of the musk coming from the cages of the big cats at the menagerie.

Closer...closer... What she was doing was not only dangerous, but highly improper, much worse than going out in public without her cincher. But she couldn't forget the feeling of his rock-hard thigh beneath her palm, or the way the big body had tensed when she'd fallen across his lap. Krisa told herself that she only meant to brush one bristly cheek, or maybe just feel the body heat radiating from his large frame into the chilly air.

"I know you're there, little girl. I can smell you."

He had the deepest voice Krisa had ever heard, like someone rubbing a handful of gravel against a stone wall. The blindfolded head lifted and pointed in her direction, that savage grin a white slice in his dark face.

Heart banging madly against her ribs, Krisa scuttled backwards, nearly tripping over the neat piles of luggage strapped to the hold's metal floor. When her nerves told her she was far enough away to safely turn her back on him, she whirled and ran down the corridor.

His deep, gravelly laughter echoed in the darkness behind her.

That night she had the dream again...

~ ~ ~ ~ ~

Large, calloused hands roved over her naked flesh, bringing her body to life in a way she hadn't known was possible. A mouth, hot and demanding, branded her own and then trailed searing kisses down her throat to lick and suck at her bare breasts. Krisa could feel her nipples hardening under the sweet pressure of his hands molding her and the sharp pleasure-pain of his teeth, nipping her tender buds and marking her creamy slopes with dark red love-bites.

She cried out, feeling her pussy grow wet and slippery for him as roughly knowledgeable fingers found their way inside her, caressing her swollen folds and thrusting to test her depth and readiness to take him. He was stroking her clit as though he knew exactly how to make her body respond to him, as though he knew her better than she knew herself. Krisa gasped breathlessly and spread her thighs wider, wanting more of him, more of his hands on her body. One blunt fingertip stroked along the side of the sensitive bundle of nerves now, he wasn't gentle but his very roughness brought her to the edge. The way he knew her body — knew exactly how to make her lose control under his rough and knowledgeable touch — was like nothing Krisa had ever experienced before. She moaned, bucking her hips up shamelessly to meet his caress, offering herself to him without reservation. Her clit was on fire, her pussy drenched with her juices and still he wouldn't stop stroking her wet, aching sex, exploring her depths with his thick fingers until she ached for something more. Something she could scarcely name, even to herself.

There was the feeling of being just on the edge of something huge and amazing. It was an edge Krisa had never managed to cross, but she had had the dream before. Every time she got closer and closer as the man with no face readied her body to receive his cock.

She knew, somehow, that once she crossed that edge there would be no going back. She would be committed body and soul to this man who was taking her so roughly and deliciously, who was forcing her body to respond to his every wish, but she didn't care. She only knew that she needed him inside her now. Needed to feel him awakening her body and rousing her soul, making her blood rise to meet his own...

~ ~ ~ ~ ~

Chapter Three

ഇ

"Well, tonight the hyperdrive engages and we'll all enter cryo-sleep. When you wake up on Lynix Prime I'll already be gone, jetting down to Lynix Omega with that brute, Teague, in tow. I suppose we must say goodbye this evening."

Captain Ketchum bowed gallantly over her hand and Krisa smiled at him in acknowledgement. They were sitting together on one of the green comfort-foam couches in the lounge, and the captain was sipping some imported Brucado scotch. Krisa stuck strictly to nonalcoholic beverages. At Briar Rose Academy one of the credos was, *A lady never becomes intoxicated.*

"Such a pity," she murmured politely, aware that Percy was watching her from the other side of the half full lounge. He was supposedly playing a game of snap-dragon with the businessmen sitting at his table, but his beady, nervous eyes were fixed in her direction. She hoped he would start winning soon so that his attention would be more on his cards and less on her and the captain.

To make conversation she asked, "Will the *Star Princess* make any other stops besides the one to drop you and...Mr. Teague off at Lynix Omega, before we get to Prime?"

Captain Ketchum shifted and took another civilized sip of the amber liquid in his glass. "Well, it's more of a slight pause for us to jet down than a stop, but I should think not. Only other planet in the system is Lynix Xi—Planet X, you know. It's between Lynix Omega and Lynix Prime, but nobody ever docks there."

"Why not?" Krisa asked with interest. She had tried to do some research on the Lynix system since Lord Radisson had bought her contract, but the Briar Rose library concentrated more on the attractive and inviting features of any particular System one might get sent to. Planets with mysterious names that no one ever landed on were largely glossed over in favor of scenic attractions and major shopping areas.

"Nobody ever goes to Planet X because nobody ever gets off of Planet X," the captain replied mysteriously. "Cloud cover's so thick you never see the sun, makes takeoffs and landings bloody near impossible, you know. Then there are the disturbing rumors about the natives that live there."

"Oh, really?" Krisa asked, feeling a little tingle of excitement race through her. "What are they like?"

"No one really knows," Ketchum said darkly. "Savages with the most barbaric customs. Strange, ritualistic religious ceremonies, cannibalism. The unfortunate souls who wind up there for one reason or another hardly ever get back to civilization. It doesn't bear thinking about." He shuddered dramatically.

"But isn't it more likely that the people who crashed there died in the crash because they couldn't see to land? That wild rumors just grew because, as you say, almost nobody ever gets back?" Krisa asked practically. She liked a good ghost story as much as the next girl but this time what Ketchum was telling her seemed a bit far-fetched.

"You can believe what you like," the captain said, looking slightly annoyed. He much preferred, Krisa had noticed, for her to hang breathless upon his every word than to actually question and discuss any of his stories. But there was a practical, skeptical side of her that couldn't always be suppressed, despite her Briar Rose training.

"Percy is nodding at me, Captain Ketchum. I believe I shall have to say good night," she said, a bit coolly. "I hope you have a very pleasant journey and your delivery of Mr. Teague goes well with no complications." She rose, shaking out her skirts and giving Percy a nod to indicate that she was on her way to bed.

"Wait, please." To her surprise, the captain reached up and caught her hand in both of his. Krisa turned quickly so that her full skirts hid the contact, hoping that Percy hadn't seen.

"What is it, Captain?" she asked, wondering if he was aware of the impropriety of the gesture.

"It's been a lovely week, Miss Elyison. I hate for it to end so abruptly." The captain's blue eyes were melting with sincerity.

Suddenly, Krisa felt rather sorry that their time together was almost over. Some of his stories had been a bit overblown, perhaps, but on the whole Captain Ketchum had been an excellent traveling companion. He had certainly livened up what would otherwise have been a very dull, monotonous trip. None of the other twenty-odd passengers had been worth talking to. Most of them were businessmen with their noses buried in the financial reports, and Krisa shuddered at the thought of spending a solid week in conversation with Percy.

"It *has* been lovely," she said. "And I'm sorry to say goodbye, Captain Ketchum."

"Then don't, at least not yet," he said imploringly, still holding her hand.

"I don't see how I can avoid it," Krisa objected. "As you pointed out yourself, we'll all be locked in cryo-sleep by tomorrow morning."

"Yes, but I have something to give you. Something I think you'll like," he said. "Meet me at my cubicle in an hour, everyone should be asleep by then."

"But, Captain, I couldn't possibly..." The impropriety of what he was suggesting, that she meet him in a private place with no chaperone, must be obvious to Captain Ketchum. Yet he was asking it anyway.

"Your Mr. DeCampeaux is coming," he said, abruptly dropping her hand. "My cube in one hour. Don't be late." He picked up his glass and took another sip, leaving Krisa to think what she would, as she followed Percy back to her sleep cubicle.

Back at her own cubicle, Krisa paced as well as the extremely limited space would allow, and changed her mind about a dozen times. On one hand, it was extremely improper to meet with a man in a private room unchaperoned. On the other hand, her sense of adventure was aroused. What could the captain possibly want?

Men only want one thing, girls. You must beware of losing your greatest treasure and never be alone with a strange man — not even for an instant. The voice of Madame Ledoux, the deportment instructor at Briar Rose, echoed in her head. But that kind of thinking certainly didn't apply in this situation.

Captain Ketchum had never been anything less than the perfect gentleman the entire week. *Yes, but you never saw him except when Percy was watching over your shoulder.* Krisa shook the thought off. She was fairly certain that she knew the captain well enough to know that he wasn't a cad or a sex-fiend.

I'll go, she decided at last. After all, Captain Ketchum probably just wanted to give her some small token or memento of their week together. Perhaps he had made a little holo-vid, which she could keep with her to remember him by, if they should never meet again.

Krisa had several holo-vids from Lord Radisson, mostly sent to her on birthdays and for Winter Solstice. But the one she had from her mother, she cherished above everything else. Her mother had made it for her when Krisa was twelve, before she had been shipped away to Briar Rose. Krisa still took it out from time to time when she was feeling low or upset. It was all she had left of her mother, who had died when Krisa was thirteen and in her first semester at the Finishing Academy. *What would your mother think of what you're doing now?* whispered that inner voice that sounded like Madame Ledoux, but Krisa ignored it.

By the time she had made up her mind it was time to go. Krisa adjusted her tight cincher took a quick look in the viewer to be sure that her hair was pinned properly in place. She was wearing an extremely large and rather sharp ornamental hairpin in her thick brown ringlets. Lord Radisson had sent as a gift with Percy and she had already poked herself with it twice. Satisfied that she looked neat and ladylike, Krisa sneaked quietly out of her cubicle.

She crept along the corridor, silently counting to herself until she reached the next to last cube which she knew to be the captain's. Taking a deep breath, she rapped quietly and heard a low voice say, "Come in."

Letting herself into Captain Ketchum's cubicle without a chaperone took more courage than she was sure she had. For a long moment, Krisa hesitated, her hand on the door switch and her heart beating hard. She had almost decided that it was a bad idea and she should go back to her own cubicle, when she heard a sudden, heavy noise in the next sleep cube. It was probably just one of the businessmen turning over in his cot, but the sound galvanized Krisa into action. Before she knew it she had pressed the switch and slipped inside Captain Ketchum's cubicle. There was a faint hiss as the door closed behind her.

It was, if anything, even smaller than her quarters. Krisa saw with some unease that the captain was lounging on the cot with his maroon jacket off and his shirt halfway unbuttoned. The open shirt showed an expanse of hairy blond chest she didn't really want to see.

"Captain Ketchum?" she said, uncertainly.

"Krisa, I'm so glad you came. I was afraid you might lose your nerve at the last moment. Come, have a seat." He patted the space on the cot right beside him invitingly.

"Captain, I'm not sure…" Krisa began.

"Nonsense. And call me Owen, please. All this formality is silly—especially when we're going to get to know one another so much better."

Krisa wasn't sure she liked the sound of that, but somehow she found herself sitting beside him on the cot, a good deal closer than they had ever been before.

"Have a drink," Captain Ketchum said, pressing a small flask into her hand. Krisa almost took a small sip to be polite, but the fumes wafting from the mouth of the bottle let her know she'd better not.

"I've told you I don't drink alcoholic beverages," she reminded him, handing back the flask.

Ketchum shrugged. "Suit yourself. Just thought you'd like to have something to loosen you up."

"You said you had something for me?" Krisa asked pointedly. Suddenly she felt very anxious to be out of the tiny, confined space with the newly informal captain.

"Indeed I do, my dear, and I'm sure you're going to love it." He grinned at her in a way that she didn't like very much at all. "Lights, dim," he said and then scooted even closer as the cube became darker and more intimate. "I've been wanting to do this from the first minute I saw you," he murmured. Leaning forward, he took both her shoulders in his hands and tried to kiss her.

Krisa was so surprised that he actually succeeded at first. There was a warm, moist pressure on her lips and then his tongue was in her mouth and down her throat, spreading the strong, bitter taste of alcohol. Krisa gagged and pushed away suddenly as the impact of what he was doing hit her.

"What...?" She wiped a forearm across her mouth in a most unladylike way before she could stop herself. "What do you think you're doing?"

"Giving you your goodbye present, my dear." Captain Ketchum's smile, which had seemed so charming earlier in the week, now looked decidedly predatory. Krisa noticed with unease that he hadn't actually let go of her shoulders yet.

"I don't understand," she said, uncertainly. Suddenly the cincher, that contrived to make her small waist truly tiny, seemed much too tight to get a good deep breath. "I thought maybe you had recorded a holo-vid or something like that for me to remember you by."

"Oh, I can give you something much more interesting than a holo-vid to remember me by," Ketchum said, pulling her closer.

The smell of his Tazzenberry cologne was strong and cloying in her nostrils and under it was the faint odor of stale sweat. Why had she never noticed that before? *Because you were never this close before,* the little inner voice whispered. But Ketchum was still talking.

"I'm going to give you a night with a real man before you get chained forever to that wrinkled old bastard who's going to be your husband. Believe me, you'll look back on this night for years to come and thank me." He tried to kiss her again but Krisa managed to get both her hands on his chest and push forcefully away.

Madame Ledoux's words for a situation like this rose automatically to her lips. "Sir," she said as coldly as possible. "You forget yourself. I must beg you not to foist your unwanted attentions on me."

Ketchum sat back, obviously surprised by her rejection. "Unwanted attentions, eh?" he asked, with a nasty little sneer. "Why did you come at all if you didn't have the same thing in mind that I did?"

"I told you, I thought you had a picture or a holo-vid for me. I never dreamed..." Krisa shivered and shook her head. "I have to go."

"Not just yet, my dear." He grabbed her arm in a hurtful, pinching grip and Krisa gasped as he dug his fingers into a tender part of her elbow. Immediately, her entire forearm went numb.

"What are you doing? Let me go," she demanded, hardly able to believe this was happening. What had happened to the charming man she had met at the beginning of the trip? Who was this stranger with a shark's smile and his fingers digging into her arm?

"I'm explaining the facts of life, Krisa, my sweet," Ketchum said nastily. "You're just an ignorant little bitch from Bride Planet so I thought I might educate you some."

Krisa gasped and tried to wiggle free but Ketchum's grip on her arm was unrelenting.

"Let me go!" she said, raising her voice.

"In a moment, when I'm good and ready. Think twice before you scream, my dear. Do you really want your chaperone, the honorable Mr. DeCampeaux, to find you in such a compromising situation?" he asked, when Krisa opened her mouth to cry for help. "I thought not," he continued, when she closed her mouth abruptly at the awful thought. "That Certificate of Virginity I know you have tucked away in your little pink carryall cube wouldn't mean a whole hell of a lot if old Percy was to start telling tales out of school, now would it?"

Krisa shook her head, feeling almost dizzy with panic as her cincher seemed to get even tighter and more constrictive. This wasn't the way things were supposed to go at all. Captain Ketchum was supposed to offer her some little token of his undying esteem and perhaps even admit that he loved her. Then she, Krisa, would make a pretty little speech about how she would be eternally sorry that she could not return his affections but that she would keep him always in her heart. Then they would both part with a bittersweet memory to cherish forever.

Stupid, Stupid, STUPID! screamed the little voice in her head. The practical part of herself that she had never been completely able to suppress rose to the forefront of her brain. *You got yourself into this, you'll have to get yourself out,* it said. *Now think of something and think* fast.

Raising her other arm, the one he wasn't currently nearly pinching in two, Krisa grabbed the large, ornamental hairpin from her hair and pulled it free, shaking out her chocolate-brown curls in what she hoped was a seductive way.

"Now that's more like it," Ketchum said approvingly. "I knew you'd see it my way once you'd thought about it. Most women do."

Most women do, Krisa thought numbly. *And* he had known about her Certificate of Virginity. Had Captain Ketchum done this before? Spent a week befriending some hapless, naïve girl who was traveling for the first time to meet her husband-to-be, then lured her into his cubicle and blackmailed her into doing what he wanted? She was very much afraid that he had. *Well, this is one girl it's not going to work on,* the grim little voice in her head whispered.

Taking a firm grip on the ornamental head of the pin, Krisa jabbed it as hard as she could into the hand that was gripping her arm.

"Ouch! You little *bitch!*" Ketchum yelped and jumped. The small cot they sat on rocked and creaked alarmingly with his movement. His grip loosened but didn't relax completely.

"Let me go or I'll do it again," Krisa said in a grim voice she barely recognized as her own. "I'm not going to make this easy for you, Captain Ketchum."

The steely look in her brown eyes must have convinced him that she was serious because he relaxed his grip enough for her to move away.

"Fine," he said sulkily, like a little boy who has been denied the toy he wants. "Run away back to your own cubicle, Krisa. But someday in the near future you're going to look back and wish you'd taken this opportunity."

"I very much doubt that," Krisa said, backing carefully away from him. She was still holding the large hairpin as though it was a blaster in one hand.

"Oh but you will," he said nastily. "Do you know what they'll do to you as soon as you sign the joining contract with the old geezer on Lynix Prime who's bought and paid for you? They'll activate that tiny little chastity chip right at the base of your neck, and if you ever even so much as *think* of another man again, it'll deliver a jolt of pure agony straight to your central nervous system."

"That's right." Ketchum nodded and smiled the nasty, predatory grin again. "You'll feel like every single nerve ending is on fire, Krisa, my dear. You won't even be able to *dream* of running away or have a single thought your husband doesn't approve of. You'll be trapped there *forever*. I hope you enjoy it every night Lord Limp-Dick tries to mount you when you think of how you had a chance at a *real* man and you didn't take it."

"You...you're lying," Krisa said in a shaky voice. Her mouth felt so dry she was amazed she could get the words out and again it was hard to get a deep breath. She wished distantly that it was permissible to loosen the tight cincher around her waist just a little. Nobody at Briar Rose had ever said anything about a — what had he called it? — a chastity chip, that was it. But then, why were they able to advertise that Briar Rose brides never ever left their husbands?

"That chip was placed in my neck for identification purposes in case I was ever kidnapped and they had to track me," Krisa protested. But the excuses sounded false and half-hearted even to her.

Without thinking about it, she raised one hand to the tiny little bump, right beneath her hairline at the back of her neck, where the chip Ketchum was talking about resided. It had been implanted her first semester at Briar Rose. The procedure had been so simple and uncomplicated that she had accepted it without question. Every one of the Briar Rose girls had one, and she had only been thirteen at the time.

"Oh they can track you with it all right," Ketchum sneered. "But it has its other purposes, as you'll find out soon enough. So go on, Krisa, my sweet. Run back to your cubicle and have a nice life as a sweet little wifey on Lynix Prime. You weren't pretty enough to be worth the effort anyhow." He pressed the door switch and jerked his head for her to get out.

Krisa stumbled out into the hall and the door whooshed shut behind her, leaving her with one last look at the distorted sneer of Captain Ketchum's formerly handsome face.

Chapter Four

ဆာ

Not true. It can't be true, Krisa thought over and over like a chant as she raced back down the long line of cubicles to her own. *They wouldn't – they couldn't. Or could they?*

Why do you think Briar Rose brides are so expensive? the practical little voice in her head asked. Krisa was beginning to wish that little voice would shut up but it went on talking just the same. *Why are they guaranteed to stay with any man that buys one for life? It's even right in their motto – A Briar Rose Wife is Faithful for Life.*

Krisa tried to push the thought out of her head but it wouldn't go. Even Captain Ketchum's monstrous attack on her faded to insignificance in the light of what he had told her about the chip in the back of her neck.

She ran to the fresher and hit the on button for the holo-viewer the minute she got inside her cubicle. Then she reached inside her proper-for-evening-wear gown and wrenched out the wretched cincher that had been constricting her breathing all night. Waiting impatiently for the viewer to warm up, she pulled up her hair and rubbed the tiny, inconspicuous little bump with the tip of her index finger. *How deep?* she thought. *How deep does it go? Is it hooked into my spinal cord?*

She wished she knew a little more biology and anatomy but such hard science classes were not encouraged at Briar Rose. Krisa wouldn't even have known as much as she did if one of the girls in her dormitory hadn't had a doting older brother who had smuggled her episodes of the drama med-vid *LifeLink* from time to time.

She had taken three semesters of butterfly collecting and one of raising herbs for use in the kitchen. That was the sum of her scientific knowledge, except what she'd been able to glean from the smuggled *LifeLink* vids and the limited school library, which tended to be heavy on romance and cookbooks and light on practically everything else. Of course, everyone knew that at Briar Rose a girl was trained to be a perfect wife, not a surgeon or a spaceship pilot or anything else that was even remotely interesting.

"Oh Goddess," she muttered as the viewer finally warmed up and she was able to adjust it to see the back of her neck. The little bump was there all right, about a half an inch square from side to side, as her questing finger had told her. But that was the limit of what sight could tell her. *How deep?* she thought again.

She knew it always stung if she scraped it with a hairpin or a brush, but now she pressed the bump experimentally with one finger, harder than she ever had before. A wave of dizzying pain drove like an iron spike into the base of her skull and Krisa actually had to clutch at the slippery sides of the little sink to keep from falling. Was this what she had to look forward to if she ever had the impudence to think for herself once she sighed the joining contract with Lord Radisson? This horrible jagged agony? *Oh Goddess, say it isn't so!*

Krisa flipped off the viewer and paced restlessly up and down the length of the tiny sleep cube. Soon she began to feel dizzy from walking in circles and had to sit down on the cot. What should she do? On one hand she had been promised to Lord Radisson since the age of thirteen. *But I didn't promise him my mind or my free will*, Krisa thought angrily. On the other hand, how could she avoid giving him those things?

Captain Ketchum was a nasty piece of work and he might be lying just to pay her back for refusing his offer. How she could have ever thought him a gentleman was beyond Krisa. She was tempted to go wake up Percy that very minute and demand the truth but what good would it do? And how could she explain her sudden knowledge of what was obviously a

Briar Rose secret—at least to the brides they brokered—to her extremely proper chaperone?

Well, if asking Percy was out of the question what else could she do? Ask Lord Radisson nicely not to activate the chip? Or what if she cut it out somehow, right now, tonight? Would she be able to hide the back of her neck until the wound healed sufficiently?

Krisa thought of the terrible wave of pain she'd experienced when she only pressed hard on the bump at the back of her neck and shuddered. Cutting out the chip would be agony and she wasn't sure she could do it. Then again, what if the chip *was* somehow hooked into her spinal cord and she botched the job and killed or paralyzed herself? What then?

Krisa put her head on her knees and cried silently, her shoulders heaving with a misery like nothing she had ever felt since her mother died. Her mother, if only she could talk to her one more time! She had been a strong woman, opposed to sending any of her daughters to Briar Rose, for she and Krisa's father had seven of them and only one son. Up until the time her mother died, Krisa had been hoping to go back home, to the other side of Capellia. But when her mother died, that hope died with her. Krisa was the oldest and the prettiest and the Bride Price she fetched would keep her family in style for a good long time. But oh, if only her mother had lived, Krisa just *knew* she wouldn't be in this hopeless situation now.

Suddenly it seemed clear to her that if she could just watch the cherished holo-vid of her mother again she could make up her mind about what to do. It was stored in her pink carryall cube in the hold. Krisa hadn't been back there since the scare she'd had the second night out.

The huge Feral had really given her a fright, talking like that when she'd been so sure he was asleep. But now she felt that nothing could be more frightening that the prospect of being controlled the rest of her life by the chip in her neck. What was one massive homicidal sociopathic killer to that?

Besides, he *was* chained up, and if he said anything to her she could just ignore him.

Krisa went into the fresher and ran herself a tall, cold glass of water and drank it all straight down. Then she splashed some more of the precious liquid on her cheeks to cool her heated face. She was perfectly aware of how expensive water was on a ship—she had probably just cost Lord Radisson another thousand credits with her little extravagance. *Who gives a damn?* the little voice in her head demanded. Defiantly, Krisa drew another whole glass. She would sip it while she rummaged in her cube to find her mother's holo. Clutching the slippery glass in one hand, she slipped out into the corridor.

She was more than a little nervous as she passed the next to last cube but from inside she heard the steady snores of a man well and truly asleep. *Sweet dreams, Captain Ketchum,* she thought sardonically, *I hope every one of them is a nightmare.* But she had to admit that if he was telling the truth, he had given her a valuable piece of information.

The question was, what would she do with the knowledge now that she had it?

Chapter Five

‰

Slipping into the darkened hold, Krisa felt her way to the stack of luggage that was hers and Percy's and began to feel around for the pale pink carryall cube that held her most treasured possessions.

"Turn on the lights if you want. Doesn't bother me."

The deep, gravelly voice startled her so much that Krisa nearly spilled her water. Setting the glass down carefully on the floor, she turned to face the manacled Feral.

"W-what did you say?" she asked, her determination to ignore the huge prisoner forgotten.

"I said turn on the lights. It'll make finding whatever you're lookin' for easier." His tone was so casual and civil that it startled her. She didn't know what she had expected from Teague, maybe threats or ravings, or more strangely oblique statements about being able to smell her, but not casual civility.

"Lights, dim." Her voice was low and hesitant but the overhead glows beamed on anyway, emitting a soft, golden radiance into the metal-lined room that greatly improved visibility. But instead of going back to digging in her carryall cube, Krisa found her eyes were once again drawn to Teague. There was just something about him that was so awful it was fascinating.

"How about givin' me a drink of that water once you find what you're lookin' for?" He spoke in the same casual tone, his head turned toward her. It was as though he was looking straight at her, despite the heavy blindfold still wrapped around his eyes.

Krisa started. "How do you know? Can you see me?" she demanded at last.

"How do I know you've got water? I can smell it. And I heard the glass clink when you set it on the floor. My nose and ears are as good as your eyes, maybe better, little girl." He shifted and the magno-locks clinked against the metal wall he leaned against.

"My name is Krisa," she said automatically. Carryall forgotten, she picked up the glass of water and moved toward him hesitantly.

"I know." He grinned, that wild white grin that had so frightened her when she first saw him. Now she compared it with Captain Ketchum's nasty leer and it didn't seem so bad. At least Teague was up-front about what he was, unlike that snake that was guarding him.

Another thought occurred to her. "How do you know my name?" Krisa edged a little closer.

"Heard you tell Ketch the first day. How about that water, now? Ferals can go a long time without, but I wouldn't mind at least one more drink before everybody else goes into cryo-sleep."

"But the trip to Lynix Omega is at least two and a half weeks." She knew that Captain Ketchum went back at least once a day with a loaded blaster to give his prisoner nutrient paste and something to drink, but she'd assumed a crew member would take over that duty while the captain was in cryo-sleep. "Won't one of the crew see to your needs while Captain Ketchum is asleep?"

"Nope. Not in their contract to handle a dangerous felon like me. Besides, they'll all be in cryo-sleep with the rest of you good girls and boys."

"Oh, that's right," Krisa murmured. She had forgotten that once the ship's hyperdrive engaged, even the captain and crew of the ship went into cryo-sleep, leaving the ship to run its set course until they woke up in orbit around Lynix Prime.

Along the way, the *Star Princess* would slow minimally to allow passengers that had stops on its route to "jet out" using the specially designed landing capsules that could be deployed during hyperdrive mode.

The only two passengers jetting on this trip were Ketchum and his prisoner, but that was two and a half weeks from now. Apparently Teague was going to be kept chained to the wall for the entire time it took to get to Lynix Omega where the correctional facility was located. Krisa remembered Captain Ketchum's little speech about "unnecessary brutality" at the beginning of the voyage and felt sick. What was leaving a man, even a man like Teague, chained in the hold of the ship without food or water for two weeks, if not brutal?

"I can't believe you're just going to be left here for two and a half weeks with nothing to eat or drink," she said.

He bared his teeth in that white, disarming grin again. "I've gone without for longer. It's no fun but I can do it— Ferals are tough. I wouldn't mind one more drink before the long haul though. Ketch didn't come in tonight for some reason. Probably wants me weak before we jet so I don't cause him any trouble."

Because he was trying to seduce me, Krisa realized, feeling obscurely guilty. *That's why Captain Ketchum didn't give Teague his rations tonight. Getting what he wanted from the "ignorant little bitch from Bride Planet" was more important than seeing to the needs of the man entrusted to his keeping.*

"I'll give you some water," she said, tentatively. She stepped forward, coming closer to him than she had since the night he'd given her such a scare. "Only, I'm not sure…" She was looking for a way to give him the glass but she realized that his bound hands were much too far from his mouth for him to be able to get the glass to his lips himself.

"You'll have to hold it for me," he said.

Krisa hesitated and he startled her by laughing, a deep, rumbling sound that seemed to come from the very bottom of his massive chest.

"I get it," he said. "Ol' Ketch probably told you I'd bite your fingers off if I got half a chance. Well, you don't have to worry, little girl. I promise not to bite. At least, not right now."

"Don't call me that, I told you my name is Krisa," she said, stung by his impertinence.

"All right, Krisa. Can I please have some of your water?" he asked so politely that she almost laughed herself.

Without answering she held the glass up to his full, red mouth and tilted it carefully. He drank in long swallows that made the Adam's apple in his corded neck move up and down rapidly and didn't spill a drop.

Seeing that he was finished, Krisa lifted the empty glass from his lips. But at the last moment, Teague's tongue shot out and licked the rim, catching her thumb in a wet, shocking motion at the same time. She made a little gasp of indrawn air and pulled her hand away, clutching the violated digit inside her fist.

"Sorry," Teague said, but there was laughter in his deep voice. Krisa couldn't help thinking he'd done it on purpose somehow—that he'd wanted to *taste* her for some reason. But that was crazy, wasn't it?

"Is…is everything I've heard about you true?" she found herself asking, still clutching the empty glass in one hand.

"Well now, that depends on who you been listenin' to," Teague replied in an amused tone. "What have you heard, exactly?"

"I heard… Captain Ketchum told me that…that you killed a lot of people," Krisa said in a hushed tone. She didn't want to ask if Teague had really gouged out his victims' hearts and eyes with his knife, it seemed rude, somehow.

"That's true," he said. And then, as if reading her mind he added, "I guess you wanna know how I did 'em."

"Well…" Krisa hesitated. "He said that…that you used a knife," she said at last, still feeling dreadfully impolite. But was there any proper way to ask how someone had preformed a murder? The topic certainly fell well outside the boundaries of Madame Ledoux's Conversational Etiquette lessons.

"When you're tryin' to get out of someplace without anybody knowing, a knife is a lot quieter than a blaster," Teague pointed out. "You just creep up behind 'em and slit their throat. No muss, no fuss. Well, actually, there's considerable fuss if they catch you at it, but you get my meaning."

"I...yes, I guess I do." Krisa's throat had suddenly gone dry and she wished for another sip of water herself. She knew she should leave the hold and stop talking to this strange, savage man but somehow she felt trapped. She was held in place by his cool, casual words, as surely as he was held in place by the magno-locks that chained him to the wall. "Did..." She cleared her throat nervously. "Did you really enjoy it?"

"No," he answered immediately, the full red mouth frowning a little. That made her feel a little better but then he followed it up with, "Didn't particularly bother me either, though."

"I don't understand," Krisa said simply. "How...how could it not?"

Teague sighed and shifted, his chains clinking against the metal wall behind him. "I'm sure Ketch told you how I killed people in detail — most of it probably exaggerated — but did he tell you why?"

"He said that you liked it," Krisa said, clutching the slippery glass tight in one hand. "That you did it for fun."

"Well, I already told you that wasn't it," Teague pointed out, sounding impatient. He shifted his head so that he appeared to be looking at her again, despite the thick blindfold. "Have you ever heard of my home planet, Al'hora?"

"No, not really. Capellia's in a fairly isolated arm of the galaxy," Krisa admitted.

"Yeah, Bride Planet's pretty far out." Teague nodded. "Guess you're going to meet your future husband, eh?" Krisa didn't answer so he continued. "Al'hora is tidally locked — ring any bells?"

"No, I'm afraid not," Krisa said humbly. She didn't want to have to go into the educational deficiencies of Briar Rose Academy so she simply said, "Tell me."

"Means that the sun we orbit has such a huge gravitational pull that Al'hora can't rotate on its axis the way most planets do. One side is always facing the sun so it's always day. The other side always faces away so it's always night. I'm a Feral, my people inhabit the night side of the planet."

"Oh, of course. Your eyes," Krisa gestured and then realized he couldn't see the motion. "The captain said that was the reason for your blindfold."

There was that white grin again, but Krisa found she was almost getting used to it. "Well, strictly speaking, the blindfold's not really necessary," Teague said.

"But I thought, Captain Ketchum said — "

"Yeah, ol' Ketch says a lot of things. Lift up the blindfold and look at my eyes."

"But won't that hurt you?" Krisa objected.

"Turn off the overhead glows first."

"Lights off," Krisa said. The overhead glows extinguished at once plunging the hold into an eerie green gloom. She set the glass down on the floor beside her and stepped forward toward the chained man again, but then she hesitated.

This close the wild, spicy scent of him was strong in her nose, and she could feel the heat radiating from his big body in the chilly hold like a banked fire. Pulling back the blindfold and looking into his eyes seemed a much more personal act than merely giving him a drink of water. The memory of him licking her thumb was still strong and somehow disturbing.

"Still afraid?" he asked, the deep voice lightly mocking.

"Would you...will you give me your word you won't hurt me?" Krisa asked hesitantly.

"I'm not exactly a gentleman, Krisa," he said dryly. "Would you take my word if I gave it?"

Krisa thought of the last "gentleman" she had trusted, Captain Ketchum, and decided again that she liked Teague better. At least he didn't try to hide what he was or pretend to be something he wasn't.

"Yes," she said firmly. "If you give me your word I'll take it."

There was a long pause and then Teague said, "You have my word. Lift up the blindfold."

Krisa felt for the edge of the thick black blindfold. It was made of a heavy feltlike material and was fitted cruelly tight around his head, cutting into his face. She couldn't find a way to untie it, and at last she had to settle for prying it up with her fingernails, being careful not to scratch Teague's cheeks as she did so.

He let out a long sigh when she finally managed to slip the heavy strip of material off. Even in the faint, greenish glow from the radiance strips, she could see the red lines the blindfold had left behind on his dusky skin.

"Better," he grunted at last, turning his head to rub one cheek against the rough material of his black tank top. "Now look at my eyes," he commanded, turning back again. Krisa looked and a little gasp of surprise escaped her.

Teague's eyes were a pure, luminous silver, glowing faintly in the dark like a cat's eyes. Also like a cat's was the vertical, slitted pupil that bisected each glowing silver orb. Krisa was reminded again of the panther she had seen as a child. His eyes were the most beautiful and the most deadly she had ever looked into.

Apparently Teague liked what he saw as well, for those glowing silver eyes roamed up and down her body in a leisurely visual tour that made Krisa blush. "Nice," he rumbled after inspecting her thoroughly. "Thought you would be." Somehow Krisa knew he wasn't talking about her personality.

"Why did you want me to see your eyes?" she asked, trying to get the conversation back where it belonged.

"Sorry, it's been a long time since I saw a woman, especially such a pretty one."

"Thank you," Krisa said, blushing harder. "Your eyes?" she said again, pointedly.

"Oh, yeah. Turn on the lights—dim, though. And watch my eyes."

Krisa realized that the ship's lights probably weren't programmed to recognize his voice print as they were for other passengers and the crew. "Lights, dim," she said, staring into the unblinking silver orbs.

It made her nervous to have so much direct eye contact with this man who she barely knew and who was known to be dangerous. It was intimate, somehow, standing over him and staring down into those eyes, though she didn't have to stare very far down. Teague was so tall they were nearly on eye-level even though he was sitting and she was standing.

The moment the overhead glows beamed on, shedding their soft, golden radiance throughout the hold, Teague's eyes flickered strangely. Suddenly, almost too fast for her to see, a black membrane swept down covering not only the lenses and pupils of his eyes, but the whites as well.

"Oh," Krisa gasped, taking a small, involuntary step back. "What *is* that?" His eyes now had a blank, alien look that she found far more disturbing than the slitted pupils and silver lenses.

"Second eyelid. It's a mutation some of us have—the ones raised in the light. In captivity." Teague's voice was a low growl.

"But I thought you came from the Night side of Al'hora," Krisa objected.

"No, I said my *people* come from the Night side. I was born on the Day side. Born into slavery — raised to serve a Daysider master my entire life. Freedom was never an option." The deep voice was thick with anger now. It vibrated his massive chest and Krisa felt from the soles of her feet right up to her head.

"That's terrible," she said with heartfelt sincerity. "Raised as a slave to serve some man who had no right to own you — "

"Oh?" Teague looked at her with those oddly alien eyes, like twin pools of midnight in his dark face. "And how was my situation different from yours, little girl? Weren't you bought and sold, just like me? I may be the one wearing the chains but it sounds to me like we're both goin' to prison."

"I-I never thought of it like that," Krisa whispered, putting a hand to her mouth. How *were* their situations different? Her family had sold her to Briar Rose for a price and the academy, in turn, had sold her contract to a man she'd never seen. A man who would own her, body and soul for the rest of her life once the chip in her neck was activated, if Ketchum could be believed. She shook her head, not wanting to think about it.

"So you killed your master?" she asked, trying to change the subject.

"Not the first one, no." Teague gave her that white, frightening grin again, but now she thought she had an idea of where some of the savagery behind that grin came from. *Born in captivity. Raised as a slave.*

"The first one died of natural causes," he said. "The *second* one I killed. Stole a ship and skipped the planet. Son of a bitch was stupid enough to have me trained as a pilot."

"Is that why you got sent to Lynix Omega in the first place?" Krisa asked.

"Among other things, but the Deep Freeze isn't the first slam I've been in by a long shot, sweetheart. See, it wasn't just that I killed him. It was the *way* I did it," Teague emphasized.

"I'm sure you heard plenty already from Ketch about my 'expert knife work'." Krisa shuddered, staring at those opaque black eyes. "How can you talk about it like that?

"How can you be so causal about it?" she demanded.

Massive shoulders shrugged, causing the chains to clink softly. "I did what I had to in order to survive. Gets to be a way of life when you're on the run," he said. "Although in my defense, my old master was the only one you could say I really 'carved up'. It got me a reputation though."

"You sound like you're proud of it," Krisa said, her throat dry.

"No," Teague said simply. "Proud I survived, maybe. But havin' the rep saved my ass more than once. Gets to be a pain sometimes, though. Look at the way they have me chained up back here. Not takin' any chances, just like Ketch told you."

Krisa narrowed her eyes, chocolate brown staring into opaque black. "You're telling me not to be afraid of you. That you're not as bad as I was led to believe," she said at last.

Teague blinked and the black, second lens that covered his eyes retracted. He stared at her with blazing silver eyes, the vertical cat's pupil contracted to a nearly invisible slit.

"That's not what I'm tellin' you at all, little girl. I'm in a good mood right now. I couldn't say what kind of mood I'd be in if these chains weren't holdin' me down," he growled.

He surged forward unexpectedly to the limit of the magno-locks, chains pulling taut behind him. Suddenly that savage face was less than an inch from hers. Krisa gasped and stumbled backwards, nearly tripping in her haste to get away. The glass at her feet tipped over and shattered with a musical crash. A messy spray of brittle shards scattered across the metal floor plates.

Teague glared at her a moment more and then subsided back onto the narrow bench behind him.

"My point is that sometimes things get exaggerated," he said in a completely normal tone of voice. The black membrane flickered back down over his eyes as he spoke and he once again looked as casual and non-threatening as was possible for such a huge man to look. "Ketch, for instance, tends to exaggerate quite a bit, especially in his own favor."

Krisa still had one hand pressed hard against her pounding heart. She glared at the huge Feral. "That wasn't funny." As if she hadn't had enough trauma for one night!

"Wasn't meant to be," Teague said quietly. "Did Ketch tell you how he caught me?"

Krisa knew she should abandon the conversation—things were getting too dangerous. In fact, she had half turned her back to go but now she turned back around.

She had been asking herself the same question all week— how had someone like Captain Ketchum been able to catch and subdue someone as formidable as Teague? Even before she'd known the truth about the captain, he had seemed to her to be more talk than action—*in most situations at least*, she amended to herself. Teague's question hooked her back in and she turned reluctantly to face him again, making sure to stay a safe distance this time.

"How did he do it?" she asked, promising herself that she would leave after she got the answer.

"He didn't," Teague said, grinning again. "He's just transporting me. I was trekking to Alpha Lyrae and had the bad luck to run into a whole frigate full of Royal Spacers. Took a whole regiment to bring me down—quite a scene—but they got me in the end. Of course, half of them won't be writin' home to tell anybody about it." He said it not as a boast but as a simple, chilling statement of fact.

Krisa noticed that the white grin had fallen away as suddenly as it had appeared, leaving his dark face blank and impassive. The expression chilled her to the bone but what he had said struck home with her.

"So he lied," she said. "Captain Ketchum *lied*." *And if he lied about one thing maybe he lied about other things too. About the chip*, she thought, hopefully. "Does he lie a lot, then?" she asked, bending down and beginning to gather the scattered shards of glass that lay around their feet.

"Not as much as some but more than others," Teague said noncommittally. "Why? What'd he tell you?"

Krisa rose and deposited the handful of glass she'd gathered on a conveniently placed box. She worked carefully and deliberately as though to make sure she didn't get cut but she was really trying to think of a way to tell him what had happened. Finally, she decided to just blurt it out.

"Tonight he tried t-to... But I wouldn't let him," she stuttered, feeling her cheeks grow hot. She looked up at Teague but his face was still impassive, not helping her in any way. "Anyway, he said I'd be sorry I didn't take the chance to be with a real man. He said that the ID chip in the back of my neck is actually a chastity chip and once he—my future husband, I mean—activates it on Lynix Prime, I won't be able to *think* of anyone else, or of trying to get away without having severe pain." Krisa took a deep breath.

"But he could be lying, couldn't he? I mean, just to be nasty? Because I wouldn't...you know?" She looked at Teague hopefully but he didn't immediately rush to support her theory as she wanted him to so desperately. Instead he looked thoughtful.

"Right at the back of your neck? Below the hairline?" he asked.

Krisa nodded.

"Show me," he commanded.

Turning she raised the heavy mass of dark brown ringlets to show him the back of her neck. It suddenly occurred to her that she had been standing and talking to him for the past half hour with her hair down and while not wearing a cincher under her gown, yet she hadn't thought of the impropriety of her actions once. She and Teague seemed to have gotten beyond the basic social niceties somehow.

"Closer," Teague growled.

Krisa half turned her head, giving him an uncertain look.

"I won't bite you—I need to *see* it," he said, exasperation clear in his deep voice.

Nerves prickling with unease, Krisa backed closer until she was almost sitting in his lap. Standing between his massive, spread thighs she could feel his hot breath blowing over the naked back of her neck as he examined the small bump closely. The sensation sent shivers racing up and down her spine and she half expected to feel his tongue, warm and wet and shocking, lick along her exposed nape at any time.

"All right," Teague said at last and she dropped her hair, glad to cover the vulnerable flesh, and turned back to face him.

"Well?" she asked expectantly.

"Can't be for sure but it looks like the same size and placement as the pain chips they put in you when you go to the slam," he said. "A regular ID chip is a fourth that big— tiny. Pain chips have to be bigger to hold the programmable part. The first one I had was supposed to be programmed to keep me from even *thinkin'* about escape without pain, but I got around it."

"How?" Krisa asked hopefully.

"I thought about it all the time," Teague said blandly. "After a while I got used to the pain. The night I went over the wall I got rid of it."

"You found someone to remove it?" Krisa asked.

"I cut it out," he rumbled. "Just another example of my 'excellent knife work'" He grinned.

"So it *can* be removed without damaging the spinal cord? I could do that, could cut it out?" Krisa felt a surge of hope.

"I wouldn't recommend it." Teague shifted, making the chains rustle and clank. He frowned. "It hurt like a son of a bitch, takin' that thing outta my neck. Nearly passed out twice and you should know I don't faint easy." The grin again. "I

55

would of waited until I got somewhere where somebody I trusted could do it for me—somebody with anesthesia and the right equipment—but they could have tracked me in the time it took me to get where I needed to be. I didn't have a choice. Why, were you thinkin' of performing a little operation on yourself tonight, sweetheart?"

"The thought crossed my mind," Krisa admitted. Now that Teague had confirmed her fears about the chip, she felt a dull kind of dread, like a ball of lead, in the pit of her belly. "But even if I managed to take out the chip…"

"What would your darlin' hubby think when you got to Prime?" Teague finished for her. "He'd wonder why the perfect wife he paid for showed up with a hole in her neck. Might as well ask him right off the bat to drop the 'honor and obey' part out of the joining ceremony vows, eh? Don't think he'd appreciate it too much."

"But if I don't then I'll be stuck forever," Krisa protested, running a hand through her tangled curls distractedly.

"Weren't you going to be anyway?" Teague asked with maddening practicality. "Did you really have plans to run away and head an expedition to the unexplored arms of the galaxy or lead a life of crime as an intergalactic jewel thief?" He smirked annoyingly.

"No, but…" Krisa sighed in frustration, trying to put her tumultuous feelings into words. "I was resigned to being married to him. Lord Radisson has owned my contract since I was *thirteen*," she said. "I knew he would…own my body, do what he wanted that way." She felt her cheeks getting hot and found she couldn't look Teague in the eyes. "But nobody said anything about him owning my mind. Nobody said I wouldn't be able to think my own thoughts. That wasn't part of the deal," she flared.

"So a man can own your body but not your soul?" he inquired dryly.

Krisa shrugged angrily. "You said yourself our situations were similar. Did *you* enjoy being a slave?"

His face darkened and the black second lid flickered briefly, exposing a quick glimpse of narrowed silver eyes. "Similar but not exactly the same, little girl," he growled. "And I think my actions made it pretty clear I didn't enjoy it." He shrugged massive shoulders, chains clinking. "Sometimes though, you have to play the hand life deals you."

"*You* didn't," Krisa pointed out, feeling more and more upset. "I don't mind leaving my home planet to go live with a man I've never met, I always knew I'd have to. But I don't want any man controlling my thoughts and feelings. There are some parts of me *nobody* should be able to touch."

"Really?" Teague said in a detached tone that incited her further. "And what parts are those?"

"Goddessdamn it!" Krisa exploded angrily, discarding propriety completely. "I don't want him *inside my head*!"

Teague looked mildly surprised. "Such language from a lady," he mocked. "I'm surprised, Krisa." But his tone was at least halfway admiring. "So basically you want to remove the chip but keep the rich husband that comes with it."

"I don't care about the money," Krisa said hotly. "But where else can I go? It's not like I have anyplace I can stay, and I certainly can't afford the price of an interstellar ticket to take me back to Capellia, even if my father would take me back. Which he wouldn't," she added, knowing it to be true.

"That's a sad story, little girl," Teague said, the corners of his full mouth twitching slightly.

Krisa felt her rage bubbling to the surface again. "I don't know why I bothered to tell you anything," she said, feeling her small hands ball into tight fists of anger. "If you weren't chained up and helpless I'd...*slap* you."

"Don't ever make the mistake of thinkin' I'm helpless, Krisa," he drawled lazily and she saw another quick flash of silver in his eyes. "Bigger and considerably more dangerous people than you have paid for the privilege of putting hands on me with their lives. I like you, but don't think that makes you any different."

"I'm leaving." For the second time, Krisa turned away from him but Teague's words stopped her again.

"I know how you can do it," he said. His deep voice was so soft it was more a vibration than a sound.

"What?" Krisa faced him again.

"How you can jettison the chip but keep the credit that comes with it. I know how you can do it."

"You have my attention." Krisa crossed her arms over her full breasts and patted one small, slippered foot on the floor.

"Listen, I'll only say it once." Teague leaned forward, his chains clinking. "I've been all over the Lynix System, even before I got sent to the Deep Freeze. There's a man in Centaura that can help you—that's the capital of Lynix Prime. Know where I mean?"

"That's where I'm headed. Lord Radisson, the man who bought my contract, is Prime's planetary envoy. He lives there." Krisa felt her heart beating slightly faster.

Teague nodded curtly. "Right, then you should be able to find him pretty easy. His name is Dr. T'lix. Alphonius T'lix— they call him the chip doctor. All you need to do is go to the Great Market—they hold it every ten-day in the Central Square in Centaura. On the west side there's a flower stall and the vendor is a tall woman with dark red hair. Ask her for blue roses from the Rigel System then hang around. She'll let T'lix know you want to see him."

"Find the woman with red hair at the flower stall on the west side of the market and ask for blue Rigelian roses," Krisa recited, nodding.

"When he comes," Teague said, "tell him Kurt Teague is calling in a favor. If he gives you a hard time, tell him to remember what happened on Pentaurus Five."

"What *did* happen on Pentaurus Five?" Krisa asked, intrigued.

"Never mind," Teague said darkly. "You don't want to know, little girl. Just remember it to tell T'lix."

"And he—Dr. T'lix—will be able to help me?" Krisa asked.

"He can remove the chastity chip and put in a dummy chip instead. He's good—removed more than a few from me. Since that first one I don't do my own surgery unless there's no other option." Teague grinned briefly.

"But, Krisa," he continued seriously. "If you're lucky, you'll be able to meet with T'lix before they activate the chip. If you're not lucky and the first Market day falls after they activate it, it's gonna hurt like hell to even remember what I just told you.

"Every step you take down to the Central Square will be like walking on live coals. When you say T'lix's name it'll be like swallowing fire. Now listen to me." He leaned forward. "*Do it anyway*," he emphasized quietly in his deep, intense voice. "Do it as soon as you can or you'll *never* be free. The longer the chip stays in your body, the more hold it has over you. Over your mind and your free will. Understand?"

"I…" Krisa swallowed hard. "I understand," she said at last. "And Teague, thank you. You didn't have to give me this information or the right to call in your favor."

He shrugged his massive shoulders, chains clinking. Krisa thought that for the rest of her life, when she heard that particular sound, or anything like it, she would think of the big Feral.

"You gave me a glass of water when I was thirsty—you didn't have to do that. Nobody else on this whole damn ship would've. I always pay my debts, it's the Feral way." He spoke as though it was a code he lived by.

Krisa thought that no matter what else he had done, there was a twisted kind of honor in this huge man. And twisted honor was better than no honor at all.

"Still," she said. "Thank you." Then she did something that surprised even her.

Leaning forward, she cupped one rough, unshaven cheek in her palm and pressed a soft, chaste kiss to his full mouth.

Aside from Captain Ketchum's very unwanted attentions earlier that evening, it was her first kiss, and Krisa had to admit she enjoyed it. It was dangerous, like daring to stroke a panther when you weren't sure if it would lick your hand or tear off your fingers with one savage bite. She felt the familiar thrill of adrenaline running down her spine, and a little ache of sadness right behind it. Surely all the kisses in her life from now on would be safe and dull.

It was over in an instant but afterwards she couldn't help running the tip of her tongue over her lips to capture the wild taste of him. She saw that Teague was licking his lips as well, with a thoughtful expression on his sharp features.

"You taste good, little girl," he growled. "Keep that up and I'll owe you another favor." Krisa saw the black second lids retract briefly and the silver eyes beneath looked both softer and more intense at the same time. She shivered, feeling the thrill along her spine again and an answering heat bloomed between her thighs and at the sensitive tips of her breasts.

"I'd better go," she said reluctantly. "I have to get to bed before the cryo-sleep sets in. I guess...I'll never see you again," she added rather hopelessly.

"Oh, I wouldn't be too sure about that, little girl," he replied teasingly. "Remember what I told you about the chip."

"I won't forget. Thank you again." She felt the urge to kiss him one more time and suppressed it sternly. It was time to get back to her normal self. *Enough impropriety for one night,*

Madame Ledoux's voice scolded inside her head. This time Krisa listened to it.

"Good night," she said. She swept the shards of glass into her hand and turned to go before a thought struck her. "Oh wait, should I put the blindfold back on you?" she asked.

Teague gave her one last glimpse at his wild, white grin. "Nah, just dim the lights on your way out. Let Ketch wonder how the hell I managed to get it off. It'll scare 'im more than he already is."

Krisa grinned back at him, liking the idea. "All right." She had a mental image of the captain shaking in his boots, with the idea that his huge prisoner was even more formidable than even he had supposed. "Well, good night then. Lights off." She turned and went back down the corridor, suppressing the urge to say anything else.

"Good night, Krisa." She heard the deep, gravelly voice floating after her down the hall. It caressed her spine like a large, warm hand and gave her another shiver. "Sweet dreams, little girl." But this last was so low that it might have been just her imagination.

Krisa tossed the glass shards into the disposal chute in her fresher, changed into her favorite nightgown and climbed into her cot. A thin, transparent plasti-steel plate extended from the foot of her bed—the stasis field generator. She relaxed as she heard the faint stuttering hiss and felt the stasis field forming above her legs and moving higher up her body, sending her into cryo-sleep.

Her last conscious thought was that she would never see Kurt Teague again.

Chapter Six

ഌ

You aren't supposed to be able to dream in cryo-sleep but somehow Krisa did anyway...

~ ~ ~ ~ ~

He was behind her this time, running those large, rough hands over her trembling body. Making her naked, making her need him. Krisa felt hot breath on the back of her neck, felt the slender curve of her body shiver with anticipation as he pressed against her back, huge and demanding like a solid wall. He was nuzzling the tender spot where her shoulder met her throat. Biting her...marking her.

His hands were cupping her full breasts, lightly at first, just teasing her sensitive nipples, erect with fear and desire, against the palms of his hands. Then more firmly, pinching her tender buds until she moaned her willingness to give him anything he wanted. "Goddess, yes...anything...anything..." she whispered but he didn't answer with words, he never did. He twisted her nipples mercilessly, sending sparks of pleasure from her breasts directly to her wet, aching pussy. Then a warm, wet mouth was lapping at them, sucking her nipples and soothing away the pain with long, hot strokes of his tongue. Just as she felt soothed, he nipped her again, sending a new shockwave of pleasure-pain that made her cry out, begging him for something she couldn't even name. Her pussy throbbed with need, the soft cunt lips spreading to reveal her swollen clit. Spreading for his fingers. Spreading for his cock.

Suddenly he was behind her again. Those large, warm hands were sliding down her body, over her slender waist and the curve of her hips and then he was parting her thighs, forcing her to spread herself for him. Blunt fingertips parted the swollen lips of her sex and rubbed against her slick folds, pressing inward. He was so close, so close to taking what must not be taken, so close to giving her exactly what she needed. Krisa moaned helplessly and rode his fingers, opening for him, submitting to him in a way that felt utterly dangerous and utterly right. Her juices made her pussy slippery and wetted both her thighs and his hand, easing his entrance into her virgin cunt. Behind her, she could feel the thick head of his cock rubbing against her inner thigh, then moving higher to slide against her inflamed clit. The broad head pressed against the entrance to her pussy, not quite entering her yet but promising that he soon would, promising to make her his completely...

~ ~ ~ ~ ~

A huge, grinding crash like the world coming to an end shattered the dream and woke her up. Krisa's eyelids stuttered open in the dim room, her limbs feeling heavy with the aftereffects of cryo-sleep. The strange dream lingered in her mind like the ghost of a fantasy that wouldn't let go. *There yet?* she thought disjointedly.

She was lying at an oddly tilted angle. In fact, the only thing that kept her from rolling out of bed was the large, curved plasti-steel plate that was hanging over the foot of her cot for some reason. It extended all the way up to her waist. Krisa squirmed out from under it and sat on the side of her tilted cot, looking at it with vague unease. Her brain was still cobwebby from the deep sleep.

It was the stasis field generator, she was fairly sure, but why was it extended only halfway over the foot of the cot? During cryo-sleep, if she remembered correctly, the generator covered the entire cot forming the stasis field and putting the sleeping person lying in the cot into a sort of suspended animation.

Had her generator only extended halfway? That might account for the strange dream she had been having when she woke up, but it would also mean that only half her body had been covered by the field and her cryo-sleep had been incomplete. The bottom half of her had been kept in suspended animation while the top half had continued aging as normal.

The top half of me is a month older than the bottom half of me now, Krisa thought groggily. The idea was too strange to wrap her head around and she pushed it out of her mind. Shakily, she rose to her feet, straightening the long white nightgown that had somehow gotten twisted around her thighs. It wasn't just the cot that was tilted, the entire floor seemed to slope slightly down and to the right. Her feeling of unease began to grow, especially as she began to feel more awake, and she remembered the deafening crashing sound that had woken her up.

The room was still mostly dark, adding to her unease. "Lights, bright," Krisa said loudly but nothing happened. "*Lights*," she said again, nearly shouting this time but there was no response from the overhead glows. Staring around frantically, Krisa noticed that the strips of radiance cells along the bottom of the faux-wood wall seemed to be growing conspicuously dimmer as she watched. As though the ship's power supply was dying.

Have to get out of here! She ran for the door which didn't immediately respond to her finger on the switch. Panic rose in chest, blocking her throat like dry cotton, as she pressed the switch again and again. Finally, with a sluggish whooshing that was more like a tired sigh than the usual brisk hiss of air, the door slid halfway open. Krisa didn't wait for it to open farther.

Wriggling like an eel, she slipped through the narrow crack, scraping the skin along her arms and shoulders and tearing her sheer white nightgown as she did so. But she barely noticed the torn gown and the sting of her bleeding arms, she was so relieved to be out of the tiny tomb of a room.

Outside in the corridor, the ship was eerily quiet and dim. Everything was tilted in a downwards slant toward the front of the ship. Krisa turned in that direction first, walking down the slanting floor, thinking to find the captain or one of the crew and ask what was happening. But as she roamed up and down the empty halls of the *Star Princess*, she became convinced that no one was there. And yet, she had a strange, ticklish sensation between her shoulder blades, as though someone was watching her somehow.

As the last effects of her cryo-sleep began to wear off, Krisa's head began to fill with panicky questions. *Where is everybody?* was quickly followed by, *Where are we?* From the tilted angle of the ship and the way the engines seemed to have died. Krisa could only assume that the *Star Princess* had crashed somewhere. But if they were on Lynix Prime, a densely populated planet, wouldn't someone have come to help them by now? Was she the only one who had woken up from cryo-sleep? And if so, why?

All right, stay calm, she told herself, trying to hold back the panic that was threatening to choke her. *If I'm the only one that woke up it just means that everybody else is still in cryo-sleep. I'll just go check it out.*

Cautiously, Krisa made her way back along the main hall until she came to the long line of sleep cubes, but the doors were sealed tight and none of them responded to her repeated attempts to activate the switches. *Good thing I got out while I did*, she thought. Just imagining being trapped in the claustrophobically tiny room she had barely managed to squeeze out of made her feel sick.

Then she wondered uneasily if she would be able to get out of the ship itself and onto whatever planet they had landed on. If the power to the inner sleep cube doors didn't work, what were the chances that the outer doors would work? And if they didn't? Why then she would be trapped in this silent ghost of a ship, for who knew how long. *What if I never get out?* Krisa pushed that thought away quickly.

Trying to control the fear that was threatening to blind her, Krisa forced herself to walk slowly and carefully back along the corridor to the hold of the ship. That was where the main hatch was, where she and Percy had entered the ship. It seemed like just a week ago they had come on board the *Star Princess*, though depending on the length of time she had been in her halfway state of cryo-sleep, it could have been anywhere from a week to a month.

Thinking about the hold made her think of Teague. Krisa wondered if the crash had happened before or after he and Captain Ketchum had been scheduled to jet down to the surface of Lynix Omega. Would she reach the hold and find the huge Feral wandering around free? It was a frightening thought. Despite their long conversation and the help he had given her, Krisa wasn't at all sure she wanted to meet him face-to-face without the restraints and magno-locks holding him down.

At last she found herself in the metal doorframe staring into the darkened hold. At this end of the ship the angle of the tilt was so steep that going forward into the hold was like climbing up a slippery metal hill. Some of the restraining straps that held the piles of luggage in place had snapped and there were loose bags and carryalls scattered near the lip of the doorway.

The radiance strips were almost completely dead here but at the far end of the hold, Krisa saw something that gave her hope. Almost hidden behind a high mound of luggage, miraculously still held intact by its straining bonds, was a faint glimmer of outside light. She had already begun to make her way toward it, climbing up the steep slant all the way, when she thought to check for Teague.

He could be hidden anywhere in the darkened space, crouched behind a pile of luggage, waiting to play a savage game of cat and mouse with her. *I like you*, he'd told her, *but don't think that makes you any different...* The thought made the itching between her shoulder blades — the feeling of being watched — come back a hundred times worse.

Almost afraid of what she might see, Krisa took a tentative step toward the darkened wall where the huge Feral had been chained. The blackness was nearly complete in the tiny space. She had to get a great deal closer than she wanted to in order to verify that the magno-locks were hanging empty and the chains that had bound him to the wall were trailing free along the narrow metal bench where he had been sitting.

"Teague?" she called without much hope. Probably the crash or emergency landing or whatever it was had happened after he and Captain Ketchum had jetted down to Omega. Still, she couldn't help trying one more time. "Teague!" she called, louder, her voice echoing disturbingly in the darkened room.

"Don't bother, my dear. I'm afraid he's long gone."

Krisa turned with a gasp, nearly stumbling on the tilted, slippery floor to see Captain Ketchum standing directly behind her. The man she had thought so handsome and dashing when they first met looked considerably worse for the wear now.

Ketchum had on his maroon jacket and black uniform pants, but the golden braid had been ripped half off and was dangling in a long, frayed rope down his side. He was dirty and disheveled and half of his face was smeared with a dark substance. Krisa couldn't be quite sure in the dim lighting, but it looked like blood.

"Captain," she said uncertainly, mindful of the way they had parted. "Are you all right? And do you know where we are?"

"Yes, I bloody well know where we are," he growled, his face twisting angrily. "Lynix Xi — Planet bloody X is where we are. That son of a bitch Teague must have changed our course somehow. I knew he'd had some training as a pilot but I never dreamed he could fly an interstellar behemoth like the *Princess*." He looked around at the tilted floor and guttering lights. "Apparently he's no expert at it anyway. He's bloody well crashed us," he said with what sounded like grim satisfaction.

Krisa had so many questions she didn't know which one to ask first. "But when did it happen? What did he do? How could he have gotten access to the controls? Weren't you covering him with a blaster?" she poured out all at once.

Ketchum scowled, his blood-smeared face wrinkling into a mask of rage. "'Course I had him covered with the bloody blaster," he spat. "Only the bastard was ready for me. Somehow he'd gotten his blindfold off and he had something sharp—I told you how he loves to use a knife—only it wasn't a knife. A piece of glass, I think."

He broke off for a moment to rub at his bloody forehead and Krisa thought guiltily of the glass she had broken in the hold. She'd been sure she had picked up every jagged shard but apparently she'd been wrong. Where else could Teague have gotten his weapon? Possibly he had even scared her into knocking over the glass on purpose—she wouldn't put it past him.

"He came for me as soon as I'd released the magno-locks, sliced the hell out of my face," Ketchum resumed. "I was forced to drop the blaster in order to grapple with him hand to hand, and I was half blinded by blood. I nearly had him but the slippery bugger managed to get behind me somehow. Threw me against a wall and I must have connected headfirst, because I don't remember anything until I heard the noise the *Princess* made when she landed. Crashed, I should say."

"So now he's gone? You're quite sure?" Krisa asked, backing away a little, as well as the tilted floor would allow. She was finding that the prospect of being alone in the darkened ship with Captain Ketchum wasn't any more appealing than the prospect of being alone with Teague had been.

"Long gone," Ketchum said sourly. "Expect I'll have a job to catch the brute again."

Krisa almost pointed out that the captain hadn't caught him the first time, but she kept her mouth shut. There was no point in antagonizing the man who was standing between her and the only exit from the ship. Instead she said, "What are we going to do? Will they send a rescue team, do you think?"

Ketchum sighed and ran one hair through his filthy blond hair, half of which was standing up in bloody spikes. "I've already tripped the ship's beacon so there should be someone from Prime along directly as soon as they notice we're missing," he said. "The problem is, the *Princess* wasn't supposed to arrive on Prime for another two and a half or three solar weeks, and depending on the type of ship they use, it could take them nearly that long to reach us with a rescue team. So, worst case scenario, say a month, month and a half before anyone can reasonably be expected to turn up.

Still," he went on thoughtfully, almost as thought he were speaking to himself instead of Krisa, "everyone else is still locked in cryo-sleep—the backup generator's seen to that. So there should be plenty of food in the ship's stores to last until they come."

Krisa could barely hide her dismay at his words. *A month and a half? What am I going to do alone with him for a month and a half?* Captain Ketchum absolutely could not be trusted. He had already proven what kind of man he was and Krisa wasn't anxious to give him a chance to prove it again.

Still, it looked like she was stuck with him and she thought the best thing to do was to try and return to their previous civil relationship. Maybe if she pretended that his attempt at her the night before they entered cryo-sleep had never happened, he would too.

"That wound looks serious. We should try to find a first aid kit and fix you up," she said as lightly as she could. "Maybe you should sit against the wall while I look for one, you look all done in with your clothes ripped up and your face all bloody like that."

"I'm not the only one with ripped clothes though, I see." He looked down at her chest and Krisa followed his eyes with her own. For the first time she noticed that the sheer white nightgown she was wearing was ripped across the chest. The gaping tear in the sheer fabric left her breasts in plain view. As though noticing the attention being paid them, her nipples came to sudden, painfully erect attention.

Krisa clutched at the gown, pulling it closed as best she could, but she could see by the predatory look in Captain Ketchum's eyes that the damage had already been done. No matter how strenuously she acted the part of the proper lady he was not going to go back to his role of the gallant gentleman.

"You look quite fetching, my dear," he remarked, taking a step closer. It forced Krisa to take a step backwards, feeling her way with bare feet to keep from falling.

"I-I'm wounded as well," Krisa said, indicating her bloody arms. "I really should find that kit. W-wouldn't want these scrapes to become infected." She knew she was babbling but she didn't seem to be able to stop.

"Oh but I think infection will be the least of your worries, my sweet," Ketchum crooned, taking another step forward, and forcing her another step back. Krisa saw with despair that she was getting farther and farther from the faint glimmer of light at the end of the ship.

"Stay away from me," she said as sharply as she could.

"Brave words, Krisa, my dear, but I notice you're unarmed this time," Ketchum sneered, advancing another step.

Krisa backed up again but this time her shoulder blades bumped something cold and unyielding. He had backed her against the far wall of the hold and she could go no farther. *Trapped!* a panicky little voice inside her head whispered.

"You know," Ketchum continued in that same, sneering tone. "I was wondering how in the galaxy I should while away the time waiting for the rescue team until I saw you wandering around the ship like a luscious little ghost in that see-through gown."

"It...it's my nightgown," Krisa faltered. She made a sudden move to the side but Ketchum was already there, blocking her way with one maroon-clad arm. He leaned in toward her, blocking the other side as well with his other arm, making her feel like a caged animal.

"Going so soon, Krisa, my love?" He smiled at her, a sharklike grin with no humor in it at all. "Don't you want to stay and have some fun? Think of all the fun we can have together in a month and a half until the rescue team arrives."

"You," Krisa licked suddenly dry lips, "wouldn't dare! You think I wouldn't tell Lord Radisson? He's a powerful man. You'll be stripped of your rank, thrown into prison—"

"Ah yes, the good Lord Limp Dick," Ketchum drawled, looking not the least upset. "Your little chaperone showed me a picture of him, did you know? Rather pathetic, that, carrying a picture of one's employer but still... He's got to be forty years your senior, my dear. Probably couldn't get it up to save his life." He laughed nastily.

"All that to the side, however, I wouldn't recommend you tell him anything at all once we're rescued. Damaged goods, you know. You'll just show him that all-important Certificate of Virginity and tell all and sundry how brave Captain Ketchum protected you in the wilds of Planet X and everything will be just fine. He probably won't even ask for a re-verification of your precious virginity. At least, you'll have to *hope* he doesn't."

He was so close to her now that Krisa could smell stale sweat and the ghost of Tazzenberry cologne wafting from his filthy skin. His rank breath was blowing in her face and she turned her head, trying to get away from it.

"You know," Ketchum said, twisting one of her long curls around a filthy finger. "I've never seen you with your hair down before. Rather lovely, especially paired with those big brown eyes in that pale little face—like a doll."

"I thought you said I wasn't pretty enough to bother with," Krisa said, finding her voice at last. Besides the fear she was feeling another emotion was growing as well—outrage that this man who pretended to be a gentleman could be so utterly savage and ruthless beneath the thin veneer of gentility he affected. How dare he push her up against the wall and tell her he intended to rape her? How dare he expect her to say nothing and just go along with it?

"Oh, you're pretty enough and I expect you know it, love," Ketchum said. "Why else would a high muckety-muck like old Radisson pay to ship you halfway across the galaxy? In all the years I've been making this run, transporting prisoners from your benighted little planet to the Deep Freeze, I do believe you're the prettiest mail-order bride I've ever, shall we say, taken advantage of."

"You haven't managed it yet," Krisa said. Ducking suddenly she nearly got under his arm but Ketchum was too quick for her.

"Not so fast, my love," he crooned in her ear, pressing her hard against the wall. She could feel the substantial bulge in his trousers digging into her thigh. "I'm only getting started. Now let's just see what else is beneath this little nightgown of yours."

With a sudden, violent move he grabbed the torn neck of the sheer white nightgown and pulled viciously. There was a low ripping noise and Krisa was suddenly exposed from neck to ankles. Ketchum stood back for a moment, one hand pinching hard into her shoulder to keep her in place, and admired his handiwork.

"Nice, very nice indeed," he murmured, his eyes roving greedily over her exposed flesh. "I think I'm really going to enjoy this, my dear."

Krisa slapped him as hard as she could. Her small hand left a vivid red print that was even visible in the darkness of the hold on the unbloodied side of his face. Ketchum jerked backwards, and she tried to take advantage of his surprise to twist free, but the hand holding her to the wall remained steady, his grip horribly strong.

"You'll pay for that," he growled, grabbing her other shoulder and slamming her back against the wall viciously. The back of Krisa's head connected with the unyielding metal and for a moment she saw tiny bright sparks of light dancing in her field of vision.

"I was going to make it nice for you, since you're such an innocent little *virgin*. But I'm beginning to think you'd benefit best from a good...hard...*fucking*." With every word he slammed her shoulders back against the wall, her head connecting every time until Krisa was sure she was going to pass out.

The dim gloom of the hold was beginning to take on a wavy, grayish cast and the tiny bright lights dancing in front of her eyes had turned into huge, exploding stars and meteors. But suddenly Krisa saw something that snapped her back to consciousness. Behind Ketchum's head, his hair spiky with blood and matted with filth, a pair of slitted silver eyes had appeared.

Teague... Her lips tried to form the name but she was too numb to do anything more than mouth the word. Still, Ketchum must have seemed something in her face because his own eyes widened and he stopped shaking her.

"Wha—" he began but then two huge hands clamped around the sides of his head, shutting him up.

"You know, Ketch, I had a feeling I shoulda finished you off." Teague's voice was a low growl that seemed to vibrate the entire room. "This is what I get for tryin' to be nice, I guess."

"Now, Teague, wait a minute—" Ketchum's blue eyes bugged out of their sockets in abject terror and the part of his face not covered in blood had gone a chalky white.

"It amazes me," the deep, growling voice continued almost thoughtfully. "How I got sent to prison for a few little homicides while a scum like you gets to walk around free. Krisa told me you already tried this once and she let you know she wasn't interested. Didn't you get the message the first time?"

The huge hands at the sides of Ketchum's head began to squeeze and the blue eyes bugged even farther from their sockets. Krisa, who was still trapped against the wall, wondered with a sick kind of fascination if Teague intended to crush the captain's head between his hands like an overripe fruit.

"I wasn't going to hurt her—I swear it!" gasped Ketchum. His face had taken on an alarmingly oblong appearance.

"Well, that's nice of you, Ketch," Teague grated. "'Cause everybody knows that rape is *completely* painless. So I guess you won't mind if I do somethin' just as painless to you." The look on his dark face was utterly terrifying and the intensity of the rage that burned in his silver eyes was unlike anything Krisa had ever seen before. The huge hands tightened until she could actually hear the bones in Ketchum's skull creaking.

"No—Teague! Wait, I—" Ketchum gasped in a high, breathless whisper.

"Goodbye, Ketch. I promise this won't hurt a bit," Teague snarled. He gave the captain's head a swift, vicious jerk to one side.

There was a sickening crunch that Krisa knew she would hear in dreams for the rest of her life and suddenly she was looking at the back of Captain Ketchum's head instead of the front.

* * * * *

"Don't faint, we don't have time," Teague ordered her, silver eyes still blazing. He casually tossed the captain's limp form to one side, as though tossing aside a used tissue, Krisa thought sickly. She leaned back against the wall, still in shock, and tried to obey him although everything kept getting blurry around the edges and swimming in and out of focus.

"Thought you always...used a knife," she said, trying to make her eyes focus on the shadowy form with the glowing eyes looming in front of her. She had only seen him sitting down—standing up he was absolutely *huge*.

Teague grinned savagely. "That's good, I like a girl with a sense of humor. Yeah, I could've." He made a sudden motion, too quick for her eyes to follow. A long, deadly looking blade as silver as his eyes appeared in his large hand. "But if I'd cut his throat it woulda gotten all over you—you were in the line of fire, so to speak. I thought you might not appreciate that." As quickly as it had appeared, the knife vanished.

"You thought right," Krisa said weakly. She tried to push away from the wall, staggered and almost fell. Her head felt four times its normal size, and when she pushed her fingers through her thick curls at the back to feel for a lump, they came away wet and sticky.

"Take it easy." A large, warm hand curved around her upper arm, supporting her. "You okay?" he asked and Krisa nodded, unsure if it was the truth or not but it seemed to satisfy him. "We're walkin' outta here fast." He turned toward the light that was still radiating dimly from the far end of the hull. "Night soon and I wanna put some distance between us and the ship before we make camp."

"W-wait a minute. We're leaving? Why? I mean, I can see why *you* have to get away but why should *I* go with you?" Krisa asked in what she hoped was a reasonable tone. Her head still throbbed and she wasn't entirely sure she might not be sick all over the floor, so she thought she was doing pretty well to say anything coherent at all. She suddenly realized that her ripped gown was hanging open, exposing her naked flesh from chest to ankles. Grabbing the ragged edges, she pulled the sheer white fabric tightly around herself.

Teague looked at her with an unreadable expression in his silver eyes. "You really want to stay here all by your lonesome, little girl? Wait for a rescue team that might never come?"

"They'll come," Krisa said stubbornly. "Cap..." The name died in her throat and she nodded toward Ketchum's limp form instead. "He said he tripped the ship's beacon. That it would only take them a solar month to find us."

Teague's face darkened at her news and he swore viciously under his breath. "Son of a bitch! Knew I should have made sure he was dead," he growled. "Well, it doesn't matter if it was a month or a week, I'd still have to take you with me."

"To use as a hostage, I suppose," Krisa said angrily. The immense throbbing in her head had subsided to a dull, persistent ache but the pain was still intense. All she wanted to do was to lie down for a while until she felt better, but she knew she couldn't. Instead she was going to get dragged through the wilds of some dangerous, unknown planet for someone else's convenience. Recently she had begun to feel that her whole life had been lived for someone else's convenience, and she was getting thoroughly sick of it.

"No, *not* to use as a hostage," Teague snarled. "Because you won't survive if I don't."

"K-Ketchum said there was plenty of food in the ship's stores," Krisa protested.

"Has nothin' to do with the food supply, unless you'd like to consider *yourself* food."

Teague grabbed her by the arm again and hauled her roughly up the steep incline of the hold's floor, until they reached the jagged hole at the end where a strange, alien light was pouring into the ship.

Krisa's eyes were dazzled by the brilliance at first but soon she could make out a deep bronze sky in which no sun was visible, hanging over what looked like some kind of a jungle below the ruined hold of the ship. The jungle, a swirl of pastel, cotton candy-like colors, was not like one she had ever seen before in the admittedly limited selection of vid-books at Briar Rose.

"Hear that?" Teague demanded. Krisa looked at him and saw that the light had caused his second eyelids to flicker down and his eyes were now the solid, opaque black she found so disturbing.

"I don't hear anythi—" she began and then a high, angry chattering sound somewhere in the depths of the alien jungle cut her off. "What...what was that?" she asked hesitantly. There was an eerie warning note in the strange call that prickled the hair at the back of her neck and set her teeth on edge. "Some kind of carnivore?"

Teague smiled grimly. "No, those are targees—soft, furry little animals about as big as your hand."

"They sound adorable," Krisa protested. "Am I supposed to be afraid of them?"

"No. But they only sound like that when a pack of soondar is near. And those *are* carnivorous—and big. They can smell blood for miles. The rest of the crew and passengers'll be safe—they're locked in cryo-sleep and sealed tight behind their sleep-cube doors. But you'd be a buffet waiting to happen, understand?" He dropped her arm and stared at her with those unreadable black eyes.

"I'm sorry, I thought—"

"I know what you thought." Teague glared at her. "Let me tell you something, little girl, if I wanted to make things easy for myself I'd leave you here for the soondar pack or kill you myself. You'll only slow me down and you got that damn chip in the back of your neck. Might as well be wearin' a big neon sign that says, 'Here I am, come and get me'. They'll be tracking you, no doubt about it." He took a deep breath and blew it out in a frustrated sound that was somewhere between a growl and a sigh. "I was halfway outta here and then I had to go and come back," he muttered.

"Then why bother?" Krisa flared, her temper suddenly getting the better of her fear. Dimly, inside her head she could hear Madame Ledoux saying reprovingly, *A lady never raises her voice.* But there was something about the huge Feral that seemed to bring out the most unladylike part of her and as he himself had pointed out, Teague was no gentleman.

"Why did you even come back in the first place if I'm such a burden, Teague?" She forgot about holding her gown modestly closed and placed her balled fists on her hips instead, thrusting her chin out defiantly.

"Heard you yellin' my name," he growled shortly. "I thought you'd be safe asleep with all the other sheep." He jerked his chin, dark with blue-black stubble, in the direction of the main part of the ship. "How come you're awake, anyway?"

"My stasis field generator was defective, I think," Krisa said tightly. "It only covered me halfway so when *you* crashed the ship I woke up. *So* sorry to inconvenience you. Maybe you should just kill me now and save yourself the bother."

The moment the words were out of her mouth she knew she had gone too far. Teague's eyes narrowed, flickering dangerously to reveal glimpses of silver beneath the black. Deliberately he stalked closer to her until he was crowding her, looming over her menacingly. She could feel the heat from his big body radiating against her exposed skin. Belatedly, she realized that her gown had fallen open again and scrambled to pull it closed.

"Don't bother, little girl. I've seen it already and let me tell you, I *liked* what I saw." The gravelly voice was thick with menace of a different kind now. A sexual heat that jumped between them like static electricity and licked over her skin in burning waves. "Do you know how long it's been since I had a woman, especially one as tasty as you?" he rumbled, reaching up one huge hand to caress her tangled curls.

"I..." Krisa's brain seemed to have frozen and her tongue felt like it was made of lead. Carefully, she backed up a step, feeling a sick sense of déjà vu. "Did...you kill Captain Ketchum just to finish what he started?" she asked finally, in what she hoped would be a strong, angry voice. Unfortunately her words came out in more of a squeaky whisper.

"I may be a murderer but I'm no *rapist*." He spat out the word as though trying to rid his mouth of something unclean. But to Krisa's relief he didn't close the distance she had put between them and force her to back up as Ketchum had.

Teague stood with his head bowed, massive arms crossed over his chest, in an almost pensive gesture for a long moment. Then he looked up at her, the midnight pools of his eyes flickering silver for an instant. "What you want to remember about me, Krisa, is that I don't have a lot of patience, so *don't test me*. Now, we're out of here in ten and you can't go in that." Black eyes raked over her tattered nightgown with obvious contempt. "I suggest you get dressed in a hurry. If you're not ready when I say go, I *will* leave you. Understand?"

Krisa nodded mutely, her mouth too dry to speak.

Teague reached down and picked up a large pack from the ground, which he had obviously dropped earlier. He turned to face the alien jungle, with its strange, pastel foliage visible through the jagged hole in the hull of the ship.

"The clock is ticking, sweetheart," he said softly. "I'd hurry if I were you."

Chapter Seven

ഐ

Krisa struggled through the strange, pastel vegetation, her throbbing head filled with the rich, pungent scent of the alien jungle. She was saying the worst things she could think of under her breath as she pushed aside pale blue vines and lavender creepers. Her vocabulary of swear words was admittedly limited but she was learning fast, listening to Teague.

The big Feral was plowing along ahead of her, cutting a trail with his huge knife. The curving blade glinted dully as it rose and fell tirelessly, hacking at the vegetation that impeded their progress. From time to time he came to a particularly tough snarl of vines and then Krisa could hear him using words that had never appeared on any of her vocabulary tests at Briar Rose.

As they pushed through the foliage, which had reminded Krisa of a big swirl of cotton candy when she had looked down on it from the hold of the ship, she reflected that she had done a lot of things lately that she never could have pictured herself doing at Briar Rose. For one thing, not only was she minus the all-important cincher that gave her a tiny, pinched-in waist, but she was presently wearing *trousers*. Wearing pants, just like a man, instead of the long skirts she had worn all her life. It was a sight so horrifying it would doubtless have caused the headmistress of the academy, Madame Sylvanna, to throw up her perfectly manicured hands and faint. *A lady is delicate, gracious, and above all, feminine.* Krisa was feeling none of the three as she followed Teague's trail.

She felt strangely exposed in the pants, which had been a pair of Percy's. She tried telling herself that at least they covered a great deal more than the ripped and ragged gown she'd discarded, but it didn't help much. Percy was a good inch and a half shorter than her, and he was narrower through the hips as well. The result was the trousers were skin tight and showed an inch of bare, scratched ankle below their neatly tailored cuffs. Krisa was wearing some of his stylish, low-ankle boots and one of his shirts too. The cuffs were rolled down to protect her arms despite the sultry heat and the buttons were bulging in protest over her full breasts.

Her current state of attire had certainly not been Krisa's idea. Teague had told her to get ready to go, but when she had returned from rummaging in her pink carryall cube in a long dress proper for afternoon or early evening wear, he had first cursed under his breath and then laughed at her.

"You won't get a yard out there wearin' that, sweetheart," he said. "Don't you have anything for outdoors?"

"*This*," Krisa insisted. "I've worn it for all kinds of outdoor activities — picnics, nature photography — "

"Whitewater needlepoint? Uphill cross-stitch?" Teague questioned sarcastically, one thick blue-black eyebrow raised nearly to his hairline. "Forget it, little girl. That might work on Bride Planet but not in the jungles of Planet X. Find something else, and *hurry*."

Krisa rummaged hopelessly through her cube, taking a few precious items, including her mother's holo-vid, until the big Feral took things into his own hands. Muttering something about women taking all damn day, he began popping open luggage containers and cubes. Pressure-compressed articles of clothing sprayed out in sudden, colorful jumbles like party favors giving up their prizes, but of course everything was much too large.

Finally he came across Percy's luggage, tastefully monogrammed in a beautiful gold cursive script, with the initials, *P.D.* "Here, put these on," he ordered, holding out a pair of trousers.

"*Pants?*" Krisa stared at him wide-eyed and shook her head. "I couldn't possibly."

"You can and you will. Here." Teague shook the fashionable tan trousers with vertical fawn and sable stripes in her direction like a flag.

Krisa snatched the offending article of clothing and glared at him in outraged silence. Finally, Teague turned his back, giving her some nominal privacy while she struggled into the skin-tight pants.

"You know," she said through gritted teeth, fumbling with the unfamiliar fastenings at the front of the trousers. "At Briar Rose Academy where I was trained, they told us that wearing men's trousers was one of the most vulgar and ridiculous thing a lady could do. Madame Ledoux always said letting a woman wear trousers made as much sense as trying to teach a cat how to read."

"Well, I'm guessin' your Madame Ledoux never had to cut trail through a jungle wearin' an evening gown or she might've changed her mind," Teague growled, looking briefly over one broad shoulder. "Believe me, little girl, you'll be thanking me before we go half a klick. There's nothin' ridiculous or vulgar about survival." That had been his final word on the subject.

That was how she'd ended up sweating under the dull bronze sky, wearing her chaperone's pants, following a man who was a known mass murderer and escaped convict, as he cut a path through the jungle of a mysterious, forbidden planet from which supposedly nobody ever escaped.

Strangely, Krisa found she didn't mind it so much.

She didn't *love* it, of course. Even though Teague was doing the dirty work of cutting trail, following in his wake was still a hot, sweaty business in the steaming humidity of the pastel jungle. She kept hearing sounds that made her jump, assuming they were coming from a pack of ravenous soondar, until Teague had growled that she should stop being so damn twitchy.

He hadn't allowed her to bring much, either. The pockets of Percy's trousers were stuffed with the bare essentials from her abandoned pale pink carryall cube. Krisa had her mother's holo-vid, a tiny compu-package of compressed toiletries and items she thought might come in handy and her all-important Certificate of Virginity.

The stiff, sharp edges of the folded document stuck out of her back pocket, and dug into the small of her back mercilessly if she leaned the wrong way, almost as if to remind her of its significance. Krisa was very aware that the big red "Certified Virgin" stamped across the stiff parchment could easily become a lie. It had in fact, nearly become so twice already on this crazy trip.

That made her think of Captain Ketchum, lying limp and dead back at the wreck of the *Star Princess* and she wondered how many certificates he had invalidated. How many virgins had he violated with his oily charm and vicious blackmail? He had said something about traveling the Capellia-Lynix route for years transporting prisoners. Who knew how many soon-to-be brides traveled from Capellia to Lynix in any given solar year? A lot, she was sure.

Despite the initial shock of seeing the way Teague had killed him so casually right in front of her, Krisa couldn't make herself be sorry that the captain was dead. In fact, she felt rather glad when she considered how many more women might have fallen prey to his wiles in the years to come.

She sighed and swiped at her sweaty forehead, jerking back quickly as a dusky rose-colored creeper whipped in front of her face. Off to their left in a dense lavender thicket, a musical hooting sounded briefly and then died. Taking a deep breath of the pungent jungle air, she allowed herself to admit that her emotions about the captain's violent end weren't *totally* selfless. In fact, after getting over her initial horror at Teague's casual violence, she had experienced an almost savage satisfaction. It felt good to see a man who had been planning to do such unspeakable things to her being dealt such deadly justice.

Listen to me, I sound like one of those thriller vids Madame Prunesia banned after finding out they weren't about rides at an amusement park, Krisa thought wryly. Absently, she raised an arm to avoid being whipped in the eyes by a lilac vine. There were vines and bushes everywhere but the pastel jungle wasn't just underbrush. There were also tall, thin treelike things that were impossibly long and slender. They waved gently in the humid air, reminding Krisa of some underwater plants she'd seen on her one trip to Capellia's Red Ocean the year she had turned nine.

When she'd asked him, Teague had explained briefly that Lynix Xi had a relatively weak gravitational pull. This allowed the slender trees, which never could have supported themselves on a higher-grav planet, to grow to tremendous heights. To Krisa they almost looked like long pink and purple fingers scraping the cloudy bronze sky. She wondered if the lighter gravity might be why she had been able to keep up the furious pace the big Feral was keeping. That or the fact that the cincher she was so used to wearing was gone.

Teague had refused to let her bring her cincher, naming it a nonessential item, despite her attempts to convince him she looked completely improper without it. "You look fine to me," he'd said shortly. Midnight eyes had raked over her, eyeing the way the white shirt bulged from the stress her unconfined breasts were putting on it, until Krisa had blushed and dropped the subject.

Now, striding along behind him, watching the muscles in his broad back jump and roll as he cut brush tirelessly, she admitted that she was breathing easier and more deeply without the cincher that had confined her from the age of thirteen. Was it really necessary, after all, for a girl to have such an abnormally tiny waist?

Despite the dull throb in the back of her head and the pain from her scratched arms, she felt alive in a way she never had before. *I may never wear a cincher again,* she thought and then berated herself for such a foolish thought. Of *course* she would have to wear a cincher again. Once she got back to civilization on Lynix Prime she wouldn't be accepted in polite society anywhere without one. She pushed the thought away and concentrated on keeping up with Teague.

They seemed to hike for hours. Krisa had never been without a dainty lace handkerchief since entering Briar Rose but now she armed sweat off her forehead in a most unladylike way. Her long, curly hair was pinned to the nape of her sweating neck with the long, ornamental pin she had worn the first night Captain Ketchum tried to attack her. Teague had laughed at its ridiculously ornate black and silver enameled handle, but Krisa had privately thought that as it had saved her virginity once, the hairpin might save it again. She had her doubts though—Teague didn't seem like the kind of a man to be put off by a jab in the hand. If he really wanted her, he'd have her, pin and Certificate of Virginity or not.

She had a brief, vivid mental picture of being taken on the ferny, overgrown floor of the jungle. Teague's large frame would be above her own, pressing her into the ground. He would open her legs and spread the lips of her pussy, exposing her to his assault. He would rub the broad head of his cock against her slippery folds, drawing moans and gasps from her lips. Then he would fill her wet, open sex with his thick cock, the same part of him she had wondered about on that first night when she had crept into the hold to watch him sleeping.

The warning chatter of a small group of targees interrupted these highly improper thoughts and Krisa was able to look up and catch a glimpse of the little creatures. They looked like powder puffs with huge, liquid black eyes and their fur matched the rest of the jungle. Decorated in splotches of mint green, powder blue, pale yellow and baby-blanket pink, they ran scolding and chattering angrily on tiny clawed feet up and down the long, thin finger-trees, marking their territory.

Krisa hoped again that the targees weren't warning of an impending attack by a pack of soondars, which she had begun to imagine might look like huge, angry panthers with lilac-toned fur. But the high, frightened note she had heard when Teague first pointed them out to her seemed to be absent from their chattering calls. With a sigh, she forced herself to relax.

If Teague thought it was a problem, he would say so, she told herself firmly as the band of pastel puffballs scolded overhead. It made her nervous to have to trust such a man with her life but what else, reasonably, could she do? And so far he hadn't done anything wrong or improper. *Just wait until you stop for the night,* whispered the practical little voice in her head. *Then we'll see about wrong and improper, Krisa.* Despite his strong statement about not being a rapist, she found the thought distinctly unsettling.

Pushing the nagging little voice to the back of her brain, she dug the fancy jeweled chronometer Lord Radisson had sent her on her fifteenth birthday out of the front pocket of Percy's trousers. She studied the delicate face for a moment, before realizing that it was still set to Capellian time. Here in the jungles of Planet X it was useless. Krisa crammed it back in the pocket of the trousers in a move that was already beginning to feel more natural and half shouted over the crashing noise of the knife demolishing underbrush to get the big Feral's attention.

"Teague!"

"What?" he growled, not bothering to turn around.

"How much longer until we get wherever it is we're going? Where *are* we going anyway?" Krisa asked. It seemed strange but there was so much to see and think about that she hadn't even considered it before. She'd just assumed that somehow, at some point, she would be able to get back to her regularly scheduled life as Lord Radisson's wife-to-be on Prime. Now she felt distinctly uneasy. Why should Teague care about her life and the way it was supposed to go? And where was the huge Feral taking her?

"River ahead about another two klicks," he grunted, still not turning. "We've gotta make it by nightfall."

Something in his tone gave Krisa a cool shiver down her sweating spine. For the first time she noticed that the cloudy bronze sky had turned a deeper color in the two hours they had been traveling. It was beginning to verge on burnt umber, which she suspected was Planet X's version of twilight.

"Why?" she asked, a little breathlessly, struggling to keep up with him and talk at the same time. It wasn't that she was out of shape, exactly, just that the nature walks at Briar Rose didn't precisely prepare one for anything as strenuous as hiking through a humid jungle for hours at a time. In fact, Krisa was beginning to think that *nothing* taught at Briar Rose prepared one for real life.

Teague paused for a moment, dropped the pack he was carrying over one shoulder and then turned to face her. He had been tirelessly cutting brush for the past two hours, hacking and slashing their way through the jungle and the state of his clothes and body showed it.

Leaves and bracken were stuck in his bristly blue-black hair and his dark face was streaked with sweat. The vines that occasionally whipped back and caught Krisa had dealt much more harshly with him. His dusky tan skin was a mass of thin red lines that looked like they must sting. The black tank top he wore was ripped where thorns had caught and torn at it and the flat planes of his broad, muscular chest and rippling abdominals showed through in several places.

He armed sweat off his face, biceps rippling with coiled tension as he did so. The casual power of his big body now that he was unchained almost took Krisa's breath away. Despite the sweat and the marks on his skin, he still looked fresh enough to cut trail the rest of the day and well into the night if necessary. It occurred to her that for a man as physical as Teague obviously was, the intense action of this rough trek through the jungle was probably just what he needed after weeks of enforced inactivity. *Better hope it wears him out, Krisa, or you might see some other kind of intense action tonight,* warned the little voice. Krisa pushed it away.

"*Why* do we have to reach the river by nightfall?" she asked again, hoping to get a straight answer.

Teague paused a moment more to take a long drink from the plasti-flex squeeze bottle of water and nutrients they had brought with them from the ship. He offered it to Krisa who shook her head. She was thirsty but she wanted answers first.

"You really wanna know?" Teague asked seriously.

Krisa nodded, feeling that funny cool shiver go down her spine again.

"Because you've got a lot of blood on you, sweetheart, and I'm not much better myself." He motioned to the myriad threadlike scratches that covered his large frame, some of them oozing thin trickles of crimson. "If we don't make the river and wash up before it goes full dark, the soondar will catch our scent. If that happens we won't have to worry about cutting any more trail, tomorrow or ever again."

"But…I haven't heard the targees make that sound that you said meant—" she began. Just then, as though cued by her words, they heard the high, angry chatter filled with the warning note she had noticed when Teague first pointed it out.

The big Feral looked up, nostrils flaring briefly. Krisa saw his black second lids flicker up to show a glimpse of silver.

"That came from the left," he said quietly and sniffed the air again. "If they get between us and the river we're dead."

"Oh…" She put a hand to her mouth, unable to hide her fear.

"Krisa." He looked at her seriously, gripping one slender shoulder in his massive hand to emphasize the point. "I'm gonna cut trail like the devil himself was after me. Stay on my leg and don't fall behind—*understand?*"

Krisa nodded, her mouth too dry to answer properly.

Teague squeezed her shoulder once and then turned. He took a new grip on the huge knife, the silver blade dripping with sticky pink and purple sap.

"Then let's *go!*"

Chapter Eight

ဢ

Teague roared ahead of her, and if she'd thought he was going fast before, now he was a machine. His muscled arm rose and fell methodically and so quickly it was just a blur in the growing twilight. She struggled to keep his broad back in sight as they ran, hacking and slashing their way through the alien jungle, trying to keep ahead of the high, wild cry of the targees.

It seemed to Krisa that the thin, wailing note that infused the tiny animals' chatter was echoing all around them. It raised the hair on the back of her neck and sent a thin, cool finger of dread up and down her spine, even as the breath tore in her throat and threatened to ignite her lungs.

The light kept getting dimmer and dimmer and she began to understand that when Teague had said, "full dark" he had meant it in the most literal sense. Because of the thick cloud cover around Planet X's atmosphere, when the last of the hidden sun's light died, they would be plunged into darkness that was a deep, pitch black. There would be no moon or stars above to guide them here. Unless they came in sight of the river soon, they would die in this strange, alien jungle, without even being able to see what was eating them.

Behind her, so close she could swear that the animals were almost sitting on her shoulder, the thin, wailing chatter rose again, a quavering chorus against the darkening sky. *We're not going to make it*, Krisa thought, hopelessly. Still she pushed on anyway. If they were going to die, at least they could die trying to do something about it, even if it was only running away.

Then Teague slacked his pace to drop back beside her. Krisa saw that they were out of the jungle for the moment and running along a narrow strip of uneven but clear land. His head whipped toward her and she managed a blurry look at him. His second eyelids were completely retracted so that his eyes blazed as full and silver as twin moons in his dark face. *His eyes!* she suddenly remembered, hope flooding through her again.

Teague would be able to see where they were going no matter how dark it got. If he would stay with her, if she could trust him not to leave her, then she still might make it. But could she trust him?

"River coming up in another half klick but there's a gorge first. Have to jump it—be ready when I say," he yelled.

Krisa saw with amazement that the big Feral wasn't even breathing very hard though she was nearly gasping for air herself. *He could be at the river by now if it wasn't for me,* she thought. *He could've been there ten minutes ago.*

She wondered if he would realize she was holding him back and leave her, but Teague just kept pace beside her. His luminous, silver eyes scanned the last thread of burnished light rimming the horizon as they ran. The darkness crept in behind them, hungry as any predator.

Then a sound like nothing she had ever heard in her life split the air and filled the night. For it *was* full night now and she was running blind. It was a low, bass roar that rumbled along the ground they ran on and vibrated up the soles of her feet, almost making her stumble. But it was more than a sound, somehow.

As the vibration licked like a rough tongue along her sweating spine, Krisa also felt—heard the roaring sound in her head. It was a hot, black sound that reverberated inside her mind, writhing behind her eyes until she felt they must be bugging from their sockets. She felt her eardrums getting ready to pop from the horrid force of the internal pressure.

"Teague!" she gasped but it came out in a breathless whisper and she realized he wasn't beside her anymore. "*Teague!*" she screamed, forcing her lungs to work. Had he left her as bait for the ravening things behind her, filling her mind with their thick, black-sounding fear? She began to slow down, exhaustion and panic taking their toll on her ravaged brain.

Suddenly a hard, strong hand gripped her arm just above the elbow. "*Run!*" he bellowed in her ear. They surged forward into the blackness, Krisa stumbling with exhaustion, while the big Feral half dragged her along. Several times she tripped on the uneven terrain and would've gone down, but the firm pressure on her arm yanked her back up again, saving her from going headfirst onto the dark, unyielding ground.

"Almost time to jump." The voice in her ear was low and calm, not panicked at all. It gave Krisa hope, but now she was nearly at the end of her strength.

"Don't…kn-know…'f…I…can," she gasped out. Just the effort of trying to communicate was making her dizzy. Her feet stumbled yet again and this time when his hand bore her up, she didn't have the strength to make them move.

"No time for this—here." Suddenly she was swept up into a pair of massive arms. Teague tossed over one broad shoulder like a sack, her head hanging down behind him. There was a jolting feeling and then their pace evened out and their speed began to increase as he ran full out in the darkness.

Krisa mustered the strength to raise her head and saw a pair of glowing purple lights bounding along right behind them in the black night. The lights winked off for a moment and then came on again and she realized with a kind of sick fascination that they were *eyes*—eyes filled with a menacing, predatory intelligence that Krisa had never seen in an animal before.

Right behind us — Oh, Goddess. Right behind us! she thought disjointedly. Suddenly, they were airborne and for a split second Krisa thought they were somehow flying. They came down with a jolting thud that would have dislodged her if

Teague hadn't taken such a firm grip on her upper thighs. Then they were splashing into a blessed, wet coolness and he was saying, "All right now, Krisa. They won't follow us here. Lost our scent and they don't like water."

Then, despite the water chilling her overheated body she was out.

* * * * *

When she woke up, Krisa wondered why she was taking a bath in her clothes and why everything was so dark. Then two silvery moons appeared in the sky above her and she realized what must have happened. She was back on Capellia with the double moons above her in the night sky. *Sneaked out again on a dare with Tisha Romella*, she thought. *Got out of the dorm all right but why am I so wet? Did it rain? Madame Ledoux is going to be so angry if I track water all over the Great Hall and she'll know it was me…*

"Krisa, you all right?" The voice was coming from somewhere close by her ear. It was a worried rumble that vibrated her head but in a nice way—not like the horrible, mind-invading roar of the soondar. *Soondar!*

Everything came washing back in a flood. She struggled until the arms that held her let go and then she was plunging deeper into wetness. Alien, sweet-tasting water with a metallic hint of copper, like a taint of blood, filled her throat as she thrashed in the darkness.

"Easy, take it easy," the voice which Krisa recognized as Teague's sounded concerned. Strong hands fished her out of the greedy water as she coughed and choked, trying to get the nauseating, sweet blood taste out of her mouth.

"Can't see," she gasped, at last finding her feet. They were standing in the shallows of the river. She was only in up to her waist, but the current pulling at her could easily drag her out farther if Teague let her go. Krisa felt its hungry tug and heard the deep, gurgling chuckle like another entity in the solid darkness, but she couldn't see a thing. It was as though she had suddenly gone blind, as though someone had painted over her eyeballs while she wasn't looking.

"Don't let go," she said, fumbling to grasp at the strong wrists that were holding her shoulders. She found them and squeezed panicky-tight. "Don't...just don't let me go, Teague."

"I won't." The deep voice was oddly gentle and then his huge hand found hers. "Come on, little girl, time to get out of the river." He tugged at her hand. Krisa tried to follow but she stumbled in the darkness again, going down to her knees in the cold, rushing water.

Without a word, Teague swung her up into his arms and she was being carried again although in a much more dignified way than she had been during their run for the river. Twin silver moons hovered somewhere above her head in the dead blackness — his eyes.

Without thinking about it, Krisa wound her arms around the strongly corded neck and let her head rest on the broad shoulder. She heard him rumble something about making camp but it barely registered. She only knew that the terror of their sprint and the disorientation of the swim had brought her to a state of exhaustion beyond any she had ever felt before. *I'm not blind, though*, she thought, reassuring herself. *As long as I can still see his eyes I'm not blind.*

For an unknown time, she slept.

She woke up once in the middle of the night beside a dying fire that did little to pierce the surrounding blackness. The blanket beneath her was damp and so was she. Krisa shivered convulsively with a sudden chill. Then she realized there was a source of heat behind her as well, one that seemed to offer more solid reassurance than the tiny flames across from her.

She snuggled back against something firm and warm that was rewarded at once by a delicious heat that seemed to penetrate her bones. A deep, rhythmic motion lulled her back to sleep. Just before she fell down under the waves of unconsciousness again, a large, muscular arm drew her even closer to the heat source, wrapping her securely close.

Chapter Nine

ഇ

"Wake up little girl, we've got a long way to go." The deep voice invaded her dream but Krisa wasn't entirely sorry. She had been having the disturbing one again. About the man without a face who touched her. That dream always left her feeling hot and strangely restless for most of the day after she had it.

She opened her eyes to the muted bronze light that diffused though the clouds of Planet X and found herself on a slightly damp blanket near the remains of a burned-out fire. They were in a little clearing, back in the pastel jungle and the deep gurgle of water to her left told her that the river wasn't too far away.

"What time is it?" she asked automatically and then realized what a silly question that was. "Never mind. Oh—this ground is *hard*," she groaned, rising stiffly.

"Sorry I didn't have time to make you a nice soft bed of moss and leaves, princess," Teague rumbled. The comment was sarcastic in a way that she was beginning to know was typically "Teague" but Krisa thought she saw the corners of his full mouth twitch just a little as he spoke. He was on the far side of the burned-out fire, rummaging in his pack. She noted that the thin red lines and scratches that had decorated his dusky skin the day before were already mostly healed. Maybe it was the effects of the river water?

Krisa looked down at her own arms hopefully, rolling up the white sleeves of Percy's shirt to do so. She was still covered with scrapes and bruises from the escape from her sleep-cube and her encounter with Captain Ketchum the day before. Not the water then. Already both incidents seemed far away, as distant as though they had happened weeks ago or to someone else entirely.

It was impossible, somehow, to sit in the warm, dark gold light pouring down from the bronze sky and think of her life as it had been not even a week ago. She could smell the lush, pungent scent of the jungle and the musical twittering, hooting and chattering going on all around her, with the faint ripple of the river overlaying it all, filled her ears. A faint breeze stirred the muted but still-vivid colors of the alien vegetation surrounding them in all directions. It was another world, Krisa decided, the life she'd left back aboard the *Star Princess*. Not one she was entirely sure she missed.

Not that the new one she found herself in was perfect by any means, despite its strange beauty. For one thing, when she tried to stretch, she felt stiff and sore. It was as though someone had thrown her over the line and beat her the way they used to beat out the huge Great Hall carpets every seven-day at Briar Rose. She uttered an involuntary groan.

"Sore?" Teague inquired, finding what he was looking for in the pack—a tube of nutrient paste.

Krisa nodded and then winced at the sharp pain in her neck. "All that running we did yesterday. I'm not exactly used to it," she admitted ruefully.

"You mean they didn't teach jungle survival skills and long-distance running at Briar Rose?" The full mouth held a hint of amusement again and Krisa decided not to answer. He would only laugh at her if she told him about the weekly nature hike that never even extended past the Briar Rose grounds or the wildflower-gathering forays they went on each spring.

"I'm stiff all over," was all she would say. "And I feel all grimy and nasty from sleeping in my clothes," she added with distaste.

Percy's clothes were if anything, even more uncomfortable today, the result of having been wet thoroughly and forced to dry on her body. The trousers looked positively painted on now, and the white oxford shirt was bulging where it tried to cover her full breasts, threatening to pop a button at any time.

"I thought you'd rather sleep in 'em than have me take 'em off you," Teague said dryly, digging out another tube of nutri-paste and tossing it to her.

Krisa blushed and nearly fumbled the tube. "I didn't mean…it's just that they've shrunk now and…" she trailed off.

"I can see that," Teague remarked, looking pointedly at the full swells of her breasts pushing against the white shirt. Krisa felt her nipples becoming stiff, standing out against the stiff material, almost as though his gaze on her was making her body react as it would to a physical touch. She wanted to cross her arms over her chest and hide herself, but she was afraid he would laugh at her. After a moment, Teague dropped his eyes, which were hooded in black again and went back to his tube of paste.

Looking down at the damage being dunked in the river had done to her clothes made Krisa suddenly wonder about the river water's effect on the rest of her meager possessions. Her hair was loose around her shoulders in a mass of dark curls but the ornate hairpin was lying on the blanket beside her—Teague must have removed it the night before. Everything in her front pockets was fine aside from the jeweled chronometer Lord Radisson had given her. It appeared to have stopped running. Her mother's holo-vid was all right, thank the Goddess it was waterproof, but…*the Certificate!* Krisa reached around hastily to feel in the back pocket of Percy's trousers and came away empty-handed.

"It's right here, sweetheart. Don't panic." Teague's voice was low and unreadable as he handed her the creased and wrinkled document across the dead fire.

Krisa took it gratefully.

"I dried it for you," he said. "Thought you might want it. Eventually." It was as close as he had come to saying he would help her get home, get back where she belonged. Hearing him say it loosened the tight, worried knot she had been carrying in her gut ever since they had left the ship and set off for parts unknown, at least unknown to her, into the jungle.

"Thank you." Krisa looked up gratefully into the blank, black eyes and then back down at her Certificate of Virginity. It had obviously been through some rough times but it was still legible. And it was still the truth. That brought back the night before in vivid detail somehow. The run through the jungle, the way he could have left her and didn't. *All* the things he could have done that he hadn't done.

"Teague," she said and he looked up again. "Thank you," she said, folding the much abused document and stowing it securely in her back pocket. "Not just for this, but for last night. You could have left me behind."

"But I didn't," he said flatly. Krisa waited but after a while she realized that was all he was prepared to say.

"Better eat your paste—we've got a long way to go today," Teague said after a while.

Krisa tasted it, grimacing at the bland flavor of the stuff. But she ate it dutifully, knowing it had enough energy and nutrients to keep her moving all day. It helped that once she got down the first mouthful her stomach realized she was ravenously hungry.

"Where are we going?" she managed to ask between mouthfuls.

Teague finished his own paste and put the tube back in his pack. "There's a village not far from here. That's our first goal."

"Village?" Krisa's heart began pounding harder. *Savages...bizarre ritualistic religious ceremonies...cannibalism,* Ketchum's voice whispered in the back of her head. Of course, the good captain had lied and exaggerated a lot, Krisa reminded herself. Then again, he hadn't lied about everything. She felt beneath her heavy tangle of hair to rub the bump at the back of her neck.

"Is— Are the people who live here…*normal*?" she asked Teague in a soft voice, half afraid some of them might be lurking in the bushes listening in to their conversation.

The big Feral threw back his head and roared with laughter. "Normal? Look at who you're travelin' with, sweetheart! Would you consider *me* normal?"

"That's not what I mean and you know it!" Krisa flared. She was tired of him finding everything she did and said amusing. "You've been here before but I haven't. I heard some pretty frightening things about the natives of Planet X. I just want to know what to expect."

Teague sobered. "They're humanoid," he said. "And as for the scary things you heard, just remember you heard some pretty scary things about me too, and I haven't killed you— yet." He gave her that sharp white grin that made Krisa feel uncertain all over again. "I'll tell you more about the Yss when we get a little closer. No point in upsettin' you right now." He got up and shouldered the pack, knife out and ready in his hand. The blade gleamed dully in the bronze light.

"But—"

"Come on. I don't care how sore you are, little girl, I expect you to keep up. I'd like to make that village by full dark and it's late in the morning already." His black eyes scanned the bronze sky as thought tracking the position of the invisible sun. "Let's go."

By the second time Teague stopped to examine the ground, as they hacked their way through the pastel vegetation, Krisa knew something was wrong. The third time she managed to catch a glimpse of something that looked like a depression in a small patch of muddy dirt—it was a print. A print the size of her head.

Krisa tugged at the back of Teague's ragged black tank top to keep him from starting again. "Teague," she said quietly. "Tell me—*please.*"

"Soondar. Trackin' us," he said shortly. "Circling around but they won't come too close while it's light."

Krisa's spine prickled with a cool fear as she remembered the huge purple eyes in the darkness and the hot-black sound in her mind that had threatened to rip her head apart like a slick, flexing fist. "But the targees," she protested weakly. "We haven't heard—"

"That's the only good news, sweetheart. Targees don't give call unless it's a pack. There's only one after us, maybe two. Probably a mated pair."

"Only one," she said faintly. "Two tops. Sure, no problem."

"We're not gonna make the village tonight," Teague said musingly. "But if I remember right, there's another river— more like a stream really—halfway to the village perimeter. We'll camp there tonight, build a big fire. It'll be fine. Come on." And he resumed cutting trail.

Krisa didn't know if she was more relieved about putting off their meeting with the Yss, as Teague had called the natives of Planet X, or more disturbed about spending another night in the open, especially now that they knew they were being tracked. But she wasn't being given much choice.

To her relief they heard the light, laughing sound of the water a long time before the sky turned burnt umber. After they had made a place in the middle of a small clearing for their fire, Krisa decided that she wanted to take a quick wash in the narrow stream. The water was a pale pinkish color that reminded her disturbingly of diluted blood, but she was hot, sweaty and sore and wanted to wash off the grime of their trek through the jungle. Teague, however, refused to let her bathe in privacy.

"I *refuse* to take off my clothes in front of you," Krisa stormed. Her temper was rising as it so readily did around the huge Feral. She was tired and hot and just wanted to wash off without having to worry about anything...improper happening. Why couldn't he let her?

"Then you don't get a bath," Teague replied mildly, but she could see the flickers of silver in his eyes behind the black second lid. "We know there's at least one, maybe two soondar on our trail. You go out there alone and unprotected, it's like wearing a big sign that says 'first course' around your pretty little neck. Or 'appetizer' in your case—I doubt if you'd make more than a mouthful for a full-grown soondar."

"I thought you said they don't hunt until dark," Krisa said accusingly, hands balled into tight fists at her hips.

"Hunting is one thing, having your meal delivered on a silver platter is another, sweetheart," he growled. "What are you afraid of, anyway? That I'll see your sweet, naked body and be unable to restrain my animalistic lust? Think I'll throw you to the ground and 'have my way with you'?"

When he said it like that it sounded ridiculous but in fact it was exactly what Krisa *had* been worried about.

"It's just not proper," she mumbled, feeling her cheeks turn scarlet. The scenario he'd mentioned had occurred to her in vivid detail more than once, as she watched his broad back flex and ripple with muscle, while following him through the brush.

"Listen, little girl, if I wanted to rape you I could have done it already," he pointed out, taking a step nearer so that he loomed over her.

Krisa held her ground.

"In fact." Teague lifted a strand of curly brown hair that had come loose from her hairpin and sniffed it, rubbing it along his cheek which was thick with blue-black stubble. "I could have done it without you even knowing it. Last night you were out like a light, I doubt having your hand bitten off by a soondar would have woken you up. How do you know I didn't do it then?"

Krisa stepped away from him, a sudden fear blooming inside her chest. She had a very vague memory of being held close in muscular arms, of sleeping with her back to a broad, warm chest. But when she'd woken that morning Teague had already been on the other side of the fire and she had assumed it was one of her more disturbing dreams. Now she had to wonder.

She looked at the big Feral's dark face and black, impassive eyes and couldn't find any clue. Surely if he had done *that* she would feel different somehow. Wouldn't she?

"If...you *had* done it," she said slowly, trying to gauge his reaction to her words. "I'd feel different today, wouldn't I? I mean, I'm sure I'd be able to tell that you'd— Wouldn't I be sore?" she asked, her eyes flickering desperately to the thick bulge in the crotch of his black trousers.

The look on his dark face became a little less blank and Krisa thought she saw a mixture of amusement and something else flicker briefly in his eyes. "Yes, little girl, if I *fucked* you, you'd know it afterwards," he growled.

Krisa flinched at the crude word. Even at midnight in the dormitory, when she was sure no one could hear her, had she dared not utter that particular expletive.

The look on her face must have angered him because Teague suddenly snarled at her. Taking a step to close the distance between them, he grasped her shoulders in both hands, fingers digging into her flesh as he stared down at her. His eyes flashed a heated silver.

"Oh, that word offends your Goddessdamn sense of propriety, does it, Krisa? Well, let me tell you somethin'—this is Planet X, not Bride Planet. We're in the middle of the *fucking jungle*, not at a finishing school for fine ladies, in case you haven't noticed. I'm out here tryin' to keep us both alive, so pardon me if I'm not too concerned about your sense of propriety. Out here in the jungle, it's more likely to get you killed than to catch you a rich husband. So I suggest you let it go for a while. *Understand?*"

"I understand you perfectly. Now take your hands *off* me." Krisa was amazed at the cool voice coming out of her mouth. His words sent a hot spike of adrenaline racing through her system, his rising temper triggering her own as it did every time.

Teague gave her a little shake and then released her with a frustrated growl. "Look, I told you I'm not going to rape you. Believe it or not, despite my criminal record, I *can* control myself."

"Well, you can't blame me for being worried," she flared back at him, rubbing her sore shoulders and backing away a step. "I've almost been raped twice already in the last month."

"*But not by me.*" His voice was a deep, angry rumble that vibrated through her, making her feel like her bones were rattling. "It's getting dark and I need to build a fire if you don't want to be a soondar snack. So decide *now*, Krisa. Do you want a bath or not?"

"Fine," she spat. Turning her back to him, she rapidly unbuttoned the soiled white shirt and let it drop, then unsnapped the catches on the trousers and shimmied out of them as well. Kicking off her shoes and feeling very conscious of his eyes on her naked backside, she waded into the stream waist-deep and began to wash as best she could.

She submerged herself to the neck in the frigid stream, getting used to the chilly water. After a while she dunked her head and let the pinkish water run through her long brown curls, making them look like a new species of water weed as they trailed in the brisk current. Despite the rather unpleasant sweet-blood taste of the water, it seemed to have a kind of natural conditioner in it. Krisa, whose naturally curly hair had always been something of a trial to fix, had to admit that her chocolate-brown locks had never been more silky or manageable.

As she bathed, she could feel Teague's eyes on her back. She dreaded having to turn around and face him head-on and naked, but she didn't see that she had much choice. Backing out of the water would be both ridiculous and dangerous. If she fell over because she couldn't see where she was going it would be painful as well.

"Are you finished?" His deep voice was closer than she had expected and Krisa's flesh prickled over with chill bumps of fear and surprise. She could feel her nipples, already hardened by exposure to the chilly water, contract painfully tight. She wrapped her arms around herself, shivering.

"Almost," she said with as much dignity as she could. Nerving herself for the inevitable, she turned around and looked him squarely in the eye. Teague was standing on the bank of the stream holding an outstretched blanket between his hands, waiting for her. There was an impassive look in his black eyes.

For a long moment she held those eyes with her own. Krisa knew she should rush up the bank as quickly as possible and wrap herself modestly in the blanket. But something rose inside her, a kind of pride—a wish to defy his expectations.

Taking a deep breath and ignoring the panicky feeling in the pit of her stomach, she dropped her arms and stood silently, waiting. Black flickered back to reveal pure, blazing silver as Teague looked over her naked, dripping body. Her long hair trailed down her back and beads of the pinkish water clung to the softly rounded apex of her pussy, the full curves of her breasts and the tightly jutting pink buds of her nipples.

"Like what you see?" Krisa asked challengingly. Her heart was drumming against her ribs and she was having a hard time getting a deep breath, but she was determined not to let Teague know how nervous those silver eyes on her naked body made her. The heat from his gaze seemed to start a fire inside her somehow and she could feel her pale, creamy skin flushing a rosy pink, but still she held her ground.

Inside her head, the voices of her vanished instructors from Briar Rose were strangely silent—perhaps they had fainted from the sheer impropriety of her act, Krisa speculated. It was a well-known fact that a true lady didn't let any man, even her husband, see her completely undressed. It simply wasn't done. *Guess I'm not a true lady, then,* Krisa thought, defiantly. It was hard to believe that only the day before she had been haggling over the right to bring her cincher and wear a dress in the jungle to avoid impropriety, but she refused to think about that right now.

"Well?" she asked again, because Teague still hadn't answered her.

He took a deep breath and let his eyes rake her body once more.

"Get up here, Krisa," he rumbled at last, shaking the blanket for emphasis. "It's gettin' dark and I need to build a fire."

Feeling in some odd way that she had made her point, Krisa climbed up the bank and allowed him to drape the blanket over her shoulders. She turned her back on him again while she dried off and dressed.

"You shouldn't have done that," he said from behind her, his deep, gravelly voice vibrating through her as she finger-combed her damp hair.

"But I did," Krisa answered him in his own oblique fashion. She was thinking of the one kiss they had shared that night in the hold, while Teague was still in chains. If she closed her eyes, she could still recall the wild taste of him that lingered on her lips afterwards. One of the girls in her dorm, Mazy Engelton, had once been sent a care package that contained candy all the way from Old Earth. The candy had a sweet, spicy flavor that was deliciously unique. *Cinnamon, that was the name of it,* Krisa remembered. That had been the flavor of Teague's kiss—wild and sweet and strong.

"Shouldn't we be making a fire?" she asked, tuning to face him at last.

Teague's eyes flashed silver and then went back to opaque black. "You need to watch yourself, little girl," he growled warningly. "There's only so much I can take."

He turned and stalked away, leaving her to follow. She helped Teague gather dried pastel sticks and brush by the armload. How in the world he had managed the night before, while she was out cold and he'd had to deal with her as well as getting a fire started? *Probably just slung me over his shoulder again and kept going,* she thought.

His immense physical stamina was still a point of amazement to her—the way he just kept going on and on without ever seeming to need a break. Did it have something to do with his Feral heritage or was it just the way he was? Krisa had never met anyone with more willpower and determination to survive. But then, she thought with a small shudder, those would be qualities needed to stay alive both as a slave and in prison.

She was still confused about why she had acted the way she had at the stream. The memory of those silver eyes on her naked body made her feel flushed and uncertain about herself. Don't think about it, she told herself sternly. What's done can't be undone. Yes, but she'd better not do it again.

There's only so much I can take, Teague had said. The memory of the heat coming from his eyes and radiating from his big body when he'd said it was enough to make her shiver again, even as she tried to push the incident out of her mind.

Krisa dumped her last armful on the growing pastel pile and saw something that made her grin, then suddenly burst into laughter. The pile of pink and purple and baby blue brush, had it been sorted neatly and had ribbons and bows to match, would have done nicely for dried floral arrangements in one of Madame Perot's classes.

Madame Perot was the art instructor at Briar Rose. She was a tiny dried stick of a lady with a face like a wrinkled fruit and hair that was dyed a dramatic black. Krisa could just hear her high, fluty nasal voice in her head saying, "Now class, today's assignment is to make le arrangement magnifique from dried jungle vines. You will be responsible for gathering your own materials for this project, so pair off and mind that you steer well clear of any ravenous soondar in the vicinity."

"What's so funny?" Teague dropped his last considerably larger load of wood and brush beside hers and gave Krisa a questioning look.

"Nothing," she said, still smiling a little. "I was just thinking about where I came from and what everybody from Briar Rose would think if they could see me now. It just seems so bizarre that I should be here with you."

"Instead of back on Prime where you belong, getting ready to marry your lord-and-master-to-be?" he finished for her in a lightly mocking tone and began lighting the fire.

At least his sense of humor was back, Krisa reflected. She was glad because it eased some of the tension between them. She could have done without his jab about Lord Radisson and the life that was waiting for her on Lynix Prime, though.

"No," she said as lightly as she could. "I wasn't thinking that at all. I was just thinking that it's so strange and different here. So unlike anything I was ever trained for at Briar Rose and yet..." She fell silent for a moment, staring at the flames licking at the pile of firewood.

"And yet," Teague prompted softly.

Krisa looked up at him and was surprised to see genuine interest in his face. It was nearing twilight, and the black second lid had retracted to show his luminous silver eyes. They were softer now than when he had raked them over her body, more open somehow.

"And yet," Krisa said slowly. "It's almost as if my entire life up to this point has been some kind of a—I don't know—

some kind of a dream. It's like I was never really alive before now. I guess that sounds crazy."

"No," Teague said but didn't elaborate. He wasn't mocking her either though, which in Krisa's view was a vast improvement. He began digging in the pack and tossed her a tube of nutri-paste. She caught it handily and sat down on the blanket she had spread beside the fire. Teague sat across from her and they ate the tasteless paste in silence for a while.

"I used to pick the lock on my dormitory and go out at night back at Briar Rose," Krisa said dreamily, looking into the crackling fire. "I didn't go anywhere because there was no place to go, just wandered around in the moonlight. It was the only time I really felt free, but I wasn't really. And I never will be until I get this chip out of my neck."

"Even then you'll be joined to Lord Radisson," Teague pointed out in his deep rumbling voice. "Think you'll like that?"

Krisa looked across the fire at him but the look on his dark face was completely impassive. "It might not be so bad," she said cautiously after a while. "After all, it's what I've been trained for most of my life."

"I was trained to be a slave most of my life," Teague said tonelessly. The light from the fire had caused his second eyelid to flicker down and Krisa could see the dancing flames mirrored in the black depths of his unreadable eyes.

"Were you ever joined?" she asked, deciding to pass over his last statement. The firelight made her feel sleepy and unwilling to argue.

Teague seemed to consider for a while but finally he said, "Yes," in a tone that made her realize no other information would be forthcoming on the subject, unless she pressed.

"Did you love her?" Krisa asked. She was trying to imagine a younger, softer Teague, but it was nearly impossible to do.

"Do you love Lord Radisson?" he countered answering her question with a question.

Krisa frowned, considering. "I don't know," she said, thinking of the holo-vids and pictures he always sent. They showed a tall, thin man with iron-gray hair and a neatly clipped goatee and mustache. He was usually dressed in an expensively tailored suit and carefully posed in front of his country estate or his black stretch hover-limo or his valuable collection of Arteezian artifacts, or some other expensive and valuable prop. Lord Radisson was a collector of rare and beautiful things and Krisa knew she would become part of his collection as soon as the joining contract was signed—just another valuable acquisition.

"He's owned my contract forever," she said, sighing and poking a pale pink stick into the fire to see the sparks fly up into the velvety darkness. "He sent me a holo-vid just after he'd picked me out and said that he'd been looking for a wife for a long time. He said the minute he saw my image on the Rose Garden—that's the name of Briar Rose's interstellar web site—that he knew I was the one for him. I was only thirteen then." She sighed.

"So I've always known I was going to join with him, but somehow it just seemed like a dream, like something that was never really going to happen. Then all of a sudden I was on the *Star Princess* and it was becoming a reality. I guess...I feel a little relieved in a way that it hasn't yet," she ended in a small voice.

"Doesn't sound much like true love to me," Teague rumbled. Krisa could see that he was grinning at her in an amused way across the fire.

"Well, how could I love a man I've never met?" she demanded, feeling irritated. "He's always sent me wonderful presents on my birthdays and Winter Solstice. Lots of the other girls at Briar Rose were jealous of me, but it never felt real. He's just been like some kindly old uncle who sent me pretty things and nice holo-vids all the time."

"If I find a way to get you back to Prime the price tag for all those pretty things is going to come due," Teague pointed out, shifting closer to the fire. "You're gonna have to sleep with kindly old Lord Radisson. You ever think about that?"

Krisa flushed, feeling her cheeks burn red at his words. "From time to time," she admitted finally. "But I try not to. There's more to joining than that. There's keeping his home in order and being a good hostess at parties —"

"Hate to break it to you, sweetheart, but that, as you put it, is a big part of joining. Not many men are willing to pay the price of an interstellar ticket from Capellia to Lynix Prime to acquire a good hostess," Teague said dryly. "But I take it you're not exactly lookin' forward to payin' the piper when the time comes." He arched one black eyebrow upwards, a sardonic grin playing around the corners of his full mouth.

Krisa frowned and tried to keep her voice steady. "How do I know if it's something to look forward to or not?" she demanded. "You know I've never…"

"Made love?" he finished for her quietly. His choice of words surprised her.

Krisa nodded, shifting on the blanket. She drew up her knees and wrapped her arms around her legs protectively.

"I don't know if I'll like it or not," she said in a small voice. She was thinking of the sexual education lectures that all girls seventeen and over were expected to attend twice yearly.

The course was taught by the school nurse, Madame Glossop, a tall, statuesque horse of a woman with horn-rimmed spectacles that hung down to her thick waist on a long beaded chain.

The main idea of the lessons seemed to be that your husband would do what he wanted when he wanted and it was the wife's job to bear it. *It is your duty, girls!* Madame Glossop would bugle, driving home the point by smacking her long wooden baton against the blackboard where a chalked image of the male and female genitalia had been drawn. This always caused considerable nervous giggling from the back of the room where the older girls who were almost at the age of consent sat. *Your duty, I say!* SMACK! *Your* Duty!

"I don't exactly think you're supposed to enjoy it," Krisa said, staring into the fire with her chin on her knees, as Madame Glossop's voice rang in her memory.

"Why not? Or is that something else they teach you at that academy you came from?" Teague demanded.

Krisa nodded once, keeping her eyes on the fire.

"Just remember, sweetheart, that's the same place that put the chip in your neck," he said, his voice low and angry.

"He's going to do it to me whether I like it or not so it doesn't make any difference what I think about it, does it?" Krisa flared, looking up from the fire to meet his black eyes.

"Let me ask you this," Teague said, his eyes fixed on hers across the fire. "Do you think of him when you touch yourself at night?"

"When I…" The question was so totally unexpected that for a moment Krisa was at a loss for words. "I never…I don't…" she stuttered.

"You're lying if you say you don't." Teague said flatly, still staring at her with that unreadable look on his dark face. "Just answer the question, Krisa."

Krisa stared into the fire, unable to meet his gaze and thought of quiet nights in the dorm when all the other girls were breathing softly in their narrow cots and she was sure none would know. She remembered the feeling of being just on the edge of something huge that she could never quite reach. She thought of the strange dreams she sometimes had about the man with no face, who made her naked and ran big, rough hands over her body. The man who made her beg and gasp and plead before he took her, sometimes hard and fast, and sometimes long and slow, but always with a pleasure that was so deep it was nearly excruciating.

"No," she said at last in a low voice, hugging her knees to her chest. "No, I don't think of him...that way. I don't think of anybody. Anybody that I know, anyway."

"I guess that's another thing you're not supposed to do at good old Briar Rose, hmm?" Teague asked, slight amusement rumbling in his deep tone. "You know, sweetheart, since you've been tellin' me about this place you came from, I've been thinking it's as bad as any slam I've ever been in. But I think I changed my mind."

"Really?" Krisa looked up from contemplating the fire, her cheeks still stained red with embarrassment.

"Really," Teague confirmed, grinning that white, irrepressible grin. "Right now I'm thinkin' it's a whole lot worse. Come on, time to get ready for bed." He stood up, stretching until his long spine cracked, and began to reposition the blankets beside the fire.

Krisa looked at him in confusion. "But I *am* ready for bed, my blanket's already spread," she pointed out, sliding one hand over the rough material. Teague had taken the emergency blankets from the ship's stores rather than the softer luxury throws from the lounge, explaining that they would stand up to the stress of travel better.

"Not there, sweetheart, over here." Teague settled back, lying on his side on the blanket and patted the space in front of him between his body and the fire.

"Look, just because we talked about what we talked about..." Krisa began angrily. "I mean, I hope you don't think because of what you saw when I was taking a bath...because I let you see me...that I'm going to turn into some kind of a...a..." But she couldn't think of a word bad enough to finish her sentence.

Teague frowned at her. "This doesn't have anything to do with what we talked about, little girl. And as for the little show you put on down by the stream, I know it wasn't anything you've ever done before. That was just you tryin' to show me

113

you're not afraid of me. I know the difference between a challenge and a come-on. Goddess knows I've had enough of both."

"Well, then why—" Krisa began, but he cut her off.

"For protection, Krisa. Those soondar are still out there somewhere. With soondar, it's always better to put yourself between fire and water because they don't like either one. Now I've got the stream at my back and the fire in front of me. If you lay between me and the fire you'll be safe. Understand?"

Chocolate brown warred with black and silver for a moment and then Krisa sighed. "Fine," she said getting up and coming around to his side of the fire. "But no funny business, Teague."

"Wouldn't dream of it," Teague said dryly as she spread her blanket where he had indicated. "Especially when I know you're savin' yourself so eagerly for dear Lord Radisson."

Krisa lay on her side stiffly, her back to the large Feral and refused to rise to his bait.

"You know, sweetheart," he continued, lying down behind her with his chest only inches from her back, so that she could feel the heat from his big body radiating against her own. "I said once before that your sense of propriety is likely to get you killed out here. That's not just because I'm only willin' to put up with so much of your ladylike crap, either. Once we meet up with the Yss, you're really gonna have to tone it down a notch or two, or we'll *both* be in big trouble."

"What do you mean? Tell me about the Yss!" Krisa demanded, turning her neck to find that he was leaning over and staring down at her in a most unsettling manner.

"Later," he rumbled. "Now it's time to get some sleep, little girl." He settled behind her, using the pack for a pillow and was silent except for his deep, slow breathing.

Krisa tried but she wasn't as exhausted from pain and fear as she had been the night before, when she hadn't so much gone to sleep as passed out. It was hard to get comfortable with only the thin blanket between her and the uneven ground, and even harder to ignore the fact that Teague was so close to her. He hadn't gotten to take much more than a quick rinse in the stream, unlike her full bath. His wild, masculine scent was strong in her nose but not unpleasant.

He had a sort of spicy natural musk, which seemed to invade her senses at once and completely, much as the heat radiating from his big body permeated the scant space between them. Krisa thought she had never met anyone who could get so completely under her skin in so many ways.

The jungle rustled around them like an animal itself, filled with frightening and intriguing noises. The velvety blackness pressed in on all sides. Krisa soon discovered that despite the sultry days, nights got fairly cold on Planet X, probably because there was no direct sunlight during the daylight hours for the ground to absorb. Despite the slowly dying fire a few feet from her, and Teague's heat behind her, she began to feel cold.

She thought of the hazy, half-memory of being snuggled close to Teague the night before. If only she could scoot back into his bone-penetrating heat and relax into sleep, but after making such a big deal about not wanting to be too close to him, she could hardly do that. She wiggled uncomfortably, wishing she could turn onto her right side but that would put her face-to-face with him, which was entirely too intimate a position.

"Settle down. Why are you so damn twitchy?" His deep voice was an annoyed growl and Krisa froze in mid-wiggle at the sound. She had thought he was already asleep.

"I'm cold," she said at last, wishing they had brought enough blankets to cover up with as well as to lie on. "And I can't sleep right without a pillow."

"Here." Teague shifted behind her and a muscular arm drew her in close, the curve of her spine fitting perfectly against his flat chest and abdomen. Krisa found her head pillowed on his thick biceps and her legs curled along the length of his own. It was exactly what she had been wishing for, but still, it was disturbing to find herself in such close physical contact with the big Feral.

Krisa stiffened against him, feeling her breath catch in her throat, but didn't dare say anything. She had provoked him enough for one night and she knew he would only be pushed so far. Just as she thought he was once again asleep, his deep voice broke into her tumultuous thoughts.

"Relax, little girl. I'm not gonna hurt you," he said, his tone oddly gentle this time. "Try to get some sleep. 'Nother long day tomorrow." Then his breathing grew deeper and more regular and Krisa knew he really was asleep.

She relaxed in slow stages, letting her eyelids drift down as the fire died lower and Teague's heat penetrated her body. There was something intensely comforting about being wrapped so close in his protective grip. He was so much bigger than she, that with his chest at her back like a solid wall and his arm wrapped loosely around her, she felt completely enclosed. He was like her own private fortress, keeping out the cold and the dangerous jungle alike.

Perfect, Krisa thought drowsily and let herself slip into sleep.

~ ~ ~ ~ ~

Large hands roamed over her body, exploring her hidden places and mapping her curves. A hot, sweet mouth covered her own, demanding entry which Krisa granted gladly. He tasted her thoroughly and then the wet heat of his tongue trailed down her throat to the soft curves of her breasts. He was sucking her nipples, taking as much of her breast in his mouth as he could while big fingers molded the other with rough gentleness.

"You taste so good, little girl," a deep voice whispered in her ear. "Can't wait to be inside you. Can't wait to fill you full of my cum. Spread your legs for me now and let me in your pussy."

Krisa obeyed without question, parting her thighs for the sweet pressure of his big fingers rubbing over her swollen clit. Her pussy lips were drenched with her juices, making her hot flesh slippery, easing his way. There was no doubt about it—she wanted this, needed it. Then he was spreading her pussy lips wide, opening her sex for his own pleasure and for hers. Two thick fingers pressed inside her, exploring her pussy, mapping her secret places where no one had ever been. He was filling her up, making her moan and gasp.

"This is where I'm gonna put my cock, sweetheart. Right here in your sweet little cunt. I'm gonna spread open your slippery pussy lips with the head of my shaft and slide into your tight,wet cunt one inch at a time until I'm all the way inside you. All the way into your hot pussy. Are you ready for that now? Ready for me to fuck you?"

Words. There were words this time and looking up she thought she could almost see his face. Almost.

"Your pussy's so wet, so ready to take me." His fingers were rubbing over her hot, slippery sex insistently, urgently. "Need to be inside you, filling you up. Need to spread you wide and fuck you, fill you up with my cum. Gonna make you mine forever, little girl," he growled low in her ear, pressing deep now but not quite deep enough.

The hot, dirty words and the motion of his fingers in her cleft made her feel so wet and hot and ready that Krisa could only moan and scratch at the broad shoulders of the man above her. The man waiting to take her, to mount her and press his thick cock deep into her wet, willing cunt. She wanted him so much she could almost feel it—could almost feel the slow slide of his thick shaft against her sex, spreading her pussy lips open for him before the broad head breached her entrance. She could almost feel him entering her, one thick inch at a time, just as he had promised. And when he was all the way inside her, so deep that she could feel the head of his cock pressing against the mouth of her womb, then he would start to thrust—to fuck. He would pound into her without mercy, she knew that and yet she didn't care. He would open her, fill her, use her cunt and she would spread her thighs wide to receive him and revel in every moment of it. Finally, he would press deep, holding her hips in his large, capable hands to keep her in place while he flooded her unprotected sex with his cum. He would fuck her to completion and she would come too, would reach that elusive edge she was always seeking and never quite able to find.

"Please," she gasped, arching up to meet him. Any thoughts of shame or impropriety were burned to ashes with the heat of her need for his big body on top of her, inside her. "Please, do it now!"

~ ~ ~ ~ ~

Planet X

Chapter Ten

೫೦

"Do what now?" The deep, amused voice broke into her dream, scattering the images that filled her head. Krisa opened her eyes to see Teague propped up on his side and staring down at her with silver eyes.

It seemed like a continuation of her dream. She had rolled on her back somehow and now, as he leaned over her, she reached up and ran tentative fingers over his strongly corded throat. He dipped his head and nuzzled her hand, the wide silver eyes never leaving her face.

Still half asleep she thought, *His eyes…his face! I can finally see his face!* Reaching up she buried both hands in his spiky black hair and pulled him down, wanting to taste the sweet, hot-cinnamon flavor of her dream again.

The silver eyes widened and then he was kissing her back, taking control of the kiss and rolling her beneath his big body to press the thick hardness between his legs into the willing wetness between hers.

Krisa arched her back and moaned like an animal, feeling the hard length of his cock rubbing against the center of her need. She cursed the stupid trousers that kept them apart, kept him from sliding inside her pussy and giving her what her body was begging for.

Just like my dream, she was thinking half deliriously, relishing the frightening, erotic sensation of being pinned to the ground, helpless beneath his big body. *Just like my dream… Dream! Oh my Goddess, this is no dream!*

The horrifying realization slammed into her dazed brain as the last cobwebs of the dream were blown away. Krisa

119

began to struggle beneath him, fighting to get away from the reality of the situation.

"Teague, stop! No… *No!*" she gasped, pressing small hands to his massive chest to try and hold him back. "Please, I didn't mean to. It was just a dream…I have sometimes." If she lost her virginity… If Lord Radisson insisted on a re-verification and it was gone…

He had the white shirt half unbuttoned and one firm breast cupped in his large hand, while he sucked fiercely against the side of her neck. Even as she tried to push him off her, Krisa could feel her body responding. She knew that soon it would be too late to stop either the big Feral or herself from giving in to the hot urges that were driving them closer to the point of no return. Even as she begged him to stop, she groaned in pleasure as rough fingers twisted her nipples, shooting sparks of pure, electric sensation down her spine to the wet heat between her legs.

"Teague, *please!*" she gasped, not sure anymore if she was pushing him away or pulling him closer. "Please—you said you wouldn't hurt me! You said you wouldn't rape me!"

The words seemed to have an effect on him at last. With a low growl, Teague gave her neck one last suck, almost a bite, and then pushed away from her and sat up. He ran big hands through his blue-black hair in a gesture of pure frustration.

"What the hell?" he snarled at last, looking down at Krisa who still lay panting breathlessly on the blanket.

"I…" Her heart was pounding so hard she could barely hear her own words. "I'm sorry," she said at last. "It's just a dream I have sometimes. There's a man…a man without a face. Or at least, I can't see his face and he…does things to me. Touches me…"

"Fucks you?" Teague growled, silver eyes savage with the need she had stirred in him.

Krisa blushed hard, feeling the deep burn of embarrassment all along her body. "I…when you woke me up

120

I thought it was part of the dream," she whispered, pulling the open halves of her shirt tight around her aching breasts. "I'm sorry, I know I started it but I thought..."

"Thought I was the man of your dreams, did you?" Suddenly he laughed, shaking his head as though trying to dispel the tension that had built up in his big body. "Well, you're not the first woman to make that mistake, sweetheart."

"I'm sorry," Krisa said again, feeling near tears of embarrassment and shame. "But it was so *real*. I could hear him talking to me. I've never heard his voice before. And I could almost see his face." She struggled to sit up and pulled her knees up to her chin, wrapping her arms protectively around them.

Teague looked at her, his dark face half angry, half amused. "You been havin' these dreams long then?"

Krisa ducked her head and studied her hands in the dim glow of the dying fire. "Years," she admitted. "I-I don't know what causes them. They just come. I-I can't seem to stop them." She didn't admit that she didn't really want to stop them, disturbing as they were. She heard Teague let out a long breath that was somewhere between a sigh and a growl.

"All right," he said at last. "I should've known you hadn't suddenly changed your mind and wanted to throw your damn Certificate in the fire."

"I'm sorry," Krisa said again, feeling the tears that had been threatening to come down her cheeks in a warm, wet flood. "I don't know what's come over me lately. It's like...being in this wild place is changing me. I never, never would have acted the way I've been acting back at Briar Rose."

"You can't help it," Teague said shortly.

She had a feeling that he wanted to take her in his arms and comfort her, but didn't quite trust himself to get so close again just yet.

"It's just your nature comin' out, sweetheart. At a place like that—at that academy, or the slam or wherever you are—

they can try to make you into somethin' you're not. But when you get away from it, the real you comes out every time. They can mold who you are on the outside, but they can't really change what's on the inside."

"What do you mean?" Krisa asked, sniffling. She wiped her palms across her cheeks and wished for just one lacy handkerchief. "Are you saying that deep down I'm just some kind of horrible...awful..."

"'Course not," Teague said roughly. He scooted closer to her and used the hem of his ragged black tank top to dry her eyes. "Just sayin' you got a hot nature, little girl. Quick to anger, quick to lust. Some people are just like that—hot-blooded. I should know 'cause I'm one of 'em. It's not somethin' you can help but it's not anything to cry over either."

"It is if it makes you act the way I've been acting lately," Krisa pointed out. She turned her back to him, facing the last glowing embers of the fire and tried to get control of herself. *What's wrong with me lately? Why am I acting this way? Letting him see me with no clothes on. Having that dream and then almost letting him...*

A low, rumbling noise interrupted her silent self-criticism. Krisa suddenly became aware that she was staring at two malevolent purple eyes, only a yard from her own, over the remains of their campfire. They glittered a deep, malicious amethyst in the darkness.

"Teague," she said through numb lips, her eyes never leaving those of the soondar crouched in the hungry darkness. She could feel the hot-black writhing pressure building in her mind again, could feel her eyes bugging and her eardrums bulging. She had a terrible urge to run—to get away—to get anywhere but here.

"I see it." Teague's deep voice was calm and controlled behind her. "Stay right where you are, Krisa. He'll try to make you run. Don't listen."

"I..." But her voice seemed to have deserted her completely. She was hypnotized by the glowing purple eyes in the blackness. *Run away, little girl thing*, the soondar whispered in a hissing, hot-black voice inside her head. *Run away and then you'll be safe. Run into the jungle, into the night. Run...*

Yes, Krisa thought. *I have to run. It's the only way to be safe.* She wanted to get up but someone was holding her back, holding her down.

"I *said* don't listen." Teague's harshly grating voice broke the soondar's spell, but Krisa was still unable to draw her eyes away from that huge, dark shape in the blackness. She had an impression of a perfectly huge cat, covered in scales instead of fur, lashing its tail. It made her feel like a weak, frightened little mouse. She could taste panic, sour and electric, on the tip of her tongue. The fire was out—what was to stop the immense creature from pouncing on them and gobbling them up in raw, wet, still-quivering chunks?

"Don't move." Teague's voice was so low she felt it rather than hearing it.

There was a low, silvery sliding sound behind her of metal coming slowly out of a sheath. Then a motion too swift and violent to follow, accompanied by a low whirring noise that passed just beside her left ear. Krisa heard a dull *thwack* that sounded horribly loud in the darkness.

The low growl rumbling through the jungle air became a jagged roar for a split second. It was deafening and Krisa was sure her eardrums would burst and her eyeballs would be so much jelly on her cheeks. Just as she felt the pressure was completely unbearable, it stooped as abruptly as it had started.

The malevolent purple lights across the fire from her died and went out, as though someone had abruptly cut the current that powered them. By the dim light of the coals that had been their fire, Krisa could see the hilt of Teague's huge knife. It was jutting between the now dull purple eyes, still quivering with the impact that had sent its deadly blade deep into the soondar's brain.

"What—" she began in a dazed voice but Teague cut her off.

"Stay here and no matter what you hear, don't leave this spot," he ordered. Standing, he took one large step over the remains of their fire, grasped the hilt of his knife. He yanked it free and disappeared into the blackness of the jungle night.

Krisa sat shivering on the rumpled blanket for what must have been fifteen minutes although it felt like fifteen hours. Knees pressed close to her chin, she clutched her ornate silver hairpin in one hand and listened, feeling blind in the darkness.

For a long time she heard nothing and then, not far off, a snapping, crashing sound in the underbrush followed by the mind-bending roar of an angry soondar. Then she heard something that sounded like Teague's voice, except he was shouting in a language she had never heard before, something multi-syllabic and guttural. His tone was rough and threatening. There was that roar again that filled her head with the snarled hot-blackness. It made her wince with pain and fear but this time it was farther off. Then for a long, long time there was dead silence, broken only by the normal sounds of the jungle at night.

Krisa's eyes wanted to return to the dead soondar across the fire. By now the embers had burned so low she couldn't see it and she kept imagining that it might come back to life somehow. Her mind kept showing her awful pictures of Teague lying dead in the jungle somewhere, with a hungry soondar ripping him to pieces, no matter how hard she tried to block them out.

Oh my sweet Goddess, what if it got him? What if he never comes back? What if…?

Suddenly, she heard a stealthy crackling sound, soft but growing gradually louder. There was something behind her in the darkness, moving. Something in the blackness that had finished with Teague and was coming for her. With a fierce, desperate scream, Krisa turned and jabbed the hairpin into the creature that was stalking her with all the force in her body.

"Goddessdamn it! Why the hell did you do that?" It was Teague, looming over her in the darkness. He pulled the silver pin from his thigh with an angry jerk and threw it down on the blanket.

Krisa nearly cried, she was so glad to see him alive and in one piece. "I thought you were a soondar," she gasped. "You left me alone and it was the only weapon I had. I thought the other one got you and it was coming back for me."

The dark face above her softened somewhat, as he dropped down on the blanket beside her. He reached behind him and dragged a couple of sticks from the pile of wood he'd been carrying and began to rebuild the fire.

"It's all right now, sweetheart," he said shortly. "I'm back."

"But why..." Krisa felt tears threaten for the second time that night and struggled grimly to hold them back. "Why did you leave me alone like that?"

Teague gestured toward the newly glowing fire. "Had to get some more wood and I wanted to make sure the other one was long gone."

"Is that what you were yelling about?" Krisa asked, her voice still trembling despite all she could do to stop it.

Teague nodded and added some more brush to the slowly growing fire. "Warned her off but she didn't want to go."

"But how— They're just animals, aren't they?" Krisa asked uncertainly. "How can you warn an animal?" But she remembered the soft, insidious voice of the soondar inside her head, *Run...run into the jungle,* even as she spoke.

Teague stopped what he was doing and stared at her steadily for a moment. "Just because they're not humanoid doesn't mean they're not intelligent, Krisa. You can't label something an animal and just dismiss it as unworthy of respect." He flashed the frightening white grin at her, making her squirm. "Matter of fact, that's the exact mistake my old master made. It was the *last* mistake he ever made."

The fire was built up to its previous proportions and he set about straightening the blankets and preparing to bed back down for the night.

"B-but, Teague..." Krisa began, unwilling to just go back to sleep after so much had happened.

"Not now," he growled arranging himself on the blanket on one side and patting the ground in front of him commandingly. "Right now we've gotta get some sleep. Tomorrow we'll be inside the village perimeters, most likely meet up with the Yss. I'll need to be in top form."

"Why?" Krisa demanded, tired of his oblique statements about the natives of Planet X. "Are the Yss really so bad? After tonight I don't see how they could be any worse than the soondar."

"A soondar will only eat you," Teague said grimly. "There are worse things than being eaten, little girl. Now *come here.*" He patted the blanket again, firmly.

Krisa didn't see anything else she could do although his demanding tone rubbed her the wrong way. But she sensed that to push him any further after both her dream and the encounter with the soondar would be foolish. Besides, all the excitement and fear had exhausted her almost to the point of collapse. Reluctantly, she lay back on her side and repositioned herself between the big Feral and the fire, making sure to keep at least several inches between Teague's chest and her back.

"Don't be stupid, c'mere." A long muscular arm reached around and scooped her close, molding her back to his front again and pillowing her head on his biceps. Krisa stiffened for a moment and then relaxed, feeling it was pointless to fight him. After all, it was true that she wanted all the safety and security she could get after what she'd just gone through.

She tried to get back to sleep, but across the fire she kept seeing the dead, glazed eyes of the soondar Teague had killed.

She felt as if the purple eyes were still staring at her accusingly and she couldn't stop hearing that hot-black voice in her head. Far off in the jungle she could hear the angry growling howls of the other soondar and she shivered at the rage and loss in their tone. *You can't dismiss something as an animal and decide it's not worthy of respect,* Teague had said. Was that all Ferals were on the day side of his home planet, Al'hora? Just animals?

The growling, rageful howl came again and this time Krisa thought she could hear a note of grief in the horrible sound. Teague had said they might be a mated pair, had referred to one sonndar as "he" and the other as "she". Could the female be mourning the loss of her mate? Krisa shuddered.

There were too many thoughts in her head and the glazed eyes of the soondar staring at her across the fire kept her from drifting off. *Never be able to sleep, not while I can see that thing. See him staring at me,* Krisa thought resentfully. Then she had an idea.

Turning onto her right side, so that she was facing Teague's chest instead of the fire and the dead soondar, she shifted to get closer to the big Feral. She curled against his body like a small animal seeking shelter and warmth. His warm, spicy musk penetrated her senses as Krisa tucked her head under his chin and pressed her face to the broad planes of his chest. Sighing, she relaxed completely at last, feeling secure in the circle of his arms despite the dangers of the night.

There was a rumbling laugh from above her that seemed to vibrate her bones, but very gently. "Comfortable, little girl?" Teague asked softly into the darkness but Krisa felt almost too sleepy to answer.

"Mm-hmm," she mumbled drowsily, snuggling to get a little closer. The arm around her back tightened momentarily in what felt suspiciously like a hug and then a large hand caressed her hair gently.

~ ~ ~ ~ ~

Warm, rough hands cupped her breasts and calloused fingers rolled her nipples, twisting and pinching with exquisite pleasure-pain that made her moan. He was below her this time, reaching up to touch her and Krisa realized that she was straddling him, her legs spread wide to sit astride his muscular hips. He pinched her nipples again and she threw back her head and groaned.

"That's it, little girl, let yourself go. Love to watch you get hot for me, love to make your pussy wet—just like it is right now."

Krisa opened her mouth to ask how he knew she was getting hot and wet between her thighs, then realized she was naked and so was he. She looked down in concern at the soft nest of damp curls that decorated the apex of her mound, wondering how this had happened, how she had lost all her clothes. Had the man with no face undressed her?

He seemed to sense her concern. "Don't worry, little girl, not gonna hurt you," he rumbled, in a strangely familiar voice. "Just wanna touch that sweet little pussy. Just wanna shove my cock inside your tight little cunt and make you come. Now spread your legs for me and come a little closer."

As always in the dream, there was no holding back. Large warm hands caressed her hips and pulled her down to him. Krisa looked down to see a long, thick shaft rising from between his muscular thighs. She wanted it inside her, wanted to feel it's thick heat piercing her pussy and thrusting deep to fill her with his cum but at the same time she was afraid. Would it hurt? Would the man with no face bring her pain as well as pleasure?

"No," he said, as though reading her thoughts. "First I need to get you ready to take me, little girl. Spread your pussy lips and I'll show you what I mean."

Obediently, Krisa reached down to open her wet sex, offering herself to him as he had demanded. She expected the man to thrust up into her pussy, opened so invitingly for him. Instead, he settled her so that the shaft of his cock thrust between her lips, rubbing against her but not penetrating her in any way.

"Now, slide," he growled, using his hands on her hips to show her what he meant. Krisa moved her pelvis back and then forward again at his urging. His shaft was pressed against his flat belly as she rubbed her open pussy up and down the length of his cock in slow, slippery strokes. Electric tingles of pleasure shot through her as her sensitive clit slid over the flared head and then back down again, almost to the base of his balls.

"Feels good, doesn't it, little girl?" he rumbled as she gasped at the warm, wet sensation of his hot cock sliding between her naked, open pussy lips. "Feels almost as good as fucking. But not quite. Do you want me to show you?"

She nodded, unable to help herself. Unable to stop even though she knew it was wrong. She wanted him in her so badly, wanted to feel him sheathed in her body, buried within her, filling her, fucking her, taking her to that place she could never quite reach on her own.

The next time she slid forward over the broad head of his cock, he shifted positions. Suddenly instead of sliding between her pussy lips, his shaft was sliding inside them. Krisa moaned as she felt the flared head breach her entrance, pressing inside her to stretch her virgin pussy wide—wide enough to take him.

"Is this what you need?" he asked her as another thick inch penetrated her sex. "You need me to fuck you, little girl, to fill your sweet cunt with my cock and fuck you until I fill you full of my cum?"

Krisa moaned assent. There were no words, no way to tell him what she needed or how badly she needed it. But he knew. He always knew.

"Sliding inside you now, little girl," he told her in that deep, gravely voice. "Filling up your pussy with my cock. Is this what you want? Is this what you need?" Strong hands pulled her down as his thick cock worked its way upward and inward, breaching her defenses inevitably.

In her dream Krisa knew it was wrong, knew she would pay for this pleasure, but she couldn't seem to stop. She arched her back, feeling the large warm hands on her hips, urging her downward. Her legs were spread, her pussy open and vulnerable, half-filled with his cock. She knew he wouldn't be satisfied until the thick length of his shaft impaled her completely, until he bottomed out inside her wet, open sex and filled her with his cum.

"Please," she wanted to say, but couldn't. "Please..." But whether she wanted to beg him to stop, or beg him to never stop, she couldn't tell. Because then he was thrusting into her, fucking her, owning her...

~ ~ ~ ~ ~

"Krisa...Krisa." A warm hand shaking her, woke her from the dream. Krisa blinked, looking up at the fiery silver orbs of Teague's eyes again.

"Wha—" She looked at him in confusion.

"You were dreamin' again," he said shortly. "Woke me up with your moaning."

"Oh." Krisa felt her face grow red with embarrassment and she could no longer meet his gaze.

"That's all right." Teague sighed and lay back down, pulling her with him. "Go back to sleep. And try to put a lid on that dream."

She curled back against his muscular chest, her body aching, but this time sleep was a long time in coming.

Chapter Eleven

ဢ

She woke up when someone poured a bucket of water over her head.

"What...how...?" Krisa rose sputtering, thinking that it had to be Maida Shepard, who was one of her best friends at Briar Rose, but just *awful* about practical jokes. Then she realized that it wasn't just her head that was wet, from head to foot she was completely soaked. The reason for this appeared to be an almost solid wall of water falling out of the sky, covering the jungle in a pounding, seething sheet of wetness.

She tried to look around but it was like opening her eyes underwater, everything was a big pastel blur. Squinting to her left, she saw a tall dark shape that had to be Teague. He had his back turned to her and was bending over to look at something on the ground.

Crawling off the waterlogged blanket, Krisa squelched around the soggy remains of the campfire and went to him. "What's going on?" she yelled, to make herself heard over the roar of the rain.

He looked up briefly and then back down at the ground he was studying. "Morning rain," he said mildly, as though the torrential downpour was nothing but a light drizzle. "Just started a minute ago after I got up to break camp."

"So this is *normal*?" Krisa asked, waving her wet arms to indicate the state of the currently waterlogged world.

Teague looked at her and shrugged. "We *are* in the jungle, sweetheart, so yes, it's *normal* to get a little rain now and again. Just wait, it'll stop pretty soon."

As though someone in the clouds above them had heard his deep, growling voice, the rain stopped as quickly as it had begun. Krisa had never seen anything like it, there was no gradual lessening of the drenching flow at all. One minute there was a solid wall of water coming down out of the sky and the next it was completely clear, as though someone had turned off a huge faucet all at once.

"There, see?" Teague said in a preoccupied voice. He went back to studying the ground and Krisa noticed a grim little frown playing around the corners of his full mouth.

"What is it?" she asked apprehensively. She was beginning to learn that if Teague was worried about something, it was probably a fairly serious situation.

Teague looked up again, the black second lid that covered his eyes flickering briefly to show silver. "She dragged him away," he said, indicating a deep furrow and a set of huge paw prints that had been nearly erased by the rain, in the muddy ground.

Krisa looked with incomprehension until it registered what he was telling her.

"The female soondar?" she asked hesitantly. "Came and took the other one?"

"Sometime last night," Teague confirmed. He stood up with a shake of his head and began wringing water out of his black tank top absently. "Don't know how she did it without wakin' me up, but I don't like it."

"What does it mean?" Krisa asked anxiously.

"Means they weren't just part of the same pack like I was hopin'. Means they really were a mated pair," Teague said shortly. He rummaged in the pack until he came up with a couple of tubes of nutrient paste. "Looks like we get a treat today, these are actually flavored," he remarked, tossing one to Krisa. She caught it without looking at it.

"So they're a mated pair—so what?" she asked, pinning her dripping hair to the nape of her neck and doing her best to wring out her own clothes. By now the fashionable striped pants and white oxford shirt would have been completely unrecognizable to Percy or his personal tailor.

"So." Teague stowed the dripping blankets and shouldered the pack, nodding his head for her to follow. "So the female will carry a grudge. I killed her male, her mate. She'll want revenge."

"Revenge..." Krisa echoed to herself and shivered, remembering the terrible howls of grief that had invaded her mind the night before. "So that mean she'll be tracking us?" she asked, hurrying to catch up with Teague. He had finished his paste and was already cutting brush.

"Somethin' like that," he said with maddening ambiguity, continuing to cut.

"B-but then what can we do?"

"Find the Yss," Teague replied. "There's one of their paths not far from here if I remember right—lead us straight to the village. We'll have to find them and prove ourselves. We don't wanna spend another night in the bush."

"Prove ourselves? What exactly does that mean?" Krisa demanded. "And don't tell me you'll tell me later, Teague. It's later *now*. I want to know what's going on."

"What's going on is you wasting time while I'm trying to get us to the path," Teague growled. But he stopped cutting brush and turned to face her at last.

"Tell me about the Yss," Krisa said, hands on her hips, the tube of nutri-paste forgotten in her hand.

Teague sighed deeply and she got the distinct impression that he didn't want to tell her was he was about to reveal. "What you need to know about the Yss is that they're a very proud people, very easy to insult. And believe me, sweetheart, you *don't* want to insult them."

"Why not?" Krisa asked, determined to know the worst.

Teague ran one large hand through his bristly blue-black hair. It had grown considerably in the time she had known him, although the stubble on his cheeks appeared to be the same length. "Let me put it this way," he said at last. "You know all the wild rumors you heard about bizarre customs, weird ceremonies, cannibalism—all that?"

"Yes?" Krisa raised one eyebrow at him, tapping her small foot in the mud.

"All true." Teague flashed her that wild, white grin, turned, and began cutting brush again.

"Teague!" Krisa almost yelled in frustration.

"Just follow my lead and do what I tell you and you'll be fine," he growled over his shoulder. Shaking her head in irritation, Krisa realized she wouldn't get anything else out of him.

They reached the Yss path that Teague had spoken of around midmorning but they didn't meet any of the path's makers until late afternoon.

Up until the Yss warriors surrounded them it was a quiet walk. As quiet as it ever got, anyway, in the jungle which was always filled with the hoots, squeals, chattering and rustling Krisa had come to pass off as normal.

Her soaked clothes had been drying very slowly and she was more than a little aware of Teague's occasional glances at the transparent material of her shirt. It clung and molded to her breasts, outlining the jut of her pink nipples which were erect from their contact with the clammy fabric.

He never said anything but there was an undeniable heat in those looks that had made her remember their near disaster of the night before, of the way his mouth had tasted so hot and sweet, and how his large hands had felt molding her breasts. The jungle steamed all around them, giving up the moisture it had so recently received to the cloudy bronze sky and Krisa felt like she was steaming herself every time Teague looked back at her.

She was walking along on the path which was a narrow, twisting thing paved with flat, pale pink and blue stones that had pastel grass growing up in the cracks between them. All of a sudden Teague stopped dead ahead of her and raised a hand for her to stop as well.

"What?" she started to ask, but he stopped her with a shake of his head. Slowly, he turned in a complete circle, the knife out and ready in his hand. Krisa watched him fearfully, wondering what new surprise was about to be sprung on them in the steaming pastel jungle. Was it the soondar Teague had said would be stalking them? But they didn't hunt during the middle of the day, did they? So it had to be the Yss.

Her shirt and trousers had dried tighter than ever and she was aware of the uncomfortable way the fabric of the shirt was cutting up under her armpits. One of the top buttons had given up an hour ago and a generous portion of her cleavage was revealed. She had been rather glad that Teague was walking along in front of her to avoid the continued awkwardness of his eyes on her body. But now it occurred to her that it wasn't only the big Feral's eyes that were going to see her in her current condition.

Remembering what he had said about not offending the Yss, she hoped that her current state of dress or undress wouldn't somehow set the volatile people off. What she was wearing would certainly have been considered highly offensive at Briar Rose. She would just have to hope that the Yss were less particular about the niceties of a proper wardrobe than Madame Ledoux.

Suddenly there was a slight rustling in the pastel vegetation surrounding them and about eight large men, at least Krisa assumed they were men, appeared in a circle around them. They had emerged so quietly from the jungle that it was a terrible shock to suddenly find she and Teague were completely surrounded.

Krisa looked wildly from one alien face to another but it was difficult to see anything. They were all wearing some kind of masks made of what looked like grass and feathers and only their pale, narrow eyes and the thin line of their lips was visible. They were tall, some she noticed with surprise were even taller than Teague, though none of them as massive or as muscular.

They were dressed in some kind of pastel leather loincloths and their skin, where she could see beneath the swirling painted designs drawn all over their long, thin bodies, was the palest mint green imaginable. They were each carrying a long spear made from the wood of the finger-trees and every single spear was pointed in Krisa and Teague's direction.

Teague stood by her side, knife at the ready and stared around them calmly, waiting. Krisa felt frozen with fear and did her best just to be quiet and small. There was no way her hairpin was going to help her in this situation and she wisely left it in her hair.

Finally the tallest of the Yss warriors stepped forward and said something in a hissing, guttural language, shaking his spear as he talked. Teague answered in the same language, his tone mild but firm and Krisa recognized it as the same language he had yelled at the female soondar the night before. The tall warrior said something else and then lowered his spear. Teague, apparently in response, lowered his knife and then all the other men lowered their weapons as well.

"It's all right," Teague told her in a low voice. "They've decided to declare themselves instead of fighting."

He turned to the tallest warrior again and began talking rapidly in the strange, multi-syllabic language while the other men came closer to inspect the newcomers in their jungle. They circled around rather like a pack of wild dogs, Krisa thought, touching, fondling and sniffing everything they could lay their six-fingered hands on. When she first noticed the extra digit it gave Krisa quite a shock and when she looked closer, as unobtrusively as possible, it appeared that it was an extra thumb, rather than an extra finger on their long, narrow hands.

She soon had other things to think about besides extra digits as the Yss warriors became more and more invasive in their inspection. While Teague stood calmly and spoke to what she supposed must be the leader of the group, long, thin green fingers poked at her and then inspected her clothing. They fingered the faded and wrinkled material and petted the rapidly disintegrating leather of Percy's fashionable low-ankle boots, which had never been made to stand up to a trek through the jungle.

Since it didn't appear to bother Teague to be poked and prodded, Krisa remained silent, though it became increasingly difficult to stand the invasion of her space. But when one of the Yss yanked the hairpin from her hair, taking some of her hair with it, she couldn't avoid making a little screech of pain.

Her rich brown curls tumbled down around her shoulders in thick profusion. All of the inspecting Yss took a quick step back, making low, hissing noises of surprise and consternation in their long, thin throats.

Teague turned in obvious irritation to see what the commotion was, interrupting his conversation with the leader. "What happened?" he demanded in a low, angry voice. "I'm trying to negotiate a place for us to stay for the night."

"H-he pulled my hair," Krisa said, pointing to the Yss who had taken her pin. She felt like a little girl telling on a playmate at the schoolyard. "It hurt—I'm sorry, Teague. I didn't mean to scream, but he surprised me."

Black brows narrowed over the opaque black eyes and Teague stepped forward to speak to the Yss who had pulled the hairpin from her hair. He gestured violently toward Krisa and then thumped himself on the chest while talking rapidly in the strange, hissing language. Then he held out his hand, obviously expecting the Yss to hand over her pin.

But to Krisa's consternation, the man shook his head and gestured first to her and then to himself with the pin. Then he made a beckoning gesture at her, as though expecting her to come over to him. Krisa stood where she was and shook her head in what she hoped was the universal signal of negation.

No way was she going over to the strange warrior—he could keep the pin as far as she was concerned.

Teague shook his head, frowning in a way that would have scared almost anyone. But the warrior who held her pin refused to give up. He kept gesturing to himself with the pin and then motioning for Krisa to join him. Then the tallest Yss, the one Teague had been speaking to in the first place, stepped forward and began gesturing as well.

"Damn it, I was afraid of this," she heard Teague mutter under his breath. Without turning his head he said loudly, "Krisa, come here right now. Don't ask any questions, just come."

It crossed her mind to wonder if he was going to give her away as a gift to the warrior that had taken her pin, but Krisa didn't let herself consider it long. Teague had saved her once from rape at the hands of Captain Ketchum and twice from being eaten by soondar. She didn't think he would hand her over like a discarded trinket to the Yss. At least she *hoped* not. Walking quickly, she crossed the space between them and stood by his side.

"What's going on?" she asked in a low, trembling voice. Teague was now glaring at the Yss who held her pin. Without taking his eyes from the big warrior, he answered in a low growl.

"The Yss believe that a woman's soul is stored in her hair. This guy is sayin' that since he had a piece of your soul," he jerked his chin at the silver hairpin, "that he's your new owner. He's especially anxious to have you because of the color of your hair—dark colors like brown are sacred to them because everything in their jungle is so light."

"Oh my Goddess," Krisa whispered faintly. "You mean he wants to own me because of the color of my hair?"

"Yeah, that's about it." Teague grinned briefly, still not taking his eyes from the angry Yss. "And I bet you thought blondes had more fun."

"Teague, this isn't funny! What are you going to do?"

"I have to prove I own you." Teague sheathed his knife suddenly and rounded on her so quickly that it took Krisa's breath away. "Listen," he growled. "Whatever I have to do I don't want you to make any protest and *don't struggle.* If you do, they'll take it as a sign that I'm not really your owner and that you want to go with him." He nodded curtly at the tall Yss who still held her hairpin.

Krisa felt as though her stomach had dropped down to her shoes. *Prove he owns me? How?* a little voice was screaming inside her head.

"But Teague—what are you going to do?" she gasped. The gasp turned into a shriek when Teague dropped his pack and grabbed her suddenly, one large hand grasping the material at the back of her shirt, and the other buried deep in her loose brown curls.

"Anything I have to," he growled and bent her back until her pale throat and creamy cleavage were completely exposed. Krisa thought she had never felt more vulnerable and helpless in her life.

"What—?" she began again but then Teague ducked his head and she felt a hot, wet sensation in the soft divide between her full breasts. She looked down to see that the big Feral was licking a long, hot, slow trail from between her breasts up over her chest. Krisa closed her eyes and gasped as she felt him reach the pulse point of her throat and bite down hard, sucking and licking, making a mark that wouldn't fade for a good long time.

"Better act like you're enjoying this, little girl," Teague growled against her throat. "Unless you want your friend there to do somethin' worse." Krisa knew he was talking about the Yss.

Gasping, she buried her fingers in the bristly black hair, pulling him closer. Teague relaxed his hold on her neck and covered her mouth suddenly in a hot, possessive kiss. Krisa opened her mouth to him, giving whatever he demanded without reservation. Then she felt those large, blunt fingertips unfastening the few remaining buttons that held the ragged white shirt closed, and palming her full, naked breasts roughly.

"Teague!" she tried to gasp, turning her head away from his hungry kiss to protest this treatment.

"I told you *don't struggle*," he growled, refusing to let her go. Cruel fingers twisted and pinched her sensitive nipples ruthlessly, sending sparks of unwanted pleasure from her tender pink buds to the growing wetness between her thighs. Krisa felt her body responding to the big Feral's touch whether she wanted it to or not. She moaned wordlessly, as ashamed of her body's reactions to his touch as she had been the night before. *Hot-natured*, Teague had called her. *Quick to anger, quick to lust.* Could he possibly be right?

"Teague..." she whispered again but this time it was less of a protest and more of a question. The big Feral seemed to understand.

"I told you I'd do anything I had to in order to prove you're mine," he growled low in her ear. "If you'd help me make the performance more convincing, I might not have to fuck you up against the nearest tree."

Oh Goddess, this is what he didn't want me to know. This is why he avoided telling me about the Yss and their customs. Because he knew he might have to do to prove he owned me to keep the Yss men away from me, Krisa realized at last. But if it was a choice between losing her virginity to Teague or one of the strange Yss men, she knew without question who she wanted to take her.

Closing her eyes to shut out everything but the sweet sensation of his hot mouth and big hands on her skin, Krisa let herself melt against him and gave in to the rough, delicious pleasure he was subjecting her body to.

Teague must have felt her complete surrender in the way her body moved against his, because the fingers on her nipples became a little less cruel.

He whispered into the side of her neck, "That's right, little girl, give it up for me. Your skin tastes so sweet, and your tits fill my hands just right." His big hands molded her breasts gently, illustrating his point. Krisa gasped, arching her back to thrust herself closer to him and give him greater access to her body.

"Teague!" she moaned his name for a third time but this time the sound coming out of her throat lacked any protest or question—it was pure submission—pure need.

The big Feral ducked his head again and this time he captured one of her aching pink nipples between his teeth, nipping lightly and then sucking hard, making her moan and writhe against him like the most shameless animal in heat. Tangling her fingers in the spiky blue-black hair, Krisa pulled him closer, wondering if her legs would hold her up when he was subjecting her to such intense pleasure. Her swollen pussy felt so wet and ready that she actually found herself hoping that Teague might have to carry out his threat of taking her up against the nearest tree, though part of her mind was absolutely shocked at the idea. And yet, she could feel the wet heat growing between her thighs, could feel her pussy lips opening almost of their own volition, aching to receive his thick cock, to have his shaft sheathed completely in her aching cunt.

She could almost hear his growling voice in her ear as he commanded her to spread her legs for him. Just the thought of that made her shiver but she couldn't help imagining what it would be like. Teague would spread her pussy lips with the head of his cock, sliding over the aching bud of her clit until he found the entrance to her pussy. She could almost feel his thick shaft breaching her entrance, sliding inch by wet inch inside her until he was sheathed balls deep in her cunt, claiming her, showing his complete ownership of her body, mind, and soul for all to see.

Teague had finished with one nipple and was starting on the other, sucking and licking until Krisa thought she was going to go crazy, when he stopped suddenly and stood up. Krisa nearly fell, would have fallen if he hadn't reached out a casual hand and hauled her up at the last minute.

"What? Why did you—?" she began but Teague only grinned at her and held out a hand, the silver pin lying in the middle of his large palm.

Krisa, who had forgotten all about her hairpin or the watching Yss warriors or anything but the intense sensations the big Feral was causing in her body, looked at it stupidly for a moment. Then she realized that she should take it and put it back in her hair which she did. Her hands were trembling so much that she did a very sloppy job.

"You all right, little girl?" he asked in a low, amused voice, black eyes flashing momentarily to show the silver underneath.

"I...yes," Krisa whispered, trying to pull herself together. It suddenly occurred to her that her shirt was still gaping open and she hastened to pull it shut and button it as quickly as possible. As she did, she noticed that the white slopes of her breasts were covered with dark red love marks. "He gave you back the pin?" she asked to cover her confusion, nodding at the Yss warrior who had been holding it.

The Yss, along with his fellow warriors, had turned and was leading the way farther along the path, presumably toward the village.

Teague grinned again. "Sure did. Said he's never seen a woman so completely owned by a man before. That was some performance, sweetheart. Wasn't sure you had it in you for a minute but you came through great."

"Thanks," Krisa mumbled, feeling her cheeks flame red with embarrassment. Apparently catching her expression,

Teague looked at her closely and then tilted her chin up with one gentle hand until she had to meet his eyes.

"Krisa," he said softly in that low, rumbling voice. "Do you remember when we started this trip I told you there's nothin' ridiculous or vulgar about survival?"

Krisa nodded hesitantly. He had told her that when he first insisted she wear Percy's trousers instead of her long dress into the jungle.

"Well, this is part of that," Teague said, still staring her in the eyes. "I don't want you to feel embarrassed or ashamed of anything we have to do to get out of here, understand? The Yss are our best bet to get off this planet in one piece, so we'll have to play the game their way for a while."

Krisa didn't understand how the obviously primitive Yss could help them secure a ride off Planet X, but she had bigger questions on her mind. "Does that mean you'll have to..." She couldn't finish the sentence but she didn't need to.

Teague's face darkened and he released his hold on her chin. "I told you I'm no rapist, Krisa," he said roughly. "Goddess knows I'll try not to, but I can't promise anything except to try and keep us both alive until we can get off this rock. All right?"

Krisa dropped her eyes again. "All right," she whispered.

How could she possibly explain that the reason she was so upset and ashamed was that her reaction to Teague's hands and mouth on her body had been no act? And that the idea of letting the big Feral invalidate her all-important Certificate of Virginity was becoming almost as appealing as it was appalling?

Chapter Twelve

ഗ

The Yss village was less primitive than Krisa had
expected it to be. A neat arrangement of conical huts built of
clay and straw were arranged in an orderly fashion behind a
high wooden fence tipped with spearlike points. "To keep the
soondar out," Teague explained when he saw her look at it
questioningly.

There was an orderly series of paths laid out along the
village streets, all made of the same flat pink and blue stones
that had paved their way in the jungle. Everywhere she
looked, Krisa saw tall, slender pale green women going quietly
about what must be their regular household chores. The Yss
women had long waterfalls of pale pastel hair in every
imaginable shade—cotton candy pink, sky blue, and palest
lilac to name a few. Here and there wiry, pale green children
played in groups of twos and threes, chattering steadily in the
strange guttural, hissing language of the Yss.

As they walked into the village, the hissing chatter
stopped abruptly and Krisa became uncomfortably aware that
she and Teague were the center of attention. The narrow, pale
alien eyes of every Yss in the village were trained on them
unblinkingly. Teague strode stolidly along, black eyes pointed
straight ahead, apparently oblivious to the attention. Krisa
tried to do the same although it wasn't easy.

The last time so many eyes had been pointed in her
direction had been at the commencement ceremonies at Briar
Rose and she had been wearing considerably more clothing at
that time. Also, she had been graduating with honors, not
going to meet the cannibal king of an alien village or wherever
the Yss warriors were taking them. It was, Krisa reflected, a
substantial difference.

At last they reached a hut in the center of the village which was built on a larger and grander scale than the others. Krisa was about to follow Teague inside when he stopped her with one large arm. "Sorry, sweetheart. Women are taboo in the chief's headquarters. Just wait here for a minute and I'll be right back."

"B-but, Teague!" But she was speaking to his broad back. Even as she watched, he disappeared past the pastel thatched door, leaving her alone in front of the grand central hut feeling horribly exposed. As Krisa had feared, it didn't take the natives long to approach.

"Vis Lieblick. Lossthinik hissthanik?" The tall, pale green Yss woman was obviously asking her a question but of course, Krisa had no idea what it was.

"I'm sorry," she told the woman who was a good three inches taller than herself and had a long, beautiful fall of butter-yellow hair. She was dressed in the same kind of leather that the warriors had worn but it was fashioned into a kind of brief top that covered her small breasts and a long skirt with a slit up the middle. She asked the question again but all Krisa could do was shrug and shake her head, hoping she wasn't offending the Yss woman.

"She say her name be Vis Lieblick, lady. What be your name?"

Krisa looked around for the source of the voice and found it belonged to a child, a little boy, she assumed by the way he was dressed, who was standing at her left elbow. He was tall, as they all were, but his skin was so pale it was almost white with only the barest tint of green and his hair was a brown almost as dark as hers, instead of being pastel as was the hair of all the other villagers. On his shoulder, half hidden by the dark brown hair was a tiny pink targee. Wide, black liquid eyes peered at her, blinking owlishly as the little puffball clung to the boy's neck.

"Who are you and how do you speak my language?" she asked, feeling grateful to have anyone at all to talk to whom she could understand.

The boy stood up straighter. "I be Ziba," he said clearly. "I know offworlder talk because I grew up in the palace of the Uneaten One—he be my sire. Now I am visiting my mother's brother and his woman." He nodded at the tall Yss woman with the pale blonde hair. "She be my mother's brother's woman and her name be Vis. What be your name?" he asked impatiently.

"Krisa," Krisa said at once, still trying to work out the weird familial relationships the boy, Ziba, had told her. Apparently he was visiting his aunt and uncle and his father was an offworlder like herself and Teague, which would explain his atypical hair and skin color. "Krisa Elyison," she added for good measure. Turning to the tall Yss woman she held out her hand hesitantly. "Very pleased to meet you."

Ziba translated rapidly in the strange Yss language and the woman nodded graciously but instead of taking her hand, Krisa suddenly found herself enfolded in a warm embrace and thin, green lips gave her a hearty kiss on the cheek before she was released. Krisa wondered if she should have kissed the woman back, though she really didn't want to. She fought the urge to wipe at the spot on her cheek where the kiss had been planted. *Easily offended*, Teague's voice rang in her head and she nodded and smiled at the woman instead.

The woman, Vis, spoke rapidly to the little boy who turned to Krisa and translated.

"She say, well met, little sister. And she say you come to her house for a bath before the feast, Krisalaison," he piped, running her first and last name together in a long mishmash of syllables. Taking her hand he began tugging her away from the central hut toward the left side of the village. Vis was on her other side also tugging. Krisa found herself being pulled away, thorough the crowd of curious Yss women and children, despite her polite and increasingly panicked protests.

"No, I couldn't...really. I have to wait for Teague...for my man to finish his meeting with the chief," she told Ziba who appeared to be listening not at all. "He'll be terribly angry at me if I leave, he told me to stay right here!"

"It's all right, Krisa."

She turned her head to look for the owner of the familiar, gravelly voice. Teague was standing at the doorway of the hut, having apparently heard the commotion outside and come to investigate.

"Teague, help me!" she yelled, feeling panicky. But he only waved a hand and nodded encouragingly.

"We've got more dealing to do in here. Go on and get a bath and enjoy yourself, sweetheart. I'll see you at the feast tonight," he called and then turning, he disappeared into the hut again, presumably to finish his business.

Krisa felt an overwhelming urge to yank free of the tugging hands and go slap the big Feral's face. How dare he leave her with all these strange alien people when it should have been obvious to him that she was scared to death? Then the practical little voice in her brain spoke up. *If Teague thought they were dangerous, he wouldn't let them drag you away, Krisa. He's inside the hut trying to make some kind of deal with the Yss chief, so maybe you'd better just go along with Vis and Ziba and try not to makes things any harder than they are.*

Krisa supposed that little voice was right—it usually was—but that didn't make the truth any easier to swallow. Making a concerted effort to relax, she allowed Ziba and Vis to pull her toward a small hut near the far left corner of the village. She promised herself that she would give Teague a piece of her mind later, when it was safe to do so.

The hut that belonged to Vis and her husband consisted of one room with pale purple and pink grass mats laid neatly across the well-swept dirt floor. Krisa noticed a sort of cooking area against one wall, recognizable by the well-used clay surface with a large pot on the top and a soot-ringed hole beneath, which was filled with glowing coals. There was also a sleeping area against another wall with a comfortable-looking collection of mats and furs made up neatly, obviously prepared for the night to come.

There were a lot more household implements that Krisa couldn't make anything out of, but the one obvious one, which Vis and Ziba were dragging her to, was a perfectly huge metal pot already half full of steaming, pale pink water. They pushed it with some effort to the center of the room and gestured at it with great pride. Apparently this was where she would get her bath. *My goodness — it's large enough to cook an entire person in*, Krisa thought. She was glad that the Yss were apparently friendly and more eager to bathe her than to eat her.

To Krisa's intense discomfort, it seemed that half of the population of the village had followed them into Vis' hut. The curious Yss were standing around, watching her with obvious interest, like people waiting for a much anticipated show to begin. Were they waiting for her to undress and climb into the pot? Easily offended or not, Krisa thought they would be waiting a long time before she would strip in front of twenty or so complete strangers to take a bath.

She turned to Ziba and tried to explain. "I'm sorry but where I come from people take baths in private. It is," she searched for the right word, "taboo for a woman to show herself undressed to others." Ziba looked at her in some surprise but when he translated to Vis, she immediately began shooing the other women out of the house. Some of them gave Krisa dirty looks and she shrugged apologetically as they left, trying to look as inoffensive as possible.

At last everyone but Vis and Ziba were gone and the tall Yss woman began to make gestures to Krisa that were unmistakably signs to undress. She looked at Ziba for some clue as to how she should act, but the boy only nodded his head encouragingly at her.

"Vis say hurry or all the heat will be gone," he said, nodding at the steaming pot. As he spoke, the tall Yss woman took the large cook pot off the clay stove, and poured its steaming contents, more pinkish water, into the bathing vessel. She nodded encouragingly at Krisa.

"B-but—" Krisa started to protest but Ziba said, "Is all right, Krisalaison. It just be me and Vis now, nobody else. Vis be heating water for the feast all day but she say you can use it for a bath instead." Translation finished, he reached up and tickled the small, fuzzy pink targee on his shoulder. It hopped up and down and Ziba began to play with the little creature, letting it scamper the length of his outstretched arms. It chattered in its high-pitched voice as it ran.

Krisa looked helplessly from one Yss to the other and decided she'd have to do it. If Vis was going to sacrifice whatever delectable dish she had been planning for the feast for her benefit, just so she could take a bath, then Krisa had better take the bath. Besides, she reasoned, undressing in front of two people was a lot better than undressing in front of twenty.

Quickly she turned her back to Vis and Ziba and shed her clothes, folding them neatly in a small pile and laying the silver hairpin on top. Then she climbed with some difficulty over the high side of the huge pot and settled up to her chin in warm water.

If someone would have told her a month before that she would be able to relax and enjoy a bath in a huge cook pot in the middle of an alien village while stark naked in front of two nearly complete strangers, Krisa would have thought them completely crazy. But she and Teague had been slogging through the heat and cold and mud of the jungle for what seemed like forever, and she had been using muscles she didn't even know she had. The warm bath was wonderfully relaxing to her tired, tense body. After a while, Krisa thought that she could almost doze off, if not for the constant chatter between Vis and Ziba and the high, continuous scolding of his pet targee.

"Vis say do you want to wash your hair and if you be wanting to she will be helping you," Ziba said after a while. Krisa looked up from the semi-doze the warm water had put her into and saw that the Yss woman had a clay jar filled with a pale purple viscous liquid in one six-fingered hand. She was gesturing at Krisa's hair with the other.

"All right," she said, feeling awkward. It didn't seem polite to refuse although the idea of letting someone else wash her hair was a foreign one. The tall Yss woman nodded and smiled, showing sharp white teeth. She scooped into the jar and approached Krisa with a handful of the cloudy purple liquid. Krisa tensed in anticipation but, to her surprise, Vis was surprisingly gentle while applying what she supposed must be the Yss version of shampoo. She found herself relaxing again as the twelve strong digits massaged her scalp, causing a weak, flower-scented lather to form.

As she worked, Vis chattered and hissed in a low, pleasant voice. Ziba translated when prompted, though he was preoccupied with his pet. The targee was fetching a tiny ball made of thin strips of leather that the boy rolled across the floor.

"Vis say never has she seen such beautiful hair," he said at his aunt's prompting. "It be a sacred color, like mine." He looked up for a moment and tossed his head proudly before going back to the game of fetch with his pet.

"Tell her I said thank you for the lovely compliment and for washing my hair," Krisa answered immediately.

After a few more hissing exchanges, Ziba said. "She say it be an honor to serve the woman of the Teague, he who does not eat."

Krisa wondered at his words. She was about to explain that Teague *did* eat, she had seen him do it on several occasions, when the boy raised his head again and asked. "Krisalaison, be it true that the Teague killed a soondar?"

Again she was surprised, but maybe Teague had told the warriors, who had spread the word as they entered the village. Krisa nodded. "Yes, I saw him do it," she said.

"Say you true?" Ziba became excited and wanted her to act it out, but Krisa declined as she was still naked in the tub. She did, however, describe the action in detail for him. Ziba became so engrossed in her description, that he completely forgot the game of catch he had been playing with his targee, until the little creature danced on its tiny hind legs and complained loudly in a squeaky chattering voice.

Vis said something and, throwing the tiny leather ball for his targee once more, Ziba translated. "Vis say there be a saying among the Yss, *only a man with a pure heart and bloody hands can kill a soondar.* Be that the Teague?"

Krisa thought about it for a moment. "Actually, I think that's a pretty good description of him...of the Teague, I mean," she said at last. Ziba nodded gravely.

Vis had Krisa dunk her head to wash out the shampoo, and then held out a long, soft piece of woven material for her to dry off with, that Krisa supposed was the Yss version of a towel. But when Krisa reached for her wrinkled clothes, the Yss woman shook her head and made hissing noises of disapproval.

"Vis say you clothes not fit for a feast," Ziba translated. "She say you wear some of hers — look proper."

"Oh, I couldn't possibly," Krisa started to protest. But the thought of the worn and dirty white shirt and skin-tight trousers changed her mind. "Please tell Vis I would be honored to wear her clothes to the feast," she told Ziba, hoping she wouldn't be sorry.

At least the shirt and trousers she had been wearing up 'til now had covered the majority of her skin. If what she had seen of the Yss women's clothing was any indication, she was shortly going to be a great deal more improper than she had been previously, even wearing Percy's trousers.

* * * * *

The feast was held in the center of the village, behind the chief's centrally located hut. There was a wide ring of grass mats for people to sit on, spread out around an open space in the middle that held an abundance of food heaped on various bone and stone and wooden platters.

When she reached the feasting ring, as Ziba informed her it was called, Krisa saw that Teague was already there. He was seated with his back to her, beside a tall, gaunt elderly Yss, whom she supposed must be the chief. He, also, had apparently had a bath and a shave. Though he had kept his black trousers and boots, he was now wearing a leather vest dyed a soft, gray-green that went well with his dusky skin tones.

She felt unaccountably shy about seeing him again after what had happened between them outside the Yss village, but Vis pushed her toward the big Feral in a businesslike way. Then her new friend went to busy herself with serving the food, as the other women of the village were doing.

Krisa walked forward, very conscious of her new clothes and wondering what Teague would think when he saw her. She *knew* what Madame Ledoux would have thought—she would have fainted dead away in a puffy bundle of crinolines and underskirts. Krisa had stopped pushing the limits of Briar Rose propriety and had broken them completely when she put on the outfit Vis presented her with.

It was a lovely, two-piece dress made of butter-soft leather that had been dyed a deep purple that Ziba informed her was called soondar eye-blue. The top and skirt were embroidered with tiny, neat stitching done in pale green that was as delicate as anything Krisa had ever seen in her advanced needlework class at Briar Rose. Krisa could only suppose that the dress had been given several coats of dye in order to achieve the deep color in this pastel world. And someone, probably Vis, had worked for hours to make the elaborate patterns in the leather with the pale green thread.

It was more than obvious that the Yss woman was letting her wear the best clothing she owned and Krisa had thanked her again and again. The smiling Vis had only nodded and bowed her head in acknowledgement of Krisa's pleasure in the beautiful clothes.

Beautiful they might be — modest they most certainly were not. The clothing had been made to fit Vis, who was three inches taller and considerably smaller in the bust than Krisa. The sling-like top, which would have supported the Yss woman's small breasts, thrust Krisa's up and out like some exotic creamy fruit on a platter, barely covering her nipples. Looking down as she adjusted the straps, Krisa could see the dark red love marks Teague had put on the slopes of her breasts during their "performance" for the Yss warriors on the path. They would take a while to fade from her naturally pale skin.

But if the top was bad, the bottom of the lovely outfit was even worse. Designed for a woman three inches taller and somewhat more slender through the hips, the long leather skirt clung to her and had a slit directly up the center which would have fallen around mid-thigh on Vis. But in order to keep the hem from dragging on the ground, Krisa was forced to adjust the low-slung waistband upwards which put the beginning of the slit almost at the juncture of her thighs.

The one saving grace of the outfit was the tiny leather thong that Vis gave her to wear under the skirt. It consisted of a small triangle of leather that tied on both sides with leather laces and barely covered her pussy lips. If anyone had given her anything like the skimpy undergarment to wear back at Briar Rose, Krisa would have turned up her nose in horror. But she had been without any undergarments whatsoever since her escape from the ship and the wild trek across the jungle with Teague. It was a far cry from her waist-pinching cincher and the silk underdrawers she was used to, but Krisa was more than glad to put on the leather thong.

Unfortunately, the thong was dyed a pale green to match the embroidery on the dress rather than the dress itself. When she walked, the pale green triangle of leather flashed at the top of the skirt's slit. Krisa thought it was probably too much to hope that Teague wouldn't notice and comment on it.

In the colorful and revealing Yss clothing, Krisa thought she looked like a holo-ad she had seen once for a club that catered to "gentlemen of leisure". Her best friend Maida had found it in her older brother's room on Winter Solstice break and had smuggled in for the other girls to giggle over. Madame Tresser, their dorm mother, had caught Maida with the ad, and she had spent well over a month in detention therapy for it. Never in her wildest dreams would Krisa have imagined herself in such an outfit, but then her wildest dreams had never included a trip to Planet X.

Walking hesitantly forward, she tapped Teague on the shoulder and waited for whatever sarcastic remark was sure to be forthcoming. The big Feral turned to look at her and his eyes widened, flashing silver. He gave a low whistle and actually stood to look her up and down.

"That's some outfit, little girl," he said at last, looking down at her with eyes that had gone from black to silver the moment he saw her. "Turn around so I can get the full effect." Feeling like the whore of Babylon, as Madame Ledoux would have said, Krisa did as he asked. She felt his sharp silver eyes on her bare skin like a brand. It shouldn't have been such a big deal, after all Teague *had* seen her naked after her bath in the river.

But there was something about the purple Yss dress that seemed to make her feel more than naked somehow. Maybe it was the way the butter-soft leather clung tightly to her curves or the flash of the pale green triangle at the apex of her thighs, but by the time she had finished her spin, Krisa felt that every inch of exposed skin was blushing under Teague's heated gaze.

"Well," she said at last, completing her turn and waiting for the comment that was sure to follow. "Aren't you going to say something sarcastic?"

Teague grinned at her and shook his head. "Sarcastic — me? You wound me, sweetheart. You know I don't have a sarcastic bone in my body."

"Oh, sure," Krisa said. The casual banter did a lot to dispel her nervousness about her appearance and she said lightly, "Would you care to help a lady to her seat?"

"I wouldn't mind if I saw any around," Teague answered, grinning widely. "But I don't see anybody here who fits that description, at least not by Briar Rose standards."

Krisa flushed deeply and dropped her eyes to her bare feet — none of the Yss wore shoes unless leaving the confines of their village. "That isn't funny, Teague," she said, biting her lip.

"Hey, sweetheart." He lifted her chin, forcing her to look into his eyes which were still a solid silver in the growing dusk. "It was a *compliment*. You've come a long way from the girl I took from the *Star Princess*, who didn't want to go out in the jungle without her corset."

"It was a *cincher*," Krisa protested. She tried to look down but Teague wouldn't let her. "It's what every proper lady wears under her clothes."

"Krisa," he said seriously, "I've been all around the galaxy and I've seen an awful lot of ladies both proper and improper but not a single one of them was as beautiful as you. You look good enough to eat." The hungry look on his dark face proved his sincerity and he stared into Krisa's wide brown eyes a long time before releasing her chin.

"Teague..." She had no idea what to say but fortunately she was saved from the embarrassing situation by a loud announcement from the wrinkled old Yss chief. Apparently it was time to eat.

Sitting beside her "man" on the thin grass mat, Krisa did her best to fold her legs modestly as she saw the Yss women around her doing. It was difficult to avoid flashing anything through the slit of her dress. The elderly chief rose and said something that sounded to Krisa like a pit of snakes getting ready to fight. It must have been a rousing speech because afterwards, all the Yss couples sitting in twos around the circle hissed approvingly and patted their hands on the ground in an odd type of applause. Krisa was careful to do what was being done around her, mindful as always of Teague's warning about not offending their hosts.

She was hoping that Teague would translate some of what was being said but he was kept busy most of the feast speaking to the old chief. Krisa began to wish that Ziba was nearby to tell her what was going on, but he and the other children were eating in a separate circle not far away. It was obvious that the groups of adults and children didn't mix much.

After the chief's speech, several of the women rose and began passing around the series of bowls and platters, serving the food onto wide, flat leaves. Krisa had thought the leaves must be some sort of placemats but they turned out to be the plates instead.

Krisa wasn't sure about some of the Yss dishes. Absolutely nothing looked familiar, but after three days and nights of bland nutri-paste, she was ready to try almost anything. As the women came around holding out various bowls and platters, she nodded eagerly to indicate her willingness to try what they offered. The one exception was when the largest platter was brought her way around the midpoint of the feast. It was a huge wooden plate piled high with unfamiliar but delicious-smelling meat.

The girls at Briar Rose weren't encouraged to eat much meat because the headmistress thought it made females too aggressive, but Krisa had always had a very unfeminine taste for it. She was more than willing to try the strange cut of juicy meat the Yss woman holding the platter was offering to her. But just as she was about to nod her head eagerly she heard Teague warn in a low whisper, "*Don't* eat the meat."

Krisa looked at him from the corner of her eye. He was staring straight ahead, apparently engrossed in something the old chief was chattering about, but he had taken none of the delicious-smelling meat himself. His leaf-plate was piled high with vegetable dishes and fruits and nuts instead.

"Why not? Is it poison?" she whispered, out of the corner of her mouth. Maybe the meat was from some animal that the Yss could metabolize but offworlders, like she and Teague, could not.

"No, but you'll be sorry if you eat it," was his oblique reply. Then he went back to his conversation with the chief as though they had never spoken.

Krisa looked longingly at the platter of juicy meat, and a bit rebelliously at Teague. Just because he knew the language and the customs of the Yss, he thought he could order her around. But she was hungry and she wanted to have some of the delicious chops and ribs that were piled high on the platter. She turned away from him and opened her mouth to accept the cut of meat the Yss woman had selected for her, only to find that the platter had moved on down the circle and she had missed her chance.

Feeling disappointed and put out with the big Feral, Krisa consoled herself with the other foreign foods on her leaf-plate. The best one was a small, round golden fruit which seemed to be almost all sweet, sunshine-flavored juice on the inside. She ate a lot of these as the only drink offered was obviously alcoholic in nature. *A lady never becomes intoxicated*, she thought dryly. Of course, a lady wasn't supposed to sit on the ground with savages and eat with her fingers while wearing a dress that would make a whore blush either, but Krisa decided she would have to pick her battles and try to stick with the ones she could win at this point.

After everyone had eaten their fill, a series of torches were lit around the circle to drive off the deepening darkness and then the chief rose and clapped his hands for attention. Pointing to one young Yss warrior and his woman, he made a brief speech and then gestured for the couple to get up.

Teague turned to her. "He's saying that since this is the young man who provided the meat for the night's feast, he and his woman will have the honor of entertaining us now," he translated in a low voice.

Krisa watched with interest as the two stood and walked to the center of the feasting ring which had been cleared of all the various platters and bowls of food to make room for their presentation. Softly, in the darkness outside the circle of flickering light, Krisa heard a slow drumbeat begin. A high, wavering flutelike sound began weaving in and out of the steady beat, causing the hairs at the back of her neck to stand up with its haunting beauty.

The young Yss and his woman stood eye to eye and circled around each other three times and then stopped, facing each other. For a moment, Krisa thought they were going to sing some kind of a strange duet, but they made no sound. Instead, the slender Yss woman, who had long, flowing hair the color of lilacs, sank slowly to her knees and began to rub her cheeks sensuously against the young warrior's thighs. The warrior reached down and caressed her face gently, and then, to Krisa's utter disbelief, he raised his loincloth and revealed what could only be his...

"I have to go," Krisa said in a low, strangled voice, attempting to rise from the circle and get away. Teague's hand on her arm stopped her at once, holding her in place with a grip that, while not cruel, was utterly unbreakable.

"You're not goin' anywhere, little girl," he rumbled. His low voice was obviously meant only for her ears and it was almost lost in the rhythmic beat of the drum. "You're gonna stay right here and watch the show politely like everyone else."

"But Teague, I *can't!*" Krisa felt almost panicked. Inside the circle of torchlight, the beautiful Yss girl was rubbing her cheeks lovingly against her man's hardened cock. Krisa couldn't believe she was being made to witness such an act. In her wildest imaginings she had never even *thought* of such a thing, and now Teague was demanding that she watch it and pretend to enjoy it like everyone else in this circle of savages.

"I can't," she said again.

"Yes," he grated, applying more pressure to her arm. "You *can*. Do you have any idea what an unforgivable insult it is to walk out during a feast entertainment? I'd have to fight the warrior, which wouldn't be a problem, but then you'd have to fight his woman which *would*. Then we'd both end up on the outside of the village wall, waiting for that female soondar to attack. Now, is that what you really want?"

"N-n-no," Krisa quavered. She was having a hard time getting anything out of her mouth at all, because her eyes kept returning to the center of the torch-lit circle, where the entertainment was still going on. Now the young Yss woman was licking along the length of her man's shaft in long, slow strokes and he was very obviously enjoying it.

"All right then," Teague growled in her ear, still keeping his silver eyes politely on the exhibition going on in the center of the circle as well. "I know it's not exactly an elective course at your precious Briar Rose, but it won't kill you to watch one blowjob. You might even take notes for your joining ceremony with Lord Radisson—most men enjoy it, as you might have noticed." He nodded at the young warrior who was making low, urgent noises at the back of his throat, as his woman continued to lick his hard cock, gilded by the torchlight.

Krisa shot the big Feral an incredulous look but he appeared to be utterly serious. Was she going to have to do *that* after her joining ceremony to Lord Radisson? She fingered the small bump at the back of her neck where the chastity chip was implanted. She was definitely going to see Dr. T'lix the minute she stepped foot on Lynix Prime. Still…would it really be all that bad? If you loved the man?

Against her better judgment, Krisa found herself watching the performance in front of her with great attention to detail. Now the young Yss woman was lapping gently at the round plum-shaped sac hanging beneath her man's cock. She tickled it with her tongue, running the tip of it all over in feather-light strokes that drew a low groan from him. Then she sucked his thick cock into her mouth, bobbing her head in time to the insistent drumbeats. The young warrior had his hands buried deep in her lovely, lilac-colored hair, urging her on. Krisa supposed Teague would say he was fucking her mouth the same way he would her pussy and blushed crimson at the thought.

She tried to imagine herself performing such a service for Lord Radisson but for some reason her mind refused to show her any such thing. Instead, she saw herself kneeling in front of Teague, unbuckling his black leather belt and unsnapping the black trousers he wore. She thought of the warm, musky scent of him and the way his thick cock would rub over her cheek before she took him in her mouth. She would start with the tip and explore him with her tongue, just as she had seen the Yss woman do. Then she would tickle the sensitive-looking sac hanging beneath it until he begged her to do more, begged her to take him inside her mouth and suck him. She could almost hear his groans and feel those large hands, sometimes gentle and sometimes rough, buried deep in her hair as he urged her to taste him, to take him deep while he fucked into her mouth. And what would his cum taste like when she finally milked him until he spurted into her warm, willing mouth? Would it be salty and hot? Would he hold her close and tight and groan out her name as he gave himself up to the pleasure she gave him?

The strange thoughts gave her a pulsing sensation in the pit of her belly and she could feel her sex getting wet and hot even though she knew it was wrong. She became aware that the hand Teague had used to restrain her was still on her arm. His calloused palm felt rough and she couldn't help remembering the way his hands had felt cupping her breasts and the hot wetness of his mouth as he sucked her nipples. Her forbidden memories and the skin-to-skin contact with him, even in such a minor way while she was entertaining such forbidden thoughts, caused her stomach to do a long, slow, lazy roll.

Krisa looked away from the young Yss couple in the middle of the circle, who were obviously nearing some kind of completion and turned her eyes toward Teague instead. He was looking at her as well, his silver eyes half-lidded with some emotion Krisa was afraid to name, even to herself. *Take notes*, he had said. *Most men enjoy it.* She wondered if she could learn to please him that way...the way the young Yss woman was pleasing her man. What would it be like to be on her knees before him, helpless and hot, taking his shaft down her throat, sucking his cock in front of everyone?

A sudden noise from the center of the circle drew her eyes reluctantly from the big Feral's and Krisa realized that the Yss couple had finished their performance and the rest of the circle was hissing softly and patting their hands on the ground in applause. Was the feast over? Krisa moved to get up but Teague's hand gripped her arm and he shook his head slightly.

There was a long pause during which no one moved and then the old chief rose once more. He made what sounded like a series of announcements that Teague didn't translate and then the feast began to break up.

Krisa got up carefully, trying not to flash too much skin and looked around uncertainly for Vis. The tall Yss woman didn't appear but Ziba did, suddenly bouncing into view in the torchlight with his pet targee clinging to his hair and chattering.

"You be the Teague, he who does not eat," he announced a bit breathlessly, raising his eyes fearlessly to meet Teague's silver ones.

"That I be, little brother," Teague replied, with a hint of a smile playing around the corners of his full mouth. "And you must be Sarskin's brat. Look too much like him for anyone else to claim you."

"I be Ziba and this be Tz." The half-Yss boy indicated the chattering pink puffball that was sitting on top of his head. "Sarskin the Uneaten One be my sire," he continued proudly. "He has told me much of the Teague. I be pleased to meet you." He held out one slim, six-fingered hand palm up, and Teague covered it gravely with one of his own large hands, palm down.

"I be pleased to meet you too, Ziba, son of Sarskin," he rumbled and Krisa swore she could see amusement glinting in the silver depths of his eyes. "Well met."

"Well met!" Ziba echoed with enthusiasm. "Vis sent me to be showing the Teague and his woman the guest hut. Follow me!" He bounded away at top speed with the chattering targee clinging to his hair. Krisa and Teague had to follow, dodging through the milling crowd of dispersing Yss as well as they could.

"Why do they keep calling you 'the one who does not eat'?" Krisa asked in a low voice, as they tried to keep up with Ziba. "They just watched you eat an entire meal in front of everyone." She thought Teague looked slightly uncomfortable.

"It's a long story," he said, taking her arm to lead her thorough a small knot of Yss villagers who were standing and talking while he nodded politely.

"I've got nothing but time," Krisa assured him pointedly. But just then they found themselves in front of a grass and clay hut that was rather smaller than the others in the village, though still neatly built. Ziba was already bouncing impatiently before the doorway.

"This be the place," he explained. "Vis say she left everything you need inside, Krisalaison. She say you need anything to let her know. You remember where she and my mother's brother stay?"

"Yes, Ziba. Thank you." Krisa couldn't help smiling at the ball of nervous energy. Ziba was much more animated tonight than he had been earlier, perhaps it was being around Teague that worked him up to such a fever pitch.

Apparently Teague thought so too, because he bent down to get a better look at the nervous child. "All right, little brother?" he asked gently.

Ziba stopped bouncing abruptly and looked at Teague, the thin face suddenly serious. "Teague who does not eat, why did you not eat my sire?" he demanded abruptly, much to Krisa's confusion. "Often has he told me of the fearsome battle you fought — the Haulder-Lenz — and how you bested him. And yet you did not eat him. Why?" He reached up to fondle the soft fur of the targee, as if for comfort. The little creature licked his hand with its tiny pink tongue.

"Well, Ziba." Teague's silver eyes narrowed, as though thinking how best to answer the question. "Your sire fought well. I thought it was better to have such a man in the walking world than to send him to the land of the eaten. Besides —" he poked the boy in the ribs gently. "He looked sour to me."

Ziba giggled and Tz, his targee, climbed to the top of his head and bounced up and down, scolding loudly in its high-pitched chatter. "Say you true?" he asked, looking relieved.

Teague rose and ruffled the boy's dark hair briefly, risking the wrath of the irate targee. "I say true, little brother," he answered, smiling.

His answer apparently satisfied Ziba because with a wave, he bounced out of sight abruptly and Krisa heard his shout, "Good dreaming, Krisalaison. Good dreaming, Teague who does not eat."

"What was that about?" she asked, when she was certain the boy was out of earshot. "Why did he ask why you didn't 'eat' his father?"

"Because I didn't," Teague replied casually, pushing open the thatched door and ducking his head to get in the hut. Krisa had no choice but to follow him.

The interior of the hut was much like Vis', only smaller. In fact, it wasn't very much bigger than her sleep cube on the *Star Princess*. There was no cooking area and the hut was largely devoid of household implements. A thick grass mat had been laid against the far wall and there were several fur and leather blankets that looked warm and comfortable. A fat clay jar with a wick in it burned with a low flame in the corner, casting long shadows in the cozy space. *Maybe cozier than I really want to get*, Krisa thought uncomfortably. She looked at the grass sleeping mat and couldn't help remembering the performance they had witnessed after the feast.

"So what exactly happened?" she asked. It seemed better to press Teague for the details of his strange status among the Yss than to dwell on the sleeping arrangements. "You fought this man—Ziba's father—and didn't kill him?" That much, at least, she had gathered from the strange conversation between Teague and the nervous, half-Yss boy.

Teague sighed and sat down on one side of the grass mat to remove his boots. "About eight years ago I was traveling with a crew of mercs from the Blackstar sector. We were delivering some goods to Lynix Prime. Now, what we were delivering wasn't illegal *per se*, but Prime has a fairly high import tax and my associates and I didn't feel the need to pay it." He grinned wolfishly and Krisa realized he was talking about smuggling.

"So." Teague settled more comfortably on the grass mat bed, his back leaning against the clay wall of the hut. "We were tryin' to take a low approach, fly under their detectors. But the idiot we had piloting took us in too low and cranked out the main shaft. It was either crash land or blow the hull, so we wound up here instead."

"Planet X," Krisa said. She crossed awkwardly and sat beside Teague on the grass mat. Vis had left her a smile pile of clothing, along with the personal effects she had been carrying in the pockets of Percy's trousers. She saw her hairpin, the chronometer and the creased but still legible Certificate of Virginity, but her original clothes and shoes were nowhere to be seen.

"Planet X," Teague echoed. "Well, three of us survived the landing — me and two others — both Drusinians. You know about Drusinians?"

Krisa shook her head.

"They're genetically engineered to be truthful, physically unable to tell a lie or break their word," Teague said.

Krisa cleared her throat delicately. "That must make for some rather interesting...*difficulties* in that line of work." A smuggler who couldn't lie would be at a distinct disadvantage, she thought.

Teague flashed his white smile again. "What do you think I was along for? Not that Drusinians need much help to twist the truth. Anyway, we landed on X and there was no way to get off again without a replacement part for the shaft. We had a one-man skiff which meant two of us were gonna be stuck here for the two, three months it took to get the part. We sent D'lan to Lynix Prime to get it and Sarskin and I stayed behind." He sighed and ran a hand through his hair.

"While we were waiting for the part, we got acquainted with the Yss and Sarskin decided he liked it here so much that he was going to stay." Teague shifted on the mat. "I guess you could say he went native. He joined with a Yss woman — several, in fact — and last I heard he'd set up a sort of little empire. A base of operations that's convenient to Prime for his 'line of work' as you put it, but located where nobody on

Prime would think to look. I'm hoping that he can help us get off this rock, he owes me a blood debt since I didn't kill him."

"You still haven't explained *why* you didn't kill him," Krisa pointed out. "Or 'eat' him — whatever that means." She had begun to go through the pile of clothes Vis had left her, and was delighted to find a pale green outfit like the one she had on that was obviously for everyday wear instead of special occasions. There was also a fluffy pink and purple tube-like thing she wasn't sure about. It seemed to be made of some kind of fur.

She looked at Teague questioningly. "What *does* it mean, anyway?" she asked.

Teague smiled at her. "Just what it says, sweetheart. The Yss custom is that if you kill a man from a tribe you're at war with, you eat him in order to take his strength into yourself. If you're feelin' especially generous, you can even share his strength with the rest of your own tribe."

"You mean..." The full impact of what Teague was saying suddenly sank in and Krisa began to feel vaguely nauseous. Despite the rumors of cannibalism, she had just assumed that all the talk of "eating" and "not eating" was metaphorical. The huge pot, big enough to cook a person in where she'd had her bath, suddenly made sense. And the feast... "At the feast tonight..." she whispered faintly, thinking of the delicious-smelling platter piled high with juicy cuts of meat.

Teague nodded. "Aren't you glad you didn't eat any?" he asked, a smile playing around his full mouth. "Told you you'd be sorry if you did."

"Oh my Goddess," Krisa mumbled, clutching the fuzzy pink and purple tube to her chest. She had come so close to taking the meat although he'd warned her not to — *because* he'd warned her not to, she admitted to herself. Of course she was relieved not to have eaten it but it was still more than a little aggravating that Teague seemed to always be right. "You could have told me," she snapped. "Instead of just saying I'd be sorry. I appreciate the warning but I'd like to know *why* I'm not supposed to do something once in a while."

"I guess 'because I said so' is never gonna be a good enough answer for you, is it, little girl?" Teague growled. "In which case you better get that chip taken care of as soon as you can, or you'll be doing what kindly old Lord Radisson says for no good reason the rest of your pretty little life."

"You don't have to remind me," Krisa flared, tossing away the fuzzy pinkish garment and turning on him. "I know what I'm getting myself into."

"Do you?" Teague's voice was a low, dangerous rumble and for a moment they locked eyes, brown clashing with silver.

Finally Krisa dropped her eyes and took a deep breath. "So you had a fight with this Sarskin person?" she said, determined to get to the bottom of the situation and not let Teague distract her with an argument.

"We had a disagreement," Teague said, his tone indicating that he would refuse to elaborate if she asked. "We had been adopted by the same Yss tribe and we ended up fighting a Haulder-Lenz to settle it—a kind of Yss duel to the death using spears. Only I didn't kill him."

"Why not?" Krisa asked. For anyone else it would have been a ridiculous question but for Teague, who had killed so many men without a qualm, she thought it entirely reasonable. "Was he a friend?"

The big Feral looked distinctly uncomfortable. "Sarskin wasn't a friend exactly but he *was* somebody you could count on if everything went to hell. A good shipmate even if he was a slippery son of a bitch. Drusinians are always looking for a way to make a credit."

Something about the way he said it didn't sound right. Krisa looked at him skeptically, she couldn't imagine Teague holding himself back just because the man had been a good "shipmate".

"If you were angry enough to fight him, you were angry enough to kill him," she said flatly. "So why...? Wait a minute—if you would've killed him, you would have had to... You didn't kill him because you didn't want to eat him!" From the look on Teague's dark face, she knew at once she was right.

Krisa felt as though she'd found a sort of chink in the big Feral's armor at last. Teague seemed so tough, so utterly invincible and ruthless, and yet here was something he wouldn't do. Of course, Krisa certainly wouldn't have done it herself either. Cannibalism, she was sure, would be strongly frowned upon at Briar Rose as being more than a little unladylike. But she didn't claim to be a tough-as-nails homicidal sociopath either.

"You'd understand if you saw him," Teague muttered, black brows drawn down low over his silver eyes. "Sarskin is this big, fat..." He made motions in the air with both hands, indicating a large belly and grimaced. "Would've taken me all month to finish him off, even with the tribe's help," he said, frowning. "I tend to get indigestion..."

"I guess it was a prospect you just couldn't *stomach*," Krisa said, feeling the corners of her mouth twitch. "You know, Teague, I had no idea you were such a *picky eater*."

"Are you laughing at me, little girl?" Teague scowled horribly, leaning forward with narrowed eyes.

"No," Krisa denied as seriously as she could. She felt a giggle wriggling to get free inside her stomach and tried unsuccessfully to hold it in. She slapped a hand over her mouth but couldn't stop the laughter from coming. The idea that the huge Feral had refused to kill someone because of a sensitive stomach seemed too deliciously funny to resist.

"Maybe I should give you something to laugh *about*." Teague pounced on her and began tickling her unmercifully. Krisa, who had always been horribly ticklish, was soon shrieking with laughter and begging him breathlessly to stop. They rolled around on the grass mat bed, wrestling and giggling until she felt like her ribs would be aching for days from his ruthless attack.

"Do you give?" Teague asked, eyes flashing silver as he crouched over her, straddling her hips. He had both her arms pinned above her head, holding her wrists easily in one large hand and he was ready to renew his assault with the other.

Tears of laughter running down her cheeks, Krisa nodded weakly. "I'm sorry..." she gasped. "No more...*please.*"

"I don't know if you've learned your lesson yet, sweetheart," he rumbled, a small smile twitching around the corners of his mouth. Keeping her wrists pinned above her head, he began to trail his fingertips along the sensitive underside of her arm, down past the curve of her breast and along the creamy skin of her abdomen, making Krisa gasp and writhe beneath him.

His hand on her bare skin felt warm...sensual. And the way he was straddling her, pinning her to the ground, reminded her of the dreams she sometimes had of the man with no face — the man who touched her...took her... Suddenly the situation didn't seem so funny anymore.

"Teague, let me up. I promise not to laugh anymore." Her voice was still breathless, but for a different reason now. Having him above her, holding her down, was both frightening and exciting. She knew she was in dangerous territory.

Apparently Teague felt the shift in mood as well. "Why should I let you up, little girl?" he whispered, almost tenderly. Warm, blunt fingertips continued to trace their way over her skin and Krisa was suddenly aware that the brief leather halter she wore had been pushed down, baring most of her breasts in their struggle. Now Teague pulled it down farther, exposing nipples flushed dark pink and hardened by excitement.

"Teague..." she whispered pleadingly, as he traced first one jutting nipple and then the other with the tip of his finger, trailing lines of fire over her flesh. She writhed beneath him, feeling helpless and hot all at once. *Hot-blooded*, she thought inanely. She shouldn't enjoy his touch on her body so much. It was wrong...so wrong. Krisa tried to twist away but he held her effortlessly, pinned in place.

"Don't struggle," he growled, cupping one full breast in his large hand and pinching the nipple teasingly, until she gasped with the painful, pleasurable sensation. "It only makes me want you more."

"You know I don't want to..." she breathed, feeling like her heart was going to pound right through her ribs. "Please don't..."

"Should I listen to what you're saying or what your body is telling me, Krisa?" he rumbled. "Because it seems to me those are two different things." Leaning down he sucked one tight, pink bud into his mouth while he pinched the other, licking and nipping, until she cried beneath him, arching her back to get closer, to give him more.

Abruptly, Teague stopped. He looked up at her, his eyes blazing. "Do you like this Krisa? Like what I'm doing to you? Is it making your soft little pussy wet?"

Krisa bit her lip. What should she tell him? She could scarcely admit the way he was sucking and twisting her nipples was making her hot and wet and swollen between her legs, could she? Did that mean she liked it? Fearfully, she shook her head.

"So this isn't doing anything for you?" He twisted her exposed nipples again, making her gasp. "Not a thing?"

Krisa shook her head again. "Not...not a thing," she gasped.

"Let me see." To her horror, Teague changed positions until he was kneeling beside her hips instead of straddling her. "Spread your legs, Krisa," he said in a voice deep with command.

"I don't...want to," she whispered in a low voice.

"I'm not gonna hurt you," Teague said, his rough voice gentling a little. "Just want to see if you're telling the truth. Here." And then warm, calloused palms were reaching under the Yss skirt and spreading her legs.

Krisa closed her eyes and let him do it, knowing it was useless to protest further. She only hoped that the tiny triangular scrap of fabric covering her pussy lips would hide her reaction to his touch.

"I don't know, little girl." Teague's deep voice sounded thoughtful. "Seems like you weren't exactly telling me the truth."

Krisa felt one large, calloused fingertip tracing the tiny triangular patch which barely hid her sex. She moaned low in her throat as she felt her pussy lips begin to open under his gentle stimulation. He was opening her, spreading her cunt wide without even taking off the Yss panties. Her tender lips felt swollen and hot as they spread and soon the only thing the scrap of fabric hid was her aching clit.

"Please," she whispered, but she wasn't sure what she was begging for.

"So hot...so wet," Teague rumbled, almost thoughtfully. His finger slid to the bottom point of the inverted triangle and dipped into the well of moisture between her thighs. Krisa gaped as he brought the slippery wetness he had collected back up to the thin fabric that covered her clit and began to trace the sensitive bump. Again and again he dipped into her pussy with just the tips of his fingers and brought the moisture up to her clit until the Yss panties were soaked with her own damp need.

"Does that feel good?" he asked at last, rubbing so that the fabric of the panties slid inside her pussy lips and caressed the aching bud of her clit.

"Yes," Krisa threw back her head and moaned. She couldn't lie any more. Couldn't pretend she didn't want this when she did, even though it was wrong.

"And are you wet?" Teague persisted, still tracing her clit.

"Yes," Krisa gasped.

"So you lied to me." Teague withdrew his hand, leaving her moaning with the loss of sensation. He glared at her, a look of anger on his chiseled features. "But the question is, little girl, are you lying to yourself too?"

Abruptly he released her and stood up, running both hands through his hair in frustration. "Think I made my point," he growled, turning his back to her.

Krisa lay panting on the grass mat bed, feeling ashamed and hot, both relieved and disappointed that he had stopped. "Teague...?" she asked questioningly, sitting up and covering herself as well as she could. It seemed like her breasts didn't want to go back into the too-small leather top and her skirt wouldn't quite cover her no matter how hard she tugged on it.

"It's time you got some sleep," he said, still not looking. "I'm goin' out for a walk. Be on *your* side of the bed and covered up by the time I get back. Understand?"

"Yes," she whispered but he was already gone.

That night she had the dream again...

~ ~ ~ ~ ~

She was on her knees before him, her naked breasts pressed against his muscular thighs. Her nipples were hard from rubbing against him. The man with no face was touching her, cupping her face tenderly in his hands.

"That's right, little girl, touch it," the deep voice urged.

Krisa looked up and realized that his cock was close to her face. She could smell his warm, masculine scent, could feel the hot brush of his skin against hers when she turned her head slightly and his thick shaft touched her cheek.

Knowing what she had to do, she reached up to take the long, hard shaft in her hand. She could feel his heat pulsing inside her palm, his thickness throbbing in time with his heartbeat. The man groaned his approval as she circled his cock with her fingers and began a long, slow stroke.

"That's good, little girl. Very good. But why don't you give it a kiss?"

Krisa looked at the thick length of him, taking in the flared head that topped the long club of his sex. Kiss it, yes, that was what she was longing to do. Just as the young Yss maiden had kissed her warrior's shaft. Parting her lips, she laid a soft, open-mouthed kiss on the broad head, tasting for the first time his salty, bitter, delicious flavor.

"Good." The man stroked her hair encouragingly. "Now lick it, little girl. Taste it, why don't you?"

There was a tiny slit at the tip of the flared head and Krisa put out her tongue and lapped at the clear fluid that was flowing from it. His taste flooded her mouth, salty and wonderful, as she explored the slit with the tip of her tongue, then opened her mouth to take the entire head between her lips.

"That's right, little girl. Suck it. Suck my thick cock into your soft, wet mouth so I can shoot my cum down your pretty throat," he growled.

Krisa bent to her task, opening her mouth wide for his thickness and taking as much of his shaft down her throat as she could. He was so thick her jaws ached with stretching wide enough to do it, but at the same time, she was aware that this act of submission was affecting her in some way. Between her thighs she could feel the aching wetness of need and desire growing. Pleasuring the man who was mastering her was somehow bringing her pleasure as well.

It was as though the man with no face read her mind. "Touch yourself," he told her. His large, warm hands were buried in her hair, guiding her gently, his thick cock fucking between her lips. "Touch yourself, Krisa. Put your hand between your legs and pet your soft, wet little pussy while you suck my cock."

There was no disobeying his tone of command, nor did she want to. As she had on the long, quiet nights in the Briar Rose dormitory, Krisa reached between her thighs and parted the wet lips of her pussy. With two fingers she rubbed slowly along the side of her aching bud, feeling the wet heat growing with every slow stroke

"That's good. Just right. Suck it, little girl. Suck my cock."

His motions in her mouth were growing stronger, faster. He stroked between her lips, the broad head of his shaft pressing against her throat and she knew that soon she would taste his cum.

Then it happened. The man above her groaned, low in his throat. His fingers tightened in her hair and a warm, salty blast hit the back of her throat, filling her mouth with the taste of him. Krisa drank eagerly, swallowing again and again. Her fingers inside her pussy moved at a faster rhythm.

She felt the warmth growing as tingling showers of sparks raced through her body. To be naked on her knees, taking his cock down her throat while she explored her wet sex was unbearably erotic. If only she could reach that peak, the place where she could never quite find no matter how long she touched herself...

"It's all right little girl," she heard the man say from above her. "Someday soon I'll take you there. I'm gonna spread open your sweet pussy and fuck you until you reach it—until you come all over my thick cock."

Krisa pulled back, letting his wet shaft slide from her mouth. She didn't know if she feared the man's promise, or longed for it to come true.

~ ~ ~ ~ ~

Chapter Thirteen

ഗ

The next few days at the Yss village passed quickly. The plan, as Krisa understood it, was to spend a few days in the village in order to throw the female soondar whose mate Teague had killed off their trail. Then they would travel through the jungle to the settlement of Teague's old shipmate, Sarskin, who had a thriving smuggling operation. Teague was hoping to get a small, fast ship in payment for the "blood debt" that the Drusinian owed him and he had promised to fly her to Prime and drop her in an area where it would be easy to get in touch with Lord Radisson. How she could explain her adventures in the jungles of Planet X to her husband-to-be was up to her—Krisa was still thinking about that. After he dropped her off, Teague planned to go somewhere he said no one would ever find him. He refused to elaborate further on his final destination and Krisa thought it best not to ask.

What worried her was the time factor. They would be spending nearly a week in the Yss village and when she found out that the trip to Sarskin's village would take a week and a half, she wondered if they might not be cutting things too close. Captain Ketchum had said that they might expect a rescue party in a month or a little more when the *Star Princess* was declared missing. But that was a generous estimate, according to Teague.

"If your Lord Radisson is really such a hotshot, he's liable to send ships that take less than a week to build momentum for the hyperdrive," Teague had predicted when she asked him. "Some of the smaller ones they have now can go straight into it, no waiting. But don't worry, sweetheart, we'll get you back to Prime before they know it and you can make up any story you want." And with that, Krisa had to be content. But

175

she couldn't help worrying that a party sent by Lord Radisson would come sooner than expected.

She knew they would be tracking her by the chip in her neck and she didn't want the signal to lead the rescuers not only to her, but to Teague as well. Still, the big Feral seemed unconcerned about it, so she tried to put it out of her mind as well.

Krisa spent her days with the Yss women, Vis especially, learning how to do the simple, routine tasks that comprised their daily existence. For a girl who had been raised never to dirty her hands, it was a novelty to build fires, grind herbs, braid rope, bake bread and do the hundred other things the Yss women did to survive. It was hard work but Krisa found she enjoyed it. She was even beginning to pick up a little bit of the hissing, chattering language she heard so much of every day.

Teague spent his days with a party of warriors, hunting the female soondar. He had explained to Krisa that if they could find and kill the beast, their trip to Sarskin's village would be considerably less dangerous. The Yss warriors were a little in awe of Teague's having killed the male of the mated pair with only a knife. It was, Krisa gathered, considered very bad luck to kill a soondar, but any man who could accomplish it was held in high esteem.

The hunting party searched far and wide, but nothing of the female soondar was seen or heard. A litter of soondar cubs—considered a great delicacy—was discovered by a neighboring, friendly tribe, according to some of the scouts. But no female that might have been their mother had been seen anywhere.

Krisa could tell, though he didn't talk about it much, that Teague was mildly troubled by the female soondar's apparent disappearance. He obviously didn't put much faith in the other warriors' hope that she might have given up her grudge and moved away to another part of the jungle.

Day by day in the slow-paced life of the Yss village, Krisa was coming to know the big Feral more and more. Teague was a fascinating contradiction of light and dark she thought she might never understand. But there was someone else in the village that was nearly as interested in him as she was.

Ziba the half-Yss boy seemed to have adopted the big Feral as an honorary older brother. What amazed Krisa was that Teague was willing to let himself be adopted. She vividly remembered the fierce, frightening man who had been chained in the hold of the *Star Princess* the first time she saw him. No mother would have left her child alone with such a brute for a second. Yet Teague was never anything but gentle with Ziba who he wrestled and laughed with during their evening suppers spent mainly with Vis and her man. Ziba climbed all over him as though the big Feral was his own private tree and it made Krisa laugh to see the half-Yss boy clinging to Teague's broad back the same way Ziba's pet targee, Tz, clung to the boy.

One night near the end of the week they were sitting on the familiar grass mats in Vis' hut finishing a delicious dinner which included, Krisa knew because she had checked to be sure, meat from animals only. She was wearing a pale blue outfit that Vis had given her and Teague and Ziba were wearing matching gray-green vests. Ziba had pestered his aunt into making him one exactly like the one his idol wore. Vis was trying to teach Krisa a little more of the hissing Yss language, when her attention was drawn away to the Feral and the half-Yss boy, who were roughhousing as usual.

Ziba was clinging to the broad shoulders and drumming his sharp little heels against the big Feral's sides, while Tz sat on the top of his head and shrieked.

"...and I will be as great as the Teague! I will slay soondar by dozens and all the men will fear me as they fear the Teague!" he was shouting at the top of his lungs.

Vis said something sharp that Krisa was sure was a command to calm down and be quieter. Teague reached around behind himself and plucked the boy off easily, sitting him down beside him at the table.

"Easy, little brother," he said, grinning a little. "Killing a soondar is more luck than skill, you know."

"I don't care about luck!" Ziba shouted, still overexcited. "I will be the greatest warrior the Yss of any tribe have ever seen! I will leave no enemy uneaten!"

"Ziba," Teague said, suddenly quiet. "What if I had thought like that when I fought your sire in the Haulder-Lenz?"

"But..." Ziba got noticeably quieter as well. "But you didn't," he finished in a small voice.

"No, I didn't. I fought him because I had to. But I didn't kill him because I didn't need to. You shouldn't kill for glory or pleasure, only for necessity," Teague lectured quietly. Krisa couldn't keep her eyes from widening. This was certainly not the way he had talked to her when she had asked about his bloody past.

"But my sire has told me you killed many men," Ziba protested, reaching up to pet Tz who was nestled at the back of his neck, nibbling at his hair.

"I have," Teague answered seriously. "But only once have I killed a man for pleasure rather than need. He was the first man I ever killed and I was very angry. But, little brother—" Teague paused for a moment and Krisa thought his silver eyes looked almost sorrowful. "Out of that first killing came all the others. Do you understand?"

Ziba nodded thoughtfully, quiet at last, and he didn't return to his former exuberance for the rest of the night.

"Teague, tell me what you were talking to Ziba about at dinner tonight." Krisa changed into her sleeping outfit while he turned his back considerately to give her some privacy.

What she was wearing was the fluffy pink and purple tube-like dress she hadn't been able to figure out their first night at the village. Vis, with some help from Ziba, had explained that it was a nightdress of sorts, though it was much different from the type of nightgown Krisa was used to. The furry tube only covered from the tops of her breasts to the tops of her thighs.

When she had learned it was made of the fluffy fur of the targees, Krisa had been upset at the thought of so many of the curious little puffballs being killed. But Ziba explained that they shed their fur regularly, which was then gathered and made into garments and household implements. Targee fur was waterproof and warm enough to keep out the chill of Planet X's cold nights.

Of course, Krisa wouldn't have had to worry about being cold at night if she was still sleeping curled against Teague's chest, as she had on their trip though the jungle. He put out heat like a furnace and didn't seem to mind sharing his warmth. But somehow, since their confrontation the first night in the guest hut, sleeping that close to the big Feral hadn't seemed exactly…safe.

Teague hadn't tried to do anything improper during their trip through the jungle, but he had been preoccupied with survival then. Now that they were safe inside the walls of the Yss village, there was time to turn his attention to other things—namely her, as the practical little voice inside her head pointed out.

So Krisa made sure she was already snuggled up, firmly on her own side of the grass mat bed with the furs tucked under her chin when she asked her question about his past.

He didn't answer so she prompted, "Teague?"

"What do you want to know?" he said at last, his back still to her. "You decent?"

Krisa nodded and then realized he couldn't see the gesture. "Yes, you can turn around now."

Teague turned, shedding his own clothes carelessly on the floor as he did. Now that they were out of the jungle, he stripped before he went to sleep, which made the practical little voice inside Krisa's head doubly nervous. She had protested this practice at first, but Teague had replied shortly that he refused to be uncomfortable just to satisfy her ridiculous ideas about modesty and impropriety.

The gray-green vest lay on the floor already and as the black trousers came down, Krisa turned and blew out the flame of the fat little clay lamp, plunging the hut into darkness. She told herself she was trying not to look, but she still caught a brief glimpse of the heavy, dark shadow of his cock between his thighs, before everything went dark. Her habit of blowing out the light before he could get completely naked had amused Teague at first, but now he didn't bother to comment.

"I just want to know why you said what you said—about killing for necessity, not for pleasure. What you told me that first night we talked in the *Star Princess* was a lot different."

Teague sighed heavily and slid into the grass mat bed beside her. Krisa made sure she kept to her own side but even so, she could feel the heat radiating from his big body.

"How is what I told him and what I told you different?" he demanded, turning on his side to stare at her, silver eyes glowing softly in the darkness.

"Well, it's a *lot* different," Krisa said indignantly. "When we talked you acted like killing people was no big deal to you—a way of life, you said. But when you talked to Ziba, when you calmed him down, you acted like it—I don't know—almost like it bothered you."

Teague sighed again. "No, I told you that doing what you have to in order to survive gets to be a way of life. For me, unfortunately, that happens to involve a lot of killing. You don't break out of the slam by sayin' please and thank you, sweetheart. It's a messy, ugly thing sometimes, trying to keep your freedom." The silver eyes looked thoughtful. "But every time I killed it was because I had to. What I was telling Ziba is that you shouldn't kill just for the fun of it."

"B-but you told him you *did* kill for pleasure. Once—the first time. Tell me about that," Krisa whispered, wondering if she really wanted to know. She felt like a child asking to be told a ghost story right before bedtime, but she couldn't seem to help herself. Teague's quiet words to the half-Yss boy had roused a powerful curiosity in her.

"Do you *really* want to know?" Teague asked flatly, echoing her own thoughts. He stared at her piercingly, the twin silver moons narrowed to slits in the velvety darkness. She felt frightened suddenly, almost afraid to move. She nodded slightly, knowing he would be able to see the gesture, even in the pitch-black hut. "Fine. Guess you do." Teague rolled onto his back, staring at the blackness above them with unblinking eyes. For a while Krisa thought he would refuse to tell her. But then the deep, gravelly voice began, speaking softly, in a tone that was more of a vibration than a sound.

"You know I was born a Nightsider slave on Al'hora, but I never told you exactly why I left. What happened that made me kill my Daysider master and jump planet."

"I guess." Krisa cleared her throat. "I guess I just assumed that you couldn't stand being a slave. You don't seem like the type to take to it, somehow."

Teague laughed dryly, a short bark of a sound that fell flat in the dark hut. "Come to that, you don't seem like the type to take to it either, sweetheart. But no—that wasn't it. Or not all of it, anyway. I was born into my first master's household, raised almost like a son because he didn't have any of his own. I was trusted, educated. I might have stayed a slave forever, I was born to it and it was all I knew."

"What happened? What changed your mind?" Krisa asked, caught up in his story despite herself.

Teague was quiet for a long time before answering. "I had a woman—a Feral like me," he said at last, after a long pause. "Nightsider slaves weren't allowed to have joining ceremonies but we belonged to each other just the same." He stirred and the fur blankets covering his large frame rustled like restless ghosts in the darkness. "Then my old master died and his estate got divided up. Slaves got sold off."

"And they separated you from y-your wife?"

He made a short, curt noise of negation. "No. But the man we were sold to had a taste for Nightsider women—for Ferals. He had me trained as a pilot so I'd be away from the estate. One day he sent me out on a long run with a shipment of goods. When I came back..." Teague took a deep breath and the silver blinked out briefly as he closed his eyes. "When I came back she told me he'd been at her—tried to rape her. Actually, she admitted he'd been trying to get to her a long time but she'd been puttin' him off. Didn't tell me because she didn't want me to get into trouble." His gravelly voice grew deeper, angry.

"I wanted to kill him, of course. Hadn't killed anybody up to that point but it didn't take me long to get the urge. Coralia—Corie, that was her name—begged me not to. I couldn't do anything about it legally, Feral slaves on the Dayside of Al'hora don't have any rights. I held off on killing him but I couldn't just do *nothing*, so... I went to him and warned him never to touch her again."

"B-but he did anyway?" Krisa asked hesitantly.

Teague made a low, angry noise in his throat. "He had me thrown me in the glow hole—a room filled with high-intensity glows that never shut off. It's a punishment for Feral slaves that forget their place. Even with our second eyelid to protect us, that much light is painful—incapacitating." His deep voice was flat now, emotionless. "When he finally let me out two weeks later, Corie was dead."

"He killed her?" Krisa asked, horrified.

"She killed herself," Teague said quietly. "Couldn't live with what he'd done to her while I was stuck in the hole. I understood. Even in captivity, it's the Feral way."

"Oh," Krisa whispered. The large form in the darkness beside her shifted and suddenly he was looking down at her again.

"Those for me?" A large hand touched her face briefly. Krisa reached up and touched her cheek, surprised to find moisture there. Hesitantly, she nodded.

"Don't bother," Teague told her, his voice growing hard. "It was a long time ago and I killed the raping bastard nice and slow before I left. That was the only one I enjoyed." He lay back in the darkness beside her.

Krisa found she didn't have anything to say to that so she kept silent. But she reached for him in the darkness, not caring anymore about impropriety. She wrapped her arms around his waist and pillowing her head on the broad planes of his chest.

After a time he held her, one muscular arm wrapping her tightly to him, as he had in the jungle.

Chapter Fourteen

ဢၣ

The week at the Yss village passed faster than she would have believed possible and before she knew it, Krisa was sitting beside Teague and listening as the old chief gave a long, hissing speech at their farewell feast. She had avoided the meat carefully this time. She watched with as much composure as she could muster as the young man who had provided it put on a post-feast entertainment with his woman in the center of the torch-lit ring.

Since the night Teague had told her his story there was less awkwardness between them, at least concerning their sleeping arrangements. Krisa now understood completely why Teague would never take her against her will. He was more than just morally opposed to rape—he actively loathed it because of what had happened to the woman he had loved so many years before.

The knowledge helped Krisa relax despite the tension between them, and the fact that she still had her disturbing dream occasionally. It was still difficult, however, to watch such a blatant display of sexuality as the Yss man and his woman were putting on without blushing or thinking things she knew she shouldn't be thinking. Wondering what doing that with Teague would be like...

The display the Yss warrior and his woman were putting on was more elaborate than any other she had yet seen. Maybe because it was a farewell feast and they were honoring their guests with their performance, Krisa didn't know. She did know that she felt compelled to watch as the Yss warrior kissed his woman and stripped down her scanty top, baring her thrusting nipples in the firelight. He sucked first one and then the other into his mouth, torturing his woman's aching buds sweetly with teeth and tongue while she moaned in obvious pleasure and wound her long fingers through his hair.

Her skirt was next to go, sliding down her narrow hips to puddle at her feet, revealing the pastel bush of hair at the apex of her sex. Kneeling at her feet, the young warrior urged her to spread her thighs which she did with no complaint. Then, delicately, he spread the swollen lips of her pussy, showing the hot wet inside of her cunt.

Krisa felt herself blush all over. She looked away from the performance for half a second, unable to stand seeing such intimate details of the Yss woman's arousal and happened to catch Teague's eye.

"Hey, little girl. You all right?" He gave her a look that was half concerned, half amused.

Krisa bit her lip and nodded at the circle of firelight where the Yss warrior and his woman continued to perform. "What...I mean why is he doing that? Showing her like that?" she managed to ask. She could understand the point of the blow job which was what she had most often seen at the feasts, it was a performance of pure pleasure. But why did the Yss man feel compelled to put his woman on display like this? Why did he feel compelled to show the most intimate part of her anatomy to the entire tribe?

"He's showing how aroused he made her, how wet." Teague's voice was pitched low, for her ears alone. "Among the Yss it's a mark of virility to make a woman so wet with desire she can't resist you."

"Why?" Krisa asked again, her attention split between the show going on in the center of the circle and Teague's dark face. The warrior was sliding two long fingers deeply into his woman's pussy now and stopping every now and then to slide the broad pad of one of his thumbs over the swollen bud of her clit. "Why does she have to be...to be...wet?" Krisa asked, and blushed again.

185

Teague shrugged his massive shoulders. "Makes it easier to get into her pussy if she's already wet. Easier to fuck her, come in her, breed her. Everything you see here is about fertility, survival of the species of the tribe. If a woman is willing to spread her legs for you, if you make her so hot she has to let you fuck her, you have a better chance of passing on your genes and your name. Watch."

He directed her attention back to the center of the circle where the Yss woman was now on her hands and knees with her bottom raised high in the air. Her legs were spread wide and between her thighs, Krisa could still see the glimmering wetness. As she watched, the young warrior positioned himself behind his woman and began to rub the broad head of his cock over the center of her wetness while she moaned and gasped.

"See the way her pussy lips open for him when he does that?" Teague said in that same, low growling voice. "He barely has to spread her at all, she's so hot she's opening for him on her own. You see," he said, taking Krisa's hand in one of his, "when you make a woman that hot, her soft little cunt gets all swollen with need—she needs to be fucked, needs to have your cock buried deep inside her pussy, filling her with cum."

"Oh." Krisa tried to take her hand back but he wouldn't let her. Her cheeks were on fire and her heart felt like it was about to pound out of her chest.

"Watch him," he commanded her softly. "Watch the way he's entering her. He doesn't just shove his cock into her cunt all at once. No—he's taking his time, sliding in slowly, inch by inch. That builds the anticipation."

Krisa watched, helpless to look away, as the Yss warrior did exactly what Teague was describing. One inch at a time the long, thick shaft slid into his woman's wet, open pussy. She cried and moaned and tried to push back against him to get more of his cock into her, obviously impatient to have him fill her to the limit. But the warrior had a firm grip on her hips, his long-fingered hand bracing her pelvis, and he forced her to hold still and submit to his fucking.

"See the way she's trying to get all of him inside her?" Teague asked. "That's because he did a good job of warming her up—she's hot for him, needs him. And that's what feels good to a woman—having a thick cock buried all the way in her tight little cunt, filling up her pussy. That feeling of being penetrated, being owned is what they need." His eyes were completely on Krisa now, not on the show, and his hands were very warm as he curled her palm around two of his thick fingers and stroked in imitation of the show that was going on in front of them.

"H-how do *you* know what feels good to a woman?" Krisa asked in a breathless little whisper.

Teague shrugged again and gave her his white smile. "I know what they've told me, what they begged for when I was fucking them. They always want it harder, deeper, want to feel my cock filling them up. Tell me, Krisa, would you like to feel that? Like to feel my thick cock sliding inside your tight little cunt until I fill you up with my cum?"

"No," she said immediately, looking away from him, her eyes on anything but the blazing fire on his dark face.

Teague looked at her for a long moment, then reached up to brush a stray curl away from her heated cheek. "Liar," he said softly, and turned his attention back to the center of the ring.

The performance was nearing some kind of completion. The Yss warrior was thrusting almost savagely into his woman's sex and she had her head bowed, her long hair hanging in her face as she submitted to his fierce fucking. She was making a high, keening wail as he drew nearer and nearer to filling her and Krisa looked down at her hands for a moment, rather than watch the embarrassing, fascinating sight.

She tried to think of something else, anything to keep her mind off the sight of the Yss couple making love and the strange feelings Teague raised in her as he explained exactly what was happening and what he wanted to do to her.

Desperate for distraction, she studied the fabric of her clothes. She was wearing the deep purple feasting outfit again. Over Krisa's protests, Vis had given it to her, as well as the other Yss clothes she had been wearing that week. The soondar-eye blue dress was too beautiful and had taken Vis too much time and effort to just give it away. She had protested through Ziba, but Vis wouldn't hear of her not taking the clothes.

Krisa had felt bad about not having anything to give in return, until she remembered the jeweled chronometer that Lord Radisson had sent her on her fifteenth birthday. Since its bath in the river the chronometer no longer worked, but it was a rich, beautiful thing and Vis couldn't tell time anyway. To Krisa's delight, the Yss woman loved it.

When Teague had seen Vis wearing the expensive chronometer on a twist of pink grass around her slender neck, he had laughed.

"Bet old Lord Radisson never expected his ten thousand-credit chronometer to wind up on some Yss woman on Planet X," he'd remarked, sarcastically. That was one thing about Teague that never changed, Krisa thought dryly, remembering his remark—his sense of humor.

Soft hissing and the patting of hands on the ground drew her attention back to the torch-lit circle where the Yss couple had apparently finished their performance. The slow beat of the drum and the thin, wailing flute that had accompanied the show had died and everything was silent. Thinking that the feast must be over, Krisa got to her knees, preparing to rise from the circle.

"No—get *down!*" Teague hissed, grabbing her arm, but it was too late. Her motion had drawn the attention of the wrinkled old Yss chief and he turned to her and Teague and began to speak in the hissing, chattering language, motioning for them to rise at the same time.

"Wh-what is he saying?" Krisa asked in a low, trembling voice, horribly afraid she already knew the answer.

"Great going, sweetheart," Teague answered, more than a touch of annoyance in his deep voice. "You just volunteered us to be next."

"What? No I didn't! Teague, you *know* I didn't."

"I know it and you know it but none of them know it," he growled, standing up and grabbing her by the arm. "Come on, little girl. On your feet—unless you want to stay down there, that is."

Krisa had been considering, with one panicked corner of her mind, just digging in her heels and staying on the ground. His remark, accompanied by the white, mocking grin, caused her to shoot to her feet in an instant. But when she stood up, she had no idea what to do. It was one thing to daydream about doing to Teague what she had just seen the Yss woman do to her man. To actually *do* it, in front of a whole group of strangers, was something else entirely. And of course, some things she couldn't do no matter how intriguing they were— not and keep her virginity intact.

"Teague, please," she pleaded in a low voice. "You know I've never... Until this week I didn't even know people did things like that to each other. Madame Glossop never said *anything* about it in our sexual education lectures." She looked up at him, putting her heart into her eyes. She was scared to death and there was no way to hide it.

Teague sighed and ran one large hand through his spiky hair. "Fine. Stop lookin' at me like that, Krisa. You know I'm not going to force you to do something you don't wanna do." He nodded his head at the Yss couple who were slowly departing the circle. "But we have to do *something* or risk offending our hosts. If you prefer, we can go the other way."

"I don't understand," Krisa said blankly, feeling horribly confused. "*What* other way?" Was it possible, she wondered, that there were even more strange and unimaginable sexual acts that she had never heard of? From the exasperated look on Teague's face, there were.

"I can't believe this," he muttered, shaking his head. "You really *are* innocent, aren't you, sweetheart? What I mean," he spared a quick glance for the Yss couple who were almost clear of the circle of torchlight, "is that instead of you going down on me, I could go down on you."

"You mean you'd put your mouth...your tongue..." Krisa closed her thighs tightly and looked at him in disbelief. "Teague, you *wouldn't.*"

He grinned wolfishly at her. "Oh yes I would, little girl, it would be a great pleasure to eat your little pussy. I've wanted to do it from the minute I smelled your sweet scent in the hold that first night you came sneakin' around."

The look on his dark face, the heat in his silver eyes and the deep, growling voice was almost too much for Krisa. She didn't want to give offense to the Yss and be thrown out to be eaten by the soondar that was stalking them, but she was on the razor's edge of panicking and fleeing the circle of torchlight anyway. Even in her most disturbing dreams, the ones where the man with no face touched her and made him ready for himself, she had never dreamed of him doing *that.* *Only because you didn't know it was possible*, a little voice whispered in the back of her head. Just minutes before, she had been fantasizing about the idea of being on her knees before Teague, pleasuring him. It had never occurred to her to wonder what it would be like to have him on his knees before her, returning the favor.

"Teague," she whispered through numb lips. "I just can't do that. I mean, *I just can't. Please...*"

He sighed again, tenderness and irritation warring in his dark face. "Fine, come with me and we'll figure out something." He took her hand and pulled her into the circle of torchlight to perform for the waiting Yss.

"But what are we going to *do*?" Krisa hissed anxiously, extremely aware of all the narrow, pale eyes focused in their direction.

"I don't know," he replied with exasperation. "All I really know is what we're *not* gonna do. You pretty much ruled out everything they'll accept, you know."

"There must be *something* else we can do," Krisa insisted, looking around the circle of watching eyes. She could sense the impatience of the seated Yss as they waited to be entertained.

Teague flashed her a grin. "There *is* — exactly what we just saw — but I'm afraid that would invalidate your precious Certificate once and for all."

Krisa blanched, wishing she could draw her hand out of his but aware that it wouldn't look right to their waiting audience. "Something besides *that*," she hissed in Teague's ear.

He rounded on her in irritation. "I don't know, sweetheart," he growled in a low, frustrated voice. "I guess I could show 'em card tricks, but I don't happen to have a deck handy. How about you entertain them with some of the valuable skills you learned at good ol' Briar Rose?"

"Like what?" Krisa demanded, looking around her nervously.

Teague snorted. "I don't know. Maybe you could put on an embroidery demonstration or a knitting show. All I know is if you don't want to do anything sexual, you'd better think of something else fast, they're about three seconds from being very offended. Didn't you learn *anything* of value at that overpriced bride stable?"

"As a matter of fact, I did," Krisa replied, stung by his criticism into having a sudden flash of inspiration. "Tell the musicians, whoever they are, to start playing again," she ordered Teague. "And tell the Yss we're about to perform a whole new form of offworlder entertainment."

Teague looked at her skeptically but turned to do as she said. Soon, the slow, steady sound of the drum was back, with the haunting flute weaving sensuously through its rhythmic beats. "What are you planning, Krisa?" Teague asked in a low voice.

"Just watch and try to follow my lead," she whispered back, trying to sound confident. Closing her eyes, she took a deep breath and tried to open herself to the music.

At Briar Rose, Krisa had taken six years of dance, three of Classic Ballroom, and three of Modern Movement Expression. It was this last class that she really excelled at—so much so that her instructor, Madame Petrosa, had recommended her for extra instruction during her last year at the academy. There had been one dance in particular that Krisa enjoyed, one that mimicked the sinuous grace of a snake that was about to strike—the Sandara, it had been called. It was this dance that she tried to let herself feel now, as she listened to the slow beat of the drum and the high wailing of the flute, like a snake-charmer's call.

Keeping her eyes shut at first, she began to move with a slow, sensual grace that seemed to flow through her limbs, turning them to liquid. Picturing herself as a snake, gliding along, intent on fascinating her prey, she began to glide in a slow circle around Teague, touching him lightly and darting away. Tantalizing…teasing…

Teague followed her with his eyes, a low, frustrated growl building in his throat and then, to Krisa's surprise, he began to follow her lead. She brushed past him, letting her full breasts touch him, her erect nipples just grazing his chest and then turned lightly, intending to make another revolution around the big Feral, only to find herself caught.

Teague's large hands were on her waist and then she felt him join the rhythm of the drums, the rhythm pulsing in her blood. Slowly, sensuously, he turned her so they were facing each other, pulling her body close to his, and began to grind against her. His hands kept her pelvis anchored to his so that she could feel the hard bulge of his cock pressing into her inner thigh, through his black trousers and her tight leather skirt.

"Teague," she whispered, her voice low and shocked. His only reply was a heated glance and a low, growling voice in her ear.

"Think you're the only one who knows how to dance dirty, little girl?" he rumbled. "Maybe you aren't so innocent after all."

He caught her right thigh in one hand and lifted it, wrapping her leg around his muscular hips. Then he dipped her suddenly so that her long hair hung down her back, almost brushing the ground. He supported her upper body with one arm while their pelvises continued to grind to the beat of the drum.

Krisa gasped in shock and unwilling pleasure as she felt the thick ridge of his cock press against her wet sex, parting her slippery folds as though the thin green triangle of leather between her legs wasn't even there. Teague thrust against her, simulating the act she both feared and craved, pressing against her ruthlessly and watching her eyes to catch her reaction.

Krisa moaned low in her throat, she couldn't help it. The thick length of the big Feral's cock was rubbing relentlessly against her sensitive, swollen clit, forcing her to react to the pleasure against her will.

"Teague...please!" she managed to whisper.

He brought her up suddenly and released her thigh so that she was standing on wobbly legs before him.

"Think it's enough?" he growled low in her ear.

Krisa tried to nod her head, but he turned her forcefully, bringing her back to his front and snarled in a low, frustrated voice, "Well, it's not, little girl. It's not *nearly* enough." He was standing behind her now, forcing her to face the circle of narrow Yss faces, outside the glow of the torches.

Reaching down he pulled up her arms and draped them around his neck, so that she was standing nearly on tiptoes.

Her breasts were thrust out from her body, her limbs stretched to their limit. Teague's breath was hot against the back of her neck.

"Whatever you do, don't lower your arms," he ordered in a low, commanding tone. Then Krisa felt his large, warm hands begin a slow journey that started with her upper arms and continued down her chest and sides. She groaned at the hot feel of those hands on the bare flesh of her waist. Then they were sliding higher to cup her breasts through the leather halter-top, and then pulling it down, baring her breasts before the circle of watching eyes. Baring her, shaming her, making her unspeakably hot.

Krisa moved to cover herself, wanting to hide her naked breasts with her hands, but Teague was there once more, anchoring her arms around his neck and growling, "What did I say, little girl? Keep you arms *up*."

Gasping, Krisa did as he said, though the position thrust her exposed breasts out, the pink nipples erect with the chilly night air. Teague ran his large hands over the ripe nubs, lightly at first and then possessively, pinching and twisting until Krisa cried out in painful pleasure. He touched her as though he owned her body, as though he could do anything he wanted with it. Touched her the way Krisa knew he had been wanting to all week, as they slept side by side on the grass mat bed, so close and yet so far away.

"Is this what you wanted, Krisa?" he demanded in her ear, his voice low and hot. "Do you like it when I touch you like this? When I show all these people who you belong to?"

"Goddess!" Krisa sobbed, turning her head to one side and closing her eyes, unable to keep them open and watch the silent Yss watching her shame.

The rough, warm hands slid lower, over her taut, trembling belly to the high slit in the purple leather skirt that showed the small, damp triangle of green leather she wore under it. Teague's palms caressed her inner thighs, warm and large and utterly inescapable, as he forced her to part them for him, though Krisa tried at first to keep them closed. He was too strong, she thought and her need was too great. *Hot-blooded*, he had said and she felt her blood rising to meet his now. Felt the pleasure in his rough, insistent touch, even as her face glowed red with embarrassment in the torchlight.

"That's right, little girl, open your legs for me," he whispered roughly, the gravelly voice thick with desire. "I want to spread your sweet pussy lips and feel how wet you are. I'm gonna show everyone exactly how hot I made you — how much you need my thick cock inside your tight little cunt."

"Teague...*please!*" But she no longer knew if she was begging him to let her go or to touch her, as the large, warm palms on her trembling inner thighs were threatening to do. Her arms remained locked around his neck now of their own volition, thrusting her naked, exposed breasts out into the cool night air, letting everyone see her shame. Yet Krisa wasn't even sure she could make herself care anymore.

Blunt fingertips drew aside the tiny green triangle, baring her sex, and then he was touching her, lightly and teasingly at first, and then harder. He was spreading the swollen lips of her pussy, so that his thick fingers could explore her slick folds at a leisurely pace. Blunt fingertips traced magical circles around her aching clit, drawing sensations from between her thighs that Krisa thought would drive her mad with want and desire. She was crying now, openly panting with need, and still he tormented her.

"Do you like this, little girl?" she heard him growl in her ear. "Like it when I pet your sweet little cunt in front of everybody like this and show them how wet you are? How does it feel to be owned like this, to have everybody know who you belong to?"

"Teague! Oh, Goddess, please!" Krisa moaned as his thick fingers slid over and around the tender bud of her clit, starting a fire in her belly that she knew could only be put out with his cock sheathed deep in her pussy. Gently, but insistently, two long fingers begin to enter her cunt, thrusting where no one had ever gone before.

"You like this, don't you, Krisa?" he demanded, thrusting deeper, but still being careful not to go too deep, not to pass the point of no return and take her maidenhead. "Do you think you'd like it better if it was my cock inside your sweet little pussy instead of my fingers? Answer me, little girl!"

His voice was harsh in her ear, but it was the slow, insistent motion of his fingers, that made her groan out a breathless assent. More than anything she wanted him...inside her, and Krisa knew she didn't care if he took her in front of the whole Yss village, as long as he took her.

The hot motion of his fingers inside her wet sex was driving her insane. She could feel that sensation building—the feeling of climbing toward some brilliant peak from where she could cast herself off and learn to fly. In all her dreams and during the furtive, silent self-explorations of the darkened dorm room at Briar Rose, she had never reached that peak. The peak she sensed she was about to reach now.

"Teague...*Teague*!" she sobbed, arching against him and spreading her thighs shamelessly, to give him better access to her pussy.

"Who do you belong to, Krisa? Who?" he demanded. He was rubbing harder, his fingers almost rough against her slippery clit, perhaps sensing the rush of sensation she was building toward.

"*You!*" Krisa sobbed, writhing against him wantonly. "I belong to you, Teague—only you!"

"That's what I wanted to hear, little girl," he growled. He bit the side of her neck possessively, leaving a mark that she knew wouldn't fade for days. "You'll be someone else's once you get to Prime but here on X you belong to *me*."

The blunt fingertips rubbed hard against her slick folds and abruptly Krisa was there, feeling the waves of unbearable pleasure crash over her, drowning deep as he took her to the peak and pushed her off, teaching her how to fly.

Chapter Fifteen

ॐ

After the blatant display at their last feast in the Yss village Krisa was certain that her Certificate of Virginity was going to be a worthless piece of paper by the time she reached Prime. Despite his personal loathing for rape, Teague would listen to the needs of her body and ignore the protests coming out of her mouth. He would take her to the hut and have her any way he wanted her. The knowledge was almost a relief.

Krisa had never known her body could burn so hotly, had never understood that the unfulfilled yearning inside her could grow so huge that she felt like she was on fire, endlessly burning but never consumed. Even though the consequences if Lord Radisson were to insist on a re-verification of her virginity once she got to Prime were extreme, Krisa couldn't make herself care.

Teague had led her by the hand to the guest house after their performance, pulling her inside and shutting the door roughly behind them. Krisa stood shivering in the center of the small space, knowing what had to come next. She would protest, of course, she had that much propriety left at least. But the huge Feral would have her anyway, would take her the way she was aching to be taken, of that she was sure.

"Strip." Teague's voice was little more than a low growl and Krisa didn't even tried to protest. With trembling fingers she pulled off the soondar eye-blue feasting outfit and untied the thongs that held the small triangle of green leather that covered her sex in place. She stood naked before him in the lamplight, shivering with cold, waiting for the inevitable.

Teague crossed the distance between them with one stride and pulled her into his arms. Threading his fingers through her long, loose hair, he pulled her head back and kissed her fiercely, plundering her mouth while his other hand roamed freely over her naked body. He fondled her breasts, pinching her nipples and cupped the wet mound of her sex, his fingers invading her cunt until Krisa moaned hotly into his mouth.

At last he pulled back. Looking at her intensely with eyes that had gone a solid, drowning silver he demanded, "Tell me you want this, Krisa. Tell me you want to give yourself to me—here, now, tonight."

She opened her mouth, wanting more than anything to say yes. To give him the permission he needed to do what they both wanted so badly, but somehow, she just couldn't say it. The voice of every instructor she'd ever had at Briar Rose seemed to rise like unquiet ghosts in her mind, whispering in horror at what she was about to do. *A lady is never unclothed before a gentleman, not even her husband... Beware of losing your most precious treasure, girls... Men only want one thing... Once lost your virginity can never be restored... It is a gift meant only for your husband and if he finds he has been cheated you may be very, very sorry...*

"Teague," she whispered weakly, shaking her head. "I just... I *can't*. I'm sorry. You can take what you want, but I can't give it to you." Reaching beneath her hair, Krisa felt the tiny bump at the back of her neck where the chastity chip resided. Though it was not yet activated, it stood for everything in her past, everything that was supposed to be in her future. "It's not mine to give," she said in a low voice. Then she closed her eyes, waiting for what was surely coming.

How often had Madame Glossop warned them during sexual lectures that men, all men, reached a point of no return? A point where nothing one did or said could stop them from taking the woman they were with. Surely Teague had reached and passed that point long before. He would take her now despite her refusal to give permission—it was inevitable.

He pulled her closer for a moment and buried his face in her neck, inhaling deeply. Krisa shivered at the feel of his hot breath on her vulnerable throat and prepared herself. Now he would do what he had vowed not to. Would spread her thighs and thrust his cock into her cunt, spreading her pussy lips with his thickness and fucking her until he filled her with his hot cum. But then, instead of lowering her to the grass mat bed and having her, he let out a low growl of frustration and released her.

"You want it, little girl. You want it as much as I do," he snarled. "Want to feel me filling you and fucking you until we both come."

"Teague..." But Krisa opened her eyes in time to see him stalking out of the hut, leaving her naked and shivering in the middle of the room.

He didn't return that night, leaving her alone to have the dream of the man over and over again...

~ ~ ~ ~ ~

"Spread for me. I want you down on your knees with your cunt open for me, little girl. Right now!" The man with no face sounded angry and the tone of command in his deep voice was undeniable.

Shivering, Krisa lowered herself to the floor, her bottom raised in the air and her thighs spread. She felt him behind her, felt his hot breath on the back of her neck as he reached forward to palm her breasts, He tugged at her nipples, sending sparks of desire shooting through her body directly to her pussy. She was already growing wet and could feel her pussy lips opening with the heat and need that obeying his commands always seemed to build in her.

"That's right." The man seemed satisfied by her submission. He bent over her, the heat of his chest radiating across her bare back and his large, rough hands caressed her sides. "Spread for me, little girl," he murmured again in her ear. "Spread your pussy open so I can get into your soft wet cunt."

But instead of his cock, she felt his fingers, long and strong and capable, thrusting into her open sex. She bit back a cry as they pierced her, pressing to the end of her channel, exactly where she needed them to be.

"Feels good, doesn't it?" he murmured. "Feels good when I finger you this way, when I fuck you with my fingers. Just think how much better it's gonna feel when I put my cock inside you instead." His fingers stroked into her, sliding in her tight wet heat as though he owned her, as though he had every right to explore her body this way. Then they withdrew and slid over her clit instead, igniting the sensitive bundle of nerves until Krisa cried out, gasping, begging...

"Soon, little girl," he promised. "Soon I'm gonna give you what you need. What we both need."

Krisa crouched on the ground below him, open and shivering with fear and anticipation. When would he do it? When would he thrust inside her and fill her with his cock as he had promised?

"Turn over." His voice was gentler this time, but there was still a steely note of command in it.

Krisa did as he asked without question, turning on her back and closing her legs instinctively.

"No...open for me. Need to see that sweet wet cunt before I fuck it." His warm hands spread her thighs, opening her to his gaze again. She wished she could see his face, could know the man who touched her like this, who tormented her so sweetly. His voice was so familiar, if she could just catch a glimpse of his eyes, she felt she would know him.

"Good girl." His fingers entered her again, this time from the front and the rough pad of his thumb swiped over her heated clit. Krisa cried out at the sharp pleasure, writhing beneath his touch as he continued to fuck into her, his thumb tormenting her over and over.

"Gonna make you come," the man with no face growled and his other hand found her breasts, twisting the nipples and making her gasp in pleasure. "Gonna make you come so hard you beg for it," he told her. "And then I'm gonna spread open that sweet wet cunt of yours and fuck you long and hard and slow. Gonna ride your pussy all night long, Krisa..."

~ ~ ~ ~ ~

"That damn dream again." Teague's voice woke her and she sat up in the darkness. He was sitting on his side of the mat, his eyes glowing a gentle silver in the black confines of the hut.

"Yes," Krisa admitted, uncertain what else to say. Had he come back to finish what they had started earlier. Had he come back to take her, to fill her, to fuck her? But there was no anger or passion in his silver eyes. Only resignation.

"Teague—" she began, but he obviously was in no mood to talk.

"Go to sleep." His deep voice sounded tired and the silver eyes blinked closed as he lay down with his back to her. "Long day tomorrow, so go to sleep, little girl."

The next day after the farewell breakfast at Vis' house they said their goodbyes to the Yss village and prepared to begin the long trip to the Palace of the Uneaten One, as Ziba proudly called the settlement of his father.

Krisa found tears in her eyes when she hugged Vis goodbye, thanking her haltingly in the hissing language she had barely begun to learn, for everything she had done. The Yss woman had touched her wet cheeks uncomprehendingly but gently—the Yss did not cry. Krisa wept for both of them, knowing she would probably never see her friend again.

"Come on, little girl. Time to go." Teague's voice was surprisingly gentle, despite the scene between them the night before. Then they left the village and found themselves back on the Yss path that led through the pastel jungle.

That first day on the path, Krisa wasn't sure if she was glad or sad that the moment between them the night before had passed. All day Teague treated her as though nothing had happened between them and it was easy to forget what had almost happened while he was teasing her with his usual sarcastic banter. But every once in a while she would feel an itching between her shoulder blades and would turn to see his eyes flashing hot silver as he stared at her. Whatever burned between them might have been put away for the present, but it was not forgotten, Krisa realized uneasily.

Things might have been different if they hadn't had Ziba with them, but the chief had asked Teague to return the half-Yss boy to his father as a favor and Teague had agreed. It was the least they could do for the Yss village that had sheltered and fed and clothed them for the past week. At least, Krisa thought, having Ziba with them helped to cut down on the tension between Teague and herself.

All during that first day the half-Yss boy skipped ahead and ran back, keeping up a steady chattering monologue that was alternately directed to herself, Teague and Tz, his pet targee. Krisa, who was again wearing Percy's old trousers and a pale yellow leather halter-top Vis had given her to travel in, wished she had half the boy's energy.

She had been apprehensive about traveling at first, knowing that the hunting parties that went out every day had never found any trace of the female soondar. But as the day went on and they had no trouble of any kind, she began to relax. That night Teague built a large fire not far from the path and made sure Ziba was close to it with his back to a small stream to be sure the boy would be safe. He spread his own blanket on the other side of the fire and then looked up at Krisa expectantly.

Feeling uncomfortable about his eyes on her, Krisa had spread her own blanket near Ziba's and away from Teague's. The half-Yss boy was already deeply asleep with his back to the fire, worn out with the excitement of running back and forth all day as they traveled. Tz was curled at the nape of Ziba's neck, pink fur fluffed out against the chilly night air. The targee blinked at her with large, sleepy liquid eyes that gleamed in the firelight.

Teague eyed her intended sleeping arrangements with a set jaw and then patted the ground between him and the fire. "Krisa, *come here*," he growled in a voice that would not be denied. She realized he hadn't relinquished the claim he had made on her the night before in the torch-lit circle at the Yss village.

Wordlessly, she got up, bringing her blanket to spread in front of Teague's. She lay down between him and the fire as she had on their first trip through the jungle and tried to relax as he pulled her close. He buried his face in her hair and she could feel his hot breath at the back of her neck as he kissed her there, biting gently with a fierce possessiveness that made her tremble.

Then a large, warm hand was pulling down the yellow halter-top and cupping her naked breasts, pinching and teasing the nipples until Krisa moaned low in her throat and tried to pull away.

"Tell me you don't want it, little girl. Tell me you don't want me to touch you like this and I'll stop," Teague growled softly into her ear. Krisa opened her mouth but nothing came out. "Didn't think so," he murmured, continuing to touch her. "Lie on your back so I can suck your sweet nipples."

Feeling helpless to deny him, Krisa did as he asked. Teague bent his head and she felt his hot breath blowing over her tight peaks for just a moment before he traced a pattern across her trembling flesh with his tongue. He kissed and nipped in ever widening circles, laving the outside of her breasts while avoiding the nipples until she thought she would go mad.

"Teague," she whispered at last, feeling her breath catch in her throat. "I thought you said you wanted to… I mean, you promised to…" She trailed off, unable to finish the request.

"I didn't promise you anything, little girl," he growled softly. "But tell me what you want and I might do it."

Krisa swallowed. "You said...you wanted to suck my nipples," she whispered at last, feeling the words catch in her throat.

Teague grinned at her. "I did, didn't I? The question is, little girl, do you want me to suck them?"

At a loss for words, Krisa nodded her head. But still Teague didn't move to do as she asked.

"No, Krisa," he said softly, "I want to hear you say it? Tell me what you want and I'll give it to you."

"I want...want..." Krisa swallowed hard, knowing it was wrong to ask but unable to control her longing. "Please, Teague, I want you to...suck my nipples," she whispered at last, her face blushing scarlet at her shameful request.

"It would be my pleasure. And yours too, I hope." Teague bent his head and sucked her right nipple, sucking as much of her breast into his mouth as he could and lapping at the stiff peak with his tongue until Krisa buried her hands in his hair and moaned.

"Goddess, Teague," she gasped, as he repeated the treatment on the other nipple. It seemed that when he sucked her like this, she could feel an electrical tingle of sensation that seemed to flow from the sensitive tips of her breasts right to her sex. Already she could feel her pussy lips getting swollen and wet and her clit was throbbing for release—the same kind of release Teague had given her at the last Yss feast.

As though reading her mind, he stopped sucking her nipples and looked at her face. "Krisa," he said in that deep, growling voice, "Do you remember what I told you while we were watching that last Yss couple at the feast? That when a man gets a woman hot enough, her pussy gets so wet it starts to open on its own?"

Fearing to say anything, Krisa only nodded.

"Well, tell me something, little girl," Teague growled, "If I made you spread your legs for me right now, is that what I'd see? Is your pussy all wet and hot for me?"

"I-I don't know," Krisa faltered, though she knew it was exactly what he would see. She felt so wet and hot and swollen that the tight material of her trousers was chafing her mercilessly between her legs. It was almost a relief when Teague pulled them down around her ankles and made her spread her thighs.

"Beautiful," he whispered, his voice unexpectedly soft as he studied her in the firelight. Krisa blushed and looked down at herself, seeing the glistening wetness between her thighs and the way her pussy lips were parting of their own volition, showing the hot pink insides of her sex in the dim light of the fire.

"Look at this." Teague traced the swollen lips of her pussy with one gentle finger, making her gasp and buck her hips for more. "Look at the way your little cunt gets so wet and open for me, Krisa. You're so hot I can see your clit without even spreading you." He demonstrated by running his fingertip along the side of the sensitive bundle of nerves, making Krisa jump and cry out breathlessly again.

Teague looked at her, his face unreadable in the fire's glow. "Does it feel good little girl, when I touch you like this? Do you like to feel my fingers spreading your cunt and petting your hot little clit?"

"Y-yes," Krisa stuttered, unable to say more.

Teague traced her clit again. "And would you like me to make you come?"

Unable to help herself, Krisa nodded. Goddess but she needed that feeling again, the feeling of his fingers tracing her clit and making her fly.

Teague leaned close and captured her mouth in a long hot kiss before pulling back to look at her once more. "Say it," he commanded. "I want to hear you say it."

"S-say what?" Krisa asked, though she was afraid she already knew.

"Say, 'Teague, I want you to spread open my pussy lips and stroke my clit until I come,'" he commanded.

Krisa shook her head. There was no way she could say such a thing. Such a dirty, improper... But Teague was withdrawing his hand. She moaned loudly. "Teague, *please*," she begged, shamelessly.

"Say it," he told her, his warm breath stirring the curls against her flushed cheek. "Say it, Krisa, if you want me to do it."

There was no other way. Looking down so she didn't have to meet his gaze, Krisa mumbled, "Teague, I want you to—"

"No," he interrupted her abruptly. "Look at me, Krisa. I want you to look me in the eye and ask me."

Lifting her chin she forced herself to meet his drowning silver gaze. "Teague," she began in a faltering voice. "I w-want you to spread my pussy lips open a-and stroke my clit until I come." She said it faster than she should have, rushing because it was so horribly embarrassing, but Teague seemed pleased.

"Good girl," he whispered, kissing her cheek. "That's exactly what I'm going to do. Now look down because I want you to watch me touch you, watch me finger your sweet little cunt until you come."

Trembling, Krisa did as he commanded. She watched as his long, thick fingers spread open the slippery lips of her pussy and saw the way he traced magical designs over and around her clit. The sight of his blunt fingertips stroking over the hot pink button at the center of her cunt was almost too much to bear. She could feel her arousal building, feel herself approaching the peak. But just as he was about to push her over, Teague stopped for a moment. Krisa moaned in protest but he bent to whisper in her ear.

"Now watch while I slide my fingers into your tight little cunt, Krisa. Watch me fuck your little pussy and imagine how it would feel if it was my cock instead of my fingers spreading you open right now."

Krisa bit her lip as his finger dipped into her narrow, virginal entrance. Watching them disappear inside her pussy and feeling the press of his fingertips against her maiden barrier was almost too much. Then Teague rubbed the broad pad of his thumb almost roughly over her ripe, aching clit and it *was* too much—too much to stand. Gasping and moaning, Krisa felt herself coming just as he had promised. Her juices flowed freely and Teague kissed her urgently as his fingers continued their delicious rhythm inside her cunt. He brought her to the peak again as he had the night before and she had to bite her lip hard to keep from crying out loud and waking Ziba and Tz.

"Love this, Krisa," he whispered in her ear, when most of the pleasure had abated, leaving a warm glow in the pit of her stomach. "Love the way you get so wet for me when I touch you, the way your pussy knows exactly what it needs from me, even if you don't."

"I know what I need from you," she tried to say, but the words wouldn't come out. Instead, she yawned sleepily.

"That's all right, little girl." Tenderly, Teague pulled up her trousers and fit her into the curve of his large, warm body. "Long day today and another long one tomorrow," he whispered into her hair.

Krisa wanted to tell him that she was wide awake and say again that she knew exactly what she needed from him. But as she drifted off to sleep, she realized that she didn't. Not at all.

* * * * *

After that, every night they traveled on the Yss path was the same. During the day Teague joked with her and Ziba and kept an eye out for the female soondar as they traveled along the long, winding path paved with flat pink and blue stones. At night, after the half-Yss boy and his pet targee had gone to sleep, he held Krisa close, kissed her and touched her until she reached the breathless peak he always brought her to.

After the first night Krisa didn't try to protest again. She wanted what he was giving her as badly as he seemed to want to give it. She put the idea of impropriety out of her head and tried not to think of how her body seemed to crave his touch more and more. Tried not to think about how even after the most earth-shattering climax, she felt an emptiness that only Teague's cock, sheathed within her to the hilt, could have filled—if only she could bring herself to ask him for it.

There were few words spoken between them at such times and the big Feral never tried to go further than touching and kissing her, though Krisa could feel his heavy shaft pressing against her through his black trousers, throbbing with need while he stroked her.

The message he seemed to be conveying was that, though he wouldn't take her against her will, he refused to lose the ground he had gained or give up the rights he had claimed over her body in the first place. Teague meant what he said— while she was on Planet X, Krisa belonged to him, and he took every opportunity to prove it.

And when he touched her that way, brought her hot and shivering to the peak every night, she stopped having the dream of the man with no face as often.

Other than the way Teague touched her, the trip from the Yss village to the settlement of his old shipmate, Sarskin, was perfectly unremarkable until their last night on the Yss path. That was the night of the attack.

When it happened, the night was almost over and the velvety darkness was receding slowly from the cloudy sky. Krisa was lying safe between the fire and Teague, encircled by his muscular arm. She had awakened a little earlier than usual and she was lying awake in the predawn gloom, thinking.

She looked sleepily into the remains of the fire, burned down to cherry-red coals and fluffy gray ash and waited for Teague and Ziba to wake up. This was their last night on the road and quite possibly her last night with Teague. If everything went according to plan he would get a fast ship from Sarskin and have her back to Prime very quickly.

Krisa felt confident that she would beat any search party Lord Radisson might have sent after her back to Lynix Prime by at least a week. And once on Prime, she intended to make the acquaintance of Dr. Alphonius T'lix, before she contacted her husband-to-be. To explain her sudden disappearance from Planet X and her appearance on Prime, she had concocted a story about kindly space-going missionaries, who had landed on Planet X to try and evangelize the savage natives and taken pity on her, bringing her to Lynix Prime unmolested, with her Certificate of Virginity intact.

Lord Radisson might insist on re-verifying her virginity, but that shouldn't pose any problem, as Teague was always very careful when he touched her...that way. So Krisa would sign the joining contract with her husband-to-be and Lord Radisson would be none the wiser about the dummy chip in her neck. Then she could live happily ever after.

Without Teague.

Krisa didn't know why the last thought made her want to cry. Teague had been so gentle that night, pressing hot-cinnamon kisses she knew she would never forget all over her face and neck, until she arched toward him, asking for what she needed with her body even though she still couldn't bring herself to ask with her voice. He had stroked her wet sex, long and slow, building her pleasure gradually and holding her off for a long time, so that when her climax came it was almost unbearably intense. Teague had caught her wild, ragged cries in his mouth, kissing her deeply over and over as Krisa had given herself up completely to his touch one last time.

Krisa stared into the dying coals and scolded herself. Yes, the past two and a half weeks with Teague had been wonderful and strange, in ways she could never have predicted when she first saw the huge Feral chained in the hold of the *Star Princess*. But it was time to get on with her real life—with the life she had been bred and raised for as the wife of Lord Radisson.

She felt the slow flow of tears warm and wet against her cheeks and gave a little half-sob in the darkness before she could stop herself. Teague made a noise in his sleep and pulled her closer. Krisa cuddled against him, breathing in his spicy scent. She tried not to think of how empty she would feel when she was on Prime and he was half the galaxy away where no one would ever find him.

Stop being so stupid. She was lecturing herself when a low noise split the early-morning gloom. But the noise wasn't coming from anywhere in the jungle—it was coming from inside Krisa's head.

Little one, the man thing has a little one, the hot-black voice that was unmistakably female snarled in her head. *I too had little ones, but when he slaughtered my mate there was no one to watch them while I hunted. Then the filthy green man-things from the village killed them.*

Krisa felt frozen in place—where was it coming from? Where was the soondar hiding in the jungle gloom that surrounded them? She started to elbow Teague awake, but then everything happened at once.

The deafening, mind-ripping roar of the angry soondar split the silence and Tz, who had been sleeping lightly, curled against his master's throat, awoke with a high, chattering scream and scampered into the jungle. Ziba, always attuned to his pet's least move, woke up with a cry the minute the targee left him. He stumbled to his feet before Krisa could stop him, and ran into the jungle after Tz, shouting in the guttural hissing Yss language.

By the time all this had happened and Krisa's elbow had connected with Teague's solid abdomen, the big Feral was already up, knife in hand, running after the boy.

"Ziba, come back. Not into the jungle!" Krisa heard him shout. Then she heard a high, triumphant roar and the soondar's voice in her head again.

Try and take him back, man-thing, she snarled. *I will carry him away where you can hear his screams but will never reach him. I will kill your young one as you killed mine. As you killed my mate!* Then there was a high-pitched wail that was unmistakably Ziba and a low, angry shout that sounded like Teague.

Krisa waded into the jungle after them, not bothering to put on the leather walking sandals Vis had given her. She knew it was probably stupid to go after Teague and Ziba unarmed, knew she might only get in the big Feral's way, but she simply couldn't wait by the fire and listen.

She stumbled through the undergrowth and pastel bracken that was becoming gradually visible as the unseen sun rose sluggishly above Planet X's cloudy horizon, praying that Teague and Ziba would be all right. *Goddess please, don't let her kill them.* Ahead there was the sound of shouting and snarling and a scream cut abruptly short that made her blood turn to ice in her veins. Yet though she ran on and on for a nightmarishly long time, Krisa couldn't find the source of the noises.

Then everything was suddenly, horribly silent and she could only hear the sobbing of her own breath in her throat as she crashed aimlessly through the underbrush of the pastel jungle. "Teague," she called as loudly as she could. She was aware that if the soondar had killed him, she might very well be next, but she didn't care a bit. "Teague, Ziba, where are you?" *Oh please, Goddess, don't let them be dead.*

But it wasn't Teague or Ziba who answered her. There was a high, squeaking chatter and suddenly a small, pink puffball landed on her shoulder from a nearby tree. Krisa was startled, she gave a breathless little scream and tried to shake it off, but then she recognized the big liquid eyes of Tz.

"Tz," she whispered softly, plucking the little animal off her shoulder and cupping it carefully in her palms. "Tz, is that you?" The targee chattered in a tiny, frightened voice and trembled in her hands. Its liquid eyes were wide and terrified. Krisa knew just how it felt.

"Tz," she whispered, feeling tears come as she stood alone in the middle of the jungle. "Tz, I can't find them anywhere and they don't answer when I call. Teague is gone and so is Ziba."

At the sound of his master's name, the little targee seemed to perk up and its trembling ceased. Krisa thought she might have been wrong but it seemed that the bright eyes were a little less terrified. "Ziba," she said again as an experiment, blinking back her tears. This time the targee's entire body came to attention and she could have sworn that it was looking at her expectantly. Krisa began to have an idea.

This is probably stupid, she told herself. *Probably watched too many animal rescue-vids at Briar Rose.* Heartwarming animal rescues vids were some of the few programs on the "approved viewing list". But stupid or not, it was the only idea she had. Carefully placing the targee on the ground Krisa said as clearly as she could, "Tz, find Ziba. *Ziba.*"

Before the half-Yss boy's name had passed her lips the second time, Tz was off in a shot, just a blur of pink fur in the undergrowth. Krisa crashed after the targee madly, not minding the vines and creepers that whipped her in the face, or the sharp brambles tearing her bare feet as she ran. She thought she had lost Tz several times, but every time the targee scampered back for her, leading her deeper and deeper into the jungle.

At last, when she had a stitch in her side and knew she couldn't go much father, Krisa followed Tz into a clearing. Stumbling, she bent for a moment to catch her breath with her hand on the trunk of a tall, purple finger-tree, only to hear the targee's insistent chatter.

"Just a minute, Tz, I can't—" she gasped, not even thinking of how stupid it was to be talking to an animal. But another noise stopped her in mid-sentence. A high, soft keening was coming from the far side of the clearing.

The sky overhead had brightened to its usual dull bronze and when Krisa looked up she could see that Ziba was sitting, half hidden in the shadows of the pastel underbrush. His head was lifted to the sky, as he made the unearthly sound of grief that sent shivers of dread up and down her spine.

"Ziba!" she cried, running behind the ecstatic, pink puffball that was Tz, who was scrambling on tiny, clawed feet to get back to his master. She crashed through the underbrush that half hid the boy, words of excitement trembling on her lips, but what she saw robbed her of all speech.

Lying in the brush to one side of the clearing was the huge form of the female soondar and lying beside her, twisted in an unnatural position, was Teague.

Neither one was moving.

Chapter Sixteen

ॐ

"Teague," she whispered through numb lips. There was no response. Krisa made herself go closer, though she had never wanted to do anything less in her life. The big body that had given her shelter and protection in the darkest jungle nights, that had given her such sweet pleasure while Teague asked for nothing in return, was silent, unmoving. His eyes were closed and though she tried to see if his chest was moving up and down, Krisa couldn't tell in the shadows of the pastel vegetation that surrounded him and the huge carcass of the soondar.

"The Teague...he will not speak. Krisalaison, he be—"

"Don't say it," Krisa said sharply, sparing Ziba the briefest of glances. His unearthly keening had stopped and Tz was on his shoulder again, anxiously licking his master's face with a little pink leaf of a tongue. She knew she should stop and examine the half-Yss boy to see if he was injured in any way, but she couldn't seem to think of anything but the still form of the big Feral lying in the undergrowth.

She made herself go closer and saw that the huge knife with the curving silver blade was still clutched in one hand although the blade was dull and sticky with a black, viscous liquid that must be the soondar's blood. But there was red blood too, she saw, moving closer—bright crimson liquid painting his dusky skin a hideously cheerful color. So much blood—too much blood. Suddenly she realized he was still bleeding.

From a rip in the black trousers, now sodden with it, blood was pulsing from a gash in his inner thigh. Krisa had a sudden flash. *If he's still bleeding, if his heart's still pumping blood, then wouldn't that mean he's still...alive?*

"Teague... *Teague!*" She knelt beside him, all hesitation gone now and slapped him lightly on both cheeks. At first he was still and silent, but then she was rewarded with a low groan. Krisa noticed with distress that the dusky tan of his skin had taken on a whitish pallor. *Well, of course he's getting pale, Krisa,* the practical voice in her head spoke up. *He's still losing blood.* Krisa looked in alarm from the broad planes of his face to the jagged wound in his thigh that was still pumping blood steadily. Teague wasn't dead yet, but he soon would be if she couldn't stop that steady flow.

Once again cursing her Briar Rose education which didn't include anything in the way of first aid, Krisa grabbed both sides of the ragged fabric and yanked, making the hole bigger so that she could see the wound better. The gash looked deep and ragged, it had probably been made by one of the soondar's claws. Desperately, Krisa pressed her hands over it, trying to halt the sticky, warm flow of crimson that leaked over her fingers. It seemed to slow after a moment but she knew it wouldn't be possible for her to keep applying such steady pressure for long—her arms ached already from pressing down as hard as she could.

Think, Krisa! the practical part of her commanded. There had to be a better way to stop the flow. She tried to remember something from all the smuggled copies of *LifeLink* she had watched at Briar Rose when she and Maida were sure the dorm mother was asleep. Hadn't there been an episode where Ben Fulsome, the handsome doctor, had found someone pinned beneath a hovercraft and had to save an arm or a leg somehow? What had he done? He'd taken off his belt and cinched it tightly. Now what was that called? *Doesn't matter if you remember the name or not—just do it!*

"Ziba," she yelled, breaking the stillness of the jungle morning. "Come here and help me."

The sharp command in her voice must have motivated the half-Yss boy, for he came over quickly enough and looked at her with wide, hopeful eyes. There was a ragged rip in the back of his gray-green vest and she realized that the soondar must have caught him there to drag him into the jungle. Thank the Goddess it had grabbed his vest and not an arm or a leg, she thought distractedly.

"Yes, Krisalaison?" he asked softly.

"Help me get his belt off," Krisa commanded. Ziba looked at her questioningly but did as he was told. Teague was dead weight, though he groaned occasionally, giving her hope that at least she wasn't too late. At last the black leather belt came free, and Krisa was able to cinch it tightly above the ragged gash in his thigh. By then her hands and arms were red to the elbows and the yellow halter-top Vis had given her had turned almost orange. As for Percy's expensive tailored trousers — if they had been in bad shape before, they were a complete loss now. Even the tips of her hair were bloody, but Krisa didn't care.

Once the belt was tightened and the bleeding stopped, Krisa turned her attention to bringing the big Feral back to consciousness. If she and Ziba were ever going to get him back to the path it would have to be with his help, he was simply too big to move otherwise.

"Teague," she said sharply, slapping his cheeks. "Teague, wake up. You have to wake up."

He groaned, eyelids fluttering, showing flashes of silver and black as he came back slowly. "Wha..." his voice was groggy and uncertain. "Where?"

"In the middle of the jungle and we have to get you out," Krisa answered with more certainty than she felt. "Come on, Teague. Can you sit up?"

Later she thought it was one of the most difficult things she'd ever done, the walk back through the thick jungle, after getting the big Feral on his feet and in motion. Teague had lost a lot of blood, more than enough to keep him unconscious or at least immobile, but by leaning heavily on Krisa, he was able to get up and start back to the camp. Neither one of them was strong enough to break trail, so they had to push through the tangled bracken and undergrowth as best they could with a very subdued Ziba in tow.

Krisa wasn't at all sure she could even find their camp, which was close by the path between the Yss village and Sarskin's settlement, but once again, Tz came in handy. The little targee put his tiny snout in the air and sniffed, then ambled off at a slow but steady pace they could keep up with and led them back to where the whole nightmare had started not two hours before.

By the time they got back, Krisa was nearly exhausted and she could see by the grayish cast of Teague's dusky skin tones and the drawn look on his face that he was as well. They stumbled out of the jungle and he collapsed wearily on the pile of disarranged blankets, the wounded leg sticking stiffly out in front of him. Krisa forced herself to dig into the stores and pull out the dried meat and fruit and several containers of water and they had a belated and much-needed breakfast in near total silence.

Teague broke the silence at last when they had finished eating. The day was beginning to get hot and Krisa was glad they were situated in the shade.

"You and Ziba will have to go on alone," he said, after taking a long drink from the plasti-squeeze bottle of water they had brought all the way from the *Star Princess.*

"I'm not leaving you," Krisa said at once. She had been using a little of the water to wash some of his blood from her arms and hands, but now she stopped, focusing narrowly on the big Feral.

"You have to," Teague replied. "There's no way I can keep going in this condition. It's midmorning already. If you and Ziba leave right now, you'll make Sarskin's compound by full dark—barely. Then you can send help back."

"And leave you alone and covered in blood most of the night, while they come back to get you? Absolutely not, Teague. You wouldn't leave me or Ziba if the situation was reversed." Krisa crossed her arms over the bloody halter-top and frowned.

Teague sighed in exasperation and shifted stiffly on the blanket. "Listen, sweetheart, if the situation was reversed I could *carry* you or Ziba and we could keep going. I appreciate the sentiment but I don't think you're up to returnin' the favor."

"I haven't done too badly so far," Krisa said defiantly, indicating his still belted leg.

Teague smiled grudgingly and nodded approval. "Yeah, I'll admit that was quick thinkin' with the tourniquet. Guess you *did* learn a few worthwhile things at your school."

Tourniquet—that's what it's called. Krisa wasn't about to admit she'd gotten the idea from smuggled *LifeLink* vids, so she only nodded stiffly, acknowledging his thanks. "The point is I'm not leaving you here alone to become a soondar snack," she said.

"So you're gonna stay here and protect me?" Teague looked grimly amused. "Listen, little girl, all you could do if you stayed is give me two more people to worry about."

Krisa was silent. She hadn't considered how exactly she would help Teague by staying, she only knew that she was determined not to leave him in the jungle alone.

"Come here," Teague said, beckoning with one large hand. Unwillingly, Krisa scooted closer to him on the blanket so that she was face-to-face with the big Feral. He looked tired and drawn and the opaque black second lid made his eyes two pools of midnight in his dark face. Teague reached out and cupped her cheek in one large, warm palm.

"Krisa," he said, the deep voice gentling a bit. "All you could do if you stayed is die with me. I don't want that. I couldn't protect you the way I'd need to in the shape I'm in now. I want you to go and take Ziba with you. All right?"

"Teague," she whispered, feeling the tears build in her throat, a hateful pressure she knew she couldn't long hold back. "I don't want to leave you here helpless."

Teague grinned, the white savage grin that had frightened her so much when she first saw him chained in the hold of the *Star Princess*. "Didn't I tell you once before not to make the mistake of thinkin' I'm helpless, little girl?" he growled softly. "Just get to Sarskin's settlement as fast as you can. If I know Sarskin, he'll have some kind of a backup ship or hovercraft stowed close for a quick getaway. The sooner you get there, the sooner you can send back help."

Kris felt a new flare of hope in her heart. Of course, Teague's old shipmate was a smuggler. Sarskin wouldn't have to send a party back on foot. "Why didn't you say so in the first place?" she said almost angrily, pulling away from his hand and rubbing fiercely at her eyes.

"Didn't think of it," he admitted. "It's easy to think of the Yss as primitive, especially after spendin' a week with them like we have, but Sarskin's always been big on havin' all the modern conveniences. Besides—" he grinned again, not quite so widely. "Maybe I just wanted to know if you cared."

"Oh, you…" Krisa made as though to slap him but he caught her wrist easily in one hand and placed the hilt of his huge, curving knife into her palm.

"Take this," he said, quietly. "In case you don't make the compound by dark."

"No, absolutely not." Krisa dropped the knife in his lap and crossed her arms over her chest. "I refuse to leave you here with no weapon. We'll make it."

"Take it, you can't defend yourself with that ridiculous hairpin," Teague argued.

Krisa shook her head defiantly. "I couldn't with your knife either. I don't know the first thing about knife fighting and you know it. We'll just *have* to get there in time.

"Ziba," she called and the half-Yss boy who had been sitting in a kind of daze across the burned-out remains of their campfire looked up at her.

"Yes, Krisalaison?" he asked, stroking Tz's soft fur with a distracted hand.

"You've traveled this path before. How far are we from your sire's village?" Krisa demanded.

Ziba sat up a bit, life coming back to his narrow, pale eyes. "A day's walk from dawn 'til dusk—if we be in a hurry as we go," he affirmed.

From dawn 'til dusk, Krisa thought distractedly. But it was almost afternoon now. They would have to hurry.

Teague must have seen the frantic determination in her eyes because he pulled her back to the blanket beside him when she tried to get up.

"Listen to me, Krisa—you'll have to pace yourself. You can't run all day in this heat without getting exhausted so don't try. Just walk fast and rest when you need to. Don't worry about me, I can take care of myself as long as I don't have you and the boy to worry about. Understand?"

"You're always asking me that," Krisa whispered through numb lips, watching the play of shadows from the overhanging leaves on his dark, sharp features. "But ever since I met you it seems like I don't understand anything anymore." Grabbing his face in both hands she kissed him fiercely on the lips, trying to put as much of her tangled emotions into the gesture as she could.

Teague was caught off guard for a moment and then he reached for her, pulling her across himself to straddle his unhurt leg. He kissed her back with an intensity that took her breath away. "I'll be waiting for you, little girl," he growled softly, letting her go at last. "Don't disappoint me." Black eyes flickered to reveal silver as he spoke.

"I won't," Krisa said, meaning it with her whole heart. Turning her head she said, "Come on, Ziba. We have to get moving."

Chapter Seventeen

ဢ

The whole day was one long, hot nightmare of walking when she wanted to be running, pushing herself and Ziba to the limit and wondering how long they had before the dull, bronze sky turned an ominous, burnt umber and then went full dark. It was going to be close, Krisa thought, but they would make it—they *had* to.

They would have too, if Ziba hadn't fallen into the pit.

"Krisalaison…there it is, the finger of the gods!" Ziba was pointing excitedly at a huge, pale monolith rising straight up by the side of the path, as they rounded a corner. "It is the sign that we be close to the village of my sire." He ran ahead excitedly, Tz chattering in his hair, to place his slim, six-fingered hands against the smooth sides of the rounded stone.

"Th-the what?" Krisa asked. She was nearing exhaustion from the grueling pace they had been traveling all day, her brain buzzing with worry and conflicted emotion. The half-Yss boy's words didn't register at first.

"The finger of the gods," Ziba repeated impatiently. "Long ago my sire saw this stone from the heavens and knew it was the place he must come. Here is where he held the Haulder-Lenz with the Teague and here he became the Uneaten One."

"So this is…some kind of a landmark?" It was at last penetrating Krisa's tired brain that they were nearing Sarskin's compound. It was a good thing too, because in the last half-hour the sky had turned noticeably darker. Slowly, she approached the stone monolith where Ziba was impatiently waiting for her to catch up, dancing from foot to foot. Tz had caught his master's enthusiasm and the little targee was chattering and shrieking with excitement on top of Ziba's dark head.

"Yes, it is sacred to my people." Ziba continued, circling around the wide base of the impossibly tall stone pillar now. "It means we be very close! Soon we—"

But the words suddenly became a scream as he disappeared behind the finger of stone.

"Ziba!" Krisa rushed around the huge stone, expecting to find that he had twisted an ankle and almost fell into a deep pit that was completely hidden from view by the base of the pillar. "Oh, my Goddess...Ziba?" Krisa knelt carefully near the lip of the pit, uncertain if it was Yss-made or some kind of a natural sinkhole. Some twelve or fifteen feet down in the well of darkness she could make out the white blur of a frightened face staring back up at her.

"Krisalaison?" Ziba's voice was faint, but at least he hadn't been knocked unconscious.

"Ziba, are you all right?"

"I-I think my ankle be hurt someway," the thin voice answered. "But Tz be fine." The high, angry chattering of his pet targee corroborated this statement.

"Can you climb back up?" Krisa asked doubtfully. Even if the boy hadn't hurt himself in the fall, the walls of the pit seemed awfully steep. Ziba tried gamely, but soon had to admit defeat. Tz had no problems with the steep sides however and the pink puffball clung to the sheer sides and chattered encouragement to his young master.

"I cannot do it, Krisalaison," the boy admitted at last, calling his pet targee back reluctantly. "But my sire's village is not far up the path. You must get help. Here—take Tz. My sire will know him." He cupped the targee between his palms and whispered softly for a few moments, then urged the little creature to climb the steep sides of the pit toward Krisa.

"I'll be right back," Krisa promised, collecting Tz and placing him on her shoulder where he sat very subdued and quiet.

"Hurry, Krisalaison! Soon it is dark and the soondar will hunt." Ziba's voice was faint but clear in the motionless evening air. As if to confirm his words, Krisa suddenly heard the high, howling chatter of a band of wild targees in the nearby jungle. The sound caused Tz to sit up straight and add his own squeaky, chattering voice to the eerie chorus, sending a cold shiver of fear down her spine.

She stood and looked around her, the sky to her left was a deep, burnt umber. The strange, orange twilight of Planet X had fallen in the few minutes she had spent talking to Ziba down in the pit. Now she had two people depending on her to make it on time. Teague and Ziba would both be easy prey for a hunting soondar once the hidden sun of Planet X dropped below the horizon.

It was going to be a race between her and the slowly sinking sun. Krisa made her way to the path and set off at a dead run.

Of course it reminded her of the first night on Planet X, when she and Teague had run for their lives from the hunting soondar pack, but it was so much worse this time. This time she was all alone and there was no one to pick her up when she got tired, or help her if she stumbled. And it wasn't just her own life she was trying to save, though Krisa was aware that there was still quite enough of Teague's blood dried into her clothes to attract the hunting soondar. This time the life of a little boy and the man she loved depended on her success. *Wait a minute – the man I love? Teague?*

But there was no time to examine the strange thought. There was only time to run and run Krisa did.

It seemed to take forever, racing the unseen sun in the sky. With every bend in the road she expected to see the welcoming torches of the Yss village and was disappointed with only another curve leading into the dusky gloom of the jungle twilight.

The breath was burning in her lungs and she was stumbling from exhaustion, the path barely visible under her feet, when Krisa at last caught sight of a group of torches in front of her. Then a blur of pale green faces appeared in the dusk, standing outside a high, pointed wooden fence.

"Lasthnk!" Krisa gasped breathlessly, hoping she was getting the slippery pronunciation right.

"Lieblick thaslink?" One of the warrior guards was questioning her but Krisa only shook her head, panting.

"Histhanik Krialaison, shebas das Teague." *My name is Krisa Elyison. I am the woman of Teague.* It was one of the few phrases Teague himself had taught her, teaching her the pronunciation before admitting what it meant, which had made Krisa angry at the time, especially when she found out what he had her saying. She motioned to the excited pink targee hopping and chattering on her shoulder. "Tz das Ziba. Please, I need to see Sarskin the Uneaten One. *Sarskin!*"

The urgency of her words got through to the warriors as well as the name of their offworlder chief's son and Krisa found herself being led through the torch light. The Yss took her to a large structure in the center of the village, built not of clay or straw, but of the same pastel stones that paved the path in the forest. This must be the palace of the Uneaten One. It was certainly more palatial than any other residence she had yet seen on Planet X.

She was dragged inside, seeing blurred glimpses of rich gelafoam furnishings, jarringly juxtaposed with traditional Yss implements, like the ubiquitous grass floor mats. Also, now that she was in a lighted area, she could see that some of the native Yss seemed to be wearing offworlder clothing but in very peculiar ways.

One of her guards was wearing what once must have been a nicely tailored pair of trousers, but he had split the seams in the legs, so that they hung and flapped free around his waist like a strange kind of skirt. Another had on a cincher, but as a type of hat, it stuck up from the top of his head comically in a fold of stiff fabric. Another was wearing a long crinoline underskirt as a type of frilly cape. Krisa couldn't take it all in, just trying made her head hurt.

At last she was led into a large, central room with marble floors and richly paneled walls. Sitting at an elaborately carved desk, jacked into an intra-orbital monitor, was a man that could only have been Teague's old shipmate, Sarskin. He was, as Teague had described him, immensely fat with long, dark brown hair tied back in a twist of grass. He had a small pink, almost girlish mouth, which was currently pursed in concentration, as he went over the figures the monitor was scrolling behind his eyes. All of Krisa's guards started talking and motioning at once and the man looked up with irritation.

"What? How am I supposed to hear if you all talk at once? One at a time." He unjacked himself carefully from the intra-orbital monitor and turned his attention to Krisa. "Well, well…and who might you be, my dear?"

Sarskin was fat enough that Krisa was glad he hadn't gone completely native. Instead of the traditional Yss loincloth and vest, he was dressed in yards and yards of rich brocade which glimmered softly in the muted lighting of the room. He had very dark eyes that twinkled in the dim light of the immense marble room. Krisa thought he looked like the fat and jolly Father Joy they always used to have at Briar Rose, handing out presents during the Winter Solstice.

"I'm Krisa Elyison, and you're Sarskin. You *are* Sarskin, aren't you?"

"Not many here call me by that name but yes, I am he. How may I help you, my dear?"

It seemed to take forever to explain but to Krisa's relief, Sarskin grasped the particulars of what she was saying almost at once and he didn't question anything she told him either. It was wonderful to see how quickly he acted on her information. Before she knew it, one group of warriors had been sent to collect Ziba, taking Tz with them and she was riding in the back of what Sarskin assured her was his fastest hovercraft. There was a second group of Yss warriors, armed to the teeth, as well as Sarskin himself, coming with her to get Teague.

But the delay with Ziba had cost her. It was now full dark and had been for the best part of an hour. Krisa knew that no matter how fast the car went, it would still take them at least two more hours to reach the big Feral. She felt exhausted both emotionally and physically, but as the loaded craft slid smoothly over the same path she had run that day, she found she couldn't allow herself to relax until she knew that Teague was safe. *Please Goddess – let him be safe.*

"Tell me about yourself, my dear. Your clothing notwithstanding, you seem to be a genteel sort of young lady. Not the sort my old shipmate would generally come in contact with, if you'll pardon my saying so."

"Oh…" Krisa looked up from her hands which were dirty from her long trip and rough from a week of working with the Yss women. There was dried blood under her fingernails — Teague's blood. *You can always tell a true lady by her hands,* Madame Ledoux's voice whispered in her ear. No one seeing her ragged appearance in the dirty, blood-splattered clothes would think she was an elite Briar Rose bride, but this man had picked up on her social status at once.

"If you prefer not to talk I quite understand. I was simply trying to take your mind off your worries, my dear," Sarskin said gently. "Let me urge you, however, not to worry overmuch about Teague. If there was ever any man who could take care of himself in any situation it's my old shipmate."

Krisa looked at him gratefully and tried to smile. More than ever he looked like the kindly Father Joy from the Briar Rose Solstice parties. Teague had spoken of the man as though he was dependable, but not very pleasant. But she found

Sarskin's large, solid presence immensely comforting somehow.

"I'm just— I had to leave him alone and wounded and it's been full dark for almost two hours now," she half whispered, looking down at her hands again.

"Ah, but Ferals have remarkable regenerative powers, as I dare say you've noticed. No matter what condition you left him, I'm sure by the time night fell he would have healed enough to be more than able to defend himself."

"You-you're not just saying that to make me feel better?" Krisa asked, wanting with her whole heart to believe him. Feeling more hopeful, she remembered the way Teague's cuts and bruises seemed to heal so much faster than her own, on their first run through the jungle.

Sarskin put one plump hand to his chest, dark eyes wide in the faint glow of the hovercraft's instruments. "Didn't my old shipmate tell you about me, my dear? I am Drusinian, we are genetically incapable of telling an untruth or breaking our word. I honestly think Teague will be fine."

"Thank you," Krisa whispered, blinking back tears of exhaustion and worry. Sarskin had been living on Planet X for eight years, she reminded herself. So if he said that Teague was probably all right, he probably was. She hoped.

"Tell me, however did you two meet?" Sarskin's plump hand found her own and held it with a warm, firm pressure that was wonderfully reassuring.

Krisa opened her mouth to make a polite reply and somehow found herself telling the Drusinian everything. How she had first met Teague chained in the hold of the *Star Princess*, her fight with Captain Ketchum, the chastity chip, the crash landing on Planet X and everything that had followed. Sarskin was silent throughout her story, only making small, encouraging noises to indicate his interest and urge her on. Krisa was surprised what a relief it was to pour out the story to an impartial and sympathetic listener as the hovercraft sped on through the blackness of the Planet X night.

"And so he took you with him, into the jungle?" Sarskin asked at last, when she described her escape from her sleep cube and the way Teague had dealt with Captain Ketchum's second attempt on her virginity.

"He saved my life," Krisa said seriously. "If he hadn't taken me the soondar would have smelled me for sure."

"Yes, a soondar on the scent of blood is quite a relentless creature," Sarskin acknowledged. "But they generally won't approach a foreign object, especially one so large and threatening as a merchant-class ship. Still, maybe Teague didn't want to take a chance."

Krisa looked at him, surprised. Was he trying to say that she could safely have stayed with the *Star Princess* until a rescue party arrived? "Still, he kept me safe in the jungle, protected me..." A lump formed in her throat when she remembered the warm shelter of Teague's big body curled around her own. She was so emotionally and physically exhausted she felt she might cry at any time.

"And he plans to just let you go back to your husband-to-be as soon as you acquire a ship?" Was it Krisa's imagination or was there a touch of incredulity in the Drusinian's voice?

"Well, yes...that is the plan," she answered hesitantly. "He was hoping to borrow a ship from you, actually," she added, uncertain if she ought to broach the subject or not.

"Oh certainly—that won't be a problem but I hope you don't think I keep my ships anywhere near the compound. There may be a delay in getting one, as I'm a little short-handed right now."

Wonderful, more delays. But Krisa found she couldn't care about that right now. "How long do you think until we find him?" she asked, anxiously.

"Oh, any moment now, I should think," Sarskin replied, releasing her hand and settling more comfortably in the comfort-foam chair. "In all probability he'll smell us before we see him. Wonderful sense of smell they have, these Ferals. Give any bloodhound a run for their credit."

"Mmm," Krisa mumbled politely. She had a quick image of Teague inhaling her scent and saying, *You want it, little girl,* and shivered.

"Fascinating species," Sarskin mused, as if to himself. "Did you know they pick a mate based entirely on smell? And once they do they're quite aggressive and almost insanely territorial. More animal than man, really."

"N-no, I didn't," Krisa answered, feeling a little uneasy. Sarskin's words stirred a memory in her mind. Someone else had said something similar to her. But who? Her overtired brain wouldn't let her remember.

Krisa put it out of her mind. Sarskin was probably just making small talk to distract her. Really, it was very kind of him, she needed distraction badly just now. She was staring out the hovercraft windows into the darkened night and one thought kept pounding over and over in her brain. *What if we missed him? Or what if he's not there?* They had been driving for quite a while now and it seemed as though she ought to recognize something, but everything outside the window was just a big, dark blur.

"They can be fairly ruthless, Ferals, fiercely loyal and ferociously competitive. I saw that for myself when Teague and I had our little disagreement. I assume he told you about *that* at least."

That got her full attention. Teague had never elaborated on what had provoked the Haulder-Lenz—the duel to the death—with his old shipmate.

"A little," Krisa said carefully. "But he didn't tell me why you argued in the first place."

Sarskin shrugged, an oddly graceful motion for such a mountainous man. "A mere impediment of culture, my dear.

A philosophical disagreement more than anything else. Water over the dam now, of course."

Krisa was disappointed—she had been hoping for something in the way of details. If anything, Sarskin's explanation of the disagreement was more oblique than Teague's had been. She opened her mouth to say so, but just then she saw something outside the window that drove everything else out of her mind.

"Stop! Stop the craft!" she yelled and the Yss who was driving, the one wearing the cincher on top of his head like an odd sort of hat, slammed on the air brakes so hard she nearly went through the windshield. At Sarskin's direction, he backed up a few yards and turned the hovercraft's high beams onto the pile of bloody, discarded blankets and the pack of supplies by the side of the path, exactly where Krisa had left them that morning.

Of Teague there was no sign.

Chapter Eighteen

ဩ

"Teague! *Teague!*" Krisa was out of the hovercraft and running before anyone could stop her. She barely glanced at the bloody blankets—he wasn't there. Therefore he must be somewhere in the jungle. *Please, Goddess, still alive somewhere in the jungle!*

"Miss Elyison, please come back! It really isn't safe." But Sarskin's well-meant warnings fell on deaf ears. All Krisa knew was that she had to find him, that he had to be here somewhere. She crashed through the underbrush blindly, calling his name over and over in a voice growing hoarse with fatigue. Vines and creepers whipped her face, but she barely noticed. Over and over she kept seeing Teague's body in that stiff, unnatural position, the way she had found him that morning by the dead female soondar. What if she found him that way again, but this time he wouldn't wake up?

"Teague! Oh, please Goddess… Teague, where are you?"

A pair of large, warm hands grabbed her by the shoulders, stopping her forward progress. For a moment Krisa struggled wildly and then a deep voice rumbled in her ear, "Right here—I'm right here, sweetheart. It's all right, settle down."

"Teague!" she nearly sobbed. She wanted to wrap her arms around him but he held her at arm's length, eyes gleaming silver in the darkness. The rest of him was invisible in the gloom.

"Don't, Krisa. I'm all covered with—"

But she didn't care what he was covered with. Struggling free with a little sob, Krisa wrapped her arms as far around the broad back as they would go and held on tight. Teague's natural musk was muted by a bitter, metallic tang and when she touched his skin it was damp and sticky. None of that mattered. Standing on tiptoes she buried her face in his shoulder and struggled to hold back the tears. Her eyes burned with exhaustion and her body trembled with released tension. He was here, he was all right.

"I ran…as fast as I could, but Ziba fell in a hole—he's all right—but it slowed me down. I was so afraid I'd be too late…"

"Hush, little girl." Teague rocked her gently, holding her close and tight. "Everything's fine, now."

Then Krisa felt the big body stiffen against her own and Teague's voice changed from a low croon to a harder tone. "Well, well, Sarskin. It's been a while."

"Longer than I had ever anticipated, certainly. Why have you made yourself so scarce, old friend?"

Krisa looked over her shoulder to see the large, dark figure of the Drusinian struggling through the underbrush, aided by two Yss. One was breaking trail with a long, sharp knife and the other was holding a halogen spot to light the way.

"I had my reasons," Teague growled, still standing stiff. He was obviously on his guard. "Do you come with peaceful intentions, Sarskin?"

"I came on an errand of mercy to rescue an old friend." Sarskin's voice was soft and appeasing. "What could be more peaceful than that?"

"You haven't answered my question," Teague growled menacingly, moving to put himself between Sarskin and Krisa. She looked at him questioningly, why was he acting this way?

Sarskin sighed sorrowfully, as though this lack of trust from his old shipmate cut him deeply. "Prickly as ever, I see. You have no need to worry about me, Teague. I come with peaceful intentions toward you and your woman."

Krisa looked at him uncomprehendingly. Hadn't she just explained on the hovercraft that Teague was only watching out for her until she could get to Prime where she belonged?

"Shut your mouth, Sarskin, and don't talk about things you don't understand," Teague snarled.

The mountainous Drusinian bowed apologetically. Again, it was an oddly graceful gesture for such a large man, though it was performed in the dense, rustling underbrush of the jungle. Behind her in the distance, Krisa suddenly heard the high, warning note of the wild targees, signaling the approach of a hunting soondar pack.

"I suggest we continue this conversation in a safer area," Sarskin remarked, apparently completely unruffled by the spine-tingling sound. "If you would follow me?" He nodded gracefully at them and turned to make his way out of the jungle, not bothering to see if they would follow.

Teague let him get a head start and then moved just as unhurriedly to follow, keeping a firm grip on Krisa's hand.

"Teague," she hissed, stumbling over a root in the darkness.

"What?" He kept her on her feet with little or no effort and then brought her closer and put an arm around her, so that he could guide her steps in the darkness. Bracken crunched underfoot as they made their way back to the path.

"Why did you act like that? He's been nothing but nice." Krisa shrugged the arm off her shoulder and stumbled again.

Teague grabbed her upper arm and hauled her upright, none too gently. He was limping heavily, she noticed. It was too dark to see if the belt was still cinched around his thigh. "I have my reasons, sweetheart," he growled shortly. "Sarskin and I go way back, don't worry about it."

"I still don't understand why—"

"Later," Teague snapped. They reached the edge of the dense vegetation and made their way out on the relative safety of the path as he spoke.

Krisa, who had been so glad to see him moments before, felt herself tightening up inside. Why did he have to treat her like this? Like an outsider, someone who didn't deserve to know what was going on? Tears of frustration and weariness prickled behind her eyelids but she refused to give Teague the satisfaction of seeing her cry.

"Fine," she said shortly, pulling away from him again. Sarskin and the Yss were already in the hovercraft, waiting for them.

Teague stopped on the path, turning to face her. In the dim lights of the hovercraft, now turned toward Sarskin's compound, she could see that his face was smeared with some black, viscous substance, as was the rest of his skin. No wonder he had been all but invisible in the blackness of the jungle. "I have a good reason for everything I do, little girl. Trust me," he said in a low voice.

Trust him. Well, what choice did she have? What had she been doing but trusting him, since the minute she stepped out of the jagged hold in the hull of the *Star Princess* and started this crazy journey? Krisa took a deep breath and decided she was just too tired to fight with him.

"What's all over your skin?" she asked instead, noticing with distaste that it was all over her as well, wherever she had come in contact with the big Feral.

"Soondar blood," he answered and laughed at the look of disgust on her face. "Told you not to hug me. It's camouflage, a hungry pack of soondar is less likely to attack another soondar than a man. I smelled like them so they left me alone."

"But that would mean you went all the way back in the jungle." Krisa shuddered at the idea of him dragging himself back to the dead soondar carcass and bathing in the huge creature's blood, after she and Ziba had gone.

"It wasn't pretty but I did what I had to do," Teague said with a shrug. "C'mon, Sarskin's waiting."

Krisa must have fallen asleep on the way back to the compound, because she only heard snatches of the conversation between Teague and Sarskin, as the hovercraft hummed above the broad Yss path.

"Good thing you heal fast. Last medic ran away with my only dependable pilot a month ago."

"...a ship. One that doesn't take too long to go to hyperdrive."

"...at least a week unless you want to get it yourself...forty klicks away...security reasons...sure you must understand."

"Fine. Day or two for this leg...soondar carcasses if your Yss want them."

"...back tomorrow and see if there's anything left...quite a feast...excited as children."

"...haven't sold any of your *children*?"

"...know I am incapable...breaking my word...quite fond of them."

"...believe it when I see it...certainly...colorful outfits."

"...let them dress as they like...at least as fond of them...you are that little girl...really taking her to Prime?"

"...her out of this."

Krisa wanted to wake up and ask what they were talking about, but exhaustion made her eyelids feel like they had lead weights tied to them. Heedless of the fact that she and Teague were getting the oily black soondar blood all over the plush upholstery of the hovercraft, she let her head drift back against the Feral's side. A warm arm pulled her close and she was lulled by the low rumble of his voice, into a deeper sleep where no dreams or sounds could follow.

* * * * *

Krisa opened her eyes slowly in the middle of a plush, dimly lit pastel room she didn't recognize. For the first time in weeks she was lying on a real mattress, the gelafoam gave slightly as she tried to sit up and study her surroundings. Pink, lavender, baby blue, mint green. Was she back in the jungle? Then why were there pearly, brocade drapes hanging from the windows and rich furnishings scattered around?

The slight movements seemed to remind her body of the abuse it had taken the day before and Krisa groaned and lay back down. She felt almost as stiff as she had after her first night in the jungle with Teague. *Teague...* Where was he anyway?

She became aware of the sound of running water and a low, rumbling hum coming from behind a closed doorway across from the vast bed she was lying on. *Singing in the shower?* she wondered hazily. Somehow, Teague didn't seem the type but then, he didn't seem the type for a lot of things she'd seen him do. He had certainly been in character the night before though, snarling at Sarskin for no good reason when the man was only trying to help them.

The object of her thoughts emerged with a puff of steam from the door she had been staring at. There were beads of water on his broad shoulders and bare chest and he had a fluffy lavender towel wrapped around his narrow hips. Krisa shook her head and tried to focus. Was she dreaming again? She had gotten used to seeing Teague in the gray-green vest while they stayed in the Yss village, but seeing him in lavender, even in this pastel world...well, it just seemed *wrong.*

"Mornin', sweetheart, or should I say evening? You slept damn near twenty-five hours, not that I blame you." Teague sat on the bed beside her a little stiffly, still favoring the leg he had injured and proceeded to towel-dry his short, spiky hair with a pink hand towel. "You ready for a bath?" he asked, conversationally. "Sarskin's got all the luxuries—hot water, overhead glows, you name it. Cold-fusion power pack out back of this place must have cost him some serious credit."

"A bath?" Krisa sat up, more slowly this time and became aware that she was a sticky, filthy, grimy mess. Teague's blood was still dried into her clothes, which were also sticky with the viscous, black soondar blood. Her hair was stiff with the stuff.

"Ugh! If I look as terrible as I feel..."

"You do," Teague said with an infuriating grin. "'S why I ran you a bath when I finished my shower. Wait a minute and I'll help you." He stood and shed the towel carelessly, treating her to the sight of his heavily muscled nude body, before he slid into a pair of black leather pants that were draped across his side of the bed. Krisa noticed in the split second before she turned her head that the jagged wound in his upper thigh looked nearly healed. Only a faint tracing of pinkish scar tissue on his dusky tan skin remained to show he had ever been injured at all.

"You...it's almost like you never got wounded at all," she said, unable to keep herself from commenting on his amazingly rapid recovery.

"Sneakin' a peek, huh?" Teague grinned again and then winced when he put weight on the leg in question. "Looks better than it feels. I'll need to stay off it a while."

"But how...?"

"Told you, Ferals are tough. Hard to kill. C'mon, bath time."

Krisa winced herself as she tried to stand and then a wave of dizziness overcame her. Teague caught her just before she would have fallen to the floor, which was carpeted in a lush, pale peach fiber that felt like silk to her tired feet.

"You're paler than usual. When's the last time you ate?" he demanded. He sat her back on the bed gently and knelt in front of her, so that they were eye-level. The black second lid flickered silver briefly, showing his concern.

Krisa thought about it. Their hurried breakfast the day before yesterday was the last meal she could remember eating. She had, of course, made certain that Ziba had some of the dried fruit and meat as they traveled, but her own stomach had been tied in too many knots to even think of eating or drinking anything but water.

"It's been a while," she admitted at last. "Is Ziba all right? He fell in some kind of a hole..."

"The mouth of the gods," Teague said. "It's what the Yss call the sinkhole beside that stone pillar they call the finger of the gods. Apparently it's gotten a lot bigger recently, Ziba probably didn't realize. He got a twisted ankle. Otherwise he and Tz are fine."

He got up and produced a glass filled with frosty, pale orange liquid. "Drink it. Nutrient shake," he said, holding the cup to her lips.

"I can manage." Irritated at being treated like an invalid, Krisa took the glass from him and took a small, experimental sip. To her surprise it tasted good, like the small round sunshine-flavored fruit she had eaten at the Yss banquets. She drank thirstily, finishing it all while Teague watched approvingly.

"Better?" he asked at last, taking the empty glass from her and setting it down.

"A little," Krisa replied grudgingly.

"Bath time then." Teague pulled her off the gelafoam mattress and guided her through the door across from the bed, into the fresher where a large, marble tub was already filled with steaming pinkish water. The warm, steamy air smelled faintly of some exotic flower.

Krisa wanted to object but when she stood up, all the blood rushed to her head, making her feel faint all over again. She did object, though, when he started unsnapping her much abused trousers, stiff with a mixture of blood and dust, in a businesslike way.

"Wait a minute—Teague—stop!"

"What?" He looked up from his task. "You wanna take a bath in your clothes?"

"No. But I can manage myself, you can leave now." Krisa tried to make her voice as firm as possible and not notice the way his large hands never left her waist.

Teague frowned. "Did you forget who you belong to while you're here, little girl?" he growled, looming over her.

Krisa felt a wave of heat wash over her. "N-no," she stuttered, backing away a step and nearly tripping over a pastel grass mat on the marble floor.

"Good because you need a bath and you're gonna get one." Teague finished with her trousers, leaving them in a crumpled heap with her much-abused Certificate of Virginity protruding limply from the back pocket. Then he peeled away the once yellow halter-top, leaving her shivering and naked in the middle of the marble floor, until he helped her into the high-sided marble tub.

Krisa was mortified despite the fact that he had seen her naked before. But once she was submerged in the hot water up to her chin, she found she couldn't hold onto the emotion. Sighing blissfully, she leaned her head back, letting the soothing water wet her tangled hair and rubbed handfuls of the steaming pinkish liquid over her dirty face. There had been baths while they stayed with the Yss, but after the first, special one in Vis' huge cook pot, they were mostly taken in the chilly, fast-flowing stream that ran beside the village. She hadn't felt anything this relaxing since her last sonic shower aboard the *Star Princess*.

Without comment, Teague poured a dollop of sweet-smelling liquid into the palm of one large hand and began to work it into her hair. "Mmm," Krisa couldn't help murmuring, enjoying the feeling of his powerful fingers massaging her scalp. He was skillful and slow, avoiding the tender bump at the back of her neck where the chastity chip was implanted.

"Like that, hmm?" Teague sounded mildly amused.

Krisa didn't answer, content to relax in the steamy bath and let him wash her hair in silence. He rinsed it, pouring the pinkish water over her head, careful not to get any in her eyes and then picked up a thin bath cloth and began to lather it.

"Really, Teague, you don't have to do that." Krisa looked nervously at the cloth in his big hand, suddenly feeling a lot more naked and vulnerable.

"Maybe I want to," he said softly. "What's wrong, little girl? You feelin' shy?" He took one of her hands and began to wash her arm in long, soothing strokes. Beneath the soft cloth, Krisa could feel the heat of his palm, as it moved toward her exposed breasts, floating gently in the warm water.

"I don't know," she said, blushing fiercely, as he palmed first one breast and then the other, paying special attention to her nipples, now painfully erect in the steamy air.

"Not like it's something I haven't seen before," Teague pointed out, motioning her to sit up so he could wash her more thoroughly. "Not like I haven't touched you here." He pinched a nipple lightly. "Or here." One large hand dipped beneath the surface of the water, brushing against her naked thigh, causing a flash of heat to course along her spine.

"I know," Krisa nearly whispered. She wanted to press her thighs tightly together to keep his hand away, but she didn't quite dare. When Teague was in this mood, he was likely to do almost anything. "It's just that—I don't know— before when you touched me you didn't...well, you weren't *watching* me. Except for that first time at the feast, I mean. It was dark...quiet." She remembered the nights in the jungle beside the glowing embers of the fire, when the big Feral had explored her body so thoroughly, with warm, capable hands.

"You weren't always so quiet, as I recall," he rumbled, stroking her thigh lightly with the bath cloth.

Krisa bit back a moan, feeling herself tremble under his touch.

"I missed touching you last night," Teague continued, his hand rising higher and higher up her leg. "Thought about how wet your tender little cunt gets for me, when I stroke you just right. Thought of the soft, hot noises you make when you come, with my fingers inside you. Wondered how that soft little pussy would taste, what it would feel like wrapped around my cock." His fingers brushed gently at the apex of her sex and she jumped.

"Teague...please!" Krisa stood up suddenly, sloshing water over the high side of the tub. "I can't...maybe it's time to stop all that," she said desperately, trying to ignore the hungry silver eyes on her wet, naked body. After the heat of the water the steamy, flower-scented air of the fresher seemed abruptly frigid. Krisa wrapped her arms around herself, feeling her skin break out into a rash of chill bumps. "I mean, I have to go to Prime soon an-and I won't ever see you again. This only makes it harder," she pleaded softly.

Teague's full mouth thinned down to a disapproving slash in his dark face. "Just can't wait to get to Lord Radisson and sign that joining contract, can you?" he asked, his voice low and savage. He stood up, grabbed a fluffy pink towel and wrapped it around her shoulders in one motion.

"Yes...no...I don't know," Krisa whispered. She felt like crying and wasn't exactly sure why. She remembered her chaotic thoughts on the path to Sarskin's compound and how hopeless and lost she had felt when she thought the big Feral might be dead.

"You'll get your wish soon enough." Teague's voice was still hard and he had turned his back to her. Krisa could see the muscles of his broad shoulders and back jumping with tension beneath his dusky tan skin. "Soon as my leg is good enough to travel I'll be going to the hideout where Sarskin stores his ships. I'll get the fastest one—it'll go hyperdrive immediately—and you'll be back on Prime before you can blink, sweetheart. Will that make you happy?"

"I don't know," Krisa said, barely able to make the words come out past the lump in her throat. "I only know it's where I belong."

"Do you?" Teague turned on her, his eyes blazing silver and slitted with anger. "Do you *really*, little girl?" Without waiting for an answer, he turned and stalked out of the fresher, leaving her alone in the echoing marble room.

Krisa sat shivering on the edge of the huge tub and rubbed her cheek against the soft towel he had wrapped her in, trying not to cry.

Chapter Nineteen

ဢ

There was nothing to do but go back to bed.

Despite her long sleep, Krisa still found herself tired, more emotionally than physically. She found a spare set of sheets to put on the gelafoam mattress, since the ones she has been sleeping on were filthy with dust and dried blood. Then she climbed beneath the covers and whispered, "Lights out," to the overhead glows. It had been so long since she had the luxury of a bed, or voice-activated lights, that it was a little hard to get used to again.

Krisa buried her face in a pillow in the darkness and let the misery overtake her. She wanted Teague badly, wanted him the way he wanted her, she admitted to herself. But after this length of time, Lord Radisson was certain to insist that her virginity be re-verified, Certificate or no Certificate. And where would she be if she gave herself to the big Feral? *Out on the street if you're lucky. Dead if you're not*, whispered the practical voice in her brain.

There were rumors of girls who had failed a re-verification of virginity for whatever reason. Rumors of what jealous husbands-to-be did in such circumstances. It wasn't as though Krisa would have any legal rights—she was literally being sold to Lord Radisson and under the laws of Lynix Prime she would be his property to do with as he chose. If he found that the Briar Rose bride he had paid so much for wasn't a virgin, who knew what he might do?

Krisa shivered in the darkness. It was better not to find out. Better to go to Prime with her virginity intact and give her husband-to-be no reason to doubt her.

She fingered the small bump at the back of her neck. What would her life be like once she was joined to Lord Radisson—once he owned her? Teague would know, he had been a slave. But she wouldn't be a slave, not exactly...would she?

When the big Feral talked about owning her, talked about Krisa belonging to him while they were on Planet X, he was talking about her body and his right to do what he wanted to her to make her hot, to make her need him. But what Lord Radisson had paid for was not only her body, but her mind and her soul. He had paid for her free will. That was the true meaning of the chastity chip implanted in her neck.

It will be all right, it has to be. As long as she could manage to get the chip in her neck replaced with a dummy everything would be fine. As long as she could still at least think for herself, Krisa was reasonably certain she could pretend to be a dutiful wife. Likewise she could pretend to Lord Radisson, if not to herself, that all of her adventures with Teague had never happened. Could pretend that she had never cared for him at all.

Trying not to think about it, she brushed tears from her eyes, rolled over in the big empty bed and tried to sleep.

~ ~ ~ ~ ~

Warm hands on her body, a hot mouth on her breasts, sucking her nipples, making her arch her back for more.

"Come on, little girl, you know you want it. Spread your legs for me." The deep, gravelly voice in her ear was familiar, so familiar that Krisa almost knew who he was. Almost. She still couldn't see his face.

"I'm afraid," she whispered, spreading her legs obediently despite her fear. Warm fingers caressed her thighs, sending a shiver through her, making her pussy so wet.

"There's nothing to be afraid of, sweetheart. I'm not going to hurt you...just going to taste you. Gonna lick your sweet little cunt until you come all over my face."

"I can't," she protested, but she made no move to shut her thighs. No move to deny him access to her body.

"Yes you can, little girl. Just spread for me and let me taste that hot, sweet cunt." Hot breath was blowing across her thighs, across her wet sex and Krisa gasped to feel a hot, wet kiss on the inside of her knee. He moved lower, licking long, burning trails down her thighs, dragging his tongue over her sensitive flesh.

Then he was there, pressing his mouth to her center. She gasped as the stubble on his cheeks scratched her tender flesh and a warm, wet tongue entered her. He parted her pussy lips, baring her completely so that he could suck her clit into his mouth, laving it with his tongue until she cried out and bucked against him.

"Please!" she begged, pressing up to meet him. "Please, I want...I need..."

"What do you need, sweetheart?" He raised his face and silver eyes gleamed in the darkness, as the man with no face loomed above her. Suddenly she could see him, really see him for the first time.

"Teague!" she gasped. "Teague, it's you..."

~ ~ ~ ~ ~

"Krisa...*Krisa*, wake up. Wake up, you're dreaming again."

"Teague?" Krisa opened her eyes to find him above her, just as he had been in the dream. There was a frown on his dark features that was barely visible in the dim room and his eyes gleamed silver.

"What are you doing here?" she asked sitting up quickly and scrambling to keep the soft sheet wrapped above her breasts. She wished she had bothered to try and find a nightgown instead of going to bed naked.

"My room too, ya know." He frowned more heavily and then sighed. "Actually, I was gonna sleep somewhere else, but when I stopped in to get my stuff you were thrashing around, having another one of your dreams. And you were calling out, moaning." He gave her a penetrating look from those blazing silver eyes. "Wonder why you were doin' that?"

"I...was I?" Krisa whispered, appalled. But as she spoke, the dream came back to her. The man with no face...he was Teague!

"You were," Teague confirmed. He had shed his vest and boots and was lying on the bed beside her, wearing only the tight black leather pants. Krisa wondered what animal had been killed on this pastel world to make those pants. As far as she knew, the only black animal that hunted the pale jungles of Planet X was the soondar.

"You wanna tell me about that dream?" Teague continued, still gazing at her intensely.

There was no way she was going to tell him that he was literally the man of her dreams, Teague would never let her hear the end of it. Krisa opened her mouth to say that she didn't remember and then thought of something else. Something she had been thinking about before she fell asleep.

"I *might* tell you some of it, if you'll tell me something. Teague," she said softly, turning on her side to face him. "You told me some of how your life was on Al'hora. But before— I mean, before all that happened was it really so..." She took a deep breath. "What's it like, being owned?"

He shifted to his side so that they were face-to-face in the darkness, the silver eyes looking deeply into hers. "Been thinkin' about Prime, huh?" he rumbled. "You want to know what it's like to be a slave? To know that you can be punished at any time for no reason except your master's whim? To know you can be starved, beaten, raped..."

Krisa cringed, shutting her eyes tightly. "Teague, *please* don't."

Strong arms pulled her close and gentle fingers combed through her curls, stroking the bump at the back of her neck. Krisa stiffened at first and then relaxed against his warmth.

"Sorry if I'm scaring you, Krisa, but that's what it's like — or was for me. When I went to my second master's house, anyway. It might be different for you, though. I'm sure the hotshots on Prime don't go in for beating and starvation quite as much as the Daylighters on Al'hora," he said dryly.

"But even if they don't..." Her voice was almost too dry to continue, but Krisa forced herself to say it anyway. "Even if Lord Radisson doesn't beat me or starve me, he's still going to do *that* to me. I mean," she cleared her throat. "I'll still have to sleep with him."

"Last time I pointed that out to you, it didn't seem to faze you too much." Teague's voice hardened a little. "I think you told me you knew what you were gettin' yourself into."

Krisa thought of her dream and shivered against him. "That was b-before I knew what was possible. I thought he would just get on top and... Teague, what we saw at the Yss feasts, you said most men liked it. Do you really think he'll want me to do that?"

"What? A blowjob?" Teague's voice was more amused now, gentler. He shifted to pull her closer, heedless of the way Krisa tugged at the slipping sheet that no longer covered her breasts.

"Yes." Krisa's voice was low and she felt very small in the darkness, cradled in the circle of his arms.

"Would it really bother you so much?" Teague asked softly. The arm that was wrapped around her shoulders moved down, circling her waist so that he could reach up and cup one bare breast in his large, warm palm.

"Well...I mean no. Not if...not if I loved him, I guess." The last word was a breathless gasp as Teague pinched her nipple, igniting her nerves as he always did whenever he touched her body. Krisa realized abruptly that they weren't talking about Lord Radisson anymore. "But h-how do I know if I love him?" she asked softly, nuzzling closer to his big body and breathing in his spicy musk. "And what if he wants to do it...the other way?"

"You mean what if he wants to taste you?" One large hand, the one that wasn't cupping her breast, dipped beneath the sheet and rested on the soft, curling mound of her pussy. "Is that what you were dreamin' about when I woke you up, Krisa? Is that why you were calling out?"

"I-I don't know." She could barely speak and her heart was pounding so hard she was sure he could hear it in the darkened room. She kept wanting to press her thighs tightly together or spread them wide for him, she wasn't sure which. It was wrong, it had always been wrong. That didn't make her want it any less.

"Don't lie to me, little girl." He breathed deeply and she could feel the tension rippling in his muscles, just under the smooth, warm skin. "I can tell how much you want it, your scent gives you away every time. That and the way you get so wet. Spread your legs — *now*."

Krisa wasn't sure what her scent had to do with anything. She only knew that when he touched her like this, when he whispered low and hot into her ear, it made her so wet, so ready. As she had in the dream, she spread her thighs obediently and felt his blunt fingertips part the lips of her pussy, dipping into her slippery heat, rubbing lightly over her clit and making her moan.

"That's it, little girl...give it up. I love the way you get so wet for me. Can't wait to taste you."

"But..." It was wrong — *dangerous* — to go so far. Krisa tried to think of something, anything that might stop him. "But what if you don't like it?"

"Don't like it?" Teague raised his eyebrows in disbelief. He withdrew his fingers for a moment and then, looking at her steadily, slid them into his mouth, licking her essence from them with obvious pleasure. "I *love* it. Love your hot, salty taste when you need to come," he rumbled. "C'mere."

He leaned down and captured her mouth, parting her lips and thrusting his tongue between them, sharing her own taste with her. Krisa moaned and leaned into the kiss, all thoughts of impropriety or shame swept away, as she experienced her own flavor mixed with the hot-cinnamon of his mouth.

At last he broke the kiss, the silver eyes burning into her own and Krisa knew he would do what he wanted no matter what she said.

"Teague," she whispered as she had in the dream. "I-I'm afraid."

"Don't be." He slid down so that he was lying on the bed instead of sitting up, leaving her leaning against the headboard. "You know I'd never hurt you, Krisa."

"I know." She looked down at him, the silver eyes bright and serious in his dark face. "Wh-what do you want me to do?"

"I want you to ride my face, sweetheart. That way I can get my tongue deep inside your sweet little cunt. C'mere." He beckoned her but Krisa held back, unsure.

"I don't understa—"

"I'll show you." With as little effort as though he was moving a doll, Teague reached for her and positioned her body so that she had a knee planted on either side of his head. Krisa could feel his hot breath licking along the insides of her spread thighs and the tender lips of her cunt, swollen with need and desire.

"Teague, I'll hurt you," she protested, grabbing the headboard to steady herself above him.

He laughed, the rumbling sound coming from deep in his massive chest and vibrating her entire body. "Sweetheart, listen to yourself. If an angry soondar couldn't kill me, how do you expect to hurt me with you soft, curvy body?" He placed large, warm hands around her waist, cradling her pelvis in his palms.

"Come down and let me taste you, Krisa," he said, his voice low and commanding. "Let me taste you and make you come the way you need to."

"Teague..." His name was a sob in her throat as Krisa finally allowed him to pull her down, spreading her thighs and making herself open and vulnerable to him.

She felt his lips first, kissing her lightly, slowly, thoroughly the same way he kissed her mouth. Then his tongue, wet and warm invading the swollen lips of her pussy, swirling endlessly over the swollen bud of her clit and making her gasp and cry wordlessly as he licked and sucked and tasted.

Krisa's hands tightened on the wooden headboard in front of her in the darkness and she threw back her head, biting her lip and trying to support herself against the onslaught of pleasure. She could feel her long hair trailing down her back and the sharp wooden edge of the headboard biting into her palms, but nothing seemed to matter except the pleasure of Teague's mouth on her there—on her hot, wet sex.

Then he stopped.

"What...?" The loss of sensation was jarring, especially when she had felt herself beginning to build toward the peak.

"Feels good, doesn't it, sweetheart?" he rumbled, heat and amusement thick in his voice.

"I...yes, yes it does," Krisa admitted breathlessly.

"Then trust me, Krisa. Come all the way down." His hands tightened on her waist, urging her lower. "Don't worry about hurting me, you can't. Just relax and let me take you where you need to go. Let me make you come."

"All right," she whispered. Forcing herself to loosen her grip on the headboard, Krisa did as he said, relaxing until she felt his hot mouth against her sensitive pussy again.

"So damn sweet," she heard him mutter and then strong hands were urging her lower and his hot, wet tongue was invading her, penetrating the slick, swollen folds of her cunt to pierce deep inside her.

"Oh Goddess! Teague!" she moaned. Unable to help herself she pressed against him, feeling his rough cheeks scratch her tender thighs as he licked and sucked and fucked deeply into her with his tongue. The penetration was so good, so right, and yet...just not enough. Krisa knew what she wanted, what she really needed. *His cock...Oh, Goddess...if only he would...if only we could...*

Just the thought of being pinned beneath his big body and feeling that thick, hard cock penetrating her, opening her as she had never been opened before, while Teague licked and tongued her was enough to push her over the edge.

Crying and shaking, Krisa came hard, grinding against him, reaching the peak he always brought her to and falling over it, as he licked and sucked her sweet, wet folds. The orgasm was so intense she saw bright-white stars exploding before her eyes in the darkened room. Suddenly she felt lightheaded and dizzy.

Teague caught her and lowered her gently to the bed beside him before she would have collapsed. Then he was kissing her again, sharing her own flavor with her, while big hands roamed restlessly over her naked body.

Goddess...so good...so sweet, Krisa thought disjointedly as she pressed herself against him, feeling the hard ridge of his cock throbbing for relief and release behind the leather pants he still wore. And even though she knew it was impossible, she couldn't help wishing for more.

So much more.

And then he was pulling away, was leaving her. Krisa cried out wordlessly, reaching for him, never wanting to let him go.

"Sorry, sweetheart." His voice was low and grating in the darkened room. "I've gotta get away. If I stay here I won't be able to help myself—I want you too much."

He sat on the edge of the bed and ran both hands through his hair—a gesture of pure frustration.

"Teague, please." Krisa scooted to the edge of the bed and place one hand lightly on the warm skin of his broad back. "That was so *intense*. I-I felt so close to you. Please don't leave me alone."

"You don't understand, do you?" He shrugged her hand off his back and turned to face her, eyes blazing silver in the darkness. "Touching you like that, tasting your sweet pussy…it's too much. I've been wantin' you for weeks now. All the nights we were traveling to get here—every time I touched you, every time I felt you tremble against me and heard you make those soft little sounds you make when you come. Krisa, you know how I feel about rape, but if I stay here, I'll fuck you. Is that what you want?" His dark face was hard and his words little more than a snarl.

The blunt words made her recoil at the same time they started a new fire in her belly. To be taken…to be *fucked*. To be spread out beneath him, open, vulnerable and feel that thick cock filling her pussy.

"You didn't answer me, little girl." Teague pulled her up and onto his lap. Suddenly she was straddling his crotch, her thighs spread wide, knees resting on the bed with nothing but the thin, black leather pants he wore between his cock and her wet, open sex.

"What?" Krisa gasped but the gasp turned abruptly into a moan, as Teague pulled her down to grind against him, rubbing the thick ridge of his cock against her swollen clit, already overly sensitive from her earlier orgasm. The feel of his mouth on her as he tasted her had been gentle, soft—but this was a whole different type of sensation—a rough delicious friction that built her pleasure quickly, almost painfully.

"I asked if you wanted to be *fucked*, Krisa." Hands spread wide on her hips forced her down farther, forced her to spread wide for him and take all the overwhelming pleasure he could give her. Teague rocked slow and hard against her, rubbing the slick leather over and over and over the tender bump of her clit until she thought she might go insane.

Krisa moaned, biting her lip, not trusting herself to say yes or no. Not trusting herself to say anything at all. Instead she draped her arms around his neck and dropped her head to his shoulder. She took a shallow, panting breath, drawing in his musk, a combination of sweat, leather and male in heat, and concentrated on enduring the intense sensations he was building in her body.

"Just think." Teague's breath was hot on her neck as he forced her to ride him. "With two quick moves I could be inside you. All the way inside your *tight...wet...cunt*." With each word he gave a hard, forceful thrust, pushing her toward another, rougher kind of climax. "Would you like that, little girl? Like to feel me spreading open your sweet, virgin pussy with my thick cock? Wanna feel me ride you hard tonight, come inside you?"

"Teague, *please!*" she sobbed, on the edge again and so *close*. So afraid of what might happen if she gave in, gave him what he was demanding.

Think of the consequences. Concentrate on what will happen if you show up on Lynix Prime and Lord Radisson insists on a re-verification of your virginity and you don't pass. But Teague was making it impossible to concentrate on anything but how badly she wanted him, needed him inside her.

"Answer me, damn it!" His hips rolled beneath her, thrusting, grinding, spreading the wet lips of her pussy and rubbing ruthlessly against her clit. Pressing deep but not deep enough. Pushing her higher and higher.

"You *know* I want to but I can't. I just *can't*," Krisa sobbed even as her climax began, overwhelming her.

"Damn you, Krisa. Damn you for holding any part of yourself back from me." Teague's voice was a deep, angry growl. He thrust roughly against her, rubbing the thick ridge of his cock brutally over her slick, swollen folds and bit her hard on the tender spot where her neck met her shoulder as she came. Krisa cried out as his sharp white teeth drew blood, not much, but enough to mix a bitter zing of pain into the exquisite pleasure of the rough orgasm he had forced from her.

Teague held her tightly for a moment more, his face buried in the side of her neck breathing hard, then pushed her off his lap and stood to leave.

"Going now." There was finality in his tone. And deep frustration.

"Sorry. I'm sorry," Krisa whispered, sinking to her knees in the silky carpet.

"So am I, sweetheart. More than I can say." And he was gone.

Krisa crawled into the bed on legs that felt like rubber and buried herself beneath the covers. Hesitantly, she touched the place where he had bitten her, marked her, as she came. It stung and throbbed but not nearly as much as her heart. Then her fingers stole around to the back of her neck and caressed the small bump of the chastity chip.

Teague would drop her off on Prime and she would never see him again. Chip or no chip her life would be miserable.

I love him. Hot tears filled her eyes and ran down her cheeks, wetting the pillow.

I love him and there's nothing I can do about it.

Chapter Twenty

ɞ

"Krisalaison!" The joyful shout echoed down the long stone corridor and Krisa looked up in time to see a dark-haired rocket headed in her direction.

"Ziba," she gasped as he wrapped his arms around her waist and knocked the wind out of her with his exuberant greeting. Apparently his ankle was better. On his shoulder Tz hopped and chattered, also clearly glad to see her.

"You were gone so long Tz and I be afraid you were sick, Krisalaison," the half-Yss boy explained at last, drawing back from the tight hug. Krisa was relieved, the light lunch she had eaten an hour before was not sitting well in her stomach and enthusiastic squeezing wasn't what she needed.

"Well, I'm not," she said lightly and not entirely truthfully. "I'm just fine—see?" She held out a hand for Tz, who hopped lightly onto it and scampered up to her shoulder to lose himself in her tangle of brown curls.

"Oh, Tz, don't—that tickles!" Krisa scrunched her shoulders to dislodge the hyper targee.

"Come, Tz."

Krisa bent down and Ziba reached up with one slim, six-fingered hand, to capture his wayward pet. He was trying to disentangle the pink puffball from her hair, when Krisa felt him go very still.

"Krisalaison, you be hurt after all," he said, tracing one finger lightly over the welted bruise between her neck and shoulder, where Teague had bitten her the night before. "Did a soondar do that?"

Krisa straightened abruptly, making Tz, who was still half tangled in her hair, scold angrily.

"No...it's nothing, Ziba. Nothing you should worry about." Krisa disentangled the pink targee from her hair and placed him back on his young master's shoulder. "Come on, show me your home."

Krisa held out a hand to him. The boy looked at her doubtfully for a moment before taking it and leading her down the corridor.

"This be the great hall for feasting," he said, nodding at a large room with a vaulted ceiling and double wooden doors as they passed. "There be a feast tonight in honor of the Teague."

"Oh?" Krisa put her free hand to her throat, remembering the cause for feasting among the Yss. Surely Sarskin who seemed such a civilized man wouldn't... Then again Teague *had* said the Drusinian had gone native. "Wh-what kind of meat did he provide?" she made herself ask at last.

"Soondar meat, of course." Ziba looked at her as though she were crazy. "You know the Teague is the one who does not eat, Krisalaison. He brings only meat from the jungle."

"Oh." Krisa felt relieved. "Of course. So the Yss went back for the soondar Teague killed in the jungle," she said. "The one that was stalking us." She shivered, remembering that hot-black voice in her head and the rage of the female soondar who had been robbed of her mate and her cubs.

"Oh, no. There didn't be much left of that one, Krisalaison," Ziba replied comfortably. "But of the second one there was much good meat. Nothing is so tender as soondar flesh—not even the meat of your enemies. And to eat of the soondar is to gain his strength. That was good hunting."

"Wait a minute." Krisa stopped him. They had been passing through a series of smaller rooms, all furnished in the eclectic style that seemed to mix rich offworlder furnishings with simpler Yss elements and now she sank down into a comfort-foam couch that appeared to be upholstered in some sort of orange fur.

"What be the matter?" Ziba asked with concern, perching on the edge of the couch beside her. Clearly he was still concerned for her health.

"I thought he only killed one," Krisa explained. "Just the one that was trying to take you away, Ziba." She remembered how Teague had been smeared with the oily black soondar blood. Camouflage, he had said, to keep the others away. But then why had it been so fresh?

"He killed another?" she asked at last.

"Of course. He said it was kill or be killed, a needful killing." Ziba had obviously taken Teague's lesson on killing only for necessity to heart. The dark head nodded gravely.

Krisa shook her head. She had thought she was in time, that despite the delays she had gotten to Teague before any of the hunting soondar could. She had been wrong.

"He could have been killed," she whispered, feeling the horror of the night overcome her again. *Killed because of me. Because I was slow…was late. But he never said anything.*

"But he wasn't. I told you Teague could look out for himself." The pleasantly cultured voice roused her out of her thoughts. She looked up to see Sarskin smiling genially as he made his ponderous way toward them.

"Hello." Krisa stood and made an awkward curtsy to the large man. Ziba took a more direct approach.

"Well met, sire," he said, grinning from ear to ear at the big Drusinian, who was his father.

"Well met, first son." Gravely, Sarskin held out a pudgy hand, palm up and just as gravely Ziba covered it with one of his own. "I need to speak to your friend, Ziba," he continued. "Why don't you and Tz run outside and play? I saw Lynza earlier and he was looking for you."

"All right." Ziba nodded at them both and ran out of the room. "See you at the feast tonight, Krisalaison," Krisa heard him howl down the echoing stone corridor as he went.

"Would you care to take a stroll about the grounds?" Sarskin offered his plump arm, covered in rich brocade, courteously. Krisa took it hesitantly. In her weeks with the Yss she had almost forgotten the customs of the civilized galaxy.

"I'd be pleased," she said, rather belatedly as they were already walking out of a large set of double doors and into a sort of garden behind the huge stone house.

Sarskin took a deep breath. "Lovely day," he remarked, leading her along a crushed gravel path, as Krisa stared in interest to either side. There were flowering plants with broad leaves in every shade of pastel imaginable, gleaming under the dull bronze sky. They were beautifully cared for and exuded the heavy, rich smell of the jungle beyond the compound into the air, but they lacked the wild beauty she had come to love in Planet X.

"You have a lovely garden," Krisa said politely, mainly to have something to say.

"Thank you, my dear. All native species from the nearby jungle, of course. I'm afraid nothing else much will grow here on X. I see you are admiring my Durba Trap plant," Sarskin remarked, watching Krisa's interest in a particularly large plant that had dusky pink flowers broader than her hand. There was a sudden motion in the leaves of the plant and then one of the flowers snapped closed abruptly.

"Oh! What was that?" Krisa jumped back from the quivering plant.

"That, my dear, was lunch — for the plant anyway. Merely another hapless durba falling prey to its enticing scent."

"But I didn't see anything. What is a durba, anyway?" Krisa asked. She watched in mild dismay as the tightly pursed, dusky pink blossom began to move rhythmically, emitting loud crunching sounds.

"No, you wouldn't have. Most of the fauna here on X has wonderful camouflage—soondar excluded, of course. Pitch black because they only hunt at night. A durba is a type of large, poisonous spider. I'm surprised Teague didn't tell you about them."

"I'm rather glad he didn't," she remarked. In fact, there had to be a lot of creatures living in the jungles of Planet X and yet Teague had never told her about anything about any of them but the soondar and the targees. *Only told you what you needed to know to survive*, the practical voice in her head whispered. Of course, would she really have wanted to know there were carnivorous plants and poisonous spiders all around? Krisa shivered.

"Are you catching a chill, my dear?"

"N-no, just thinking..." Krisa groped for words.

Just then one of Sarskin's Yss warriors walked by, with an expensive-looking silk scarf wrapped around his waist. To the ends of it he had tied two pink satin, high-heeled lady's slippers that would have been proper for a ball at Briar Rose. They dangled and slapped against his bare green thighs as he walked.

"I was just thinking that your, um, people dress very colorfully here," Krisa said at last.

Sarskin laughed, a warm, pleasant sound that shook his mountainous physique from head to heels. "Yes, rather amusing, isn't it? I first imported the clothing for my wives—I have six, you know."

Krisa struggled to control her reaction to this announcement. Well, Teague *had* said his old shipmate had gone native and joined with more than one Yss woman. But *six*? It seemed a bit excessive.

"I wanted them to dress properly but it was hopeless," the large man continued. "The Yss warriors appropriated most all of the fancy dress clothes I brought, and they wear them however they like, think it brings them status to have

261

'offworlder skins'. A bit like children playing dress up, don't you know." He chuckled again and urged her to continue their stroll along the garden path.

"Since then I have given up on getting my Yss women to wear the latest fashions. I suppose their native costumes are more comfortable in this heat. You seem to have gone native yourself, Miss Elyison, if you don't mind me saying so."

"No, of course not. I-I didn't have much choice," Krisa admitted, blushing a little. Someone had cleaned and mended all her clothing and she was wearing the mint-green everyday outfit Vis had given her. She hadn't thought for a long time how she looked in the skirt and halter-top combination that the Yss women wore, but now Sarskin's comments made her feel exposed.

"It's quite all right, I've gone more than a bit native myself," Sarskin said kindly. "Although I do believe I have a bit more frippery left that my warriors didn't get into, which just might just fit you. If you like, I'll have it sent to your rooms for the feast tonight. You're under no obligation to wear it, of course."

"Of course," Krisa murmured, concentrating on the sound of her leather sandals crunching on the gravel path and the warmth of the hidden sun beating down on her bare shoulders. "That would be…most kind of you, Mister Sarskin."

"Just Sarskin, please, my dear. And it is the least I can do. I very indebted to you and Teague both for bringing Ziba safely home again. He is my eldest, you know, and very bright."

"Yes, he is," Krisa agreed, smiling. "A very sweet little boy too."

"He seems to have a genuine affection for you as well, my dear. And he is not the only one." He stopped walking and turned to look at her, giving her a penetrating glance from those dark brown eyes.

"I-I don't know what you mean," Krisa faltered, pretending to study a lavender vine climbing the side of a larger, pale blue plant. In the distance she could hear two of the Yss who were tending the garden speaking in their low, hissing language. It made her miss Vis.

"I mean Teague, of course. I must say, Miss Elyison, that I have never seen my old shipmate so taken with a woman before and I flew with him for several years before we had our little...falling-out."

"The Haulder-Lenz." Krisa looked at him expectantly. The dull, bronze light gave his long, dark hair reddish highlights that Ziba's didn't have. "Teague won't talk about it. Wh-why did you disagree?" It seemed a pale word to use to describe a duel to the death, a polite, Briar Rose word. But somehow, when she was near the portly Drusinian, Briar Rose mannerisms and language she had almost forgotten in the past month came back to her.

"As I said, it was a disagreement based on a difference of opinion. I thought I saw great opportunity for advancement when we landed here. I wanted to take some of the Yss natives offplanet, give them a taste of the civilized galaxy. Teague...disagreed. Rather strongly I am afraid. After he won the duel, he left me alive on the condition that I would abandon any such plans. Naturally I agreed and I cannot break my word to him, as you know."

Krisa nodded. It seemed a strange thing to disagree over, the education of a few Yss offplanet. She couldn't understand why Teague would care about such a thing. She opened her mouth to ask more, but Sarskin cut in smoothly.

"As I was saying, my dear, I have never seen my old shipmate more taken with a member of the fairer sex. And now I see he had marked you." He nodded casually to the bruise on her neck and Krisa blushed and covered it hastily with her hair.

"That was an accident," she said, leaning down to pick an innocent-looking pale green flower.

"I shouldn't do that if I were you, my dear. The sting of the slindir blossom is quite painful," Sarskin said, watching her motion. "And, Miss Elyison, Ferals don't do *anything* by accident. Marking of the skin is a mating ritual among them. Oh yes," he nodded gravely. "I know their customs and their ways, they're not that much more civilized than the Yss if you want to know the truth. If Teague marked you there had to be a reason. Are you quite certain he intends to take you back to Lynix Prime once he gets the ship I have promised him?"

"He's never lied to me before," Krisa said slowly, standing up and stepping away from the pale green plant. *But he's good at withholding information, isn't he, Krisa? The dangerous poisonous plants and animals in the jungle he never told you about...killing the second soondar.* "I don't believe he means me any harm," she said with as much conviction as she could, looking Sarskin in the eyes. "He's never," she blushed, "taken advantage of me in the way he could have all this time we've been away from civilization."

"That's quite a good thing, considering that your Lord Radisson will be looking for you soon, if a rescue party isn't already somewhere on X, which wouldn't surprise me at all," Sarskin remarked casually.

"Oh." Krisa put a hand to her throat. "Do you really think so?" If Lord Radisson found her before she could get to Prime and have the chip removed.

"Nothing is more likely, but that's neither here nor there. I understand why you want to avoid them until you can meet Lord Radisson on your own terms." He touched the back of his own neck, indicating the chip. "But I'm trying to warn you, my dear. Teague is a fine fellow but he's wanted nearly everywhere in the galaxy and not for minor indiscretions either. Ferals are savage when provoked, quite animalistic. If something they feel belongs to them is threatened they can exhibit an almost berserk-type rage."

Krisa remembered the bulging blue eyes and the sickening crunch of Captain Ketchum's neck as Teague killed him. *But he did that to save me, not because he thinks he owns me,* her mind protested. *Who do you belong to, little girl?* Teague's voice growled in her head in return. And Sarskin had seemed to think Teague had "marked" her on purpose. Krisa still wasn't sure how she would explain the purplish welt where he had bitten her if it didn't fade by the time she got back to Prime and Lord Radison.

"I see by your face that what I am trying to tell you has made an impression," Sarskin remarked, watching her closely. "I'm just saying that you ought to be careful of what you do and who you trust, Miss Elyison. I am, as I said, forever indebted to my old friend. But I wouldn't like to see anything bad happen to such a lovely young lady. I think the best place for you is back on Lynix Prime with your Lord Radisson, living the life of comfort and privilege you were raised for. Don't you agree?"

"I-I suppose," Krisa said carefully. "Are you...saying that Teague might try to take me with him, wherever he's going?"

"I feel it's entirely possible," Sarskin said, a grave look passing over his plump face. "If he's begun to have possessive feelings for you, and I think it's clear that he has." He indicated the purple welt on her neck. "Possession is what passes for love among Ferals, I'm afraid."

"But...I just don't think... I don't feel Teague would break his word to me. He promised to take me to Prime," Krisa protested. Her heart was pounding. Teague take her with him? The idea had never even occurred to her. Sarskin's words of caution seemed to open a whole new realm of possibilities.

What would it be like? A life on the run with the big Feral, traveling all over the galaxy. *A life of uncertainty and fear,* whispered the practical voice in her brain. *No – a life of freedom. A life with the man I love,* she insisted to herself.

"Miss Elyison, are you all right?" She looked up to see the mountainous Drusinian staring at her with concern.

"Fine, I'm fine. Still a bit fatigued, that's all," Krisa said, trying to cover her confusion. "Actually, if you don't mind I think I'll go back to my room and get ready for the feast tonight."

"Very well. But think about what I've said, will you, my dear?"

"Yes, I certainly will. Thank you." Krisa pressed his arm urgently. "Thank you very much."

Chapter Twenty-One

❧

Teague could take me with him. We wouldn't have to go back to Prime at all. Krisa's head reeled with the possibility, as she walked slowly back to her room. It seemed silly that she had never considered it before. But then, she had never really let herself realize exactly how she felt about Teague before last night.

But how does he feel about you?

The thought stopped her cold. How *did* Teague feel about her? Oh, Krisa knew he wanted her—wanted her with the same white-hot need she felt for him. But did that deep sexual craving mean love? Was Sarskin right about him "marking" her on purpose the night before? She couldn't just walk up to the big Feral and say, "Oh by the way I've decided to run away with you because I've realized I love you", could she? What if he didn't feel the same?

Her thoughts were interrupted when she found herself at the door of her room and realized Teague was already inside.

The big Feral was standing on the far side of the room, looking out of place among the plush pastels in his black leather vest and pants. He had his back to her, broad shoulders hunched, staring at something on the bed.

"Hello, Krisa," he said, not turning around.

"Good afternoon, Teague." The words seemed stilted, forced in some way. But she hadn't seen him since the night before, when she had been spread out naked on his lap. The memory made her blush hard.

He turned at last, an annoying smirk on his dark face when he saw her red cheeks. "What's the matter, sweetheart? Feelin' shy?"

"No," Krisa lied, lifting her chin defiantly. She might be in love with him but he could still be one of the most infuriating people she had ever met. Why did he always have to bait her like this?

"Not having any regrets?" he asked more softly, moving toward her. His feet made no noise in the thick peach carpeting.

Krisa shook her head, forcing herself to meet his eyes which were a blank, unreadable black in the slanting late afternoon light.

"Well, maybe I have a few," he said, the smile falling abruptly from his face. He stroked the curtain of chocolate-brown curls away from the side of her neck, and studied the deep purple welt his teeth had left there the night before.

Krisa's heart began beating triple time beneath her ribs. *Oh Goddess! Is he sorry he marked me? Does that mean he doesn't want me after all?*

"It's all right," she said, trying to pull away.

"It's *not* all right." Teague pulled her against him, one arm around her waist and the other buried in her hair, so that he could study her neck more closely.

"Let me *go*." Krisa pushed against his broad chest with absolutely no result.

"Not until I see what I've done to you," Teague rumbled warningly. "Be still, little girl."

Krisa stopped struggling since it wasn't doing any good and let him tilt her head to look at the purple welt marring her creamy skin.

"I didn't mean to do this, didn't mean to leave a mark." His warm breath on the sensitive skin of her neck sent a tremor of desire along her nerves, but his words made her heart sink. So he *didn't* want her the way she wanted him.

"It's all right," she said again, dully. "You were…upset."

Teague gave a short bark of laughter. "Upset, huh? Yeah, I guess you could say that." He leaned down and placed a soft, warm kiss over the bruised skin and Krisa shivered helplessly against him, feeling her body react to his touch as it always did. Teague kissed her neck again, lapping softly at the hurt spot with a warm, wet tongue, as though he could kiss the bruise away.

"Teague...*please*." His hot mouth on her neck reminded her of the places he had kissed and licked her the night before. Krisa could feel herself rapidly losing all control of the situation and her own emotions.

He pulled back at last and looked at her seriously.

"I promised I'd never hurt you and then I did it anyway. I'm sorry, Krisa, I didn't mean to."

"Sarskin said you did. He said you did it on purpose." The moment the words were out of her mouth, she wanted to call them back. But it was too late. Teague's dark features hardened and he pulled away from her.

"He did, did he? Have you been havin' a cozy little chat with my old shipmate? What else did he say?"

"He said you marked me, that it was a Feral ritual that meant you wanted t-to own me." Krisa struggled to keep the desperation out of her voice, to speak in a firm, steady tone. She looked at Teague, trying to gauge a reaction to her words. His face had gone blank, the black eyes opaque and unreadable. Abruptly he pushed her away.

"I know you're naïve, Krisa." He sat heavily in a nearby chair that was upholstered in pale baby blue. "But you can't trust everyone you meet."

"I don't," she said, stung by his rejection.

"No I guess not. It's pretty clear you don't trust me even after everything we've been through," he flung back.

"Why didn't you tell me about the second soondar you killed? Before we got to you that night?" Krisa shouted. "You told me you were covered in blood for camouflage. You could have been killed because I was too late!"

"You didn't need to know, sweetheart," Teague growled. "I can take care of myself, what happened to me was never your responsibility. And I *wasn't* killed so what's the point of tellin' you about something that would only make you upset?"

"The *point* is to tell me the truth for once." Krisa thought of something else the large Drusinian had told her.

"Sarskin told me that night we were coming to pick you up that soondar won't usually come near a foreign object, especially one as big and threatening as an interstellar ship. He seemed to think I would've been safe if you'd left me in the *Star Princess* in the first place."

"Usually?" Teague snarled, standing up from the chair and looming over her. "No, I guess they *usually* don't. Except that after a week or two even something as big as the *Princess* might stop being so threatening. Especially when the smell of fresh *blood* is comin' from it." He ran a hand through his hair.

"But I guess I should've taken the chance and left you there. Stupid of me to think you'd rather come with me and live than stay inside and wait for the rescue party, while you were beaten and raped and probably eaten one dark night!"

"That's not... I didn't mean..." Krisa clenched her hands into fists, feeling her nails dig into her palms. Why did things always go wrong when she tried to talk to him?

Teague had paced away, apparently too angry to talk to her, but now he turned again, eyes blazing silver with emotion. "Can't believe after everything we've been through you still don't trust me. What makes you so sure you should take that Drusinian's word over mine?"

"Because he *is* a Drusinian," Krisa flared. "You told me they couldn't tell a lie or break their word."

Teague sighed and slumped into the blue chair again, running both hands through his spiky blue-black hair. "So that's it," he muttered. "Look, Krisa, maybe I didn't explain very well. Drusinians are some of the slipperiest sons of bitches you're ever gonna meet in this galaxy. They can't lie but they're damn good at twisting the truth. Makes them some of the best businessmen around. What else did Sarskin tell you? C'mon—give."

"Just th-that I should be careful because Ferals are possessive and he didn't think you would let me go, didn't think you'd really take me back to Prime. He said..." Her voice dropped so low she could barely hear it herself. "He said that Ferals equate possession with love, that you'd want to keep me, take me with you." Krisa looked down at her hands, unable to meet those blank, black eyes, when her own were so full of hope.

Teague snorted in disgust. "Love? What does that fat Drusinian know about love? He's got six wives—six! What does he know about giving yourself to one person for life?"

"I know all that," Krisa said angrily. "But I didn't know...he seems so nice..."

"Of course he does. Sarskin has always been a personable bastard, a real charmer. Seems like a great guy until you get to know him. Unfortunately it can be too late by the time you do. Did he ever tell you why we fought? Why I had to challenge him when we first landed here?"

"The Haulder-Lenz? No—and you haven't either. He just said something about sending some of the Yss offplanet for education." Krisa crossed her arms, waiting to hear the truth.

"Oh they would have gotten an education all right. Sarskin had the bright idea to start slaving them out—the Yss women especially—to interstellar brothels and other interested buyers."

"But...he wouldn't...he *couldn't*. They adopted him, adopted both of you. He joined with their women, had children."

"That doesn't matter to Sarskin." Teague was pacing up and down the peach carpeting as though he was tying to wear a hole in it. "He might not have slaved out the tribe that adopted him, but the other neighboring tribes would have been fair game. Drusinians are big in the slave trade. They're so civilized and superior they don't think of other cultures as being much more than savages and if there's a profit to be made they'll make it, never mind how those 'savages' feel about it." Teague stopped pacing for a moment and took a deep, angry breath.

"I had to stop him. I didn't mind going along with his smuggling schemes—that's small shit when you're wanted over half the galaxy for multiple homicides. But I draw the line at slavery. I think you know why." He glared at her.

"Yes," Krisa said quietly, through numb lips. "Yes, I-I can see why."

"All right." Teague ran both hands through his hair. "What I'm trying to tell you is that Sarskin's a nice enough guy as long *as you keep an eye on him*. He's friendly and useful—we're getting a ship from him—but don't trust a Goddessdamn thing he tells you. Drusinians are bound by their word, which is why it's so hard to get a straight answer out of them, they'll twist things every time."

"So…you're saying everything he told me—"

"Forget all of it." Teague gave her a level glare. Krisa's heart sank. "And try to trust me, at least a little. I got you this far, didn't I?" he demanded. "If I say I'll get you to Prime, then I'll damned well get you there."

"Teague, I'm sorry. I should never have listened—"

"No, don't apologize." Teague frowned. "Sarskin can be damn convincing. He probably told you that I'm just some kind of an animal. Some vicious, unpredictable beast. You can't trust a soondar not to rip you to shreds and you can't trust a Feral to keep his word, is that it?"

Krisa nodded her head, feeling the dull burn of shame in her heated cheeks. What he was saying was entirely too close to what Sarskin *had* said to her, about Ferals in general and Teague in particular, for comfort.

"Thought so." Teague nodded, a curt gesture. "And you ate it up because my old shipmate is so damn *civilized*." He strode over to the bed where an assortment of clothes were laid out. "Look what he sent you, Krisa." He lifted a delicate, ivory lace gown into the air between them. It had a high collar and tiny pearl buttons that would climb all the way up to her throat if she put it on. The gown would have been proper for evening wear at Briar Rose or anywhere else in polite society. It would have been perfect for Lynix Prime.

"Go on." Teague threw the gown at her and Krisa caught it purely out of reflex. "Put it on, it's even got a nice high collar to hide the place I 'marked' you," he sneered. "Rejoin the world you were meant to live in all along. That's what you want, isn't it? You can't wait to get to Prime and wear clothes like that every day. It's a wonder they bothered with the Goddessdamn chip in your neck at all, they don't need it to make you act the way they want you to." His voice was an angry growl, almost a snarl. Krisa was reminded obscurely of the snarled, hot-black voice of the soondar inside her head.

"Teague, that's not fair and you know it." She was crying now, tears streaming down her cheeks unheeded. She clutched the beautiful lace dress to her chest, her hands tightening in the delicate material.

But the big Feral was furious again, past hearing anything she had to say. "Just remember something, sweetheart." He leaned down, glaring at her with eyes that had gone full silver with barely controlled rage. "I know who you *really* are. It doesn't matter what you wear or how you try to hide it—I've seen your true nature—the heat you try to keep locked inside."

He leaned closer, hands on her shoulders and pulled her in for a savage, breath-stealing kiss. His mouth on hers was bruising and hurtful and still Krisa felt her body react to his touch. The dress in her hands forgotten, she leaned into the kiss, giving as good as she was getting, wanting to show him somehow that he was wrong about her, wrong about what she wanted.

Teague pulled away so abruptly that she nearly fell. "That's the *real* you, Krisa, and you're never gonna be happy trying to deny it." He turned and headed for the door.

"Teague, wait..."

"What?" He half turned, hand on the ornate brass knob, eyes a solid, midnight black again.

It was on the tip of her tongue to tell him how she felt, what she wanted, but it was obvious he didn't feel the same. He had told her to disregard everything Sarskin had said, had scoffed at the idea of "marking" her as his own. He didn't want her the way she wanted him, so there was nothing to say.

Krisa shook her head in mute misery.

"The feast is in an hour," Teague said coldly, nodding at the lace dress she still clutched in her fists. "I suggest you put that on and come out on time. We wouldn't want to give offense on our last night here."

Krisa found her tongue at last. "Last night? But—"

"Didn't my old shipmate tell you a rescue party has been spotted back by the wreck of the *Princess*? Had the news from one of his scout ships today."

"He said it wouldn't surprise him if they were already here," Krisa whispered through numb lips. Unconsciously one hand crept to the back of her neck to rub the small bump at its base.

Teague sneered. "Told you he could never give a straight answer about anything. How long d'you think it'll take them to realize you're not on board the *Princess* and start homing in on your chip? Two, three days at the most. Tomorrow morning I'm going for Sarskin's fastest ship and I'll be back tomorrow evening to collect you, so you'd better be ready to go."

"Why can't I go with you to get the ship?" Krisa asked desperately. The idea of staying anywhere that Lord Radisson's men could show up at any time made her feel like she was suffocating. *But that could be anywhere you are as long as you're got that chip, Krisa.*

"You'd only slow me down. It's a rough path and besides, Sarskin refuses to let you see the location of his ships. That chip makes you a security risk, sweetheart. If you told the wrong person what you'd seen, you could bring his whole operation down. He may like you enough to warn you about me, but that doesn't mean he'll let you get in the way of his precious profits." Teague turned to go again.

"But…"

"What's the matter?" he asked, turning back. Krisa could see the muscles in his jaw clenching as he spoke. "Afraid I'll leave you? Take the ship and jump planet. Let you take your chances with Lord Radisson and the chip?"

"No, that never entered my mind." Krisa felt her temper bubble up, overcoming the tears.

"So glad you can trust me at least that much," Teague growled. "Now get dressed, the feast is in less than an hour. You're mine, for at least one more night, so you'd better show up and act the part."

He left, slamming the door behind him.

Chapter Twenty-Two

ဢ

"You son of a bitch!" Krisa gave vent to her temper in a most unladylike way. She threw the only thing she happened to have at hand, the lovely ivory lace dress, at the door as it slammed. It hit the door with a soft, unsatisfying rustle, and lay in a small heap of silky fabric at the base of the thick wooden door, while Krisa fumed. Pacing up and down the thick peach carpeting she called the big Feral everything she could think of under her breath, using words she hadn't know existed a month before. The irony of the fact that she was using vocabulary she had learned from Teague to curse him out wasn't lost on Krisa, it made her angrier than ever.

"Play the part, don't give offense," she snarled under her breath, snatching the ivory lace gown from the floor at last and stomping over to the bed to see what else Sarskin had sent her. There was a pair of silk stockings and some dainty, high-heeled shoes covered in tiny pearls that looked as though they would just fit her. And of course, there was the all-important cincher to pull her figure into a perfect hourglass shape under the ivory gown.

Muttering angrily, Krisa put everything on, pulling the cincher viciously tight to make sure her waist would be extra-tiny under the lovely dress. She buttoned every minuscule pearl button right up to her chin and twisted her hair, which she had been wearing loose around her shoulders for days, into a tight and proper chignon at the nape of her neck. She secured it with the ornate silver hairpin that had come all the way from the *Star Princess* with her. Then she marched into the fresher and slapped on the full-length holo-viewer in the corner of the marble room.

A girl from another life stared back at her. A girl with a lovely gown, proper for evening wear that was buttoned right up to her chin. A girl with a tiny waist and every hair neatly in place. A prim and proper Briar Rose bride that any man would be glad to claim.

Any man but Teague.

Krisa stood glaring into the holo-viewer, watching as the perfect girl's face crumpled and tears poured down her cheeks. Teague didn't want her—not the way she wanted him. She supposed she had been stupid to think he would want an inexperienced girl like her tagging along after him wherever he went. *Probably just slow him down, trip him up.* After all, he would be trying to stay one step ahead of the law everywhere he went. There would be a price on his head, just as there would be on hers if she ran away from her obligations and defaulted on the Briar Rose contract.

Stupid idea anyway, wanting to run away with a wanted ex-convict and known murderer instead of going to live a life of luxury and security on Lynix Prime where you belong, scolded the voice of Madame Ledoux inside her head. Except Teague was so much more than that. He was...there was no way to explain what he was. He reminded Krisa of a puzzle box she used to own as a little girl.

On the outside the box looked ordinary enough, it was made of plain, dark brown wood, worn smooth with the passage of time and many hands. But when you opened it, there was a secret compartment inside and inside the compartment, if you could find it, was a tiny switch that caused the whole box to open into a different box and *that* box had another secret switch and so on and so on. Teague was like that—he kept surprising her, kept doing and saying things she couldn't have predicted and wouldn't have expected.

Krisa supposed it was one reason she had fallen in love with him. What did she have to look forward to on Lynix Prime but a life of dull security and sameness day after day after day for the rest of her life? Assuming she could get the chastity chip out of her neck, of course. She supposed she could expect some fairly severe pain unless she could get that taken care of.

Thinking of the chip made her remember Teague's angry words. *It's a wonder they bothered with the Goddessdamn chip in your neck at all, they don't need it to make you act the way they want you to.* But the chip wasn't activated. There was no one forcing her to act or think or dress herself this way—the Briar Rose way. Not yet.

Krisa looked at herself in the viewer again. The lace dress was prim and proper—too proper—and her hair was pulled up so tightly it made her head ache. The lovely pearl-encrusted shoes pinched her toes and sent sharp pains through the arches of her feet, which had become accustomed to the comfortable leather sandals the Yss wore. But worst of all was the damned cincher. It constricted her breathing so that she felt she was constantly gasping for air and held in her naturally voluptuous breasts, hiding their curves behind its unyielding material. It made her look as though she was pinched in two, which was exactly how she felt while she was wearing it.

The girl in the mirror—that perfect Briar Rose bride—wasn't her anymore. In the month since she had decided to take her chances in the jungles of Planet X with Teague she had changed. She'd seen and done things that would have made her gasp and shudder and feel faint just to think about during her life at Briar Rose. Those experiences had changed her—*Teague* had changed her whether he believed it or not. She would never be the same person again, no matter how tightly she pulled in her cincher, or how many perfect parties she threw for Lord Radisson's guests at his country estate on Lynix Prime.

No matter what else happened to her, some part of her would always be the girl who had sat down to a cannibal feast and run through the jungle with a soondar on her trail. The girl who had raced a sunset to save the man she loved and performed shameless acts in public to entertain a crowd of savages. Who had performed those same acts and worse and enjoyed every minute of it with the big Feral in the privacy of their room.

That's who I really am — that's what Teague meant when he said he knew the real me — the heat I keep locked inside.

Krisa looked in the viewer a third time. Once she got to Prime that person, the person she really was, would have to be stowed away like a dress that was out of fashion. A dress so beautiful you couldn't bear to part with it, but one that could never be worn again. But there was no one here on Planet X to make her do that. Not now. Not yet.

What am I doing?

Angrily, Krisa ripped the pin out of her hair, letting it fall loose around her shoulders in abundant curly brown waves. Then she grabbed both sides of the ivory lace dress's high collar and yanked. Delicate fabric ripped and tiny seed pearl buttons flew everywhere, zipping through the holo-field, distorting her image, and ricocheting off the marble walls to patter onto the floor. Krisa kicked off the sharp-toed, pinching shoes and pulled down the silk stockings, making huge, satisfying runs in them with her violent jerks. Last of all she yanked off the offending cincher, threw it on the floor and kicked it into a corner.

She might have to act a part once she got to Prime, but she'd be damned if she'd do it one minute before she had to.

And I'll be damned if I'll leave without letting Teague know exactly how I feel. Even if he doesn't return those feelings.

One last night as his woman. One last night to show the man she loved what she wanted, what she was capable of. If she didn't take advantage of this last chance, Krisa knew she'd regret it the rest of her life.

And she didn't intend to go to her prim and proper life on Lynix Prime as the dull and boring wife of Lord Radisson with any regrets.

* * * * *

Every head in the feasting hall turned when she entered the room and Krisa knew why. She was dressed in style—Yss style—and she felt both utterly exposed and utterly beautiful. She was wearing a special dress—one Vis had given her over many protests. It was a ritual mating outfit she had been sure she would never wear it because, even by Yss standards, it was very revealing. Now she was glad that her friend had insisted on making it a present.

The dress was a deep, indigo color that was sacred, as were all dark colors, to the Yss. With Ziba translating, Vis had made her understand that the material was dyed using the refined blood of the soondar, which was such a deep blue it appeared black. The material itself had a soft, velvety texture that felt like short, lush fur rubbing against her bare skin.

The top half of the dress cupped her breasts and pushed them high, plunging into a sharp vee at the front and rounding gently at the cups which barely covered her nipples. If Krisa took a deep enough breath, the dusky rose arcs of her areolas were revealed on either side. The bottom half was an abbreviated skirt that showed her long, slim legs right up to the thigh. The customary Yss slit up the center showed a tiny patch of the same velvety soft material barely concealing her pussy lips.

What made the outfit really special was the pale gold thread embroidered over almost every square inch of its fabric. Vis had tried to explain the markings to her when she gave Krisa the clothes in the first place. As far as Krisa could gather, they were fertility symbols, markings to draw the eyes of the man you wished to mate with, the man you wished to possess and be possessed by. The embroidery had a special significance for her tonight and she felt both beautiful and wanton in the Yss mating gown. To complete the outfit, she wore traditional Yss sandals that laced up to the knee.

Krisa held her head high as she paced regally into the echoing room with its high vaulted ceiling and broad windows that let in the deep, burnt umber light of the Planet X sunset. As was the Yss custom, everyone was seated in a large circle on woven mats on the floor. The center of the circle was filled with many platters of food, the biggest of which was piled with fragrant, steaming meat that was a deep blue color—the second soondar Teague had killed.

The guest of honor was sitting at the far side of the circle, facing her. The moment she walked into the room, his black second lid flickered back to reveal blazing silver. Krisa could feel his eyes on her every step of the way as she walked gracefully around the circle and made her way to him. She was Teague's woman tonight—this last night they had together—and her place was by his side.

There was complete silence for a moment as she walked around the wide circle and then a low hissing began in waves from the seated Yss. Slim, six-fingered hands patted the floor in appreciative applause. Krisa nodded her head in acknowledgement of the praise. She might not fit the Briar Rose standard of propriety, but tonight she epitomized the Yss idea of beauty perfectly and she knew it.

"What the hell do you think you're doin', sweetheart?" Teague growled when she had settled herself gracefully and the feast was underway.

Krisa looked at him with wide, innocent eyes. "I'm playing the part just like you said, Teague. Aren't I supposed to belong to you, be your woman?" She shifted closer to him and reached across his body so that her breasts brushed his arm suggestively, feeling his muscles bunch and tense as she did so. Taking one of the small, sunshine-flavored fruits, Krisa bit into it, her eyes never leaving Teague's silver slitted ones. Sweet, sticky juice leaked down her arm. Krisa lapped it up, trailing her pink tongue in a slow, sensuous motion along her forearm, never breaking eye contact as she did it.

Teague's eyes widened, then narrowed and his nostrils flared as he watched her perform her little show. *Scenting me*, Krisa thought, taking a deep breath she knew would display the creamy swells of her breasts. *Smelling my heat.* And she could smell his as well. This close to his big body the heat that radiated from him carried a deep, spicy musk that was uniquely Teague. The scent seemed to intoxicate her, like a drug that pulsed through her veins, making her feel reckless and hot. From the look on his face, Krisa knew the significance of the Yss fertility symbols embroidered all over her outfit weren't lost on him either.

When he finally spoke, Teague's voice was a deep, warning growl. "This is a dangerous game you're playin', little girl." The menacing rumble seemed to vibrate through every part of her body and Krisa felt her heart skip a beat. Was she going too far? Maybe—but there was no way in hell she was backing down now.

Giving him a level gaze that she hoped didn't betray her racing pulse she said, "I'm not afraid, Teague. I know what I'm getting myself into."

"You sure?" Teague frowned and there was a blazing heat in the silver eyes that made something deep inside her clench with fear and desire. "I'm not kidding, Krisa. Don't push me tonight or you're gonna regret it."

Krisa just looked at him, keeping her face carefully blank despite the spikes of adrenaline racing through her veins. She intended to push Teague tonight—push him hard—but it wasn't quite time for that yet. For now she could enjoy the feast and the feeling of heat his eyes raised on her exposed skin.

Pretending to be very interested in the food, Krisa took some of the deep blue soondar meat as the tray was passed. It had a strong, wild flavor, unlike anything she had ever tasted before. The Yss believed you took in the strength and characteristics of the animal whose meat you ate. Tonight Krisa hoped they were right. She would need every ounce of strength and courage she could get to do what she planned on doing.

The feast seemed to take forever but it couldn't have been that long. The burnt umber light faded away to be replaced by soft glows that lit the inner circle, gleaming from the pale, narrow Yss eyes all around her. Krisa's stomach felt tight with tension, but she forced herself to eat at least a little, knowing she would need the energy.

As she ate the strongly flavored soondar meat, Krisa recalled what Vis had told her when she had given her the special dress dyed in the huge creature's blood. *The soondar mate for life*, Vis had said. *When the female soondar finds a male she wants she stalks him, follows his scent until she finds him alone. Then she entices him, makes him want her. He cannot resist her. They mate for many days, bonding. May your mating be as long and as deep as that of the soondar.* It was a polite thing to say among the Yss, a wish for a happy, fulfilling joining. A hope for a relationship that lasted a lifetime, but Krisa had only one night.

A sudden silence in the great feasting hall made her look up. The feast was over—if no one moved in the next few seconds everyone would disperse quietly, and her chance would be lost.

Krisa stood up.

"What the *hell* do you think you're doing?" Teague growled, for the second time that night.

Trying to keep her voice calm and light, Krisa answered him. "You provided the meat for this feast, Teague. You're the guest of honor and it's your duty to provide the entertainment as well. Isn't that right?"

"This isn't like the Yss village we stayed at before, Krisa. It's not required that we do anything for entertainment," the big Feral growled, his eyes glowing in the dim light.

"Well, maybe I *want* to entertain them," Krisa said lightly. Then she let her voice drop, taking on a low, purring tone. "Come on, Teague. It's our last night here, let's make it a show to remember." She held out a hand to him. The big Feral stared at her, his eyes gone black and unreadable for a long moment. Then, finally, he got to his feet.

There was a low, sighing hiss of anticipation from the assembled Yss. From somewhere the rhythmic drumbeat and haunting flute that always accompanied such performances began.

Krisa led her man to the center of the circle, from which all the platters and bowls had been cleared, leaving a large open space. Teague stared at her. She could see the muscles of his big arms and broad back bunching and jumping with tension beneath the black leather vest he wore.

"Now what? What did you have in mind, sweetheart? Another dance?" he asked sarcastically. But Krisa only shook her head.

"Just wait—you'll see," she whispered. She stood still for a moment before him, letting the music flow over and around and through her. Letting the primitive rhythm pulse in her blood and take her where she needed to go to make this work. Then, very slowly, she began to move.

Keeping her eyes on her target she glided silently along the smooth stone floor, trailing fingertips lightly along his shoulders, chest and back as she moved. She felt like a female soondar on the prowl for a mate. There was a wildness in the air as she circled him, a reckless heat singing through her veins. Just for tonight Teague was more than her protector, more than her man. He was her prey and she stalked him, keeping her eyes fixed on his boldly, as he turned his head to follow her movements, letting him know what she wanted, what she needed from him.

A low growl was building deep in his chest and suddenly Teague struck, quick as a snake, pulling her to him, large hands biting roughly into her bare shoulders. "I'm warning you now to stop this, Krisa. If you keep pushin' me I won't be responsible for what I do." His face was dark with anger and barely controlled heat.

Krisa slithered out of his grasp, as slippery as a snake herself and began circling the big Feral again. "Maybe I don't want you to be responsible," she purred softly, brushing her cheek against the broad back, feeling the warmth of his skin through the black leather. "Maybe I'm tired of us both acting so damn responsibly," she continued, standing in front of him to unbutton the vest with teasing slowness.

"You don't know what you're saying, what you're askin' for," Teague rumbled. "But if you don't watch out, little girl, you're going to get it anyway." His breathing was harsh and rapid in the echoing room. Krisa could smell his musk, leather and sweat and spice, as she popped open the last button and ran her hands caressingly up and down the broad, well-defined planes of his chest.

"That's what I'm hoping for," she whispered softly, letting her hands trail down to the tense muscles of his lower abdomen, to play teasingly with the waistband of the leather pants.

Teague's eyes widened and he grabbed her by the shoulders again as he suddenly understood her intention, but he was too late. Krisa had already unsnapped the stiff material and was pulling open the black leather to reach inside.

"Krisa, I'm warning you...don't!"

"Don't what?" she asked, using both hands to claim her prize while she looked him directly in the eye. The feel of him, of the long, thick cock in her hands, was like nothing she had ever touched before. Hard as a stone and yet warm and alive and throbbing in her palm. And the skin that covered it was smooth and softer than velvet, softer than rose petals as she caressed him, measuring his length and thickness with her small, careful hands. Krisa tried to get her fingers all the way around it and when she couldn't do that, she stroked the length of the shaft from the broad, plum-shaped head to the base, thick with coarse, curling hair, that scratched against her fingertips when she touched him there.

"*Don't,*" Teague begged again. There was a hoarse urgency in his voice that a part of her knew she ought to listen to. She was doing what he had warned her not to, pushing him to his limit and beyond. *Every man has a point of no return, girls,* Madame Glossop's voice echoed in her head. *A point after which protests and pleading are futile.* Krisa wanted to see the big Feral reach his limit, wanted to push him into crossing the line just once.

Slowly, her eyes never leaving his, she sank to her knees before him in the pale circle of light.

"Krisa," he breathed, a low, tormented sound that was barely audible above the low beat of the drums and the high wailing of the flute. "I'm beggin' you…don't do this."

"But I want to," she whispered back. The stone floor was hard on her knees but she barely noticed it. Teague's hands pinched into her shoulders, trying to keep her back from him, but she ducked her head forward. Remembering what she had seen at the other Yss feasts they had attended, she stroked her cheek lightly along the heated length of his cock.

His musk was strong here—intoxicatingly spicy. Delicious. Krisa rubbed her face against him, feeling the hot silk of his shaft like a branding iron along her cheekbone, forehead, throat. She bathed in the scent of him, relished his fire, the wild masculinity that pulled her so strongly. Tonight Teague was hers and she intended to enjoy him to the fullest.

Taking the thick cock in one hand she rubbed the rose petal-soft head along the moist curve of her lips, looking up to see the heat in those half-lidded silver eyes as she did so. *Mine,* she thought, as Teague's hands released her shoulders and buried themselves in her hair instead, urging her on. *All mine. Even if we never see each other again after tomorrow, you'll never forget this night when you belonged to me, as I belong to you. As I will always belong to you, in my heart.*

Deliberately, she parted her lips and laid a soft, open-mouthed kiss on the broad crown—an opening—an invitation. Teague made a deep, almost painful noise low in his chest, the sound vibrating her body as she did it again. There was a clear, sticky fluid leaking from the tiny slit in the plum-shaped head and Krisa's tongue darted out to capture a drop, swirling slowly around the warm, dusky skin, tasting him.

Delicious, she thought, finding his salty-sweet flavor as intoxicating as his strong, musky scent. Opening her mouth carefully, she took all of the broad head inside, lapping and sucking gently, experimenting to see what pleased him. Teague groaned out loud, fingers twining in her hair as she sucked him. Lifting her eyes for a moment, Krisa could see that his head was thrown back, the cords standing out in his strong neck as he struggled to endure the exquisite sensation of her hot, wet mouth on his cock.

How does it feel? Krisa thought triumphantly. She remembered the deep, painful pleasure Teague had put her through the night before and felt her pussy throb between her legs. Now she was giving him back a little of his own medicine and revenge was very, very sweet. Struggling to open her mouth wide enough to accommodate him, she leaned forward, taking him deeper, though there was no way she could get his entire long, thick cock into her mouth.

Teague groaned again and she felt his thickness throbbing against her tongue and the roof of her mouth. *Any minute now.* Krisa had watched enough of the Yss performances to know what came next. Moving her head in a slow rhythm to slide him in and out of her mouth, she waited for the salty spray against her tongue. Waited for the fingers in her hair to tighten as he reached release and gave her what she was searching for.

But the moment never came.

The fingers in her hair tightened, but instead of pulling her forward, they yanked her back, pulling her free of him in one desperate motion. Krisa looked up, half drugged with the pleasure of pleasuring him, bewildered. "What?"

"No." Teague's eyes were little more than metallic slits in the dim room. "Not like this," he muttered. He stuffed his bulging cock back into his trousers and fastened the leather with a few quick motions. Then he reached down and caught Krisa under her arm, jerking her to her feet.

"What—" she asked again, her heart in her mouth. Looking up into those angry, burning eyes she felt real fear for the first time that night. Had she really thought she wanted to push Teague over the line and beyond? Had she really?

"Not like that," Teague growled again, shaking her slightly for emphasis. "If I come in you, Krisa, it's going to be deep inside your sweet, little cunt after a long, hard ride. I'm going to fuck you, little girl, and I don't mean your mouth."

"Teague..."

"Shut up," he grated. "Just shut up, Krisa, before you make it worse for yourself." He was dragging her out of the lighted circle now—the Yss were moving silently aside to give him room to pass.

Krisa looked wildly around for anyone, anything that could help her, but only blank alien eyes in pale, narrow faces stared back. Sarskin, whom she had seen briefly at the beginning of the feast, was gone now, where she didn't know. There was no one to help, no one to care if she shouted or struggled. An old saying of her grandmother's flashed through her mind—*Having sown the wind, you shall reap the whirlwind.*

Krisa was on her own.

Chapter Twenty-Three

80

"Teague, no! Teague, I didn't mean to." The words poured out of her mouth and fell on deaf ears, as he dragged her along down the curving stone corridors back to their room. Krisa felt nearly ready to panic. If she couldn't make him listen to her…couldn't make him see.

I only wanted to pleasure him – wanted to make him understand the way I felt, just once before it was too late. When she had planned her little seduction Krisa had envisioned herself before him, on her knees, with his big hands buried in her hair and his cock pumping hungrily into her mouth, as she drove him over the edge the way he always drove her. She had imagined Teague's deep groans and the salty spray over her tongue as he gave in to the pleasure she was giving him. But she had never, ever, pictured him dragging her off the floor and into their room as he was doing now. Everything had gone horribly, horribly wrong.

"Teague, *please!*" she gasped as he shoved open the door and pushed her roughly inside before slamming it closed behind them.

"It's too late," he said. Fingers biting into her arms he swung her around to face him and claimed her mouth with a punishing kiss. Despite her fear or maybe because of it, Krisa felt her body react to his. Twining her fingers in his thick black hair she pressed herself against him, feeling her breasts crushed against his chest and opening her lips for the demanding assault of his tongue. Big hands roughly roamed over her body with an urgency that wouldn't be denied any longer. The low top of her Yss outfit was ripped down and cruel fingers twisted her nipples until she moaned into his mouth, signaling her submission.

289

Krisa could feel him rocking against her, pressing his barely contained thick cock against her pussy, grinding hard with a promise of more to come shortly. Much more. Very shortly. *Remember your Certificate. Remember the consequences!* The panicky voice in her head was like a fire alarm. Abruptly, Krisa tried to push away but it was like pushing against a brick wall.

"Teague." She turned her head to the side to escape his brutal kisses. "Teague, I'm sorry. I just wanted to show you how...I felt. I didn't mean for it to go this far."

"That's too damn bad, sweetheart. It *has* gone this far and it's about to go a lot farther." His eyes were narrowed, shining slits in the dim room and the massive chest was heaving with barely controlled emotion, fingers still biting into her upper arms.

Krisa tried to think of something, anything she could say to stop him, to halt this disastrous chain of events she had set in motion. "Teague," she gasped at last, holding his gaze with her own, letting the fear and uncertainty she felt fill her face. "You said... You promised you wouldn't rape me."

He threw back his head and laughed, a deep, grating sound that made her tremble with its wild fury. "You get on your knees and suck me in front of everybody at the Goddessdamn feast and now you want to talk about *rape*?" he demanded, eyes blazing a metallic silver. He shook her once for emphasis and Krisa felt her teeth click together and tasted warm, coppery salt, she had bitten her tongue. "Oh no, little girl, the time for that kind of talk has passed," Teague assured her.

He turned her roughly, so that her back was to him and pushed her toward the huge bed in the center of the room. Boosting her up, so that she was on her knees on the mattress, he stepped up behind her and wrapped arms like warm steel cables around her waist.

"We have a saying about rape on Al'hora, sweetheart. Wanna hear it?" he whispered low in her ear, cupping both her bare breasts in his large palms. "Well, do you?" he demanded, rolling her nipples between thumbs and fingers, shooting sparks of pleasure-pain down her spine to the soft vee between her legs.

"Wh-what?" Her voice was little more than a breathless whisper and she was half aware that she was arching her back to push more of her breasts into his hands, giving in to the overwhelming sensations he was putting her through.

"It goes something like this—'You can't rape the willing'," he said softly and she felt the thick bulge in his leather pants press menacingly against the back of her thigh. Nervously she pressed her legs together but Teague felt her do it and growled warningly in her ear.

"I-I'm *not* willing. I'm trying to tell you *no*," Krisa protested weakly, knowing it was a lie even as the words left her lips.

"I'm through listenin' to what you say, little girl. Right now I can only hear what your body is telling me," Teague grated. "Now spread your legs for me, Krisa. Spread them right *now*."

"Please..." She was almost crying now, filled in equal measure with need and doubt, feeling like she couldn't get a deep enough breath. Teague's hot mouth brushed the back of her neck, biting and sucking the tender skin at her nape and the heat of the big, hard body behind her overwhelmed her with his harsh demands.

"Spread your legs for me, Krisa," he insisted and then, in a softer tone, "I'm not going to fuck you...yet."

"Th-then why?"

"I'm proving a point," he growled low in her ear. "Spread your legs for me, little girl, I wanna feel your sweet, little cunt. If you aren't hot and wet and ready for me, I swear I'll leave you alone." Big hands reached in front of her, parting her thighs despite everything Krisa could do to stop him.

"But… But what if…" Krisa couldn't finish the question. She knew, and knew the big Feral knew, what he would find when he pulled aside the tiny triangle of fabric covering her pussy.

"What if you *are* wet? Wet and ready for me?" he rumbled, deep in his chest. "Why then I'm gonna fuck you, little girl. Just like I promised. Gonna fill you up long and hard and slow. Gonna make you mine, so spread your legs and let me in."

Crying softly, helpless before his demands, Krisa felt her legs part for his big hands and then the tiny scrap of soft cloth that went with the Yss outfit was being ripped away with a violence that made her shiver. Huge hands spread wide to cup her trembling inner thighs, framing her naked pussy for an instant, pulling her backwards so that the hard bulge of his cock dug into her from behind, letting her know what to expect.

"Teague…oh, Goddess…" Krisa whispered brokenly.

There was no reply but his harsh breathing against the back of her neck and then thick, blunt fingertips were invading her, parting the wet lips of her pussy and driving into the hot, lush entrance to her body. Teague rubbed hard twice against her throbbing clit and Krisa's hips bucked suddenly in a whip-crack orgasm that left her breathless and gasping.

She had never been so wet or so ready before.

At last Teague spoke, still rubbing firmly over her slippery folds as he did, making her cry and grind against the invading fingers. "You know what this means, Krisa," he growled, low in his throat, his breath hot at the back of her neck. "It means I'm gonna have to fuck you now."

"All right. All right, Teague," she said at last, her voice low and accepting. Wearily, she sagged back against him, letting herself rest against the broad chest and muscular torso, letting him support her. "All right, do it. I can't stop you, I don't want to." *But Lord Radisson. Lynix Prime. Lost*

Virginity...Recertification. Shut up, she told the little voice inside her head. *Just shut up.* She was tired of fighting, tired of holding out when what she wanted, what she *needed* was to feel Teague's thick cock sheathed to the hilt inside her body, filling her, fucking her, marking her as his own, even if it was only for one night.

She might regret it in the future, but Krisa knew she would regret it more if she didn't give in to the demands of her body now. The decision had gone beyond her, just as it always did in the dreams she had of the man with no face—the man who turned out to be Teague. It was fate—destiny. She could give herself to him or try to hold herself back, but either way he would take her. Krisa preferred a willing surrender.

"Teague," she whispered, pressing back against him, rubbing against the hard insistent bulge of his cock deliberately. "Whatever you want, whatever you need...take it. I-I want you to."

He growled, a low, inarticulate sound that rumbled up from the bottom of his deep chest and vibrated his entire body, then nuzzled against the back of her neck, breathing her scent in deeply, as though inhaling some kind of a drug. *The scent of my heat*, Krisa thought. *The scent of my submission.*

Then he was stripping away the remains of the Yss feasting outfit, making her completely naked. The soft material landed with an unimportant rustle on the floor and big, warm hands were running up and down her naked body, petting her arms, thighs, belly, the small of her back, cupping her breasts and sliding over her inner thighs, touching every inch of her while Teague lapped hotly at the side of her neck.

"Mine, Krisa. Have to make you *mine*," he whispered. "Tried to let you go but I can't—I *can't*."

"I don't want you to," she said, feeling the words strip away any pretense, leaving her soul as naked and vulnerable as her body. "I-I want you to take me."

He didn't answer her with words. Instead she heard the sound of him shedding the leather pants and vest and then he was pressing her forward to her hands and knees on the firm, gelafoam mattress. Krisa bit her lip and spread her thighs even wider for him. The position made her feel primitive—*hot*. Like a female animal in heat about to be mounted. She could feel the big Feral looming over her, but she couldn't see him, couldn't stop him. She could only wait, open and vulnerable on the bed for him to take her.

"Listen to me, little girl." Teague's breath was hot in her ear as he leaned over her, covering her naked, trembling body with his own. Krisa felt the head of his thick cock, hard and ready for her, brush against the inside of her thigh as he spoke, branding her with his heat.

"I-I'm listening," she whispered back, barely able to get the words out.

"Need to fuck you now," Teague whispered. "Have to be inside you...can't wait anymore. But I know it's your first time, I'll try not to hurt you."

Warm hands were putting her into position, pressing her down so that the synthi-cotton sheets, which had seemed so soft before, chafed against her hypersensitive nipples and her bottom was high in the air. Then the broad, plum-shaped head of his cock was rubbing insistently over her slippery sex. Not to penetrate—not yet, Krisa realized—but to get him wet enough to enter her trembling, virginal entrance. *Oh my merciful Goddess, he's really going to do it!*

"Teague," she whispered. "Teague, I'm *afraid*."

"Don't be." Large hands soothed her back, rubbing firm, comforting circles over her skin, which had broken out in a sudden rash of gooseflesh. "Gonna break you in real sweet and easy, sweetheart. It might hurt a little just at first..." He gripped her hips firmly, holding her in place. Then the broad head of his cock began to ease inside her, pressing the swollen lips of her pussy aside to enter her wet passage, crowning in the entrance of her body. Krisa gasped, feeling herself stretch to accommodate his girth. "But once you're over that little pain," Teague continued, still pressing deeper, entering her one wet inch at a time. "Once I'm deep inside you," he continued, "once my cock is all the way into your sweet, tight cunt then...well, then I'm gonna ride you hard, little girl. Understand?"

"I..." Krisa had to take a deep, shuddering breath before she could finish. "I understand," she breathed at last, trying to open herself wider for his invasion.

"That's good because I have to make you mine now." Teague's fingers tightened on her hips, making her sure she'd have ten finger-shaped bruises the next day and he began to push deeper into her tight entrance. Another thick inch of his cock slid into her and another. Suddenly Krisa felt him nudge against something, some barrier inside her body and then, with a sudden sharp pain that was gone almost before it arrived, he was through it.

She gave a strangled little gasp and Teague stopped his steady assault for a moment to pet and kiss her back, running soothing hands over her quivering sides as though she were a wild creature he wanted to tame.

"Easy, little girl, easy," Krisa heard him murmur, his voice deep and gentle. "You ready for me to go on?"

"Y-yes." She was moaning now, making a low, steady noise in the back of her throat that she couldn't seem to help. It was an overwhelming sensation—being fucked like this for the first time, having his thick cock invading her pussy, filling her, owning her.

Hands tightened on her pelvis once more and then he was pressing deeper, filling her completely until the wide head of his cock kissed the end of her channel.

"In you now, Krisa..." She heard him breathe, his voice low and hoarse with barely restrained lust. "All the way in you now. Can you feel it? Can you feel my cock filling you up?"

An inarticulate sound of assent fell from her lips. Never could she have ever imagined such a feeling — the feeling of being joined so completely, of being mastered and fulfilled at once. Warm palms slid forward along her lightly sweating sides to cup her full breasts, hanging like ripe fruit beneath her body.

"Ready for me to fuck you now, little girl?" Teague's breath was hot in her ear. "Ready for me to fill you up with my cum and make you mine? Mine forever?"

Something about the words, the way he said them, made her tremble inside, made her wonder if there was a deeper meaning somewhere. But the feel of Teague's big body covering her, surrounding her, invading her, drove every other thought out of her head. There was no room in her mind to think, no room to question — there was only room to feel.

"Teague," she breathed softly. "Teague, *please...*" The sheets were rough under her palms as she gripped them tightly between white-knuckled fingers, bracing herself against what she knew was coming. Teague had promised to ride her hard and she knew he wasn't lying. The big Feral had been waiting for this moment for a long, frustrating time. With so much tension and passion built up between them, it was bound to be a rough ride. She fully expected to be sore from the coming onslaught when all this was over.

She wasn't disappointed. With a muted roar, Teague drew almost all the way out of her slick channel and thrust back in, driving his thick cock into her tight, wet cunt like a battering ram, forcing a cry from her lips as he repeated the action again and again.

Krisa cried out, losing her balance under the fierce assault. Her hands would no longer support her and she was forced to go down on her elbows, a move that spread her pussy even wider to Teague's pounding thrusts. Pain burst through her and pleasure too — a deeper, more consuming sensation than she had ever felt and the beginnings of an orgasm so fierce Krisa was afraid it would burn her to ashes with its intensity. She turned her head and bit her lip until blood flowed, tears squeezing from beneath her tightened eyelids, as she tried to endure the overwhelming sensations.

Teague had been working her in silence, concentrating on building a slow, deliberate pulse within her body with his punishing strokes, but now he began speaking in a low, hoarse voice that seemed to penetrate her mind the way his cock was penetrating her body.

"Love to fuck you, Krisa," he growled, and she felt the hands cupping her breasts shift and rough fingers were tugging and pinching her nipples, heightening the sensations between her legs. "Been wanting to shove my cock inside you from the first minute I smelled your sweet scent in the *Princess*."

Krisa moaned, unable to give a more intelligent reply to his confession.

"You don't know how hard it was, all those nights in the jungle not to pin you to the ground and spread your legs and fuck you, little girl," he rumbled, still stroking inside her. "Fill you up with my cum and claim you right there." Teague licked a long wet furrow up her back, along the groove of her spine, never stopping the rough motion of his fucking as he did it.

Krisa gasped at the push and thrust of his cock inside her pussy and the feel of his tongue on her skin. "Why...didn't you?" she moaned, amazed that she could say anything at all.

"Wanted you to trust me. Wanted you to submit to me just like you are now with your sweet ass in the air and your pussy wet and spread for me, ready to be filled by my cock. Wanted to hear you cry and moan underneath me while you opened yourself for me completely. Does it feel good, little girl? Is this what you wanted, the way you need to be fucked?" he demanded, speeding up the intensity of his thrusts, pressing her into the mattress so that Krisa was sure an imprint of her face and arms would be there forever.

"Yes...yes, Teague," she sobbed, abandoning any pride or dignity she had left. His rough love was pushing her faster and faster toward the peak, building the pleasure inside her until she couldn't think about anything else. "This is how I want you. This is how I need you," she gasped. "Inside me...so *deep* inside me!"

"That's good, little girl, because that's what I need too." Teague released her nipples and Krisa felt one large hand slide back to her pelvis and then dip between her legs. "Gonna come in just a minute, Krisa," he whispered roughly. "Gonna fill your sweet cunt up the way I need to, but I wanna feel you come first. Can you do that for me, sweetheart? Can you come for me while I'm buried inside you?" Blunt fingertips rubbed over the wet place where they were joined, caressing the slippery, swollen bud of her clit and sending electric jolts of pleasure through her body.

Krisa cried out, arching her back as her body obeyed his order and the fierce orgasm pounded through her. Large, white blossoms of light exploded before her eyes and she trembled uncontrollably. Her wet sex helplessly spasmed around the thick invader, his cock piercing her to the core. Teague's rhythm inside her quickened as he felt her reaction.

"That's it, little girl, come for me," he growled, still rubbing over her slick folds with knowledgeable fingers. "Come for me...let me feel you come."

"Oh... Oh, Teague! Feels so... Oh!" Krisa's hair hung in her face in a long, silky curtain obscuring her sight but she didn't need to see anything just then. The only thing she wanted was to go on feeling this incredible pleasure—her body's sweet submission to the man she loved—the only man she would ever love.

With an inarticulate growl, Teague pulled her up, supporting her with strong arms around her waist as he plunged as deeply into her as possible, seating himself to the hilt in her tight cunt. He nuzzled his face against her neck, pushing her hair aside to bare her throat. Krisa leaned back against him, knowing what he needed, giving him the side of her neck that was unmarked. She cried out as she felt his sharp, white teeth sink into her again, drawing blood while he filled her to the limit.

The feel of him pulsing into her, claiming her body completely, coupled with the stinging pain of his bite, sent a second wave of orgasmic pleasure racing through Krisa's veins. She moaned helplessly, a scrap of paper caught in a flood, carried away on the tide of sensation and need.

Teague held her tightly for a moment, his broad chest slick with sweat and pumping like a bellows against her back. Then slowly, not withdrawing from her body, he lowered them both to the bed where he wrapped warm arms around her as though he never intended to let her go.

"You're mine, little girl," Krisa heard him growl softly in her ear. "Mine now, don't forget it."

Yours now, she thought, beginning to regain some of her ability to think—to reason—as the crushing tide of pleasure ebbed leaving a dull, throbbing ache behind. The enormity of what she had done, what she had allowed him to do to her began to penetrate her brain. *Yours now, here on Planet X, Teague, but whose will I be tomorrow? And how will I explain my lost virginity to Lord Radisson on Prime?*

Chapter Twenty-Four

ॐ

"I hurt you." Teague's deep voice was flat in the dim room.

"N-no. Not so much," Krisa denied, trying to stifle a sob. She was still cuddled close in his arms, her back to his front. The deep, even sound of his breathing had convinced her that he was asleep, that it was safe to give in to her overwhelming emotions.

"Then why the tears, little girl? Here, turn around." He rolled her over, until she was lying on her side, facing him. There was grave concern written on his dark face and glinting in the silver depths of his eyes. "Well?" He cupped her cheek in one hand, wiping away a tear with his thumb.

"It's just…it's just that I can't go to Prime now."

"I know." His voice was quiet and unconcerned.

"So glad to see you're worried about what happens to me," Krisa said, stung by his apparent lack of distress for her future. She pulled away from him and sat up in bed, dragging the sheet up to cover her breasts.

Teague pulled it back down again. "Don't bother," he growled. "I've seen it all, no point in tryin' to hide any of it from me now, Krisa."

"I know you've seen it all. You've had it all." The accusing words bubbled up from a deep spring of fear inside her and had to come out. "You just took the only thing that could guarantee my future."

"You've still got your precious Certificate of Virginity," he pointed out, sitting up beside her. His dark face was like a thundercloud.

"After all this time, lost in the wilderness with Goddess knows who, Lord Radisson is sure to insist on a recertification of my virginity. This—" Krisa leaned over and pulled the limp piece of parchment out of the night table drawer, where she had kept it carefully folded. "Is worthless. *Worthless.*" She held the document up before his eyes and very deliberately ripped it in two, right down the middle.

Teague grabbed her wrists in a punishing grip, making her drop the crumpled paper. "What are you sayin', little girl? You sorry about what we just did? Regret giving yourself to me?"

"No," Krisa nearly shouted. She yanked free of him, rubbing her wrists angrily. "No, I-I wanted to do what we did as much as you. Needed it as much." She blushed, embarrassed to admit her need for him, but continued doggedly. "But what am I supposed to do now that I can't go to Prime? Where am I supposed to go, Goddessdamn you?"

"Where you're goin' is with me." Teague spoke in a tone of finality that brooked no argument.

"I...*what?*" Krisa wasn't sure she'd heard him right.

"I *said* you're comin' with me to Alpha Lyrae and that's the end of it," Teague growled, eyes flashing.

"H-how dare you? You promised me you'd get me to Prime. You said you wouldn't try to take me with you." It didn't occur to Krisa that she was arguing against the very thing she wanted, she only knew that his proprietary tone had gotten her temper up again. "You said I could trust you," she accused.

"Yeah...well, that was before," he growled. "Before I had you—*marked* you. You're mine now. I'm sorry if you're gonna miss livin' in the lap of luxury with dear Lord Radisson, but that's too damn bad, 'cause you're coming with me."

"You know I never gave a damn about having a lot of credit or living in style," Krisa yelled.

"Well, why else are you so anxious to go sign the joining contract with that old bastard?" Teague took her by the shoulders and shook her once, hard. "I *know* you don't love him."

"No—I love *you!*" The minute the words were out of her mouth, Krisa wanted to call them back. Why had she revealed something that made her look so stupid and needy? She waited for Teague to laugh or curse but instead he pulled her closer. He stared into her eyes, studying her face with a fierce intensity that made the pit of her stomach jump and twitch.

"Say that again," he commanded in a low voice.

"I said, I love you," Krisa said defiantly, lifting her chin to meet his silver eyes squarely. Let him think what he wanted.

"Do you? Do you really?" Teague was still looking at her, a strange expression growing on his dark face.

"I wouldn't say it otherwise. I keep my word, unlike *some* people," Krisa snapped.

Teague sighed heavily and let her go to run a hand through his hair. "Look, when I made you that promise to get you back to Prime, I meant to keep it. But now...I can't. I just can't."

"Because you've had me? Because we..."

"Made love, fucked, call it whatever you want." Teague frowned irritably. "Look, Krisa, I knew the minute I saw you, the minute you pulled back my blindfold and trusted me not to hurt you, that I would do anything—*anything* to have you. But I also knew the kind of life I lead isn't real easy for a girl like you to get used to. So I swore to myself I wouldn't touch you, wouldn't let myself go too far. Because I *knew* that if I ever took you all the way, I could never let you go."

"Then why did you act like you didn't want me? Why did you pretend you didn't mark me on purpose?" Krisa rubbed her neck where the purple welt he had put there the night before was still very visible, though there was surprisingly little pain. Soon she would have a matching one on the other side.

"Because I didn't," Teague growled. "What Sarskin told you is true, all right? Marking *is* a Feral ritual—we don't do it unless we've found the woman we want to mate with for life. Last night when you wouldn't let me have you, I...well, I kinda went a little crazy. I think part of me was determined to make you mine somehow, even if I couldn't actually..." He let the sentence trail off.

Krisa didn't know whether to laugh or cry. Teague was offering her everything she wanted on a silver platter. But was he offering it for the right reasons?

"So," she cleared her throat. "So if we hadn't made love just now, you would have just let me go? Just dropped me off on Prime and forgotten about me?"

Teague laughed, a short, harsh sound. "Truthfully? I don't know, sweetheart. Don't know if I could've let you go even if we hadn't made love. I was gonna do my damnedest, though, because I'd promised you. But forget about you? Never. You're burned into me." He pressed one large hand over his chest. "Here. Couldn't forget you if I wanted to. Which I don't."

"Teague, are you...trying to say you love me too?" Krisa looked at him earnestly, trying to read the emotion in the metallic depths of his eyes.

"Love you?" He sighed and leaned back against the headboard. "Yeah, guess you could call it that."

"What's that supposed to mean?" Krisa asked in exasperation. "Either you love me or you don't." She crossed her arms over her chest, waiting.

Teague sighed again and pulled her close to him, despite the fact that she remained stiff in his arms. "Guess I do, then. It's just that there isn't a word in any language to describe what I feel for you, little girl. Love, lust, want, need—need more than anything, I guess." He looked down for a moment and his voice got softer.

"After...Corie died I never thought I'd feel for anyone again. Thought that part of me died with her. Never expected to find what I needed in a little girl from Bride Planet, who didn't want to go into the jungle without her corset."

"I *told* you it's a cincher," Krisa scolded gently. She let herself melt against his big body, let him comfort her with his heat. "But why didn't you tell me sooner if you knew all this time?"

"Because *you* didn't know. Didn't seem to feel the same." Teague pulled her even closer, tucking her head beneath his chin, so that Krisa could hear the muffled thump of his heart. "Besides," he continued. "It's a dangerous life—livin' on the run. I'll always have a price on my head and once you default on your contract you will too. Once we get to Alpha Lyrae we'll be okay. They have a non-extradition policy. It's gettin' there that's gonna be risky."

His mention of her Briar Rose contract made Krisa think of the chastity chip. Her hand stole up to the back of her neck, fingering the small bump anxiously. "Teague, what about the chip? They're on Planet X right now, tracking me. How are we going to get away clean when I've got this stupid transmitter in my neck?" She looked up at him.

Teague shook his head. "Don't worry about it, sweetheart. I've got a few tricks up my sleeve. They won't catch us."

Krisa frowned and pushed away from him. "No, I won't be the one to put us at risk."

Teague scowled. "Well, we don't have a whole lot of choice right now."

"Yes we do." Krisa fingered the bump on the back of her neck and tried not to think of the iron spike of pain that had driven into her skull when she only pressed it too hard. She looked up at Teague. "I want you to cut it out. Now. Tonight."

Teague gave her an incredulous look and tried to pull her close again. Krisa resisted.

"You don't know what you're askin' for, Krisa. It's pain like you wouldn't believe. Better to wait until we can find somebody qualified that'll put you under and do it right."

"I don't want to wait," she insisted. "I don't care if it hurts. I don't want to risk Lord Radisson's men finding us. You..." she swallowed hard, "you took out your own, and you're always talking about your 'excellent knife work', Teague. You can do it, I know you can."

Teague sighed and rubbed his face tiredly with one large hand. "Yeah, I can do it, but I wish you wouldn't ask me to. That kind of pain... A little love bite on the neck is one thing." He touched the place where he had marked her earlier that night and Krisa blushed. "But this... I don't want to hurt you, sweetheart. Don't want to put you through it."

Krisa took the large hand in hers and twined their fingers together. "Teague," she said softly. "I understand how you feel, but you have to admit our chances of getting away from here undetected are a lot better without the chip. Y-you said you loved me. I need you to do this for me. Please."

He looked at her closely. "You're determined, aren't you?"

Not trusting her voice, Krisa nodded.

He nodded with decision. "Fine, lie on the bed on your stomach and pull your hair out of the way."

Krisa lay down, pulled her hair to one side, and buried her head in a pillow, determined not to watch whatever it was the big Feral was doing. *Don't think about it*, she ordered herself, but it was terribly hard not to. She wished she would have had the luxury of finding a medic or a "chip doctor" like Alphonius T'lix, the man Teague had referred her to on Lynix Prime, but they couldn't afford to take a chance with Radisson's men already on the planet. Everything inside her said this was the right thing to do and the right time to do it.

If Lord Radisson's men traced the chip and caught them, it would look like an escaped felon kidnapping a helpless girl, no matter what either of them might say. Krisa would be taken back to Prime to her husband-to-be, assuming he still wanted her after he realized she was damaged goods, but Teague would be taken back to prison or summarily executed. She knew Teague was willing to risk himself for her, but she wasn't willing that he should do it. Much better to get the damned chip out now, before they were traced.

No matter how much it hurt.

Despite her determination not to see Teague's preparations for her "surgery", Krisa still managed to catch a glimpse of the long, curving blade of his knife, before she shut her eyes tightly. There was a slight jostling as the big Feral got back on the bed with her and straddled her hips, leaning over her back.

They were both still naked and Krisa could feel the heat radiating from his big body to warm her own. It was strange, she thought, that this same position which had been so pleasurable just a little while ago, should now be filled with dread.

She was so tense she nearly shrieked when Teague bent over her, but instead of the cold kiss of sharp steel on her neck, she felt his warm, wet tongue instead.

"What are you doing?" she squeaked, as he continued to bathe the back of her neck and the tiny bump covering the chip methodically, with long, caressing strokes.

"Ferals have a natural antiseptic in our blood and body fluids. One reason we heal so fast," he explained, stopping for a moment. "This way you'll heal clean, no infection. Okay?"

"All right." It was all Krisa could do to get the words out.

"You changed your mind, sweetheart?" Teague kissed the nape of her neck lightly, reassuringly. "I won't be upset."

"No." Krisa started to shake her head and then thought better of it. "No, do it, Teague. I want you to."

"All right. I'm gonna be as quick as I can. Want you to keep your hands by your sides and hold on to the sheet hard. You feel like you need to scream, do it,just try not to move. This is a sharp knife. Got it?"

"Yes." She tightened her grip on the sheet on either side of her and braced herself, feeling the synthi-cotton pull between her white-knuckled fingers. *Please Goddess, let him get it out quick, please just let him…*

When it came, the flare of white-hot agony was almost too much to bear. Krisa had expected pain but this was in an entirely different category. The sensation that was currently tearing through her nervous system made any other pain she had ever felt no more significant than a stubbed toe.

A line of fire was being traced down the back of her neck and spreading like molten lava throughout her body down every limb, to throb at the tip of each separate finger and toe. Every nerve was crackling like a wire jammed full of electric current, screaming that she was dying, drowning, burning, smothering. On fire…she was on fire and nothing could put her out…

It seemed to go on and on, time stretching like taffy and there was a shriek building in her throat, one so high and frantic it wouldn't even be audible once it left her. Krisa felt the strong synthi-cotton fabric rip between her fingers with a low purring noise and every muscle in her body was tensed to the breaking point. She bit her tongue hard for the second time that night, but didn't feel it. She was only vaguely aware when her mouth flooded with warm, salty bitterness that she had done it at all.

Dimly she heard Teague talking in a low, frustrated voice, saying something about the chip resisting removal, but none of it penetrated her brain, which was completely taken up with the hideous, all-encompassing torment.

Then there was a shooting spike of electric pain that traveled from the base of her skull all the way down to her heels and the world was eaten in a silent, merciful blackness.

* * * * *

"...over now. It's all over now." Someone was holding her close and something wet and warm and soothing was bathing the back of her neck. Krisa was reminded of how her mother had put a damp cloth on her forehead when she was little and had a fever. Next she thought of Madame Glossop's soothing herb poultices, which were applied for every complaint from headache to "womanly pains". But the arms around her waist were like warm steel bands and the voice whispering in her ear was low and soothing and masculine. The person tending her was neither her mother nor Madame Glossop, she suddenly realized. It was Teague.

"Where...what...?" She could barely form the words, they came out as the vaguest whispers. She tried to move and became aware of a dull, persistent pain that started at the base of her skull and pervaded her entire body. It was like having a headache all over. She tried to move again and groaned.

The arms around her tightened a fraction. "Hold still for a while. You had a worse time than I thought you would." Teague's deep voice sounded concerned in her ear.

Krisa tried again and found she could form words if she concentrated, though her lips felt numb and cold. "What happened?"

"Chip resisted removal. It wasn't activated yet but it was pretty well enmeshed in your muscle. Took longer to get it out than I thought. Sorry, sweetheart."

"'S all right," Krisa murmured. At least it was gone. Wasn't it? "Where?" she asked. Teague understood.

"Right here. Open your eyes a minute."

Krisa did and after a moment the dim bedroom swam into focus. She saw Teague's large palm in front of her face. Lying in the center of it was a fingernail-sized bit of coppery, mangled metal. She noticed with distaste that there was blood in the grooves of the twisted chip. *My blood*, she thought, feeling queasy. But she was also relieved that the hateful chip was out of her neck and destroyed, breaking her last link to Lord Radisson and Briar Rose.

"Glad it's gone," she whispered, closing her eyes again. "Teague, I hurt."

"I know, little girl. If I'd had any idea it would be so bad for you I wouldn't have done it. But once I started I had to finish. The chip was broadcasting pain signals pretty strong there toward the end, so you may be sore for a while."

"Feels like…headache…all over," Krisa said.

"Yeah, you'll be sore for a few hours because the chip activated all the pain centers in your brain," Teague explained. "Best thing is to try and sleep through it." The warm, wet sensation that had woken her up in the first place began at the back of her neck again. Krisa realized he was licking her there, tending the small wound he had made to remove the chip. It would have seemed a strange and alien concept to her only a month ago, but now it just felt soothing and right. Still, she didn't want to sleep, didn't want to miss out on the last few hours with Teague before he left to go retrieve the ship Sarskin had promised them.

"Don't wanna sleep. Wanna talk," she protested, though she was filled with a bone-deep weariness like nothing she had ever known. She stifled a yawn.

"Nothin' to talk about." Teague pulled her close as he had all their nights in the jungle and tucked her head under his chin. "Don't worry, I'll wake you up before I leave in the morning."

"Promise?" Krisa stifled another yawn, feeling the deep ache in her body dragging her toward sleep.

"Promise." Teague's deep voice was firm and his presence behind her was warm and comforting. Eyelids stuttering closed, Krisa relaxed into sleep.

* * * * *

A hot mouth on the side of her neck woke her. As she came to consciousness, Krisa became aware of large warm hands caressing her naked body gently. They cupped her breasts, rubbing lightly over nipples, suddenly erect with desire, then traced lower over her trembling belly to brush the quivering mound of her pussy. Krisa found she was already wet for him.

"Mmm." The sound escaped her lips as blunt fingertips spread the tender lips of her sex and delved into her heat, rubbing lightly over her sensitive clit.

There was rumbling laughter from somewhere above her. "You feelin' better, little girl?" Teague asked. He rubbed a cheek rough with stubble against her own, causing her to squirm beneath him.

Krisa took a minute to take stock of herself and realized that she was feeling much better. In fact, she was feeling remarkably well considering the painful removal of the chastity chip. Then Teague's thick fingers found their way inside her wetness and she felt even better.

"Well?" he rumbled again, fingers still working in a long, slow motion that seemed designed to drive her insane.

"M-much better," Krisa whispered. She arched her back, reaching to get more of him inside her. She loved the feeling of Teague's strong fingers stroking into her newly opened body. She felt owned, cherished, loved.

"Wish you didn't have to go today," she whispered, arching her back more and spreading her thighs wider for him. The position opened her completely to him. It made her feel utterly vulnerable and utterly right to give herself to the man she loved this way.

"I'm not gone yet." Teague nuzzled the side of her neck again, nipping gently along the shelf of her jaw and lapping softly at the marks he had made on her the night before. "You feel well enough to give me a sweet goodbye?" He moved so that he was over her completely, his big body between her spread thighs while he continued to stroke her.

"Mmm, as long as you promise not to be gone too long."

"I'll come back as soon as I can. We'll be off this rock and on the way to Alpha Lyrae come nightfall," Teague promised. "You ready for me?"

"You know I am." Krisa wiggled beneath him, relishing his wild, musky scent and the heat from his big body that drove away the early morning chill.

"That's good, little girl, 'cause I'm ready for you."

She felt the blunt head of his cock replace his fingers and then he was sliding into her, filling her with his thickness as he had the night before. Making her hot, making her his completely.

"Oh," Krisa gasped softly. He was more gentle this time, less urgent. His strokes were long and sure inside her, building her pleasure with a breathless intensity that left her feeling weak. She thought if she lived to be a thousand she would never forget this moment, it was burned in her memory forever.

Teague loomed over her, a large, warm shadow in the darkened bedroom just beginning to grow light from the dull, bronze radiance of Planet X's hidden sun. His eyes were a soft, glowing silver, filled with love and need, as his big body moved over her, inside her. As he stroked into her, he caressed her legs, sides, arms, neck—every part of her he could reach and he buried his hands in her hair to pull her close for hot-cinnamon kisses.

She reached the peak just moments before he did, felt her pussy spasm around his cock and heard Teague's low groan as he cradled her close and let her climax trigger his own. He pulsed into her, pressing deep, filling her with his seed. She was whispering something over and over in a low, breathless voice. Krisa didn't understand what she was saying until

311

Teague pulled back and whispered, "Love you too, little girl. Always. Don't forget it."

In the growing light, he got up and dressed in his leather pants and vest, then sheathed the long silver knife stained a rusty brown with her blood. Krisa didn't want him to go. It seemed they had been so long in coming together. Now that they had finally reached an understanding of whom they were and what they wanted, he had to go. She begrudged any time away from Teague, even a day for him to go get the ship.

"I'll miss you," she whispered when he leaned down for a kiss before leaving.

"You're still tired from yesterday. Sleep. I'll be back before you know it. And don't worry, I made Sarskin give his word to look out for you and make sure you're safe while I'm gone." Teague cupped the side of her face in one large, warm palm and gave her one last, lingering kiss. "Love you."

Krisa thought she would never get tired of hearing those words. "Love you too," she murmured, nuzzling her cheek into his hand and leaving a soft kiss in the calloused palm. He left, closing the door softly behind him. *He'll be back soon, he promised.*

She couldn't understand why the faint *snick* of the door latch catching should bring the sting of tears to her eyes and make it so hard to swallow.

Chapter Twenty-Five

ॐ

"My lord, my lord — in here!"

Krisa sat straight up in the large bed, registering the fact that morning had faded into afternoon while she slept.

"My lord..." The high, nasal whine was familiar and it was getting closer.

Something was very wrong. Krisa decided to make a dash for the fresher. She leaped out of bed and was in the act of crossing the room when the heavy wooden door banged open. She froze, uncertain of which way to turn. She was suddenly dreadfully aware that she was completely naked.

Framed in the doorway was a face from another lifetime, one Krisa had never thought to see again. Percy DeCampeaux, her old chaperone, turned three shades of red and averted his eyes, as though the sight of her naked body might cause sudden and incurable blindness. Beside him in stark contrast to Percy's thin frame stood the portly figure of Sarskin. The Drusinian smiled a little sadly at her and then looked politely away.

"Stand aside." The sharp, commanding voice coming from behind the two men was new but it sent a wave of gooseflesh over her exposed skin.

"My lord, I don't think —"

"Never mind what you think, Percy. I said *stand aside*."

Sarskin and Percy moved out of the way, like two wildly uneven curtains being drawn from across a stage, unveiling with agonizing slowness, a tall, lean figure with iron-gray hair and a neatly trimmed goatee and mustache to match.

Lord Radisson.

* * * * *

"M-my Lord," Krisa stuttered, feeling herself blush scarlet with shame and confusion. She tried to drop a curtsy and then realized that she had no skirts to spread because she was still completely naked. She made a quick grab for the edge of the synthi-cotton sheet, meaning to wrap it around her body, but Lord Radisson came forward, moving at what seemed like a horrible speed for an older man and snatched it away from her.

"No," he said in a voice that would have frozen the center of a star. "I will inspect what damage has been done to my merchandise." He stalked in a circle around her, his bearing stiff with barely suppressed rage, as he took in the "damage".

Krisa stood rooted to the spot, thinking of how she must look to him. She was naked and no doubt wild-looking, with her hair down around her shoulders and love marks on both sides of her neck, not to mention the healing wound at the base of her hairline where the chastity chip had been removed.

She crossed her arms protectively over her chest, eyes down on the floor, her mind running in useless circles. *Where is Teague? Is he safe? Will he come for me? How in the name of the Goddess did they find us?*

Cruel fingers bit into her jaw, forcing her chin up so that her husband-to-be could examine her neck more thoroughly. Krisa gasped as he jerked her head to first one side and then the other, examining the purple welts left by Teague's teeth. Then he forced her chin down and parted her hair to stare for a long moment at the back of her neck.

"My lord..." Due to the uncomfortable tilt of her head, Krisa couldn't see his face, but Percy's voice sounded shocked—almost wounded. In his thin, nervous hands she could see the ripped remains of her Certificate of Virginity and the twisted, coppery chip now brownish with her own dried blood.

"Very well." Lord Radisson released her suddenly and stood back. Krisa dared to look at him and saw that the scowl on his face had been replaced by a look of icy calm. "I think it's fairly obvious what happened here. Kidnapped, raped, bitten, for the Goddess' sake."

"It wasn't like that at all," Krisa protested, but Lord Radisson acted as though she hadn't even spoken.

He turned to Percy. "Has the battalion I dispatched captured the Feral?"

Krisa felt her gut churn at his words. Teague—they were after Teague!

"If they haven't they will surely have him soon, my Lord," Percy replied eagerly.

Just being in the presence of this forbidding man, her intended husband-to-be, brought back all of Krisa's Briar Rose associations so strongly, they felt like a hand at her throat. But now she stepped forward, forgetting her nakedness and her inhibitions both completely.

"Please, you don't understand. *Teague didn't hurt me.*" She laid one hand beseechingly on Lord Radisson's immaculate black sleeve. He jerked his arm away, scowling as though she had smeared him with some unspeakable filth instead of only touching him.

"You don't know what you're saying. After what this man, this *Feral* has done to you. Despoiled you, ruined the bride that was to be my crowing glory." His stern features crumpled and for a moment he just looked like a sad, old man.

"Lord Radisson, please...don't hurt him. I-I love him!" The moment the words were out of her mouth, Krisa knew they were a colossal mistake. The sad look in Radisson's steely gray eyes was replaced instantly with anger so cold it gave her goose bumps.

"Percy, she doesn't know what she's saying. You know what to do." He snapped his fingers and suddenly Percy was at her side, still blushing but gripping one arm determinedly.

"Let me go!" The shock of seeing her intended husband-to-be was wearing off and Krisa began to feel panic overwhelm her sense of offended propriety. *If they take me away, back to Prime... If they hurt Teague...* She yanked at the arm Percy was holding, but he held on grimly, not giving an inch despite his obvious embarrassment.

"I'm sorry, Krisa," he said and she felt a sudden, sharp pain in her arm. She looked down to see a wicked-looking injector in his other hand, the tiny, multiple needles dripping with some clear fluid that was also running down her arm. "I blame myself," Percy said in a low voice.

"I second that sentiment." Lord Radisson sneered briefly and then turned to Sarskin. "Her virginity is obviously gone, sir. The price we agreed on has just been halved."

Krisa stared with wide, uncomprehending eyes at the fat Drusinian. Teague had told her that he had extracted Sarskin's promise to take care of her, to see that she came to no harm. A Drusinian couldn't break his word, so how...?

"You," she slurred. The pastel room was growing fuzzy around the edges and she was beginning to feel decidedly dizzy, but she made a special effort to focus on the large form clad in bright silk and brocade in front of her. "How cou' you? M...Teague saved Ziba...your son... He din' eat you. You tol' me...indebted to him."

"But of course, my dear," Sarskin purred smoothly. "Percy, perhaps you'd better let her sit down." Percy draped a sheet around her shoulders and sat her on the edge of the bed, before turning back to Lord Radisson, who had begun to bark orders at an alarming rate. The room continued to swim in and out of focus. Krisa concentrated fiercely on staying alert.

"How?" She stared at the brightly colored blob. "Why?"

"I am assuming you want to know how I was able to break my word and lead the good Lord Radisson here, Miss Elyison." Sarskin bowed gracefully and used the gesture as an excuse to make certain that Lord Radisson was busy dictating commands to Percy, who was scribbling as fast as he could with a light stylus on a compu-pad.

"The fact of the matter is that I haven't broken my word at all," the Drusinian said, turning back to her. "I promised my dear friend, Teague, that I would see to your safety and comfort. But where in the galaxy could you be more comfortable and safe than with your rightful husband on Prime? It's where we both agreed you belong, if you remember our conversation in my garden yesterday. I never would have initiated the call that brought your Lord Radisson here if we hadn't already spoken about it."

Krisa started to deny it and then remembered with horrible clarity that Sarskin *had* said something about the best place for her being on Prime. And she had agreed with him, too distracted with her own thoughts and too polite to disagree. Had she unwittingly given him permission to ruin both her life and Teague's? She wanted to scream but her tongue didn't seem to be functioning anymore.

"As for Teague's part in the whole process, I must confess that it is quite regrettable." The portly Drusinian shook his head sadly, his neck like a fat tube of sausage as it rotated. "I am, as I said, most indebted to him. But while I promised him a ship, I did *not* promise there wouldn't be a battalion of the Royal Space Corps to intercept him halfway to it. I *have* secured Lord Radisson's promise that my old shipmate's death will be both swift and, as nearly as possible, painless."

His death? Sweet Goddess, no! Fuzzily, Krisa shook her head, feeling as though she was moving under water.

"Oh yes," Sarskin continued, just as though she had spoken out loud. "As indebted to Teague as I am for preserving my son's life, I'm afraid there was nothing I could do to save him. Lord Radisson fairly *insisted* on having the man you'd gone off with. And he offered such a substantial reward for information leading to his capture, well, if you understood the Drusinian nature, my dear, you'd see there was nothing else I could do." His fat face contorted into an expression that was meant to be sad, but looked more predatory to Krisa's fuzzy vision.

"Also, with my old friend deceased, all of my promises to him will be nullified. Surely you can see the freedom that affords me."

"S-s..." Krisa sounded like a snake with a lisp, her mouth seemed to be made of lead. Finally she managed to get the word out. "Ssslaver," she whispered. With Teague dead, there was nothing to stop the Drusinian from slaving out women from all the surrounding Yss tribes. The thought of those beautiful, slim green women condemned to a life of sexual subjugation and slavery for one man's greed made her sick. She wanted to spit on Sarskin but she was fairly certain her mouth wouldn't cooperate with her. Instead she forced it to say one more word.

"S-sick." She glared at Sarskin as well as she could, with facial muscles that felt like rubber. Everything in the room seemed to be growing dimmer, less substantial.

"Of course you are, my dear, as I am myself. It's a most regrettable occurrence. Teague, of course, will be missed by both of us," Sarskin said, deliberately misunderstanding her. He glanced behind him. Apparently Lord Radisson was wrapping up his orders to Percy, for Sarskin leaned in close for a moment.

"I've told Lord Radisson how you were abducted and forced to behave in ways you normally never would in order to preserve your life. He thinks you were an unwilling victim in Teague's sick games. If you are as intelligent as I know you to be, you'll keep up my little fiction. It was the best I could do for you." He gave her a warning look and then his expression softened. "I really do like you, you know. I believe you're the first civilized person I've met since my self-imposed exile to this nasty little world. You may not see it now, but you'll be much better off on Prime."

Krisa shook her head in slow, exaggerated swoops of negation. The air around her felt thick, like honey or some kind of syrup and she didn't think she could hold her eyes open much longer. "W-wr-wrong," she finally managed.

"You may think so now, my dear," Sarskin began and then everything faded to black.

Chapter Twenty-Six

ॐ

"…said, wake her up. I want her to hear this. Do we have a feed?" The words were fuzzy, indistinct. A low hum at the back of her mind. *That voice should be important. Why?*

There was a stinging pain in her arm and Krisa was instantly, painfully alert. Her head throbbed and her eyes felt like the natural lubrication in their sockets had been replaced by sand.

"There, my dear." It was Percy at her side again. He was patting her hand, which was strapped down to a soft surface. Krisa turned her head, not wanting to see his simpering face. She was dressed and inside a ship of some kind. It wasn't only her hand that was restrained—her entire body was strapped into a luxurious blast couch, upholstered in a fine, gray velvet material. The entire ship, as far as she could see, seemed to be decorated in shades of gray and deep maroon, a picture of understated elegance.

Near the front of the small ship she could see the tall, stiff figure of Lord Radisson. He was leaning over and barking at what must be the pilot, who was sitting at the controls.

"Do we have a feed?" he was asking impatiently, leaning farther over the pilot's shoulder and peering at a large screen that was currently showing only grayish static.

"Regrettably, my Lord, only audio. The dense vegetation must be interrupting our visual signals."

"Never mind, audio will have to do then." Lord Radisson raised his voice, addressing the screen. "Humphreys, can you hear me?"

There was a crackle and pop of static and then a distant voice said, "Yes, my Lord. Reading you loud and clear."

"Have you got him?" Lord Radisson leaned closer until his long, narrow nose was almost brushing the screen. Krisa had a moment of unreality, when she thought he had better be careful, or he might fall in and get sucked up in the gray field of static. Then the meaning of his words sank in.

Teague — my Goddess, they've got him.

"I say, have you—"

"Right here, my Lord." There was some indistinct muttering in the background and the voice said, "What? Can't see us?" And then louder, "I have the big brute right here beside me in manacles, Lord Radisson. All systems go."

"Never mind your idiotic lingo." Lord Radisson sounded impatient. He turned to Percy for a moment. "Is she awake?" Then he glanced at Krisa and his face hardened. "Good, I see that she is."

"Sir? Lord Radisson?" The crackling, static voice was suddenly interrupted by a low, growling tone.

"I *said*, take your fuckin' hands off if you don't wanna lose one."

Krisa's heart sank. There was no mistaking that voice.

"That's him?" Lord Radisson asked.

"That's him," the other voice confirmed.

"Krisa? Can you hear me?" It was Teague again.

Krisa struggled to sit up but the straps holding her to the tasteful, gray blast couch made that impossible. "Teague!" she yelled, trying to make her voice heard across the room. "Teague, *run*. They're going to kill you!"

"Krisa?" She couldn't tell if he had heard her or not.

"I love you!" she shouted, not caring that Lord Radisson's face had gone as cold as an iceberg.

"Can't you shut her up?" he hissed to Percy who was already scrambling to get a hand over her mouth. Krisa twisted her head violently to avoid him but he caught her anyway.

"Hold still and be *quiet*, Krisa. You're only making things worse for yourself!" Percy looked very red in the face with the effort of keeping her quiet.

"Hang on, sweetheart! I'm coming for you, I promise."

"That will be quite enough of *that*." Lord Radisson's voice cracked angrily through the cabin of the small ship. "Humphreys, do it. Shoot him!"

Krisa struggled wildly and bit the hand plastered over her mouth as hard as she could. Percy yelped and pulled his wounded palm away. "*No!*" she screamed. "*Teague!*"

"Do it, I say," Lord Radisson insisted. "Humphreys, at once. I insist!"

"Yes, my L—" There was the flat crack of a blaster being discharged and then sudden silence.

"My Lord, we appear to have lost the feed," the pilot said tonelessly.

"Never mind, never mind." Lord Radisson looked satisfied now, almost smug. He dusted his hands together, as though he had done the actual killing himself and it was a job well done. "We've heard all we need to hear, haven't we, my dear?"

"You—" Krisa was stunned. A single thought kept running through her mind. *I don't even know if he heard me. Don't even know if he heard me say I love him.*

She had never really hated anyone before, not even her father when he insisted she go off to Briar Rose over her mother's protests. But now the emotion she felt inside her was red-hot, a rage as vivid as the agony she had experienced when Teague removed her chip. Lord Radisson had just executed the only man she had ever loved and he had the nerve to stand there with that smug, self-satisfied expression on his cold face and look pleased about it.

"I'll... You..." Some of Teague's choicest words rose to her lips and Krisa put her new vocabulary to good use. Percy's eyes widened at her language and he clamped his unwounded palm across her mouth, shaking his head.

Lord Radisson simply stared at her, a look of distaste growing on his cold features. "To think I waited eight years and paid four hundred thousand credits for that," he muttered.

"My Lord...the effects of the drug. I'm certain she doesn't know what she's saying," Percy babbled, keeping his hand clamped tightly over her mouth.

"Oh, she knows what she's saying all right, Percy. A lifetime of good breeding wiped out in a month. Or was she always such a foul-mouthed little guttersnipe?"

"My Lord, I assure you, no," Percy protested. Krisa tried to bite him again but he produced the injector from his pocket and there was the by now familiar stinging sensation in her arm. The world began to get fuzzy around the edges and Krisa felt herself starting to float despite her rage and grief.

Lord Radisson frowned. "It doesn't matter anyway, as you'll be disposing of her the moment we get back to Prime. The way she is now and minus her virginity, she's worthless to me."

"But my Lord, only think of what people will say, the gossip alone..." Percy's voice rose to a positive squeak. "With the proper conditioning...no one need know that she wasn't rescued from cryo-sleep the same way the rest of us from the *Star Princess* were. With another chip, perhaps a more advanced one this time..."

"You may have a point, Percy. I'll be a laughingstock if anyone finds out the truth." Radisson scowled, looking like an angry, gray blob to Krisa's drug-distorted vision. "But another chip, however advanced, is not the answer. No, I think a full memory wipe is in order. A neural implant should do the trick nicely. Contact my surgeon the minute we make orbit around Prime and make sure he understands the need for discretion."

"A neural implant? But Lord Radisson, the dangers. That is to say, there have been rumors of...*complications.*"

"Do you think I give a damn, Percy? If I'm to maintain the pretense you suggest, I'd rather be married to a pretty idiot than that raving thing with a foul mouth." He jerked his chin angrily in Krisa's direction. "Just see to it, and I'll hear no more about it." He strode out of her line of vision, apparently heading for one of the other plush, gray blast couches.

The room was fading in and out alarmingly. Krisa knew the drug was about to take her under, no matter how hard she tried to fight it. Dimly she heard the flat, emotionless voice of the pilot asking everyone to strap down for blastoff. They were headed for Lynix Prime, where her memory would be wiped clean.

She had a brief, vivid recollection of helping to dust the wide, imported mahogany wood table at Briar Rose, as punishment for sneaking out of the dorm at night. *Everything, be sure every speck of dust, every fingerprint is removed, girls. I want to see my face shining in the wood when you're done.* Madame Wisk, the head housekeeper had been quite adamant that she and the other girls receiving detention did the job right.

Now she would be wiped clean of memory and personality, would become a blank, reflective surface in which Lord Radisson could see himself.

Fine, do it. If Teague's dead then there's nothing for me to remember anyway. The thought followed her down into the blackness.

Chapter Twenty-Seven

&

~ ~ ~ ~ ~

"Krisa." The man had shining silver eyes set in a dark, forbidding face. He lifted a hand and cupped her cheek in his palm. His skin was so warm...

"Krisa," he said again. There was deep sorrow, a longing in his voice that made her eyelids sting with unshed tears. She had a feeling that she ought to know him, that he was important to her somehow. But why? Why?

"Krisa," he said a third time. His name, the name of the strange, silver-eyed man, was on the tip of her tongue, was as close as the warm palm on her cheek, but she couldn't...quite...remember... There was a sharp, burning pain in her temples.

~ ~ ~ ~ ~

"Perla! *Perla!*" She woke up with tears in her eyes, her head pounding. Her nurse was there at once, her kindly, wrinkled face creased with concern.

"Yes, my sweet? Was it the dream again?" She sat on the side of Krisa's luxurious, satin-lined sleeping couch and took one of Krisa's hands in both of her own. Her touch was cool and soothing, her skin so worn by age that it was as soft as a baby's.

Krisa sighed in relief. "Yes, the same one. The man with silver eyes—he knows me but I don't know him, even though I feel I ought to. And Perla, he looks so *sad*. What does it mean?"

"Well now, it's just a dream, lovey. Most often they don't mean a thing, so don't you fret yourself." Perla patted her hand reassuringly and blotted Krisa's eyes with one of the sweet-smelling hankies she always seemed to have handy when Krisa needed one. "It's morning anyhow and time to get up. You don't want to be a slug-a-bed today for his Lordship has requested you have breakfast with him. Now, isn't that fine?" Perla's wrinkled face fairly glowed with the compliment to her charge. Lord Radisson didn't often request Krisa's presence anywhere.

"That's...wonderful," she said, struggling to show the excitement and enthusiasm she knew Perla expected. Lord Radisson was responsible for all the good things in her life. Her lovely clothes, the sleek blue hovercoach that took her shopping to anywhere she liked, the beautiful bedroom done in rose-pink silks and satins, imported all the way from Old Earth—all of them came from him. And yet, somehow, Krisa couldn't bring herself to like the man much, though Perla reminded her constantly of his generosity.

Any time Lord Radisson requested her presence Perla got so excited, the old nurse liked to fuss over every little detail of her appearance. Krisa didn't care for Lord Radisson as she knew she ought to, but she liked her nurse very much. For Perla's sake she tried to pretend that she was thrilled at the prospect of eating the first meal of the day with the cold, silent man who always watched her as though she were a dog that might jump up and bite him at any second.

"Well then, what's to wear?" Perla hopped nimbly off the satin-lined couch and scooted over to the large walk-in closet, in one corner of the spacious room, where all of Krisa's best clothes were kept. Perla had been Lord Radisson's nurse when he was a child and he had spared no expense on rejuvie treatments to keep her healthy and vital, so she moved surprisingly quickly for a woman well into her second century.

Kris sighed and resigned herself to getting up and facing another day. She pushed aside the rose-silk curtains that hung around her couch and formed a snug cocoon for her in the cavernous room at night.

Another day and yet every day here, in the vast, beautiful house on Lynix Prime, seemed to be about the same. She rose, bathed, ate, shopped or not, buying anything that caught her fancy. Sometimes she wandered the extensive grounds with their lush purple grass or played with some of the amusing pets Lord Radisson had imported all the way from Old Earth, just for her. In the evenings she had dinner, always the finest cuisine and sometimes Lord Radisson would call her into his library to sit by the fire at his feet while he read. Krisa would stare at the fire and Lord Radisson would stare at her, always with that same look, that wary, watchful look as though he was wondering if he could trust her or not.

Krisa sighed again, making aimless patterns in the silky, deep rose carpet with her toes. It felt so soft, almost as soft as the fur of a... Krisa frowned. The fur of a what? None of the pets Lord Radisson had gotten for her had soft fur. Krisa ticked them off in her head.

There was a gray pony that she rode sometimes, with a long, coarse mane and tail, beautiful fish that filled the pond by her window with flashes of gold and orange and blue, an amusing bird with long white feathers that could talk and would sit on her shoulder once in a while. But wasn't there an animal, hadn't she seen one or had one or known someone who had one, that was small and soft, with a high, chattering voice? Krisa winced at the sharp pain in her temples. *Why can't I remember? Why does it hurt when I try?*

"Perla," she called, still drawing patterns in the carpet with her toes. "What's the name of that little animal—you know the one—it could fit in your hand and it looks a little like a powder puff?" She reached up with one hand absently to massage her aching temples.

"Sounds like a dream animal, my sweet. A funny little pet you can play with in your sleep." Perla's gray head was buried between dresses as she dug around at the bottom of the closet for the slippers that matched the apple-green silk dress she had picked for Krisa to wear. "And it's time to get your head out of the clouds and come get dressed," she added sternly. "I've already laid out your stockings and cincher."

Sighing, Krisa went.

The clink of silverware on fine china seemed nearly deafening in the silence of the cavernous dining room with its vaulted ceiling and marble floors. It seemed to Krisa that she could remember another room like this one, but in that room there had been no table and chairs. *The people sat on the floor.* She shook her head, trying to think past the shooting pain that accompanied such thoughts. *Sat on the floor? That didn't make any sense. And yet...* She set down her knife and fork and closed her eyes, fingers rubbing at the sides of her aching head. Flashes of pale, narrow faces and slitted alien eyes. *One of them was my friend. She gave me a bath in her stewpot.* Krisa frowned. *That's crazy.*

"What are you thinking of?" Lord Radisson's harsh, dry voice startled her into opening her eyes and dropping her hands to her lap. He was staring at her with that same watchful expression on his pale, stern face, giving her a look that seemed to see right through her somehow. Krisa felt embarrassed although she didn't know why.

"I-I was thinking of what a lovely day it is," she stuttered. It didn't seem wise somehow to tell this stern man her real thoughts.

Lord Radisson stared at her long and hard across the shiny surface of the table. He was wearing a severely tailored black suit and his hair and goatee were freshly trimmed. Krisa squirmed under the relentless gray eyes, wondering what he saw when he looked at her that way.

"Come here, child," he said at last, motioning her to walk around the table and stand in front of him. Krisa did it at once, though there was hardly anything she could think of that she wanted to do less.

"Yes, my Lord?" she said, uncertainly, looking fixedly at his sharp, beaky nose. It was a trick she had learned somewhere—stare directly at someone's nose and it looks like you're looking them in the eye, only you're not. It was a useful trick whenever you were in trouble and had to convince someone of how sorry you were. Where had she learned that? *There used to be a place filled with girls. Girls like me...waiting...for what?* Her head hurt.

"Perla tells me you have bad dreams sometimes. Nightmares," Lord Radisson said abruptly, shattering her thoughts and throwing her into confusion.

"I-I do sometimes," Krisa stumbled, feeling uncomfortable. The tight cincher she wore made it hard to breathe. She had a sudden, irrational desire to rip it off, but suppressed the unladylike urge fiercely.

"She says you wake up crying. Tell me, girl, what do you dream?" He reached up and caught her chin in a firm, pinching grip, forcing her face down so that he could stare into her eyes intently.

Krisa looked into the icy gray depths and tried not to blink. Lord Radisson's breath was heavy with the bitter odor of his morning caffeine brew. Instinctively she knew she must not tell him about her dreams of the man with the silver eyes, though how she knew that wasn't clear. But how much had Perla said?

"Well?" He was still staring at her fiercely.

"I-I don't know, my Lord," Krisa faltered, deciding to risk a lie. "I can't remember much. I just wake up feeling terribly sad. It's silly, really." She gestured nervously with one hand, hoping to placate him. "When I live in such a beautiful place and have everything any girl could possibly want."

Lord Radisson studied her eyes for a moment longer and then abruptly released her chin. "Very well," he said at last. "I suppose it is not your fault if you have a bad dream now and again. Perhaps it is time to forget the past and move on to the future."

"My Lord?" Krisa looked at him uncertainly.

"Yes, it is time, especially if I ever expect to produce an heir." He seemed to be speaking more to himself than to her at this point. He looked up. "Krisa, you will attend me in my rooms tonight after dinner." He reached up and fingered the sleeve of the green silk dress she was wearing. "Wear something...pretty."

"My Lord." Krisa curtsied submissively and went back around the table to pick at her breakfast. She suddenly had no appetite. She felt, in fact, as though someone had dumped a large lump of ice into her belly. Deep in her brain a low, growling voice spoke. *The price tag for all those pretty things is gonna come due, little girl.* Who did the voice belong to and why did the words send a helpless shiver along her spine and a spike of pain through her head?

"His Lordship tells me you're to attend him tonight." Perla was plainly bubbling over with happiness at the wonderful news.

"Yes," Krisa said and then couldn't think of anything else to say. For some reason her thoughts kept returning to the man in her dream—the man with the silver eyes and warm hands. What would it be like, "attending" Lord Radisson? She supposed she would find out tonight.

"Well, come on." Perla gestured impatiently to the spindly chair with the poofy pink cushion that was placed in front of an old-fashioned mirror. Krisa would have preferred a holo-viewer but the mirror was a valuable antique and Perla had impressed upon her how fortunate she was that Lord Radisson cared for her enough to put it in her room.

Krisa plopped onto the poofy cushion and stared at the hollow-eyed girl in the mirror. Her cheeks were very thin, despite the rich foods served on a daily basis in the big house and her skin was very pale. It seemed to her that when she first started looking in the mirror, her skin was a rich, tan color and her cheeks were pink, but that had faded over time. There used to be marks too, on the sides of her neck...hadn't there? She vaguely remembered them, but couldn't remember how long it had taken to fade.

Days seemed to run into each other, filled with routine and sameness until it was impossible to keep track of how long she had been in the big house. She had a vague idea that she hadn't always lived here, but whenever she tried to explore it, her head hurt and her mind veered off in another direction. She often found herself thinking of something else entirely, like going out to play with the gray pony, or counting the fish in the pond. It was terribly frustrating.

"Now, how are we to fix your hair tonight?" Perla bustled around behind her, laying out jeweled hairpins and gold and silver combs.

Suddenly Krisa felt like she was going to burst. "Do we have to worry about my hair just yet?" she asked. "After all, dinner isn't for hours and I should...go out and do some shopping, find something pretty to wear." She hoped her old nurse didn't see the shiver that passed through her as she said it.

"Well now, I think that's a lovely idea. Just let me get my wrap and we're off." Perla patted her shoulders and turned to go.

"Perla, wait. Couldn't I...go alone? Just this once?" Krisa pleaded. As much as she liked the old nurse, she longed to be out of the house without a chaperone. It seemed to her that if only she could be completely by herself for once, she might be able to think.

"Well, I suppose it couldn't hurt just the once. Want to buy something special I suppose and you're feeling shy." The old nurse chuckled. "Mind you, my sweet, there's nothing you could buy would shock old Perla, but if you've a mind for a bit of privacy, just take the hovercoach and be sure to stay in the restricted shopping area. It's ten-day today, so all the vendors will be out with their wares, but mind you stay away from the Great Market, nobody but common trash goes there. All right?"

"I promise," Krisa said with relief. "I won't put a toe out of line. Thank you, Perla."

"Oh, go on." Her nurse made a shooing gesture. "Just be sure you're back in time to fix up properly. It wouldn't do to keep Lord Radisson waiting."

"No...no, it wouldn't." Krisa felt the horrible, icy chill in the pit of her belly again. "Don't worry, Perla. I'll be back in plenty of time."

* * * * *

The smoky blue hovercoach hummed silently through the streets of Centaura, headed for the restricted shops where only people of a certain credit limit could enter. The district was famed across Lynix Prime for its multiple security measures. *Safer Than Your Own Backyard*! proclaimed a wide, spooling holoposter with an arrow pointing the way.

Krisa sighed and sank back into the plush upholstery, watching the world unwind beyond the hovercoach's tinted windows. Centaura was a very modern city, the streets laid out in an orderly fashion, all except the old canal district where the Central Square was. Krisa had never been there but she had heard about it from Perla often enough, how trashy and common the people who lived and shopped there were. It was ten-day today, the canal district would be packed, filled with vendors selling their wares, common people buying, children with sticky faces crying...

Suddenly, despite her promise to Perla, she wanted to go to the Great Market more than anything. She already had as many "pretty" things as she needed to wear. Maybe she could get something else. Maybe some...flowers? The idea felt right somehow in a way she couldn't explain to herself.

"Coach," she said aloud. "Change destination."

The hovercoach pulled to the side of the road in one smooth motion. "New destination, Mistress Krisa?" a soft, sexless voice asked.

"The canal district. I want to go to the Great Market at the Central Square."

"Negative, Mistress Krisa. You are not authorized to go to dangerous areas without supervision. Mistress Perla or Lord Radisson must accompany you and neither is present."

"Fine, I'll walk." Krisa tugged on the latch of the door closest to her but it wouldn't open. She yanked harder. "Let me out!"

"Negative," said the smooth, sexless voice of the hovercoach again. "I am sorry, Mistress Krisa but I cannot allow you to leave for such an unsafe destination. It would be against Lord Radisson's orders."

Krisa thought hard. The old canal district wasn't that far from the restricted zone, at least she didn't think so. At any rate, they were both downtown. She would let the hovercoach take her to her original destination and then walk from there. That way if anyone came looking for her, the hovercoach's log would show that she had gone exactly where she had told Perla she was going. It didn't occur to her to wonder why anyone should be looking for her or why her sudden whim to buy flowers at the Great Market now seemed vitally important. She only knew she had to get there.

"Drive on to the restricted area," she told the hovercoach. She fingered the small silver bracelet that linked her to the mechanism. "Drop me off at the very first shop and take yourself to storage. I'll signal when I need you."

"Very good, Mistress Krisa." The coach resumed its smooth motion. As unobtrusively as possible, Krisa slipped the slender bracelet off her arm and tucked it between the velvet-lined cushions.

"Excuse me, could you tell me, I'm looking for the Great M—" Her fellow Centaurans gave the apple-green silk dress mistrustful glances and hurried on by, not stopping to answer her questions. Krisa sighed and trudged on, the bright Prime sunshine beating down on her head like a heavy golden hammer.

Finding Central Square was proving harder than she thought and no one would look at her or speak to her because of the ridiculously rich clothes she wore. She had long since taken off the emerald jewelry that went with the dress and stuffed it into an inner pocket of her cloak, hoping not to attract the wrong kind of attention. Now she trudged along, her feet in their thin slippers aching on the rough paving of the narrow streets, trying to follow people who looked like they had business at the Market.

Worse than the ache in her feet was the pounding in her temples. *A flower stall… West side of the market… Woman with red hair… Blue roses…* Krisa knew that voice—the one that was giving fragmented directions inside her aching skull—it belonged to the man with the silver eyes. But what did it mean? And why did her head ache so fiercely whenever she remembered another snatch of information?

At last she reached a tall arching stone gate and inside was a huge square, bustling with people of all descriptions. Voices were raised, customers haggling over prices, and vendors extolling the virtues of their wares. Surely this was it. With relief, Krisa walked under the huge stone arch and pressed into the crowd.

"West side," she muttered to herself. "Which side is west?" Then she remembered the stone lettering inscribed on the stone archway. "North gate" it had said. She bore to the left, pushing past crowds of people. After her time in the big house with only Perla and Lord Radisson for company the press of bodies, the noise of the crowd and the stench of unwashed flesh was almost too much, but Krisa held her breath and kept going, trying to concentrate past the pain in her head.

Then she saw it. *There! There it is!* Beside a small, wooden cart selling fried dough was a stall filled with brightly colored blossoms and standing beside it was a tall, red-haired woman. She had her back to Krisa and was bent over tending some of the blooms. Krisa hurried forward eagerly, passing a child with a honey-smeared face and the people lined up for the greasy-smelling delicacy at the other cart. She was ready to tap the red-haired on the shoulder and the words, *blue Rigellian roses* were on the tip of her tongue.

"Hey now, missy. What's a pretty thing like you wanderin' around lost-like out here in the Great Market?"

A heavy hand fell on her shoulder and before she could utter so much as a muffled shriek, a huge, dirty palm was clamped over her mouth and she was being dragged away.

* * * * *

"...me go!" Krisa gasped as the filthy palm finally released its hold on her mouth. Whoever had grabbed her had dragged her away from the flower stall and into a dim, dark corner of the market, down a blind alley and around a corner which appeared to be deserted. She turned to face her attacker, wishing for some kind of weapon. She had a dim memory of fighting off someone once with a hairpin, but her long hair was confined in a net today, covered in delicate seed pearls.

The man who was blocking her exit from the alley was big and dirty with a flattened nose and lank, greasy brown hair clinging to his scalp. Narrow, yellow eyes regarded her with amusement and some other emotion she didn't want to think about.

"Well now, ain't you just the prettiest little thing I've ever seen," he cooed gently, taking a step toward her.

Krisa shrank back against the stone wall behind her. "Please." She shoved a trembling hand into the pocket of her cloak and drew out the emerald necklace and earrings that went with her dress. "This is all I have, take it and leave me alone. Please!"

The yellow eyes widened and the dirty man snatched the sparkling jewelry from her outstretched palm. He examined the treasure closely and then thrust it into an inner pocket of his ripped and ragged vest.

"That's nice, my sweet." He smiled at her approvingly and moved closer. "Very nice. Maybe almost as nice as what you've got under that pretty green dress." He moved closer yet, suddenly pinning her against the wall. The breath gusting into her face was thick with the odor of rotten teeth. The man grinned, revealing a few blackened stumps, as though to prove he came by the stench honestly.

"Leave me alone! *Help!*" Krisa struggled to get away but he had her trapped, wrists pinioned in one hand, her palms scraping the rough stones of the wall, drawing blood from the abused flesh.

"Scream all you like, missy. T'aint no one to hear you." The filthy face leered into her own, the yellow eyes and blackened teeth filling her vision.

"That's where you're wrong." The man was suddenly yanked off her and thrown to one side of the alley. "Leave now if you want to live." The deep, gravelly voice belonged to the biggest man Krisa had ever seen. He loomed in the shadows of the alley like a dark god, his shoulders as broad as the wide stone arch over the marketplace, his slitted, silver eyes glittering with rage.

Her attacker took one look at the fierce stranger and bolted from the alley, taking her emerald jewelry with him, but Krisa didn't care. She only had eyes for the huge man with the silver eyes.

"Hey, little girl." The deep voice was surprisingly gentle. The man took a step closer and Krisa backed up in fear, clutching her wounded hands to her chest. This was the man in her dreams, of that she had no doubt. But who was he and what did he want?

"I'm surprised to find you out here without even a hairpin to protect yourself." The man took another step toward her and Krisa realized she was backed into a corner. "Don't look at me like you think I'm gonna eat you up. I told you I'd come back for you, didn't I?"

He bent down and concerned silver eyes peered into her own. A sharp, wild musk filled her head, tickling a memory somewhere in her brain. This man...he was...he was...the name was on the tip of her tongue, she could almost hear it in her head. If only she could think past the stabbing, shooting pain in her temples!

"Krisa." The huge man took her by the shoulders and shook her once. "Krisa, why don't you say something?"

"Please." She barely recognized the voice as her own. "Please, you're scaring me. Who...are you?"

"Who do you think?" He shook her again. "It's me, *Teague*."

The name triggered such a hideous wave of burning, stabbing pain that she couldn't see anymore. The large man wavered in her vision and then faded, along with everything else, to blackness.

Chapter Twenty-Eight

වා

"…injected with neuro-nanites. Formed a neural block in the temporal lobes, where memory is stored. Not like a chip, Teague, look."

Teague… The name sounded very familiar to her foggy brain and yet, the moment she thought it, a spike of pain drove through her temples like a jagged piece of glass. Krisa gasped and a small, weak scream escaped her lips.

"You okay?" The tall, silver-eyed man bent over her, causing Krisa to shrink back in fear. A look of frustrated tenderness crossed over the dark face and he pulled back. "Not gonna hurt you."

"No," the other voice said and a small, red-haired man came into view on her other side. Krisa realized she was lying in a dim room on some sort of table. She tried to sit up but gentle hands pressed her back down. "Don't try to move, my dear," the red-haired man with the puckish face said softly. "Just try to relax and rest." He turned back to the dark man.

"As I was saying, these neuro-nanites are clustered around the memory centers of her brain, unlike a chip. The good news is there's no tracking device. The bad news is they're completely irremovable. Look here at the express C.T." He directed the big man's attention to a device he was holding. It looked like some kind of medical instrument with a row of controls and a flat screen about three inches across at the top.

"See those tiny, bright specks in the temporal region? They're actually forming a block, keeping the memories from getting through to the cognitive portion of her brain. If anything does get through, it comes at a price. I'm sure you remember how painful thinking of escape is when you've got a pain chip in your neck. Well, this young lady will have the same sort of sensation if she manages to remember anything the programmer who injected these nanites didn't want her to." The small man shook his head. "I've heard of memory wipes and neural blocks, but I've never seen one this complicated. She's lucky she can think at all."

"But then...there has to be *something* you can do. This is important, T'lix." The big man gestured abruptly, throwing huge, black shadows on the opposite wall and Krisa shrank back from the sudden motion.

"I'm sorry." The red-haired man moved away, carefully placing the handheld device on a countertop that held an array of other instruments on its cluttered surface. "But if what you've told me is correct, just trying to remember your name engendered pain so severe it caused a syncopal episode. Think of what you'd be putting the poor girl through, Teague. I can see that you feel strongly for her and I'm sure at one point she felt strongly for you. But that's all gone now—erased." He turned to face the dark man again. "If you love her, the best thing you can do is return her to Lord Radisson to live a comfortable, pain-free life."

"No!" Krisa struggled to sit up and this time when the large man came near to help her she didn't shrink away. "No, please," she said, looking from the dark, oddly familiar face with the silver eyes to the concerned frown of the doctor he had called T'lix.

"What is it, sweetheart?" The gentle endearment seemed to jog another memory loose inside her skull and Krisa winced against the pain. The dark man bent over her and she reached up to grasp the sides of his vest, relishing the sting of rough leather against her wounded palms.

"Please," she said, concentrating hard, trying to think past the pain. "Please, I don't know you. I don't know you, but I dream about you almost every night. Please don't take me back to Lord Radisson. I-I hate it there. Whoever you are, wherever you're going...take me with you."

Chapter Twenty-Nine

ℰᴈ

The trip to Alpha Lyrae was a long one because Teague was taking his time, doubling back from time to time and making sure no one was following. He wasn't too concerned about this, he explained to Krisa. He himself had been presumed killed, the execution reported by none other than Lord Radisson. The brigade of Royal Spacers who were supposed to have done the job were supposedly lost in space, the debris of their ship had been found in orbit around Planet X. Actually, Teague explained, what had been found was the spare parts most Spacer vehicles carried in case of emergency, jettisoned from the airlock and fried by the engines to make them look like the remains of an exploded ship.

Krisa didn't ask what had really happened to the men who were supposed to have killed Teague. The grim look in his silver-black eyes was enough to let her know that anyone who crossed this strange man she had decided to go with, mainly on the strength of her disturbing dreams, was in for trouble.

As for herself, though the neuro-nanites continued to block the many memories Teague promised her they had together, at least she had no locator chip placed in her neck this time. Teague speculated that the stolen emerald jewelry and the traces of her blood from the scraped palms on the stone wall of the alley would probably work in her favor. His hope was that Lord Radisson would assume her dead and not bother to search to confirm it. Krisa hoped he was right. She didn't remember much, but she knew she didn't like the cold, gray man she had left behind on Lynix Prime.

No matter how strange and forbidding Teague might be, he treated her gently and considerately. Sometimes he told her a little about their past together, though it seemed like the most far-fetched fantasy imaginable to Krisa. It was hard to believe that they had run through the jungles of an uncharted planet together, that huge, telepathic carnivorous beasts had chased them, that they had lived with cannibals and a dozen other things that Teague told her.

But she never got the sense that the big man was lying and every once in a while, something he told her would jog a memory and with it, a horribly sharp, shooting pain. When that happened, Teague would stop at once and make her lie down until the agony passed. Then Krisa would have to coax and plead to get him to talk to her again about the past.

Teague had gone back to the place they had been staying, the place Lord Radisson had taken her on Planet X, to complete what he called some "unfinished business". The look in his silver eyes when he said this made Krisa shiver for some reason. He had saved some of her personal effects, including a ripped-up Certificate of Virginity, a long silver hairpin and a holo-vid of someone he told Krisa he believed was her mother. One day when he was busy plotting a new route in the Navi-Com, she took the vid into her sleeping chamber, which was right beside Teague's and watched it.

She activated the small, battered device and sat on her gelafoam mattress, her knees pulled up to her chin and her arms wrapped around her legs as it hummed into life. Suddenly there was a 3D holo of a woman's head in front of her. Krisa could see at once why Teague had believed this to be her mother. The woman had the same chocolate-brown eyes and curly, brown hair that she had. Except for the lines of care and worry etched around the tired eyes and beautiful, full mouth, Krisa might have been looking at herself. The resemblance was there, but Krisa felt no sudden stab of recognition at the sight.

"My darling Krisa," the woman began, in a soft, beautiful voice that was only slightly marred by the scratchy quality of the recording. "You're twelve now, over halfway grown. In just eight more years you'll reach the age of consent and be a woman. I hope I'll be there for you on that day. I want to see you and your daughters and their daughters grow into beautiful, graceful, strong women as well. But we're not there yet, it's many years in the future.

"What I want to tell you, Krisa, is that even though you're still a girl, I see all the qualities in you already that will make you a woman to be reckoned with, a woman I can be proud of. You're intelligent and thoughtful and you're not afraid to be your own person. Krisa, if you don't remember anything else your mother ever tells you, I want you to remember how much I love you and how proud I am to have such a strong, independent daughter."

That was it, the holo flickered and went out leaving Krisa to stare at the spot on the coverlet where the woman's head had been, the words of the recording echoing in her head. *So proud, she was so proud of me and I can't even remember her.*

Krisa rested her forehead on her knees and wept for all she had lost. For the memory of her mother and her time with Teague, for most of her life which she couldn't remember at all and for the tiny pieces that managed to make it past the neural block that came at the price of the blinding pain in her temples. For the lost emotion that went with the lost memories.

She had an idea she had loved Teague once, loved him with a white-hot intensity and a physical passion that was unsurpassed. But that was gone now, leaving her with only a vague longing that was more of a ghost of an emotion than an emotion itself. They slept in separate rooms in the small ship, though she was certain they hadn't slept separately in the past. Teague seemed unwilling to force a physical relationship, though Krisa turned around sometimes and caught him looking at her with a longing that bordered on hunger in his deep silver eyes.

Thinking of those silver eyes, so unreadable at times when the black second lid covered them and so vulnerable at others when she caught him looking at her unexpectedly, Krisa cried herself to sleep curled on her bed…

~ ~ ~ ~ ~

"Krisa." His arms were open and she went to him willingly.

"Teague," she whispered when he had drawn her close and tucked her head under his chin, a position that made her feel wonderfully safe. "Why don't I know you anymore?"

"It's not your fault, sweetheart. Don't let it bother you." But the deep voice was terribly sad.

"It does bother me." Krisa pulled away and looked up. "Because I want to know you. The way I did before and I want you to know me. Teague—touch me."

"You shouldn't ask for things like that, little girl." The deep voice had become a low growl and the silver eyes blazed. "You don't know what you're asking for, but you're gonna get it anyway if you're not careful."

"Teague…I'm not afraid." Krisa did her best to make herself believe it. "I said I'm not afraid!"

~ ~ ~ ~ ~

"Not afraid of what?"

Krisa opened her eyes with a shock of recognition and saw his eyes hovering above her head like twin silver moons in the gloom of her sleep chamber. Teague was sitting on the side of her bed peering down at her intently. At first she shrank back, but then she remembered her dream. Could it hold some sort of a clue to getting past the neural block, to the return of her memory?

"I'm not afraid of you. Not afraid to have you touch me," she whispered, meeting his gaze with an unblinking intensity of her own.

Silver eyes looked into hers. Krisa's heart began to beat faster.

"What are you talkin' about, little girl?" Teague asked at last. The deep voice was gentle, but it carried an undertone of warning that she knew she could ignore at her own peril. She decided to answer a question with a question.

"Teague," she whispered, sitting up against the molded headboard of the bed. "You've told me a lot about the things we did and saw while we were trapped on Planet X, but there's one thing you never talked about. While we were there did you ever...did we ever...make love?"

Teague turned from her roughly and made as if to get off the bed, but her light touch on his arm stopped him.

"You've seen the Certificate of Virginity all ripped up the way it is," he muttered at last. "You did that, Krisa. You ripped it up, can't you draw your own conclusions from that?"

"I can, but I want to hear you say it. Tell me about it, about what we did. Show me." Krisa's heart was beating so hard she could feel it in every part of her body and she was suddenly, vividly aware of the musky, masculine fragrance that Teague carried with him everywhere, invading her senses. But she had to ask, had to know.

"You don't know what you're askin' for," he growled, just as he had in the dream.

"No, but I'm not afraid to find out," Krisa insisted.

"You're lying." Teague turned to her and took her by the shoulders. "I can smell your fear in the air all around us and your little heart's about to pound out of your chest. You don't know me anymore, Krisa. Don't ask me to do things you'll regret later."

"I know I used to love you," she whispered and licked her lips nervously. "I know I want to again. I want to remember how I felt about you, want to remember my past—our past, Teague. I thought maybe if you touched me...held me..."

"Don't ask me to do this." Teague closed his eyes briefly, a look of near agony coming over the strong features. "You don't understand, Krisa. I lost you once, I couldn't stand to do it again. I was gonna give you until we got to Alpha Lyrae to get back your memory and then if you couldn't I was gonna let you go your own way, if you wanted to. But if you push me into doing this, I won't be able to stop. And when it's done, I won't be able to let you go. Ever. Understand?"

"Maybe I don't want you to stop. Maybe I don't want you to let me go." Krisa didn't know where the words were coming from, but they sounded right in her mouth. She could taste his masculine spice in the air, hot like a pepper on the tip of her tongue, could breathe in the musk from his big body and feel his heat radiating against her skin. Suddenly, though she didn't know him as she had before, she wanted him. Wanted him badly. Her body responded to him whether her brain understood why or not. They needed each other—they belonged together.

"I should go." Teague moved to get off the bed again and again Krisa held him back with the lightest touch.

"Let me prove it to you," she whispered, the words rising from some place inside her, deeper than memory. She was wearing a one-piece silky gown that hugged her curves. Teague had bought it for her on one of their stops to what he considered to be a "safe" world, one where Royal Spacers rarely landed. Because the cincher she had been wearing when he took her from Prime was so uncomfortable, Krisa no longer wore it, so there was nothing under the flowing material that hugged her curves but a brief pair of silk panties.

She took Teague's large hand in hers and tugged the skirt of her dress out of the way, to place his palm over the warm, damp patch of silk that covered her pussy. "Feel me," she whispered, arching her back to press more of her heat into his palm. "Feel how wet I am for you, Teague. Feel how much I want you to touch me."

"Krisa…" Her name was little more than a groan and she knew he was close to breaking. She raised her hips again, rubbing against his large, warm hand, feeling her wet pussy lips open like a flower beneath the thin silk. Teague's fingers curled almost convulsively around the edge of the flimsy material and Krisa's breath caught in a gasp when she felt blunt fingertips brush the slippery heat of her wetness.

Then Teague was growling, low in his throat. He ripped the flimsy panties away, in a move that seemed to trigger a memory of times past. Krisa felt a sharp pain in her temples, but pushed it away fiercely, unwilling to let anything intrude on this moment with Teague. He had been her lover once and now she was certain he would be her lover again.

"Off," he growled and raised the silky dress over her head, baring her completely for the blazing silver eyes.

"Teague," she protested, suddenly shy. She tried to cover herself with her hands but he had her pinned to the bed, arms above her head in a way that made her feel unspeakably bare, unspeakably hot.

Don't hide yourself from me, little girl." His deep voice was hoarse with emotion. "You may not remember it, but I've seen and tasted every inch of you and I can't wait to do it again." He dipped his head and rubbed cheeks scratchy with stubble against the tender slopes of her breasts, making Krisa writhe and squirm beneath him. Then a hot mouth was capturing her nipples, sucking, licking, nipping, torturing them with almost unbearable pleasure until Krisa was moaning and crying beneath him.

When Teague had marked the creamy curves of her breasts with multiple dark red love bites and Krisa thought she couldn't take any more, the dark head began to move down her chest and abdomen to her quivering belly and exposed pussy.

"Teague, I don't think…" she gasped breathlessly.

He looked up, silver eyes shining like alien coins in the dimness of her room. "You don't think what, sweetheart? Don't think you want me to taste your tender little cunt? Well, that's too damned bad. You gave up control of this situation a while ago, in case you didn't notice. It's been months since I touched you and I'm not gonna stop until I'm done, understand?"

"I..." Krisa could barely breathe past the fear and pleasure he was causing her. "I understand," she whispered at last.

"Good, now just lay back and enjoy yourself, little girl. You don't know how long I've been waiting to do this." He dipped his head again, the bristly blue-black hair scratching against the sensitive skin of her bare abdomen, as his knowing tongue circled her navel in a promise of things to come.

Large, warm hands spread her thighs and Krisa gave a strangled little moan when she felt hot breath blowing against the wet lips of her pussy, swollen with need for him. Blunt, knowledgeable fingers spread those lips wide, baring her most intimate secret. Then a warm, wet tongue was invading her, circling her aching clit relentlessly, before plunging suddenly into the slippery depths of her slit to tongue her as deeply as he could.

"Teague!" His name was a wail in the dimness of the cabin. Krisa buried her small hands in the spiky black hair and ground herself against him, pressing up to get more of that wonderful tongue inside her. Scratchy cheeks abraded her tender inner thighs, and she reveled in the sensation, knowing she would be marked by his pleasure. She could feel something building inside her, a wave of pleasure that was threatening to crest, if only he could push her a little higher, a little harder.

But the intense pleasure Teague was giving her was bringing back memories in broken, jagged fragments, like shards of pottery working their way out of the sand of her unconscious. And like jagged shards they hurt as they came, sending shooting pains to her temples which were becoming harder and harder to ignore. Krisa knew instinctively that the pleasure needed to be deeper, needed to match the pain in order to bring any result.

"Teague," she moaned, tugging on the spiky hair. "Teague, *please*. I need more...need you inside me..."

She didn't have to ask twice. She never knew how he managed to get his clothes off so quickly, but in what seemed like the next heartbeat he was naked under her and she was sitting astride him, her wet, open pussy poised above the thick club of his cock. He didn't need to ask if she was ready, he had made certain of that already. It was with a feeling of relief that bordered on pain that Krisa felt him pierce her, felt the thick cock spreading the lips of her pussy to make room inside her for him, felt large hands encircle her waist and bring her down firmly as he thrust deep to fill her with himself.

Teague began to thrust, pulling out of her and pushing back in, with a brutal urgency that forced a deep, jagged pleasure to spread throughout her body and sizzle along her nerve endings. His hands were still clamped around her hips and Krisa reached down to grasp his muscular forearms, trying to ride out the intense sensations of his cock in her cunt as the memories began pouring back.

She was on the Star Princess *and there was a dark man blindfolded and chained to the metal wall of the hold... She was feeling the bump at the back of her neck, knowing what it meant for the first time since the chip had been implanted... She was wriggling to get through the door of her sleep cube, trying to get free in the tomb-like silence of the ship... She was running through the jungle with Teague cutting trail ahead of her... She was hearing the targees' eerie howling chatter and seeing the pulsing purple eyes of the soondar hot on their trail in the absolute blackness of the Planet X night... She was sitting down to a feast in the Yss village, meeting Ziba and Vis all over again...*

Racing the sunset to save Teague...dancing before the gathered Yss not once but twice... Feeling Teague's hands on her body, making her helpless and hot... Tasting his spice as she took him in her mouth and deep in her throat... Feeling his tongue inside her for the first time... Feeling him spread her legs to mount her...feeling the deep thrust of his thick cock as he breached her virginity and claimed her for the first time as his...as he possessed her utterly.

"Teague... Oh, Goddess, Teague!" The pain of her returning memories and the pleasure of his thick cock inside her peaked at the same time. Krisa felt herself tilt over the edge, felt something give inside her, as Teague thrust deep and held her rock-solid and steady, to pump her willing, open pussy full of his seed. Suddenly she remembered everything. *Everything!* It was too much. Sobbing with a heady, overwhelming mixture of pleasure and pain, Krisa collapsed on the broad chest below her.

Chapter Thirty

ॐ

"Krisa, you awake?" A warm hand shook her gently and Krisa mumbled something unintelligible and turned over, snuggling closer to the big warm body beside her. They had made love for hours the night before and she was worn out. It was almost as though Teague was afraid she would forget the hard-won memories she had reclaimed through their loving and wanted to reinforce both their place in her head and his own place in her heart.

"'M tired, Teague. Can't it wait?" she muttered irritably, when he continued to prod her. "You wore me out last night, let a girl get a little rest, will you?"

"It's not about that, sweetheart." There was a low rumble of laughter in his deep voice. "Though I can never get enough of that sweet cunt of yours. But there's somethin' I think you oughta see."

"Right now?" she grumbled. But she could tell by his tone that the big Feral wasn't about to give up any time soon. Sighing, Krisa got up and wrapped the sheet she had been tangled in around her shoulders. Trailing the end of it along the plate-metal floor of the ship and wincing at the cold on her bare feet, she followed Teague, who hadn't bothered to get dressed, into the Navi-Com.

"Well?" He was standing, completely naked and pointing to the large view-screen that dominated the room.

"Hmm?" Krisa rubbed sleep out of her eyes. What she had been mostly looking at was her lover's perfectly sculpted and deliciously nude body. At Teague's insistence, though, she raised her eyes to the view-screen and saw a small, round shape about as big as her fist but getting visibly bigger all the time. The shape was blue and green with white swirls and she suddenly realized she was looking at a planet spinning slowly in the void of space, coming closer and closer to fill the view-screen.

"See that?" Teague grinned at her, a wild white smile that filled her with joy.

"What is it?" Never taking her eyes off the screen, Krisa moved over to press against his side and Teague pulled her in and draped a warm arm around her waist. He leaned down and planted a soft kiss on her forehead as she watched the planet grow.

"That, little girl, is Alpha Lyrae. We're almost home."

Why an electronic book?

We live in the Information Age—an exciting time in the history of human civilization, in which technology rules supreme and continues to progress in leaps and bounds every minute of every day. For a multitude of reasons, more and more avid literary fans are opting to purchase e-books instead of paper books. The question from those not yet initiated into the world of electronic reading is simply: *Why?*

1. *Price.* An electronic title at Ellora's Cave Publishing and Cerridwen Press runs anywhere from 40% to 75% less than the cover price of the exact same title in paperback format. Why? Basic mathematics and cost. It is less expensive to publish an e-book (no paper and printing, no warehousing and shipping) than it is to publish a paperback, so the savings are passed along to the consumer.

2. *Space.* Running out of room in your house for your books? That is one worry you will never have with electronic books. For a low one-time cost, you can purchase a handheld device specifically designed for e-reading. Many e-readers have large, convenient screens for viewing. Better yet, hundreds of titles can be stored within your new library—on a single microchip. There are a variety of e-readers from different manufacturers. You can also read e-books on your PC or laptop computer. (Please note that Ellora's Cave does not endorse any specific brands.

You can check our websites at www.ellorascave.com or www.cerridwenpress.com for information we make available to new consumers.)

3. *Mobility.* Because your new e-library consists of only a microchip within a small, easily transportable e-reader, your entire cache of books can be taken with you wherever you go.

4. *Personal Viewing Preferences.* Are the words you are currently reading too small? Too large? Too... ANNOYING? Paperback books cannot be modified according to personal preferences, but e-books can.

5. *Instant Gratification.* Is it the middle of the night and all the bookstores near you are closed? Are you tired of waiting days, sometimes weeks, for bookstores to ship the novels you bought? Ellora's Cave Publishing sells instantaneous downloads twenty-four hours a day, seven days a week, every day of the year. Our webstore is never closed. Our e-book delivery system is 100% automated, meaning your order is filled as soon as you pay for it.

Those are a few of the top reasons why electronic books are replacing paperbacks for many avid readers.

As always, Ellora's Cave and Cerridwen Press welcome your questions and comments. We invite you to email us at Comments@ellorascave.com or write to us directly at Ellora's Cave Publishing Inc., 1056 Home Avenue, Akron, OH 44310-3502.

erridwen, the Celtic Goddess of wisdom, was the muse who brought inspiration to storytellers and those in the creative arts. Cerridwen Press encompasses the best and most innovative stories in all genres of today's fiction. Visit our site and discover the newest titles by talented authors who still get inspired - much like the ancient storytellers did, once upon a time.

CERRIDWEN PRESS

www.cerridwenpress.com

Discover for yourself why readers can't get enough of the multiple award-winning publisher

Ellora's Cave.

Whether you prefer e-books or paperbacks,

be sure to visit EC on the web at
www.ellorascave.com

for an erotic reading experience that will leave you breathless.